I0668662

RIPPED

TO

SHREDS

A Ripple Effect Cozy Mystery
Book Three

Jeanne Glidewell

Book design by eBook Prep
www.ebookprep.com

Cover and Book design by eBook Prep
www.ebookprep.com

January, 2017
ISBN: 978-1-61417-993-1

ePublishing Works!
www.epublishingworks.com

DEDICATION

There is no one I could rightfully dedicate this third Ripple Effect mystery to other than Janet Wright. Not only is Janet a neighbor and one of my closest friends, she's also my co-conspirator in crime. One day, while helping me set up my new "critter cam" by a pond near a section of timber, she suggested I write a story involving a game camera like my own. Together we planned a murder that afternoon and I hope you enjoy the tale that was inspired by our discussion. It barely resembles the plot we'd scripted that day, but then, none of my mysteries have ever ended up the way I thought they would. It seems as if there's always a twist at the end I hadn't anticipated.

ACKNOWLEDGEMENTS

I'd like to thank my friend, fellow author, and proofreader, Shirley Worley, for giving my manuscript a once-over, and my editor, Judy Beatty of Madison, Alabama, whose skills are so very beneficial to me. My gratitude is also extended to my longtime editor and friend, Alice Duncan, of Roswell, New Mexico, a very talented and professional editor whose contact information I'd be happy to pass on to any writer who requests it by sending me a message via my website, www.jeanneglidewell.com. Alice is also the author of the award-winning Daisy Gumm Majesty and the Mercy Allcutt series; must-reads for any cozy mystery fan. Both ladies are wonderful individuals and I'm very appreciative of their efforts to teach me proper English and correct grammar, along with encouraging me to resist the urge to make up words at will. Unfortunately, most of their valiant attempts are in vain. By now, I'm sure they've both figured out it's like explaining calculus to a cockatoo.

I'd like to thank the best sister I could have ever asked for, Sarah Goodman. As my first line of defense, Sarah's the only person I can totally rely on to be painfully honest and tell me my story sucks, when indeed it does. As an avid cozy reader, I can trust her to give me great advice, like when my story morphs from a cozy mystery into a science fiction or horror novel. Sarah, my only sibling, is also the person I can count on for support and encouragement when it comes to my writing career. I know, without a moment's doubt, she will always have my back. Love you, Sis! Thanks so much for all you mean to me, and all you do for me!

And I would be amiss if I didn't also thank my incredible publishers, Nina Paules, of eBook Prep, and Brian Paules, of its sister company, ePublishingWorks. One of the best days in my writing career was the day they accepted me as a client, and I've thanked my lucky stars to be part of their team every day since.

CHARACTER LIST

Rapella Ripple—Just because this feisty senior citizen is well beyond her spring-chicken days, doesn't mean she's not an audacious ball of fire. Given her intrepid spirit and meddlesome tendencies, it's no wonder she lands herself in one awkward situation after another. Despite the occasional humiliation, and frequent wrong turns, nothing short of a massive coronary will stop her. But will that deeply ingrained tenaciousness pay off?

Clyde "Rip" Ripple—The other, more pragmatic half of this full-time RVing couple. As a career lawman, he wants to catch the killer as much as his wife, but goes about it in a more sensible, level-headed way. Will he get the opportunity to watch his fellow sheriff eat crow after she blows off his offer to assist in the investigation?

Cora Beaufont—The Ripples' niece who resides in Buffalo, Wyoming. She's holding down the fort while her husband is away on business. Cora's the person responsible for talking her aunt into buying a motion-sensor camera and later pays for Rapella's entry in a wildlife photography contest. Cora could not have imagined how that challenge would turn out. But will her thirty-dollar investment pay off?

William "Slick Willie" Beaufont—Cora's fourteen-year old son whose talents include playing baseball, auto mechanics, and conjuring up clever schemes. There's a good reason his Uncle Rip refers to him as Slick Willie. Will his idea to help track down a poacher pan out?

Beata "Bea" Whetstone—Co-owner of the Rest 'n Peace RV Park, a campground surrounded by the Bighorn National Forest. Bea's not the most pleasant person to be around, so when she goes missing it's anyone's guess who, or what, is behind her disappearance. Did someone despise her enough to want her dead?

Boonie Whetstone—Beata's husband and business partner. There's reason to believe he might have had a hand in his wife's disappearance. But could it be because he has another woman waiting in the wings to replace her?

Richard "Ranger Rick" Myer—A park ranger who befriends the Ripples. Rip and Rapella have to put their fondness for the man aside to determine if he had a strong enough motive to kill Beata Whetstone. Was he friend or foe of the victim?

Janelle Tyson-Simms—The gold-digging woman Boonie was seeing behind his wife's back before Bea's grisly death. Did she want to snag Boonie badly enough to eliminate her competition?

John and Barb Harris—Animal activists who are staying at the Whetstones' campground. They're upset when Beata kills a bear on the park's property. But were they ticked off enough to kill her?

Desireé Myer—Ranger Rick's ex-wife, who's also the victim's sister. The shop she owns in Buffalo is the last sort of store Rapella would want to patronize. But Rapella is so determined to track down Bea's killer that she'd walk through fire in search of the truth. Desireé and Bea's mother has been diagnosed with terminal esophageal cancer, and the sisters are both in line to inherit a fair amount of dough. Was there a compelling enough reason, whether personal or monetary, for Desireé to want her sister out of the picture, as well as out of their mother's will?

Leo and Charly Brown—The owners of the Sweet Sixteen RV Park, located two miles west of the Rest 'n Peace RV Park. Before Bea's disappearance, the two determined rivals had engaged in an all-out tug of war for customers. Were the Browns determined to get in the last punch?

Jaclyn Wright—The sheriff of Johnson County, Wyoming, who shows an offensive lack of respect for Rip Ripple. Rip refers to the stern, no-nonsense woman as "battleaxe", and her sense of superiority only strengthens his resolve to solve the case. Which sheriff will come out on top in this rivalry?

FROM THE DESK OF
JEANNE GLIDEWELL

Dear Reader,

I have a habit of apologizing in advance when presenting someone with a gift, having convinced myself they are going to hate it. In this same vein, I'd like to apologize up front if you find yourself horrified by my use of bordering-on-absurd grammar that goes against the grain of what your fifth-grade English teacher taught you, or when I invoke my creative license to employ a word that somehow got overlooked by every dictionary ever compiled, abridged or not. I am blessed with two incredible editors, but one cannot expect these ladies to turn water into wine. Only God can perform miracles, and clearly he has more important issues to take care of.

You may also think the idea of a sixty-eight-year-old amateur sleuth doing risky or impetuous things in her efforts to track down a killer is a far-fetched notion. But if you do, isn't that the very premise of the entire "cozy mystery" genre?

So, if these things disturb you, my mysteries are not for you. My objective is to entertain you on those occasions when you need something to while away your time; as you sit squeezed into an airplane seat for the duration of a long-distance flight; while you're sprawled out on a beach chair, soaking up the sun with your e-reader in one hand and a margarita in the other; or when you just want to relax, all snuggled up in your recliner in front of a roaring fire with your favorite furry friend curled up in your lap. If you find yourself in one of these situations and are not offended by the work of an author who chose archery and racquet ball classes in college in lieu of English and grammar whenever possible, then sit back, kick off your shoes, and let me tell you a story.

Happy Reading,
Jeanne

CHAPTER 1

"Screech! Screech! Screech!"

"What the—?" I started to ask Boonie Whetstone, the owner of the Rest 'n Peace RV Park, which was nestled amid tall pines in the Bighorn National Forest. He was in the laundry room with me, emptying quarters out of the washing machines into a three-pound coffee can. He'd later wrap and resell them to customers who needed them to do their laundry, he'd said. Now that was a recycling plan I could really appreciate.

"Screech!"

"What in the world was that?" I asked. I'd dropped my basket of clean clothes, startled by the eerie noise. "It sounds like a woman screaming out there in the, um, out there in the—"

"Boonies?" Boonie chuckled at his pun after finishing my sentence for me. As I bent over to collect my clothes, many of which would have to be refolded, he replied to my inquiry. "Could be a number of things. A screech owl, perhaps. Maybe even a female mountain lion."

"Screech! Screech!" The high-pitched wail emanated from within the not-so-distant forest again.

"Yeah, my guess is a lion," Boonie said with a knowing nod, as if telling me there was a wild baby bunny running amok in the woods. If there *was* a bunny running out there, it was probably because a mountain lion was chasing it, intent on devouring the poor little thing for lunch.

"There are mountain lions that close to us? Couldn't they come right into the campground?" I asked nervously.

"Yes, of course. The elevation's eighty-nine hundred feet here, and this campground is surrounded by woods, which are naturally inhabited by a lot of dangerous forest-dwelling animals. In fact, my wife had a close call with a cougar herself not long ago. We don't have a fence around this RV Park because acquiring one high enough to prevent a large cat from breaching it would cost us a pretty penny. Better to lose a customer now and then than to shell out a boatload of money to keep the predators at bay." He laughed and winked, not at all concerned about the possibility of having feral, customer-eating felines in the vicinity.

The handsome, dark-haired man had a muscular but lean frame from all the hours of strenuous labor that went in to maintaining a campground. He looked as if he could take down a cougar bare-handed, but a sixty-eight-year-old woman like me would be no match for the dangerous creature.

"Lose a customer now and then? Not very encouraging, I'm afraid. I appreciate your sense of humor, Mr. Whetstone, but maybe you really should invest in a fence."

As if he hadn't heard me, Boonie went on to explain. "Female mountain lions or cougars will scream like that when they're calling out for a mate. Their mating season usually runs from December through March. It's mid-April, but they'll mate at other times of the year on occasion."

"Well, there goes the 'Rest 'n Peace' aspect of your park, Mr. Whetstone," I said with a shudder. When we'd first arrived, I'd thought the RV Park's name was a clever idea for such a quiet, serene campground, but now I found it more ironic than cute.

"Don't worry. They're not apt to bother you. Wouldn't hurt to carry a can of pepper spray when you're out and about on the grounds, though. We sell some in the store for just that reason. Probably not all that effective, but it gives our customers a little peace of mind, anyway."

"I'd settle for a little peace of mind at the moment. I'll go buy a can right now while my last load is drying."

"Sorry, ma'am. The store's closed on Sundays. Only the check-in desk is open."

Swell. "Not apt to bother you" and "not all that effective" were not comforting phrases to me, but it beat having nothing at all to protect myself. I didn't have pepper spray to carry on my way back to the Chartreuse Caboose, our thirty-foot travel trailer. What I had was a spray bottle of *Shout*; a stain remover, not a cougar remover.

"Screech!" I heard again twenty minutes later as I took a step outside. Its source appeared to be frightfully close. I quickly stepped back inside and closed the door, giving myself a few extra minutes to bolster some courage. Leave it to Rip to request a site at the farthest end of the campground. "Closer to nature," he'd said. *Closer to wild, treacherous animals, too*, I thought. *And, at the moment, too blasted far from the laundry room for my liking.*

I knew I couldn't stay in the laundry room forever. When I'd left the trailer, my husband had been watching our team, the Texas Rangers, who were in the process of getting routed by the Kansas City Royals. He was no doubt snoozing on the couch by now. I'd have to move as briskly as possible returning to the trailer. If I came face to face with a cougar, my only option would be to try and "Shout it out", and that wasn't a very reassuring concept.

I managed to make it back to the trailer in record time. And that's taking into account I had to stop once to pick my clean clothes up off the gravel and shove them all back into the basket in one big wad. When a toddler I'd just passed shrieked for her mother, I'd come completely unglued. I'd flung the basket, armed myself with the bottle of Shout, and assumed a defensive posture, all in the space of a second-

and-a-half. The young child, now terrified of me, was a cute little girl, and I prayed she wouldn't become an hors d'oeuvre before momma took her back inside their motorhome.

When I entered the trailer we'd painted chartreuse, with yellow, green, and brown sunflowers to give it even more style, my husband of nearly fifty years, Clyde Ripple, better known as Rip, was just waking up from his nap. There were four or five cheese puffs scattered across his chest as if he'd fallen asleep mid-snack. He was intrigued, but not all that apprehensive, about having big cats in the area. "I had assumed there were imposing animals in the forest, but figured most of them were more afraid of humans than we were of them. Most only attack people they see as threatening. But we can pick up a couple cans of that pepper spray tomorrow if it makes you feel better. Are you still planning to go garage-sale shopping with Cora today?"

"Of course. She's picking me up in about an hour. Willie will hang out here with you while we're gone. In the meantime, I need to fold these clothes for the third time and put something in the slow cooker for supper. Rump roast sound okay?"

"You bet! My rump's about to waste away to nothing, you know." We both laughed. Rip had put on twenty pounds since retiring from law enforcement six years ago, and he wasn't exactly emaciated back then. A year after his retirement, we'd sold our home, rid ourselves of most of our belongings, bought the Chartreuse Caboose, and hit the road as full-time RVers.

At the present, we were in northern Wyoming. My late brother's daughter, Cora Beaufont, and her husband, Dirk, live in Buffalo, just east of the Bighorn National Forest, a formidable mountain range.

Cora's father, Dusty, the youngest of my four brothers, passed away ten years ago when Cora was twenty-nine. She and I had always been close. Dirk, an engineer for a large oil company, was spending three months in Ingleside, Texas, overseeing the construction of a large oil rig. We decided it'd be a good time to visit Cora and our great-nephew, fourteen-year-old William, or "Slick Willie", as Rip called him. We'd keep the two company while Dirk was away on business. I was looking forward to an enjoyable stay in Wyoming with my favorite niece nearby.

"Hey, Aunt Rappie! Over here!" Cora called out from across the crowded garage. Story, Wyoming, a town not too far north of Buffalo that fewer than a thousand folks called home, was having a city-wide garage sale all weekend. We'd already been to three places and found nothing of interest. Many of the same people we'd seen at the other sales were now shopping at this one, as well. Clearly, we were all on the same circuit. When I approached Cora, she was holding up a camouflaged box the size of a brick. "Here's what you need!"

"What is it?" I asked.

"A game camera!" I'd told her on our way to town about the screeching I'd heard in the forest. "You can attach it to a tree in the woods and get photos of any kind of critter that passes by. The lady who lives here told me it's motion-activated. It takes color photos during the day and infra-red ones at night. Cool, huh?"

"Yeah, *real* cool. Except that'd involve actually walking into the woods where a mountain lion might be waiting to stalk me like a newborn moose. No thanks, sweetheart!"

I had to admit, though, the possibility of capturing a photo of the critter making the spooky sounds was enticing. Unfortunately, at times, my curiosity was stronger than that of our fifteen-pound cat, Dolly. And you know what curiosity did to the cat, don't you? I turned my attention back to Cora as she tried to sell me a game camera that didn't even belong to her.

"You really need to buy this thing, Aunt Rappie. Take Uncle Rip with you to set the camera up and then check it for photos occasionally. He does own a gun, doesn't he? After all, he was a county sheriff for six or seven years."

"Ten, actually. But I'd never let him shoot an animal," I said. "Except maybe with his pellet gun, just to scare it off."

After much debate with Cora, and even more with myself, I decided to invest in a like-new "critter cam". I hadn't planned on spending my entire twenty-dollar wad on only one item, but it was exciting to think about what kinds of critters I might get photos of in the forest. I could feel my enthusiasm mounting.

Little did I know at the time that my new critter cam would snap a photo of a critter of the two-legged variety; one even more menacing and lethal than a mountain lion.

CHAPTER 2

"Good morning, dear," I said to the middle-aged lady at the counter as I walked into the Rest 'n Peace RV Park's little store. Glancing around, I saw a wall of shelving units with a vast variety of RV supplies displayed on them. The majority of the store was dedicated to toiletries, cleaning products, snacks and food items, and everyday household necessities. The remainder of the store was filled with souvenirs of every kind, from Bighorn National Park t-shirts to cheesy "I stayed at the Rest 'n Peace RV Park" bumper stickers that no one in their right mind would actually affix to their vehicle.

"If you say so," was the lady's sourpuss response to my cheerful greeting. She looked perturbed, as if someone had slipped a ghost pepper into her breakfast burrito. The biggest part of the burrito remained uneaten on her desk behind the counter.

I am one of those people who have the annoying habit of trying to brighten the moods of people who appear down, unhappy, or depressed, all three of which appeared to apply to this lady. So, with this noble goal in mind, I said, "I'm Rapella Ripple. It's nice to meet you. My husband and I are really enjoying this delightful campground."

"Good for you."

Strike one in my attempt. "And I must commend you on your wonderful shower houses. I'd have to say they're some of the cleanest we've ever encountered."

"I fired the work camper in charge of cleaning them yesterday. I found her attitude to be disagreeable."

A bundle of joy like you found the work camper disagreeable? How ironic! I thought, but didn't say.

Strike two. One more strike and I was giving up on my mood-brightening objective.

"That's too bad," I said, trying desperately not to come across as insincere as I felt.

"Yeah, whatever."

"And what did you say your name was?" I asked in my friendliest phony voice.

"I didn't," she replied.

I stood speechless for a few seconds. Most folks introduce themselves when someone makes a comment like mine. So after studying the nametag hanging crookedly from her collar, I took the liberty of introducing the lady to me myself. "Oh, I see it's Bea Whetstone. You must be the co-owner of this lovely park."

"It's only one syllable, pronounced Bee, not Be-a. It's short for Beata," she informed me as if it was a comment she'd made a zillion times before.

Beata was an attractive woman, I'd have to admit. She had short blond hair with a lot of red-highlighted strands, pale green eyes, and an unblemished olive complexion. Bea Whetstone was about my height of five-eight and appeared to be in her mid-forties. She had a trim, well-toned physique like her husband, Boonie. And her tan, which I would guess was sprayed on, was very becoming as it contrasted with her itty-bitty white and pink tank top that left little to the imagination. But she wore a frown that took away from what otherwise would have been a classically beautiful appearance.

"Pretty name for a pretty lady." I forced myself to spit out the compliment. I felt it best not to start out on the wrong foot with the co-owner of the campground in the event I needed a favor from her in the future.

Rip and I had served as work-campers on numerous occasions in the past. This stay most likely wouldn't be one of those times during which I found myself bored and restless and wanting to offer to help out around the park for a cut on our site fees, or a little extra spending money. For one thing, we weren't staying long enough to make it worth the while. Plus, it might not take this woman long to realize I wasn't always all that agreeable either. Still, I had no desire to burn a bridge I might later want to cross.

"Thanks! The meaning of the name Beata is blessed," Bea replied, even though I hadn't inquired. She actually sounded amicable and turned her frown upside down for a moment. Her straight pearly-white teeth were on exhibit just long enough for me to recognize the fact she was truly a stunning creature. Super-model material, in fact. But the moment was fleeting and her frown reappeared. It seemed almost as if the mere effort of smiling was painful for her.

"You don't say!"

"Or 'the bringer of joy'," Bea added solemnly. I could sense she was very proud of her given name even if its meaning could not have been any less fitting.

"Why do you go by Bea rather than Beata? Beata's such a nice name. And unique, as well."

"So is Bea."

"Yes, of course," I agreed quickly. I hadn't meant to imply otherwise.

"And it's much easier and quicker when I have to pen my signature," Bea explained.

"I understand." I didn't understand one iota. If leaving two letters off her signature saved such a significant amount of time for the lady, one would have to assume that when she wasn't busy snarling at customers in her campground store, she was walking the red carpet somewhere, signing autographs for her multitude of fans.

Being persistent in my effort to improve her disposition, I told her my little anecdote about being scared spitless after hearing the eerie screeching while doing laundry the previous day. I instantly regretted sharing the story with her when she didn't appear to find it amusing—or even interesting, for that matter.

Unfortunately, I was never one to give up easily. I'd noticed a unique gold tennis bracelet on her right wrist. It was an inch or so wide, and had several gems imbedded in it. I decided to try one last time to bring a smile to her face. "What a beautiful bracelet you're wearing. Real gold?"

"Of course." Bea's response made it clear she was affronted I'd even suspect otherwise. Although I'd never wear a bracelet with a real diamond the size of the one the bracelet boasted, I decided it'd be a waste of time to ask Bea if it was genuine. I knew the answer would be a scornful "of course".

"Do the gems represent anything in particular?"

This time Bea showed a softer side, almost nostalgic, as she explained the significance of the large diamond and two smaller emeralds. "My birthday is in April and my twin brothers were born in May. It had been a gift to my grandmother but she gave it to me many years ago. She said wearing it would bring me good luck."

"Oh, goodness!" I gushed, with much more enthusiasm than the situation called for. "That is such a heart-warming story. Your grandmother must have been a real sweetheart."

Bea shook her head in denial. "Not really. She was a hateful old shrew. However, this bracelet *has* seemed to bring me luck nonetheless."

Strike three. Or was it four? Maybe even five, I thought. *Obviously, Bea's apple had not fallen far from the hateful old shrew tree.*

My efforts to brighten her disposition had been futile and I decided to get down to business before the ill-natured woman brought my cheerful mood down to her level. "So, Beata, I'm here to buy a can of pepper spray so I won't be snarfed up by a mountain lion, or not without at least putting up a fight. Boonie told me you sold it here in the store, and I thought carrying some around might ease my anxiety when I'm out and about on the park's grounds."

"If you say so. It'll be twenty bucks."

"Twenty dollars? Seriously?" I asked the lady as she reached for her half-eaten burrito. "You're charging twenty dollars for this little can of pepper spray? I saw this exact brand online for just over ten."

"Then go order some online and get out of my hair so I can enjoy a little peace and quiet while I eat my lunch."

After her rude remark she took a bite of her breakfast, chewed and swallowed it, and then sneered at me as she added, "Or you can save a few bucks if you'd feel safer carrying around a bottle of Resolve Stain Remover, which we sell here for five dollars. It's very comparable to Shout, you know, and just as effective at fending off wild animals, no doubt."

I again regretted sharing my story with her and was appalled not only by her mockery, but also that she'd charge her customers five bucks for a bottle of Resolve that they could pick up at Wal-Mart for under three. But I really did want the comfort of having pepper spray with me and didn't want to drive to town looking for another store that'd be apt to carry wildlife repellant. The peace of mind it would give me was worth twenty bucks. Even if, number one: it cost me as much as my new critter cam had; and two: the rather pathetic weapon wasn't likely to do anything but antagonize a hungry mountain lion or a protective mother bear. And a pissed-off lion or bear was ten times more perilous than the threatening animal would have been if you hadn't just sprayed its nose and eyes with the irritant. Still, I was in a blissful state of denial and wanted the pepper spray for what little comfort it would provide me. To be honest, I was also disgusted with myself at how much I was prepared to give for it at that moment.

"All right, Beata," I said. "I guess you have me over a barrel. I'll have to remember to make a trip to town for any other items we might need while we're here. I always try to be conservative with our hard-earned money and just hate being taken advantage of by opportunistic business owners."

"Good for you," Bea replied. By this point I wasn't sure which one of us was the more disagreeable. But to my credit, I had valiantly tried to cheer her up and somehow allowed her to cheer me down instead.

Just then the back door of the shop opened and Bea's husband, Boonie, walked into the store. He greeted me in a friendly manner before informing his spouse he needed money to go fill up a gas can. He told her, "If I don't get the outer perimeter mowed soon I'm going to have to rent a brush hog and baler."

He was exaggerating, and I laughed politely at his facetious comment and then cringed when Bea replied, "Yeah, whatever. 'Bout time you got off your lazy butt and did something productive 'round here."

Her spiteful response went in one of Boonie's ears and immediately whizzed out the other like a bullet. Boonie was obviously accustomed to being slighted by his wife because her foul remark didn't appear to affect him. Whistling a popular George Strait tune, Boonie removed a fistful of bills from the cash register and exited out the door he'd come in just a few moments earlier. Before the door closed behind him, with sarcasm dripping off each word, he said, "Always a pleasure to see you too, my love."

The resentful exchange between the Whetstones left a sour taste in my mouth. Rip and I might not always agree on everything, and what couple did? But even when we did have a difference of opinion, we never treated each other with such blatant contempt. I had to wonder what Boonie had ever seen in this woman. It was feasible her personality had grown more repulsive over the years due to an unhappy marriage. But, if I were a betting person, I'd wager Bea was born with her obnoxious demeanor.

As I set the small aerosol container on the counter, I remembered Rip had told me to pick up a water regulator while I was at the campground store. The water pressure at our site was extremely high and had a tendency to surge even higher on occasion. Rip was worried it might bust the water lines in our trailer. The ideal range was between forty and fifty pounds of pressure, and this park's water pressure was well beyond those levels.

Many RV parks had built-in regulators on their main water lines to keep the water pressure consistent at all the sites, but this one did not. I soon learned why not having a built-in regulator was beneficial to this particular business establishment. It became evident to me the Whetstones' retirement account was being substantially funded by the sale of individual regulators when Bea placed the regulator down on the glass counter, and said, "Twenty bucks."

I studied the shiny brass gadget to see if I could determine why it was so much higher than the previous ones we'd purchased. It seemed to have all the same features, which basically amounted to nothing more than a female hose thread on one end and a male one on the other. We'd never paid more than ten dollars for a water regulator in the past, so naturally I was even more surprised when Bea added, "It's a used one."

"Twenty for a used one? Good grief! How much is a new one?" I was floored.

"Twenty bucks."

Are you freaking serious? I wanted to ask. But I chose to take the high road and resisted the urge to respond angrily.

"So you're telling me this used regulator is the same price as a brand new one?" I inquired with an unmistakable hint of disbelief in my tone. For a short while I was concerned I might be more in need of hearing aids than my husband, who rarely wore his ultra-expensive pair. He'd purchased them a year after he retired on the premise "he'd never be able to hear what I said to him without them." Clearly, he'd quickly realized he really didn't give a rat's behind what I had to say. After a couple of weeks of routinely utilizing them, he'd tucked them away in his toiletry bag and now only fished them out when we were scheduled to be in the presence of people whose words he really did value. For Rip that was a rare occasion.

After Bea ignored my inquiry, I asked her again, louder this time. "New and used regulators cost the same here?"

"Yes. This used one's the same price because it's like brand new." Bea responded without even having the decency to look embarrassed by the highway robbery she was committing. She went on to justify the price. "The Bankstons, from Arkansas, bought it here when they arrived last week and forgot to remove it from the water spigot when they left. Happens on a regular basis. Chances are you'll forget to take this same regulator with you when you head out, too, and I'll resell it here in the store. For twenty bucks." For once, she sounded delighted. A bit too gleeful, in fact.

I'd have been more offended by her comment if not for the fact it was the exact reason I was in the store requesting a water regulator that morning. Rip had left our last one behind at the Summerlan RV Park in Raton, New Mexico, where we'd stayed overnight on our way to Wyoming. This would be the third regulator we'd purchase in the last year alone. As the lady had said, leaving them behind at campgrounds happened on a regular basis, since they were only used when water pressure was an issue.

"Wow! You could make a decent living just selling the same handful of used regulators over and over again for twice the price a person could buy a brand new one anywhere else."

"Yep! It's called capitalism, lady. And, in my book anyway, it's also called astute business acumen."

"We apparently have different tastes in reading material because it's called 'greed' in my book," I countered. "But, once again, you have me over a barrel. We need it to protect the water lines in our trailer because the water pressure here is quite high. Ridiculously high, in fact."

"Imagine that."

I made a mental note to ask Rip if he knew whether or not a campground could intentionally raise their water pressure to such a lofty level that their customers would be forced to attach pressure regulators between the campground's spigots and their water hoses to protect their RV's water lines. It would certainly increase the sale of regulators in the campground's store. And Bea Whetstone didn't appear to be above adopting such a lucrative practice. All in the name of "capitalism", of course.

Even if I had the desire to be taken on as a work camper at the Rest 'n Peace RV Park, my chances had lessened significantly, I realized. And that was just fine with me. I couldn't in good faith charge a customer twenty bucks for a used water regulator, even if I hadn't been the one responsible for its exorbitant price.

Shaking my head in disgust, I pulled my Mastercard out of a back pocket and waited silently as Bea rang up my purchases on her cash register. She asked, "Before I total this up, do you need any Aqua-Kem? I have the three-packs on sale today."

"Really?" We were halfway through our last bottle. It'd be nice to restock the holding tank chemical at a reduced price. "How much are they on sale for?"

"Twenty bucks."

I gasped. "Does every item in your store cost twenty bucks? Are those twenty-dollar Butterfinger bars on that rack over there next to the chest freezer? Would five postcards cost me an entire C-note?" I smiled as I spoke to appear as if I were only kidding. But I wasn't. I'd be danged if I'd pay twenty dollars for another marked-up product in the Rest 'n Peace RV Park store.

Beata neither returned my smile or replied to my derisive questions. Instead, she appeared totally indifferent. "Want any or not?"

"No thanks, Beata. Maybe later if our supply runs out." I was outwardly friendly, but boiling inside.

"Yeah. Whatever."

Despite my unsuccessful efforts to make this woman's offensive manner more upbeat, I had remained as affable as possible. But under my breath, I wasn't so gracious.

I will squat in the woods amongst an army of cougars and bears to go to the bathroom before I'll buy toilet chemicals from you, is what I had wanted to say. But I bit my tongue and remained civil. Little did I know at the time, that very scenario of squatting in the woods to relieve myself would actually come to pass in the near future. However, it wouldn't be because I wanted to save a few bucks on toilet chemicals.

"In fact, Beata, I'll probably pick some up in town later on this week." I had intentionally used her full name, despite the fact I'd had to make the time and effort to articulate two unnecessary syllables.

"All right. Makes no nevermind to me. It's first come, first serve. When the three-packs are gone, they're gone." Bea acted astonished I hadn't jumped all over her featured bargain item that was on sale for twice what it cost anywhere else.

"I'll keep that in mind." *Don't hold your breath, Miss Congeniality.* I couldn't resist adding, "I doubt they'll be gone any time soon."

I could swear I tasted blood in my mouth from biting my tongue so hard, and for so long, to prevent myself from becoming as rude and insufferable as Bea Whetstone. Now all I wanted to do was get away from her as quickly as possible.

"That will be $43.80 with tax."

"That's absurd, I'll have you know!" I grasped my credit card and the receipt I'd signed out of Bea's hand before stuffing the duplicate copy into a small plastic bag along with the two items I'd purchased.

It was apparent the woman could care less about her customers. Her next snide remark left me itching to throw my new "used" brass regulator at her head. She said, "Good luck with the pepper spray. As far as I'm concerned, it ain't worth a tinker's dam, but if it makes you sleep better at night, so be it."

I felt my fear level ratchet up a notch after Bea voiced the same pessimistic opinion of the product as her husband had the previous day. The campground was situated in a mountainous terrain and almost completely encapsulated by dense woods. There had to be scores of potentially lethal animals, stalking and preying on weaker targets, within yards of the tree line surrounding the campground. Suddenly, I felt like the campground was hosting a luncheon for predators and I was a juicy slab of meat on display in the middle of an all-you-can-eat buffet table that was offering a delectable selection of human body parts for its dinner guests. I shivered from head to toe as I turned to walk away.

"But hey!" Bea said, as I cautiously opened the door to exit the store. "Ain't none of us getting out of this world alive anyway."

I almost choked on the breath mint I'd placed under my tongue to get rid of the bad taste the campground owner had left in my mouth. *When can I expect you to start bringing the joy, Beata?* I badly wanted to ask. *I'd really like to be present to witness that anomaly.*

On my walk back to the trailer with my can of pepper spray cocked, loaded, and ready to fire, I couldn't get Bea's last remark out of my head. It was true none of us will get out of this world alive, but it's also true that some of us will get out of it a lot quicker than others. I'd soon discover Bea's comment had been eerily prophetic.

CHAPTER 3

"Hey, Rip, look what the cat drug in." I swung open the door to welcome Cora and our nephew, William. As I spoke, our chubby grey tabby, Dolly, looked up to make sure I wasn't spooning an extra helping of tuna-flavored morsels in her bowl. I knew she'd never go to the trouble to drag anything into the trailer unless it was edible. Willie joined his uncle on the couch, and Cora sat down in a chair across from me at the kitchen table. "There was something in this morning's paper I wanted to show you, Aunt Rappie. The article I circled might inspire you to get your new camera set up in the wilderness around here. Perhaps in the vicinity of where you heard those eerie screeches the other day."

"It's going to take a little more than a newspaper article to inspire me to willingly walk into the cesspool of man-eaters populating what you call the 'wilderness' surrounding this campground. The fact that 'wild' is a fitting first syllable for both 'wilderness' and 'wildlife' is not merely a coincidence, you know."

"How about the opportunity to win as much as twenty-five thousand dollars in a local contest? Would that make the idea sound more appealing?" Cora smiled impishly.

"Okay, now you have my attention." My curiosity was instantly piqued at the prospect of winning a bundle of cash.

Rip, who'd been listening in while taking apart two of his handguns to clean, looked up from where he sat on the couch and spoke directly to Cora. "You do realize that your aunt would likely saunter through the Serengeti Desert naked, with a bleeding baby gazelle draped around her neck, for that kind of prize, don't you? Please don't encourage her to do something she and I might both later regret."

Rip was teasing, of course, but the expression he wore suggested differently. He knew me well enough to know my weaknesses. He also realized that for a person like me, who was tighter than the bark on trees in the wilderness Cora had referred to, the prospect of winning a pile of money was akin to dangling an apple in front of a hungry jackass's nose.

"Hush," I said to Rip. "Why don't you show Willie the safe and proper way to clean a gun while Cora and I chat?"

Rip, Cora, and Willie all laughed at my expense. After Willie walked over and parked his too-thin frame on the opposite end of the couch from his uncle, I turned back to Cora. "So, sweetheart, tell me more about this contest you read about."

Cora spread a page from the latest edition of the *Buffalo Bulletin* on the kitchen table, and we sat down on the bench seats across from each other. "Johnson County Nature Photography Contest" was the headline. I skimmed through the article that gave details about the competition, which included the grand prize of twenty-five thousand dollars Cora had coaxed me with. The prize for second place was ten thousand dollars, and the third place recipient would receive a respectable five grand. Honorable mention honors would award five-hundred dollar pre-paid Visas to five additional participants.

"See why I was so excited?" Cora asked. She was obviously enthused about the opportunity and wound up like a jack-in-the-box about ready to pop out of its lid. I, however, could feel a sense of dread beginning to simmer inside me.

"Well, honey, yes and no. The prizes sound quite overwhelming, naturally. However, the danger involved in trying to capture an award-winning photograph leaves me a little underwhelmed, I'm afraid."

"I can understand your hesitation, but like I said before, you'd be perfectly safe if you took Uncle Clyde with you. He can take along one of those guns he's cleaning." Cora pointed toward the couch where Rip and Willie were intent on their task. Cora was the only person I knew who could get away with calling Rip by his given name, which she only did on rare occasion. He'd been the namesake of a great uncle on his mother's side. But he'd never been very fond of the great uncle or the name Clyde. So when a young friend of his nicknamed him "Rip" in grade school, the moniker stuck, and he was perfectly content with that.

"Honey, I don't want any wild animals killed on my behalf. Just as we are, they are all creations of God."

Rip chimed in again to assure me there'd be no need to kill, or even wound, anything. "A shot in the air or over its head would deter the animal and make him flee with no physical harm to us or the animal. Don't let that aspect keep you from entering the contest if you're interested in competing, Rapella. Sounds kind of fun to me."

"Aren't you the one who just advised Cora not to encourage me?" I asked.

"Yes, but in this case, I don't see any real risk in getting involved. I've noticed you've been restless the last couple of days, and this would give you something to do. Not to mention, I think we'd both enjoy the challenge of competing in the photo contest."

With Rip's approval and support, I began to feel a little spark of excitement. I had to admit it would be fun to see if I could capture any interesting images on my new critter cam, whether it was an award-winning wildlife photo, or not. "Okay, Cora. If I do decide to enter the contest, what would I need to do next?"

Cora had come prepared. It was apparent she'd been fairly certain she'd be able to appeal to my adventuresome spirit. She reached into the pocket of her windbreaker and pulled out an entry form. She instructed me to fill in the blanks and mail it to the address given at the bottom of the paper.

I soon realized she'd been even more confident than I'd anticipated when she reached into her pocket again and withdrew a postage-paid envelope she'd earlier prepared for me. I was even more surprised when Cora reached in a third time to retrieve a check for thirty-dollars made out to the Wyoming Travel and Tourism Department.

"What's the check for?" I asked.

"It's the entry fee."

"You didn't tell me there was a cost to enter. I'm not sure it's worth it, given my chances of winning a contest of this nature."

"Doesn't matter. It's my gift to you. Happy Easter, Aunt Rappie!" Her response was accompanied by a sly grin. "Besides, it's a small price to pay for an opportunity to see you win a monetary reward of such an impressive amount. I know how much enjoyment you'll both get out of the challenge of capturing an award-winning wildlife photograph."

I wasn't fooled by my oh-so-clever niece. She knew I'd never have agreed to enter the photography contest if I'd known there was a fee involved, no matter how badly I wanted to compete. She also knew I'd been on edge, with little to do to keep myself occupied. I was not as fortunate as my husband, who could entertain himself all day with a six-pack of beer, a bag of those ghastly pork rinds, and the TV remote within arm's reach.

I hesitated. I was still unsure I wanted to waste thirty dollars of my beloved niece's money. I wasn't wearing rose-colored glasses, after all. Realistically, I had about as much chance of beating out dozens of experienced photographers in a wildlife photo contest as I had of beating out dozens of Kenyans in the marathon taking place in Boston the following Monday.

I was on the brink of handing her back the form, check, and envelope, and turning down her proposal, but the expectant expression on Cora's face made me decide to accept the challenge instead. I had sensed she'd be disappointed and possibly offended if I didn't agree to give it a whirl. Not to mention that the ever-increasing boredom of one nondescript day after another was beginning to get to me. When having a load of dirty clothes to wash becomes the highlight of your day, it's time to look for something more stimulating to do.

"Okay, sweetheart. You win. I'm in." I vowed to myself that if, miraculously, I was awarded a monetary prize, Cora would get a healthy portion of it to repay her for her ill-advised investment and undue confidence in me. I pulled the critter cam out of the storage compartment under the bench seat where I'd stashed it and set it in the middle of the table. "Now, I just need to figure out how to work this silly contraption."

"That shouldn't be a problem," Cora said. "Get the instruction manual out and we'll look through it."

"I got this at a garage sale, honey. Remember? It didn't even come in a box, much less have a manual with it."

"Oh, yeah. I forgot. Well, I guess you can look it up online." With a dubious tone to her voice, Cora said this in the same manner she'd ask me to assemble a nuclear reactor. Clearly she didn't have much confidence in my ability to accomplish anything related to the Internet or any of the new-fangled electronic devices.

I was anxious to prove to her I was at least somewhat computer-savvy. Granted, there were a few things I hadn't learned yet; like where that damn "cloud" was that everybody talked about and what "face-timing" someone was all about. But, still, for someone born before the color TV was invented I thought I did remarkably well.

"Oh, yes, of course. I'll Google it. Great idea!" Our fifty-year-old daughter, Regina, had gifted us with an iPad, and I'd learned how to make use of it the previous fall while visiting our friends at the Alexandria Inn in Rockdale, Missouri. I wasn't proficient with it by any means, but I could Google any subject, play a couple of my favorite online games, and utilize the camera, calculator, and weather app. Better yet, I had learned how to ask "Siri" questions I was too lazy to research on my own. Knowing how to accomplish those few tasks was sufficient for our needs. After all, for nearly a year we'd been perfectly content just utilizing the tablet as an over-sized coaster on the end table.

"You sure you can handle it by yourself, Aunt Rappie?"

I set the camera down on the table. "No problem, sweetie. I'll find the manual online later. Right now I'd like to visit with you and Willie while you're here. How about we catch up while I throw together a little something for lunch?"

"Did someone say lunch?" Rip asked. "Willie and I are both starving. The only difference is that Willie can put away enough food to feed a small village in Africa without gaining an ounce. I, on the other hand, can eat a handful of peanuts and have to unzip my jeans to catch my breath. What's up with that?"

"What's up with that, dear, is that Willie's body is in perpetual motion while yours is vegetating on the couch for a minimum of eight hours every day." I chuckled to show I was just messing with him.

"Quit wasting time sassing me, woman, and get to cooking!" Rip replied good-naturedly.

"Why can't you use your cell phone?" I heard Rip ask Willie a short time later. Cora had joined the fellows in the living room and I was in the kitchen making toasted cheese sandwiches to serve with a bowl of leftover potato salad I had in the fridge. I felt obligated to do whatever I could to put a little meat on Willie's bones, even though I knew he'd burn off the calories before the food had even settled in his stomach.

Rip and Willie were involved in a conversation about why Willie was grounded from using his smart phone for a week, a penalty the typical teenage boy considered to be equivalent to capital punishment.

"I was grounded from my phone for engaging in a little entrepreneurship. I needed a new pair of shoes and mom refused to buy them for me. So I took the initiative, and—"

"Hold on there, Buster Brown." Cora interrupted her blond curly-haired son with just a hint of amusement in her voice. "For starters, you didn't 'need' yet another pair of Nikes. And, furthermore, I wouldn't refer to what you did to obtain money for them as 'entrepreneurship'."

"But mom—"

"Don't 'but mom' me, William Michael. What you did was wrong and you know it!" She turned her attention to Rip. "Willie wanted a pair of these gaudy-colored tennis shoes that cost a hundred and twenty-five dollars. I've never spent that much for a pair of shoes in my life. Not to mention, he already has a closet full of similar shoes."

"A lot of them don't fit," Willie cut in.

"The way you're growing, in two months this pair you want won't fit either. Why don't you donate the ones you've outgrown to the Salvation Army store so some underprivileged boy who'd appreciate them can make use of them. And don't interrupt me again. It's uncouth and inconsiderate," Cora chided her son. She'd always been stern but fair with her only child. She then continued. "I made the mistake of telling him the only way he was getting a pair of the ridiculously expensive sneakers was if he earned the—"

"Aha! So, you're admitting it was your fault, and not mine?" Willie cut in.

I had to restrain myself from giggling. You've got to give the kid credit. He did have plenty of spunk, which was a trait I've always maintained he inherited from me.

Willie was not finished talking back to his mother. "And they are not called sneakers, Mom. I'm not a kid, you know. Besides, I—"

After Willie butted in a second time, Cora gave him a look that shut him up mid-sentence without her having to utter a single word. I wouldn't swear to it, but I'm pretty sure that God-given talent was passed down to her DNA make-up from me as well. Regina had always complained that I had a look that could melt iron. I listened as Cora went on with her story.

"So he decided to take advantage of Mr. Wilson, a widower who lives down the street from us. My insensitive son thought he'd try and weasel the money to buy the shoes out of our wonderful neighbor, a kind old gentleman who treats Willie like he's his own grandson."

"Mr. Wilson calls me Dennis the menace," Willie said with a chuckle. "And I did weasel…er, I mean win the money, but Mom wouldn't let me accept it."

"Win?" Cora asked in a scornful tone.

"Well 'win' is more fitting than 'weasel'. What I mean is that it's not the way you're telling it, Mom," Willie said in his own defense. "I certainly intended no harm to Mr. Wilson."

"Okay. Then you tell the story." Cora folded her arms and sat back in the recliner. Her eyes sparkled and her lips curled in her unsuccessful attempt to appear disapproving.

"Well, you see," Willie began. "Mr. Wilson had just bought a brand new truck, and every time I stopped by his house he complained about its fuel efficiency. Then a few weeks ago he heard about some amazing new additive that claimed to boost the vehicle's fuel efficiency by cleaning the injectors and combustion chamber deposits, which theoretically would reduce friction and wear in your pressure fuel system. I, of course, was skeptical."

"As I would be," Rip said. "But I've always been pleased with the mileage my Chevy truck gets. I have several friends who drive other types of trucks and none of their fuel efficiencies can match mine."

Willie's ambition had always been to be an auto mechanic and restore older model vehicles after he graduated from a nearby trade school. If he didn't get drafted by a major league ball team, he'd always add. I felt like auto mechanics was a vocation that would suit him well due to his natural intrigue about anything that's motor-driven. He was a gifted student, enrolled in a program for early graduation. He always sounded incredibly mature when he discussed the subject of vehicles and the engines that powered them. Even Rip occasionally conferred with his young nephew when he had an issue with the Chevy.

"Go on with your story, son," Rip prompted Willie. He'd call the boy "son" since the day Cora had given birth to him.

Willie cleared his throat a couple of times and appeared slightly embarrassed as he continued. "So, you see, I started siphoning gas out of Mom's car every few days and pouring it into Mr. Wilson's gas tank after dark. I know where he hides his spare house and truck keys under a rock by his garage. He started doing that last year after he locked himself out of his house with his key ring lying inside on the kitchen counter."

"And your trickery is the thanks he gets for trusting you enough to show you where he hides his keys," Cora broke in to remark.

"Come on, Mom. He knows I'd never steal his truck or go into his house uninvited. And please don't interrupt me again. It's uncouth and inconsiderate." His barb hit home as Cora grimaced and Rip and I did our best not to chuckle at the way Willie had thrown his mother's reprimand back in her face.

"So, back to what I was saying before I was so rudely interrupted." This time neither of us could squelch a snicker, but we got control of our amusement quickly as Willie went on with his tale. "After a few days of adding gas to his tank, Mr. Wilson was ecstatic about the increase in mileage he was getting due to what he thought was the addition of the new addictive."

"And, meanwhile," Cora said. "I was wondering why I was having to fill up my tank nearly every other day. I even made an appointment with the service department at Sheridan Motors, which I later had to cancel when I discovered the true reason for the car's sudden reduction in fuel mileage."

"Sorry about that," Willie said with an ornery smirk before turning back to his Uncle Rip. "So then he started boasting about averaging thirty-two miles to the gallon, and encouraging all the old guys he has coffee with every morning at the cafe to add the additive to their tanks too. That's when I knew I had him right where I wanted him. Knowing Mr. Wilson has a fondness for gambling, I told him I didn't think there was any way in hell—"

"William Michael!" Cora spat out in dismay. "Watch your mouth! You shooting for another week without your phone?"

"Oh, sorry. I meant to say I told him there was no way in the world he could continue to get that kind of mileage once the truck got accustomed to having the additive added to the fuel. Sure enough, he said, 'Wanna bet?' So I bet him one hundred and twenty-five dollars he couldn't average over twenty-five miles a gallon before his Chevy had gone through the next full tank of gas."

"Uh-oh," Rip said with a snort of laughter. "I can see where this is going."

Willie smiled and continued. "So after we made the bet, I started sneaking over to Mr. Wilson's house again after he'd gone to bed and began siphoning gas out of his truck every night and putting it back in Mom's car. Not a lot each time, you see. Just enough that he began getting agitated that his fuel gauge was dropping a lot faster than he thought it should."

At this point everyone was laughing. Even Cora couldn't contain her amusement and was chuckling right along with us. "Too smart for his own good. And mine!"

"And people wonder why I call my nephew 'Slick Willie'. I'm impressed by your ingenuity, son, despite the fact it was a sneaky thing to do to the poor guy. So what happened next?" Rip asked after he managed to stop chuckling.

"As usual, Mom ruined everything."

"It's in the job description of 'mother', darling," Cora replied.

Willie rolled his eyes dramatically. "Mr. Wilson would have made good on the bet, I'm sure. But Mom started getting suspicious when suddenly she could drive forever without her gas gauge ever dropping."

"I'd also been smelling gasoline fumes in the garage," Cora added. "I guess it's hard not to spill a few drops when you're pouring gas into a fuel tank using a gas can."

"Yes, it's tough to do, Mom. I spilled very little under the circumstances." Willie beamed with pride. "So, to make a long story short, I had to apologize to Mr. Wilson and admit to pulling a prank on him. He wasn't upset about it either. In fact, he thought it was really funny and was considering trying the same trick on old Mr. Dudley who lives across the street from him. And that, Uncle Rip, is why I'm grounded from my phone. Cruel and unusual punishment, don't you think?"

Before Rip could reply to Willie's question, Cora said, "You're lucky I didn't ground you from using your phone for a month, you little rascal."

From the warm look Cora exchanged with her son, it was evident they had a close and loving bond. Then Cora turned to us. "But I did cave in and agree to get him a pair of those silly-looking sneakers for his upcoming birthday."

"They're 'kicks', Mom, not 'sneakers'. But I really do appreciate you buying them for me." Willie then turned his attention back toward us, and with a grin he said, "See? Mom's not nearly as mean as everybody says she is."

Willie hollered when Cora's purse walloped him in the back of the head. He hadn't even seen it coming.

CHAPTER 4

"Already?" Rip asked. "Didn't you just do laundry a couple of days ago?"

"It's been four days, actually. And I'd appreciate not having to go up to the laundry room as often if you'd be thoughtful enough to stop using towels showering and quit changing into clean clothes," I replied in jest.

"Trust me, darling. You wouldn't appreciate my 'thoughtfulness' for very long. You'd be begging me to take a shower after the trailer began to smell as if there were a decaying possum in one of the trailer's under-carriage compartments."

We shared a laugh before I hoisted up my full laundry basket and stepped outside to trudge up to the far end of the campground where the laundry room was connected to the shower houses. To be fair, Rip had offered to drive me. But I had no desire to appear as if I were too old and decrepit to make it there on my own, even if it meant risking life and limb with only an over-priced can of pepper spray to protect me. And, of course, a half bottle of Shout. If nothing else, whoever discovered my body could use it to remove the blood stains from my clothes before donating them to Goodwill.

Before I stepped off our concrete patio, I reached for my belt to ensure that the pepper spray, my lame excuse for a weapon, was secure in its new leather case. At my request, Rip had trimmed down an old gun holster he no longer needed to create a carrier for the spray container. It worked splendidly, and I was rather proud of my own resourcefulness. Even Rip seemed impressed with my clever idea.

Wanting to cover the space between our trailer and the laundry facility as rapidly as I was able, I walked briskly down the gravel road between rows of full hookup RV sites. I wanted to spend as little time as possible on the imaginary buffet table, you understand. I wasn't keen on spending two hours of my day on such a boring endeavor to begin with, but I knew if I put it off one more day I'd have to haul two baskets to the laundry facility tomorrow. Besides, I had nothing else to do with my time that day.

For many years we had lived in a brick ranch home in Rockport, Texas, and I never thought of doing laundry as an undesirable chore. I could toss a load in the washing machine and stay busy accomplishing another task, or reading a cozy mystery on our screened-in porch, until it was time to move the load to the dryer. Very little time or effort was needed.

But since we'd become full-time RVers a few years ago, laundry had taken on a whole new significance. We couldn't afford one of those fancy-schmancy RV's that came with a washer/dryer combo, and if you can believe it, occasionally a fireplace as well. Hauling dirty clothes to the campground's laundry room and waiting while they washed and dried was a dull and time-consuming task. It was one of the few aspects of living in our beloved Chartreuse Caboose that didn't agree with me. Laundry and cooking in a child's Magic Chef-sized kitchen were my only major complaints. Otherwise, I loved the freedom of the road and not being tied down to a house full of material items that had no real significance in our lives. Simplifying our lifestyle had actually enhanced it.

I came out of my reverie in a split second when I heard something rustling in the woods no more than twenty yards from my location, which was fifteen or so steps from the laundry room door. I covered the distance in five steps, all taken in the span of two-and-a-half seconds, and then slammed the door behind me. I immediately turned toward the window to see if I could spot what might have made the racket at the edge of the forest. Nothing out of the norm could be seen as I scanned the tree line through the glass pane. The undulating waves of my racing heart were beginning to ebb when I had the bejeezus scared out of me again, as an unexpected high-pitched female voice from just inches behind my ear startled me. "Are you all right, ma'am? You look spooked."

Breathing heavily, I felt my heart's rhythm soar, more from fear than exertion. As soon as I could catch my breath, I assured her I was fine.

"I thought I heard a wild animal near the tree line, but it was most likely just my mind playing tricks on me," I explained, feeling flushed. To ease my embarrassment, I joked. "Just an overactive imagination of a silly old lady, I guess."

She smiled and told me she had also heard odd noises emanating from the woods as she was walking to the laundry room. I flinched when she added, "But I have no intention of paying twenty bucks for a useless can of pepper spray. The owners carry it in the office only to take advantage of anxious customers who are too foolish to realize it would serve no purpose should they be attacked by a cougar, bear, or even charged by a moose."

"Oh, my goodness! Charged by a moose?" I instinctively pulled my jacket around my waist to hide my pepper-spray holster.

"Yes. They are huge animals, you know, and have been known to charge people when they feel threatened or someone gets between them and their offspring. Of course, just like with bears and cougars, pepper spray would only further antagonize them."

"Swell. Good to know."

Without formally introducing ourselves, we began to exchange small talk as we both concentrated on sorting out our piles of towels and soiled clothing. I marveled at the swanky pantsuit and exquisite diamond ring the woman wore to do laundry. In contrast, I wore an old stained and tattered sweat suit I'd picked up for a quarter at a flea market over a decade ago. It wasn't stained or tattered when I'd first purchased it, mind you, or I'd have tried to bargain the seller down to a dime.

Although she seemed like a pleasant enough woman, my laundry room companion's manner was a little hoity-toity for my taste. But chatting with her was not only a way to while away the time, it was also very illuminating.

"I just arrived yesterday and haven't had time to shop for a few things I forgot to pack. Can you believe that wicked witch in the office charged me five bucks for this single-load box of detergent?" The striking woman shook her head in obvious disgust as she spoke.

Even though Bea Whetstone wasn't my favorite person by any means, I considered replying that I thought "wicked witch" was a little too harsh a description of the campground owner, but then thought better of it. I wasn't in the mood for a confrontation that morning and "wicked witch" wasn't really that much of an exaggeration.

"I know how you feel. I've had to pay a king's ransom for a couple of necessary items in the store myself. Mrs. Whetstone doesn't seem to be a very personable hostess, especially considering she owns a business that requires a person to be as accommodating as possible and to interact with customers on a continual basis. But maybe she's just had a tough go of it recently."

"'Not very personable' is an understatement if I ever heard one," the tall, willowy brunette said. She appeared to be about the same age as the woman she was bashing. They were both in their mid-forties or so I'd guess. "At least Boonie is amicable, friendly, and has a laid-back personality. How he can stand being married to Bea is beyond me."

"Have you stayed here before?" I asked, curious about the familiarity she seemed to have with the area and the park owners.

"No. It's my first time in Wyoming." The annoyed woman with long, wavy dark-brown locks appeared to have formed strong opinions of the Whetstones having just arrived the previous day, but I didn't feel inclined to comment further on the touchy topic. I was happy when she changed the subject, and said, "I'm from Illinois. Chicago, to be exact. I live on the right side of the tracks, I might add."

"I gathered that. You wear nicer clothes to do laundry than I do to attend weddings."

"I'm sure you're a lot more comfortable than me, though. Even in clothes that look like they were pilfered from a sleeping hobo. I wish I felt comfortable going out in public in rags. No offense intended." I started to protest at her description of my outfit. How could I not take offense at a remark like that? Yes, the clothes I was wearing were old, and perhaps a bit shabby, but insinuating they were rags and akin to a hobo's wardrobe was insulting. Before I could respond heatedly to her rudeness, she asked in a friendly voice, "So, where do you call home?"

I hesitated for a moment before deciding I was in no mood to squabble with a stranger about the condition of my outfit, and would rather ignore her offensive remarks and answer her question about my hometown. "Rockport, Texas. It's a quaint little coastal town just north of Corpus Christi. A small drinking village with a fishing problem, they like to say."

"Sounds delightful," the woman said with a smile, after a polite chuckle in response to my play on words.

We worked quietly side-by-side for a few minutes before the other lady began to converse again. While we were seated in cheap plastic chairs at a folding table across from a half dozen commercial dryers, she commented on her plans for the remainder of the day. "I'm not looking forward to having to unhook the car by myself, but I need to go to town to pick up a few necessary items. I want to buy some laundry detergent for one, so I don't get gouged in the park's store again."

"Can't your husband unhook the car, or at least assist you?"

"No, unfortunately my husband passed about six months ago. This is the first time I've taken the RV on a trip by myself since his death. I just needed to get away for a couple of weeks, you see."

She sounded fed up more than emotionally upset, but I immediately felt sorry for her. Other than her hair, I thought she bore a strong physical resemblance to Bea Whetstone but didn't think she'd appreciate me telling her that. Bea's short mop of strawberry-blond hair was the only real feature that set them apart. Both tanned ladies had admirable physiques and were even a tad taller than my five feet, eight inches.

"Yes, of course. I'm so sorry for your loss, and I can understand why you needed to get away for a spell. It must be a tough adjustment for you, and I sincerely wish you the best. As for your car, I'm certain my husband would be happy to assist you, or unhook it himself. Currently he's doing nothing more than making sure the couch in our trailer doesn't levitate off the floor on its own accord." I attempted a little humor to lighten the exchange. I hated to volunteer my husband in situations like this, but felt sorry for this widowed lady, despite the disrespectful way she'd referred to my clothing. I couldn't imagine life without Rip and didn't want to ever have to experience it. My goal was to die before he did, but I was realistic enough to know that God might have different plans.

The slender lady smiled in response to my offer, and after declining it, she related a humorous anecdote about a vacation she and her late husband had once taken to the Black Hills in South Dakota. She told me that one evening while in Deadwood she'd asked him if he'd mind unhooking the car so they could go out for supper even though they were just staying in that RV park overnight.

"He replied to me in his usual delightful joking manner, 'But of course, my dear Jan. You know I always go where I'm towed'."

I laughed at the quip her husband had made and vowed to myself to remember the story long enough to share it with Rip. I started to respond, but a loud shout outside startled us both. We ran to the window and saw Bea Whetstone standing outside the office with a six-shooter in her hand. Our eyes immediately shifted in the direction the silver-handled, gold-barreled gun was aimed and both gasped when we saw a large black bear and a young cub standing on the edge of a gravel road between the campground and the tree line. I immediately thought the approaching bears had to have been behind the creepy rustling noise I'd heard just before arriving at the laundry room. I swallowed hard, knowing if I'd been just a few minutes later, I might have come face-to-face with the imposing creatures.

The sun glinting off the gun's gold-plated barrel reflected on Bea's face, illuminating her determined expression. She appeared tense, but resolute.

Bea's bellow had stopped the two bears in their path. What I presumed was the cub's mama stood up on her back legs and tucked her young one behind her in an obvious attempt to protect her offspring from harm. Within seconds, twenty or more people had exited their units and gathered to see what was causing the disturbance. Several took their cell phones out and began videoing or taking photos of the incident, no doubt anxious to share with their family and friends the excitement of observing a mama bear and cub in the campground.

Jan, my fellow laundry room inhabitant, and I stepped outside the door just far enough that we could watch the events taking place outside with the other onlookers. We stood motionless as the mama bear, sensing danger, took several cautious steps backward, maneuvering her cub into the safety of the forest as she retreated. She was clearly more afraid of humans than we were of her. Therefore, we were all stunned when Bea emptied her weapon, discharging all six cartridges, and dropped the female bear just as she was about to disappear inside the tree line. The large bear took a couple of shallow breaths before her body stilled. She'd died almost instantly, for which I was relieved. I can't stand to watch any living creature suffer.

It seemed as if every person viewing the scene screamed in unison at their dismay of the unnecessary carnage they'd just witnessed. Naturally, I had no desire to be approached by the massive bear, which now laid lifeless on the ground, or any other wild animal, for that manner. But I was appalled that Bea shot and killed the bear when it was evident that, rather than adopting a threatening posture, the sow was in the process of retreating.

I swallowed hard at the heartrending sight of the orphaned cub who approached the body of the prostrate bear and tried to awaken its mother by nudging her with its nose. I held my breath in fear Bea was going to kill the baby too. I think she was seriously considering it when a man and woman pounced on her from behind and grabbed the gun from her hands. There was absolute chaos and wild hysteria in the campground for a few minutes. I wanted to slap the cruel campground owner and demand to know why she felt it necessary to kill the animal after it'd become apparent the mama bear was not posing a threat to anyone.

Thirty-some people were now scattered around the common area, standing in shocked silence: their mouths agape, their eyes as wide as tea cup saucers, and their bodies motionless, as if frozen in time. Mrs. Whetstone briskly scanned the crowd before shouting out, "The show's over, folks! Now there's one less bear who'll be trying to get in our trash dumpsters."

A murmur circulated through the crowd. It was clear nobody could believe what they'd just witnessed, and not one person made a move to depart from the scene until Bea stomped her feet and barked, "Time for all you gawkers to go back to your RVs and mind your own business!"

"Oh, my goodness," Jan whispered to me. "She's yelling at the very people who put food on her plate with the site fees they pay. Can you believe that woman's audacity?"

"No, I can't. Nor can I believe she killed that defenseless cub's mother. Could it be she killed that poor sow only because she was ticked off about bears raiding the park's dumpsters? Reckon that's what put a Bea under her bonnet?"

"Who knows. From her remark, it sure sounded that way. Like I said, she's a wicked witch!"

Within fifteen minutes the carcass of the dead bear was loaded into the back of a truck and the crowd had dispersed. Emotionally drained, Jan and I returned to finish our work in the laundry room. We were both too upset to chatter, so went about our duties silently. As I folded the clothes I'd removed from a dryer, my eyes welled up with tears, concerned for the welfare of the cub who now had no mother to protect it.

What kind of person would gun down an animal whose only intention was protecting her young, a natural maternal instinct of nearly all of God's female creatures? I was on edge as I walked back to the welcoming comfort of the Chartreuse Caboose and felt bile rise up in my throat as I passed the pool of blood left on the ground by the slain bear. I realized that I was now in total agreement with Jan's description of Bea Whetstone. Although it goes against my grain to call people unkind names, the woman truly was a wicked witch.

CHAPTER 5

"Was that my stomach growling?" Rip asked as I rinsed off the breakfast dishes. "If so, it's because it's not sure if it will make it to lunch. It's touch and go already."

"That noise was from the motorhome firing up in the site next to us. Trust me, honey. You're not going to dry up and blow away any time soon. You can inform your stomach it can look forward to a grilled chicken salad in a few hours."

"Oh, yum. I can hardly wait to tear into a chicken salad. Are you trying to kill me, woman?"

"No, on the contrary, I'm trying to prevent you from killing yourself. Dr. Herron just started you on cholesterol-lowering medication, and she warned you that your last lab results indicated you're at higher risk of becoming diabetic if you don't change your diet and increase your exercise immediately."

"That's exactly why I hate going to see doctors," Rip countered. "I was perfectly healthy when I arrived at her office, and a total wreck knocking on death's door when I left. It's all the doc's fault!"

"Yes, of course it is, dear. I always have thought Dr. Herron was responsible for all of your health issues," I said dryly. "In fact, I'm not sure she isn't just making it all up to keep you coming back."

"You're just standing up for her because my doctor's a female like you."

"Yeah, that's the reason. You bull-headed buffoon!"

Our bantering was all in good fun, but my concerns about his health were genuine. Dr. Herron had not been joking when she warned him of impending ill health if he didn't make dire changes immediately. In line with her suggestions, for breakfast, we'd each made do with one slice of unbuttered wheat toast and a shared grapefruit. We both needed to drop a few unwanted pounds. Actually, it was more than just a few in Rip's case. He could lose twenty pounds overnight and his arteries, heart, back, and knees wouldn't miss them one bit. Nor would his wife!

Until recently, I'd let him eat about anything he'd wanted following his hip replacement last August, so he could concentrate all his complaints on the pain and suffering from the surgery, as men are wont to do. But the scales had begun groaning louder and louder each time he stepped on them, and I knew it was time for both of us to resume a healthy eating regimen. Rip's primary physician, Dr. Herron, had verified that conclusion at Rip's check-up before we left Rockport for Wyoming in late winter.

At that appointment, which Rip had felt was totally unnecessary, the no-nonsense doctor had warned him his high cholesterol and off-the-chart triglyceride levels put him at greater risk for a stroke and heart disease. She told him he needed to reduce his saturated fat, carbohydrates, and sugar intake. My stubborn husband had scoffed at her advice, saying man could not live on carrots alone. He also pooh-poohed her suggestion to join a gym so he could exercise more.

An unhappy camper, Rip was missing his customary bacon and cheese omelets, which in the past seven or eight months had been routinely served with an English muffin, laden with butter and lathered in strawberry jam. He clearly wanted to make sure I appreciated the sacrifice he was making to help me keep him alive for at least another week.

"It's not fair," he grumbled. "I feel weak. I think I could actually pass out if I don't get some *real* food in my stomach soon."

"Then pass out quietly, dear. All your squawking is getting on my nerves."

Rip was now fully invested in the pity party he was throwing for himself in the living room, grumbling that his stomach thought his throat had been cut. As usual, I was unmoved by his bellyaching. It was his health I was most concerned with, even if he didn't appear to be worried about it at all. Finally, I'd had enough. "Would you like a little cheese with your whine, darling?"

"Yes, yes, and hell yes!" He enthusiastically replied. "And a handful of crackers to accompany the cheese would be welcome, as well. In fact, I'll take anything you have to offer, as long as I can stuff it in my mouth."

"Why don't you stuff that throw pillow you're leaning on in your mouth? It may not appease your stomach, but at least it'd plug up your pie-hole."

"Humph! Neither you or Dr. Herron care about my misery and anguish, do you?"

I ignored his grumbling and dried my hands on a dish towel before joining him in the living room. I picked up my iPad to see if I could locate an owner's manual online that'd explain how to use my new critter cam. "How about we go search for a good location in the woods to set up this new camera? It will take your mind off eating."

"I doubt that, but I'm game if you are."

"Great. Just let me see if I can find some instructions on how to operate it first."

"We don't need instructions. How difficult can it be? It's a camera, for goodness sakes. It should be self-explanatory."

"Um, yeah. But—"

"Trust me, I'll figure it out. It's not like I haven't used a camera before, you know. I had to take photos of crime scenes for years. It's the exact same thing."

"Was the department's camera motion-activated? Did the victim have to come back to life and wave at the camera to trip the shutter release? Did the only item a burglar didn't steal have to roll off the coffee table? It is *not* the exact same thing, Rip."

"Don't be ridiculous. I can figure it out, honey. It's not rocket science, for goodness sakes." Rip exuded confidence, but that didn't prevent the flashbacks I was suddenly experiencing.

"*Listen here, Rapella. How difficult can it be to fix this lawnmower?*"

"*Come on, Rapella. I really don't need instructions to repair the dishwasher.*"

"*Seriously, Rapella? You, of all people, want to waste money on a mechanic when I can fix this transmission malfunction myself?*"

"*Trust me, sweetheart. I can get this DVD player working perfectly. Like new, in fact.*"

In each case, a few days and many profanities later, the lawn mower, dishwasher, transmission, and DVD player had indeed all worked perfectly. *Like new, in fact*, as Rip had promised. But that's only because all four *were* brand new after Rip had declared that the faulty ones he'd tried to repair were worthless and unfixable pieces of crap. On each occasion, all that was left of the faulty device was a box full of miscellaneous parts he'd removed in his attempt to repair it and later didn't have a clue where they'd come from or how to return them to their rightful place.

But, I didn't want to dissuade him and have him change his mind about accompanying me into the deep, dark, and totally horrifying woods. So I choked back a sarcastic retort on the tip of my tongue and, with fingers crossed behind my back, said, "Okay, dear. I guess I'm ready if you're certain you can figure out how to set the camera up and make it function properly."

"I couldn't be more certain!"

* * *

"What do you reckon 'burst' means?" Rip asked. "Or 'delay'?"

I remained silent. Not only was I already irritated with him, I knew he'd pay no attention to any opinion I voiced anyway. He'd fiddled with the camera while I nervously paced in circles around the pine tree he'd chosen to attach it to. Attach it after, of course, he'd figured out how to set and activate it to trip the camera's shutter whenever the motion sensor was triggered. My head was spinning on my neck like a merry-go-round as I tried to keep my concentration fixed on our surroundings and off the unimaginable amount of time it was taking Rip to figure out how to operate the camera.

He'd been randomly pushing buttons and turning dials on the critter cam, more accurately referred to as a game camera, for over half-an-hour. Pushing random buttons and arbitrarily turning dials in an eenie-meenie-miney-mo fashion is exactly how he frequently screws up the settings on the remote control, forcing us to watch reruns of the *Three Stooges* for hours on end until some seven-year old stops by and re-programs it. Rip thinks the trio of screwballs are hysterical. But after about fifteen minutes of watching their nonsense, I'm ready to throw a brick through the TV screen.

Thinking back to Rip's earlier statement, I was thankful now that utilizing the camera *wasn't* rocket science. If it were, the critter cam, and the two of us, would probably be orbiting the moon by now, having been rocketed into space by Rip's haphazard fiddling with the device. It would have given an entirely new significance to the term "space junk".

At this point, I realized from years of experience my husband would never be able to duplicate the procedure even if he did manage to get the camera set properly. But I kept that thought to myself. I was more interested in getting back to the safety of our travel trailer than anything else, and a bout of bickering would only delay, or possibly prevent, that desirable outcome.

"What 'burst' says to me is how bright the infrared flash illuminates if motion is detected at night," Rip reasoned, talking to himself more than me. "And what 'delay' says to me is the amount of time it takes for the shutter to open after that motion has been detected."

"Whatever you say," I replied. Unable to contain my annoyance any longer, I added, "But what both 'burst' and 'delay' say to me is that you should have listened to your wife and let her Google the instruction manual for you to study before we left the trailer. That way you wouldn't have had to wing it once we got out here in the woods, thereby making us vulnerable to attacks by wild animals for a much longer time than necessary."

As expected, Rip ignored my response. Although activating the camera seemed as if it might turn out to be nothing more than a time-consuming catastrophe, he'd had no trouble deactivating his selective hearing at a moment's notice.

Rip was a stubborn man, determined to save face. He was not going to throw in the towel if there was still an unlikely chance to prevent having to swallow his pride and admit I might have had a valid point. This was a man who'd once driven four counties out of our way rather than stop so I could walk into a convenience store and ask for directions.

When I realized it could be a good long while before he needed my assistance to strap the camera to the tree trunk, I sat down on a bed of pine needles and leaned my back up against a large rock. The warmth of the sun shining through the tree limbs was on the verge of lulling me to sleep when the snapping of a branch about twenty yards behind me nearly made me wet my pants. Even Rip was startled by the unexpected noise and reached for the forty-caliber pistol in the holster attached to his leather belt. *Only to run the animal off, unless it becomes a life or death situation for us,* he'd promised. I wanted an approaching animal scared off, not mortally wounded, as Bea had mercilessly done to the mama bear the previous day.

"I don't like this location. Too close to the campground." We heard a man's voice say, but couldn't make out what a softer female voice said in response. It sounded to me as if she'd mentioned something about a saw, claw, or jaw, but I couldn't be certain. I also thought I'd made out another word she'd said, like "tack" or "tap". Rip couldn't hear the woman's voice at all because his hearing deficiency was most prominent in the higher-pitched tones. It was an issue I was always reminded of when he claimed to not have heard me ask him to do something he'd had no desire to do in the first place.

The voices were getting harder to make out as the distance between us appeared to get greater. The only other word I could decipher was the male voice saying "valley".

"What kind of idiots would be out here in the middle of the woods?" I asked.

"Besides you and me?"

"Well, uh—"

"Maybe they've entered the photo contest too and have visions of twenty-five thousand buckaroos dancing in their heads like you do," Rip said. He sounded more frustrated than amused. "I think I've got this thing ready to strap to the tree trunk now. Let's get it done and get the heck out of here!"

I couldn't have agreed more. But strapping the game camera to the tree was easier said than done. I was afraid that at any given moment he'd drop kick the entire contraption into the mountain stream that meandered through the woods not far from the pine tree Rip had been cursing for the last twenty minutes. I'd actually witnessed him booting a golf club into a pond one day after whiffing three straight shots from the edge of a sand trap. So I had first-hand knowledge of how disgusted he could get when aggravated.

He controlled his temper this time and continued fiddling with the straps. Finally, he rubbed his hands together and said, "There! Now if I can arm it without causing it to slide down the tree or tilt over again, we've got it made."

I clapped my hands and was backing away from the tree when a loud, shrill "SCREECH" made me trip over my shadow and fall on my rear end. Fortunately, there was just enough padding there to keep me from breaking my tailbone. A broken butt was not something I was anxious to deal with.

Once I'd gotten back up on my feet, my first instinct was to sprint away from the direction from which the sound had originated, but Rip advised me to stay next to him. He was the one with the weapon, he reminded me, and the hip replacement surgery he'd undergone eight months ago was not going to allow him to outrun a bear, or any other animal, except possibly a pissed-off sloth.

He told me that in a situation like this, one should not panic. He said, "The worst thing to do when approached by a wild animal is to run away from it."

Not panic? I couldn't promise that, but I definitely was not going to run. Especially when we didn't know which direction to flee since we weren't entirely sure from which direction we'd come. If I sprinted off erroneously, I'd likely beat the bears back to their den, where they'd devour me as if I'd been delivered by room service on a silver platter.

Although I didn't say so out loud, I felt confident that due to that aforementioned surgery of Rip's, I could outrun my husband and, naturally, it was the one pulling up the rear who was most at risk of being mauled, killed, and/or eaten by the animal you're fleeing. Not that I wanted him to be attacked or injured in any way either, you understand. Survival of the fittest is an appropriate phrase that comes to mind. Just saying…

But, fortunately, outrunning Rip was not an issue that day. Luck was with us and he was able to retrace our path well enough that we emerged only seven RV sites down from where we'd initially entered the woods. The frightful screeching noise we'd heard was enough to make me want to forget the idea of winning a photo contest and sacrifice the twenty bucks I'd spent on the critter cam. And for me, that's saying a lot.

I assumed Rip was just as reluctant as I to ever step foot inside the terrifying woods again. But I soon realized the scary sound we'd heard had only served to encourage him when he remarked, "I can't wait to see if we capture any wildlife photos on the camera, maybe even that critter we heard screeching right before we headed back. Didn't Cora say she could download the photos on the memory card to our iPad for us to look through?"

"Yeah, but—"

"Good. Let's give it three days. Then we'll go retrieve the camera and check it out. I think there's a way to tell how many images have been captured on the memory card from the display on the camera. Why don't you find the owner's manual online so I can study it in the meantime?"

"Gee, why didn't I think of that?"

"That's amazing!" I exclaimed. "Eight hundred and forty-seven photos!"

I was so excited I could barely contain myself as I watched Cora upload the photos to our tablet. I just knew my critter cam had captured an award-winning photograph of the female mountain lion Boonie had assured me belonged to the screeching noises emitting from the woods surrounding the Rest 'n Peace campground.

After reading the manual during the three days' wait Rip had allotted before checking it, he'd figured out how to operate the camera. When we'd returned to the pine tree and removed the camera from the tree, Rip had said, "I'm going to mark this tree with a ribbon. If we capture any wildlife photos here, it's likely a great location to set it back up in the future."

"Set it back up?" I'd muttered uneasily. I thought this was a "one-and-done" type of endeavor. *Shouldn't I already have a twenty-five thousand dollar winning photo on the memory card?* I had wanted to ask. In retrospect, it's just as well I kept the inquiry to myself.

We were waiting patiently to preview all the photos the camera had taken as Cora went through the process of uploading them on our iPad. She dutifully explained each step as she performed it, as if seriously thinking either Rip or I would remember them by the time ten minutes had passed.

A short time later, as we clicked through the photos one by one, we began to get confused. We were baffled by the first thirty or so photos that seemed to be taken of the same viewpoint sideways, upside down, and at every other possible angle. The next few photos showed what looked like skin, perhaps the palm of someone's hand.

"It's like someone was jacking with our camera," I said.

Cora and Rip agreed. There was no other way to explain the photos. We all gasped in unison when the inseam of a pair of jeans was spotted in a subsequent photo. I turned to Rip, and said, "I'll bet that couple we heard talking in the woods came across our camera. They might have even been stalking us, waiting for us to leave so they could mess with the critter cam."

"That sounds a little far-fetched, Rapella. Even for you," he replied. "Keep clicking through them."

The next two hundred photos showed different scenes, ranging from a cloud in the sky to a pile of animal scat on the ground. Rip echoed my thoughts when he remarked. "It looks like somebody was walking with the camera."

"They took the camera off the tree?" I asked. "How odd is that?"

"Odd's not the word for it. Returning it to the exact same spot later on is even odder." Cora shook her head in disbelief. "Why would someone take your camera, walk around with it, and then bring it back and reattach it to the same tree they'd removed it from?"

Cora looked confounded as I shrugged my shoulders in response. Then as Rip clicked on the next file, she exclaimed, "Hey! There's someone's shoe! Someone's definitely walking with the camera and doesn't realize it's still on."

"Maybe we'll figure out who it is in the remaining images!" I was angry that someone would mess with our camera and, like Cora, perplexed as to why they'd steal it and then return it to the exact spot they'd found it.

"You can! Even I know who it was." Willie spoke up for the first time, all the while rolling his eyes. "Good grief, and to think I'm the kid in this foursome."

"How?" Rip, Cora, and I asked in stereo.

"It's not that odd, after all," Willie said with a mocking tone. "Look down, Aunt Rapella. That's your shoe in the photo! See the red stitching around the heel that's identical to the shoes you're wearing? And the earlier picture was of Uncle Rip's blue jeans, the same pair he's wearing now. See the matching purple stain on his pants leg?"

"Duh," Rip replied, as we all glanced from my sneakers to his Levi's. He slapped Willie on the back and said, "Sorry, son. Senior moment. I think it's clear that the three days we believed it was on, it was actually off. Then when I thought I'd turned it off when we went out to retrieve it, I'd actually turned it on. All eight hundred and forty-seven photos are of us carrying the camera home this morning, starting with me turning it on when I thought I was turning it off, and removing the camera from the tree."

"Jeez, Louise," I said. "That was a wasted three days."

"Don't look at it that way, Aunt Rappie," Cora said to console me. "Look at it as a learning experience. Give it another try."

"She's right," Rip said. "What do you say, Rapella? You game?"

"Oh, heck, why not?" I consented. "As someone recently told me, ain't none of us getting out of this world alive anyway. But, I have to admit, I'd prefer dying in my sleep on my one-hundredth birthday, as opposed to being gnawed on this afternoon by a mountain lion like I was a piece of beef jerky."

He reviewed the online owner's manual again, before reinserting the memory card into the camera and erasing all the photos on it by pushing in and holding two buttons on the control panel of the camera at the same time for three seconds, as the manual instructed. He then set the camera to take a burst of three photos in rapid succession after a five-second delay each time motion activated the shutter. "Okay, honey. Let's go. I've studied the manual and know how to operate it now. It's ready to turn on as soon as we get it reattached to the tree."

Three days later we found ourselves sitting at the kitchen table again, reviewing the twenty-seven photos on the memory card from our second attempt. Cora had stopped by to upload them for us. We were disappointed again when each photo showed a blurry streak across the sky from when a bird had flown within the camera's motion detection range. The only things in focus in the whole lot were a few tail feathers of an owl that were picked up by the infrared light at night, and the red head of a cardinal flying in bright sunlight.

"Well, at least we had it set up perfectly," Rip said.

"Yeah, right," I replied dryly. "Perfect if we were hoping to get an amazing shot of a giraffe's head while it strolled past our camera in the forest. I say we give up and—"

"This time we need to lower the camera's angle to catch sharp images of land animals, not blurry ones of birds in flight." As usual, Rip had totally ignored me.

Three days later, after clicking through the two hundred and twelve photos on the memory card, I found myself growing even wearier of the endeavor.

The first few images were encouraging: a yellow-bellied marmot sniffing the lens of the critter cam. They were fuzzy and hardly of award-winning quality, but I was excited to see an actual varmint in a few of the photos. I thought of them as a preview of coming attractions as I anxiously clicked on the fourth .jpg file, which was an image of the south end of the marmot as it ambled away. The fifth image was of nothing more than a single strand of tall grass.

Naturally, I was disheartened when the next two hundred and nine photos were of the same blade of grass that had apparently been buffeting around in the wind. It'd been captured in a photo each time it moved vigorously enough to set off the motion detector.

I was ready to pitch the camera in the same meandering stream that days earlier I'd worried Rip might boot it into, but Rip was still not ready to throw in the towel. With undue optimism, he said, "We're getting closer. But you were absolutely right about adjusting the camera's angle."

I pulled our cell phone out of my back pocket and asked, "Do you mind repeating that part about me being right so I can get it on tape?"

Rip grinned broadly, and replied, "Well, it was bound to happen sooner or later, you know. And, by the way, video *tape* became obsolete before the turn of the century. Try a little harder to stay up to date, sweetheart. You need to be on top of things like I am."

"And this is coming from a man who asked me last night where our answering machine had gotten off to?"

"Yes. And I'm still waiting patiently for your answer."

"Fine. I'd hate to make you wait any longer. Our answering machine is in technology heaven. I think it 'rusts in peace' right next to the push-button phone it used to be connected to."

Our playful banter lifted my spirits. But they plummeted again when Rip said, "This time we need to try to aim the camera higher, but not as high as we had it before. It should be over the top of the foliage in the near vicinity and at the correct height and angle to capture a taller land animal, such as a mountain lion or bear. If we keep trying, we're bound to get a decent wildlife photo eventually."

My husband's stubborn trait had always managed to push my buttons, and I found myself getting increasingly annoyed with his bullheadedness.

"Whatever," I said in a huff as I shook my head.

* * *

Three days later, on a cool Thursday morning in the mountains, we cheered at a washed-out, silhouetted image of an unidentifiable four-legged critter's rear end. Because, after all, our bar for success had been set very low after several unsuccessful attempts. Studying the expression on Rip's face, I could tell he was already thinking about our next shot at it. I feared his mulish streak was just getting warmed up.

"Stick a fork in me, dear. I'm done! We've already given it four tries, and in my opinion, that was four tries too many." Even as I spoke, I knew my words were falling on deaf ears, both figuratively *and* literally.

"Just one more time," Rip pleaded. I was more than ready to immerse myself in a new activity, but my obstinate husband wanted to give it five days on a fifth attempt, convinced the four-legged critter was a mountain lion and would one day soon return to pose charmingly for the camera. Charmingly enough, in fact, to take the grand prize purse in the wildlife photo competition. The contest deadline was only two weeks away, Rip reminded me. I wanted to slap the optimistic smile off his face.

CHAPTER 6

"Hello again. Fancy seeing you here," Jan greeted me nonchalantly early Saturday afternoon when I ran into her in the laundry room again. She was clad in a silk workout suit, and glistened with perspiration, as if she'd just finished jogging. Even then she looked quite chic; fresh and fit as a fiddle. I, on the other hand, looked like I'd been robbing homeless bums again.

"Good afternoon, Jan. We must be on the same laundry schedule."

"Looks that way, doesn't it?" Jan was in a cheerful mood, as was I. Rip and I were looking forward to our afternoon cocktails ritual and a quiet night at home. Jan hung up a sleeveless top, and then asked, "Say, have you heard the news?"

"What news?"

"Bea Whetstone is missing." The casualness of the Illinois native's reply was the same as if she were telling me that the local Lion's Club was putting on a chili feed to raise money for a new rest stop along the Cloud Peak Skyway, a scenic byway between Buffalo and Ten Sleep. Nothing about the woman's manner indicated a reason for concern, so I felt no immediate cause for alarm either.

"Missing?" I asked, somewhat confused by the term Jan had used. "What do you mean by 'missing'?"

"No one can find her. Boonie was going around to each site this morning asking each camper in turn if we'd seen her. You must have not been in your RV at the time."

We had spent the morning in town, watching Willie's baseball team beat a team from Worland, six to five. Our nephew, who was Buffalo's third-baseman, knocked in the winning run with a double off the right field wall. For a wiry kid, he had a good stroke and an even better eye. He rarely went down swinging.

"We were at a ball game in town. What's going on? How in the world could Bea be missing?" I asked. I suddenly felt a twinge of concern, but not panic.

"Dunno. But Boonie said she'd gone to the office to take care of some business after supper last night, and he hadn't seen her since. He mentioned that she always waited until ten o'clock to run each day's credit card batch. Then she'd record that day's sales in the park ledger before locking up the store and office. But when Boonie woke up this morning, Bea was nowhere to be found. Apparently he tosses and turns all night. He said all his restless fidgeting made it hard to tell if her side of the messy bed had been slept on."

"You mean Boonie went to bed without making sure Bea had returned home safely? There's a fair distance between the office and their home, and we know for a fact that there are dangerous creatures that come into the campground at will. And that's just of the four-legged variety. The two-legged kind can be even more perilous at times."

"That same thought crossed my mind too. From what Boonie told me, Bea often awoke early in the morning and would go for a hike in the forest. But she'd always returned in time to open the store at eight."

"She hiked in the forest alone?" I asked, marveling at her courage, as well as her dedication to stay fit. "Isn't that a little foolish? Not to mention, potentially hazardous to one's health?"

"Yeah. But, Boonie said she usually carries a small handgun for protection, And, as we witnessed a while back, she wouldn't hesitate to fire a gun at a bear, or at any animal that crossed her path, most likely. According to her husband, she'd had a close call with a mountain lion about six months ago."

"And yet she still goes walking in the forest by herself?" Now I was marveling at the breadth of Bea's stupidity.

"Looks that way," Jan replied before she had to go cram more quarters in the dryers.

The Whetstones lived in a small log cabin of about twelve hundred square feet, nestled back into a cluster of aspen trees in the far northwest corner of the property. There were no outdoor lights illuminating the path from the campground office to the Whetstones' rustic little home. I had to admit it was a cozy, but secluded location.

As I sat there waiting for my washer to stop spinning, I mused about where the missing woman could have disappeared to. Had she gone for a hike and had another unexpected encounter with a cougar that didn't end well for her? Or, conversely, had she never made it back to their house the evening before? More likely, I thought, she was at a friend or relative's house and had not told Boonie of her plans. Someone could have picked her up early that morning before her husband had awakened.

I assumed working in the office late at night was probably a routine she and Boonie were both accustomed to. If it'd never been an issue in the past, he probably felt comfortable in assuming she'd come to bed when she'd finished up with her customary evening paperwork. Or, maybe, he didn't give a bee's behind whether his surly wife made it home, or not.

"I'd think the most logical explanation for her absence is due to a lack of communication," I said. "One day, before we retired, I was on the way back from grocery shopping and got delayed for three hours by a multi-car accident that happened directly in front of me. After the wreck, the highway looked like a war zone with emergency equipment everywhere, and it took a long time to clear the road. We didn't have a cell phone back then and I fretted the entire time that Rip was worried half to death and, as a police officer, might even have put out an all-points bulletin on me. After all, the chore took several hours longer than it would have otherwise, and I knew Rip would have expected me home a lot earlier."

"So, what happened? Did your husband have half the police force out searching for you?" Jan asked.

"No. As it turned out, he hadn't even realized I wasn't in the house the entire time. So much for worried half to death. But my point is, mix-ups like that happen all the time."

"Yeah, I know. But they don't happen as often as they used to before nearly every person over six years old carried a cell phone. My guess is whatever happened to her, happened in the woods on her morning hike." Jan seemed certain Bea had suffered an animal attack. The very idea sent a chill up my spine.

"Do you reckon a bear got her? Or a mountain lion, perhaps?" I asked.

"Dunno," the lady said. Almost gleefully, she added, "Maybe."

"She may have ticked off an entire community of forest inhabitants when she ruthlessly took out one of their own," I said. I was still seething at the cold-heartedness of the woman when she killed the mama bear and left her cub with no parent to protect it.

Jan nodded silently. Her next remark seemed a bit cold to me. I flinched as she said, "Couldn't really blame them for seeking revenge."

"Well, let's pray she's all right." My voice was trembling a bit. I'm not sure if I was more unnerved by the news of the missing campground owner, or the fact the lady telling me about it showed no concern whatsoever about the woman's well-being. It went without saying that Jan wouldn't be kneeling down beside her bed to send up a prayer on Bea's behalf anytime soon.

But I would. "So, there's still no clue or idea where she might be?"

"Dunno," was Jan's unruffled reply.

"Has Boonie searched the woods where his wife liked to hike? You know, just in case she's been immobilized by an animal, or something else entirely, and needs to be rescued before it's too late?"

"Dunno" seemed to be her go-to response as she repeated it once more, and then added, "Don't think so."

"I assume there's no real, and undeniable, evidence of an animal attack. There isn't, is there?"

"Dunno. Don't think so." Jan seemed to have clammed up all of a sudden.

"Has Boonie filed a missing person's report?"

After Jan replied with "dunno" for the fifth time in the same dispassionate tone, I said, "I'll bet she shows up somewhere unharmed. Probably nothing more than a case of miscommunication between the couple, as I said before."

I hurriedly finished folding my laundry so I could rush back to the trailer and tell Rip about the disappearance of the campground's co-owner. If not a miscommunication, my guess was that Bea Whetstone had left of her own accord. Boonie had seemed like a decent fellow in my dealings with him, even though the one interaction I'd witnessed between the pair had been tense. But who really knew what went on behind closed doors when it came to another couple's relationship? Just keeping one's own marriage strong and on an even keel was a full-time job at times.

Like Jan, Rip had been unmoved by the news of the missing woman. And, like me, he'd felt confident she'd show up soon, if she hadn't already been located. "You wouldn't believe how many times in my career a missing person is reported, only to show up at a friend's house an hour or so later."

"Reckon the Whetstones' marriage is going through a rough patch right now? Remember what I told you about her rudeness to him the other day in the store?"

"It's really none of our business either way, Rapella. No sense getting tongues a 'wagging by gossiping about the couple's relationship."

My husband could be a real killjoy. I certainly had no intention of gossiping about the Whetstones and told him so. "Merely discussing the events of the day with one's spouse is not the same thing as gossiping, I'll have you know."

Rip picked up the remote control and turned the volume up a notch, clearly not interested in discussing the subject with me any longer. He was effectively drowning me out with an old rerun of *The Rifleman*. Chuck Connors was twirling his shotgun like it was a drum major's baton. He was ready to mount his horse and chase down a cattle rustler when I walked out the door. With any luck at all, I would happen upon someone who *was* interested in talking about Bea Whetstone's disappearance.

CHAPTER 7

When we'd captured nothing of significance on the game camera after the five allotted days, Rip decided we needed to move the camera farther into the woods. All we'd managed to photograph was the back half of a cottontail bunny. As we viewed the photo, I realized that the bunny may have already been consumed by something higher up the food chain. I hate to admit it, but I was getting so impatient I briefly wished the bunny *had* been fleeing a hungry cougar. At least we'd have had a fair chance at capturing an image of the feral cat sprinting by.

Rip was discouraged too, but not to the point of giving up on the venture. "Maybe we'll capture something a little more interesting if we change locations."

I'd been even more reluctant to enter the forest than normal after waking up in the middle of the night soaking wet following a dream about Bea Whetstone being chased down by an angry sleuth of bears.

I don't know about you, but I find the word "sleuth" an odd choice to describe a group of bears. But it sounds more fitting than its alternative, a "sloth" of bears. There was certainly nothing sloth-like about the bears in my dream, tearing through the forest at break-neck speed with only one goal in mind: to seek vengeance against the evil creature who'd shot down their friend while she was protecting her baby.

At Rip's insistence that, if need be, he could scare away any wild animal with his gun without harming it, I took a leap of faith and followed him far into the woods once again. And for a couple of terrifying minutes, I regretted that decision.

The forecast that morning had called for a sixty percent chance of rain, so we both wore red ponchos I'd picked up at Wal-Mart while we were staying at a campground in Eugene, Oregon. It seemed as if Eugene's entire annual average of rainfall, almost forty-two inches, fell during the month we were there.

Wearing our ponchos, we were marching down a well-worn path when Rip reached out and grabbed my arm so abruptly it startled me. Out of instinct and natural reflexes, he grabbed his weapon and pushed me behind him just as I noticed what he'd already seen: a black bear and three cubs in the path ahead of us. One cub was quite a bit smaller than the other two. All four bears were standing still and observing us quietly.

"Stay behind me," Rip said. "Don't run. The sow's going to have to get through me before she can get to you. If she rushes me, run back to the trailer as fast as you can. If I'm forced to use my gun, shooting birdshot over their heads will probably scare them off. But, if not, I'll do everything I can to keep them occupied so you can put some distance between you and them."

I was touched by my husband's vow to protect me. I felt a sense of shame for having ever considered whether or not I could outrun him if we were being chased by a wild animal.

We'd heard you want to make yourself look as large and intimidating as possible when confronted by a bear. Rip decided our best bet was to stand side-by-side and hold our over-sized ponchos as far out from our sides as we could so together we'd look like an immense red monster with four legs, at least two of which were shaking badly. I'm surprised the right half of the red monster was even able to remain upright.

After about fifteen of the longest seconds in my entire life, the mother bear turned and sauntered off at a ninety-degree angle, away from our intended destination, nudging the playful cubs to keep them moving along ahead of her.

"Phew!" I said. I was panting and trying to catch my breath, as if I had just run down a purse snatcher. "That was a close one! Let's get the heck out of here."

"No, we'll be all right. She won't bother us and is going off in the other direction, anyway." Rip shoved the gun back into its holster.

If I didn't love him so much, I'd have wished mama bear had smacked Rip around a little—without seriously hurting him, of course. Just enough to knock some sense into the stubborn fool's thick skull. Meanwhile, I'd have broken the land-speed record sprinting back to the campground, which at that moment seemed a million miles away.

"Oh, good grief. All right," I consented only because we'd already walked a good distance and would have to retrace our steps back to camp either way. "Did you notice how small the one cub was compared to its siblings?"

"Yeah, I did. My guess is that the mama bear adopted the cub whose mother was killed by Bea that day. It's not uncommon with bears, and a lot of other animal species, for a female to adopt orphaned babies. That'd explain the size difference too. The little one was obviously born later than the other cubs, and to another female bear. It was too much smaller to just be the runt of the litter."

"I hope the runt was the orphan then. Brothers from a different mother, huh? That would be awesome!"

We zigzagged our way through the trees and abundant foliage and located a different spot deeper into the forest where the vegetation was not quite as dense. After Rip decided he'd found the perfect location, he attached the camera to the trunk of a large sycamore tree. As I paced nervously, I urged him to quit lollygagging. My pulse had still not returned to normal.

I was distracted by a whistling sound behind me. I felt my heart rate soar even higher, and quickly extracted Rip's new Bushnell binoculars from the leather case hanging from his belt to look for the source of the eerie sound. Scanning the area, I saw nothing out of the ordinary, so I leaned the field glasses against the base of the tree where they'd be handy if I heard the noise again. After a few quiet minutes, I decided the noise had been a figment of my over-active imagination. I attributed it to my anxiety about the earlier bear encounter and the fact we were lingering in the woods a lot longer than I felt comfortable with. Satisfied with this deduction, I resumed pacing.

"I'm about done here, honey," Rip assured me when he noticed my restlessness. "I know you're nervous. I'm a bit jumpy myself. You can go on and head back if you'd like and I'll catch up with you shortly."

I considered his suggestion with mixed emotions. On the one hand, I wasn't wild about walking alone in the woods. A protective mama bear might only scoff at half a red monster, and a wobbly one at that. Plus, I was not entirely certain from which direction we'd come. On the other hand, I couldn't get out of those woods fast enough. But I knew walking in the wrong direction would serve absolutely no good purpose whatsoever.

"Which way is the campground?" I asked, praying Rip had paid better attention to our path and the direction our trek through the forest had taken us, or at least possessed a better sense of direction, than I did. An unanswered prayer, I soon discovered.

"Um, well, let's see," Rip mumbled. He glanced around and finally pointed toward a cluster of juniper trees, a decision based solely on a wild-ass guess, I could tell. "That way, I'm pretty sure. I'm not positive, though. I assumed you were taking note of our route so I could concentrate on a finding a good spot for your camera and keep an eye out for bears."

"You think I wasn't keeping an eye out for bears? I had *both* eyes watching for wild animals, one searching straight ahead and the other scanning the forest behind us. And that's no easy task." I could have predicted getting lost in the woods would somehow be my fault. It always seemed to work out that way when blame was being assigned. *Dang it!* I thought. *Where's a bag of Reece's Pieces when you need one?*

There was no consolation in knowing that, unlike a couple of mature adults, the young kids in *E.T. the Extra-Terrestrial* had the good sense to mark their trail so they could retrace their steps easily and accurately. I reluctantly walked away in the direction Rip had randomly chosen. Soon he was on my heels and chastising me for not keeping track of the twists and turns we'd made earlier while snaking our way through the forest.

"I should have known better," Rip grumbled. He wisely left off the last part of his statement, which would have been, "than to trust you". He didn't leave off the "patting himself on the back" part, however. "Probably a dang good thing I thought to bring a gun with me."

I'll see to it you get a medal, I wanted to say, but thought better of it. *Too bad you didn't also think to mark our trail with pieces of candy, or at least pay heed to the route you took to lead us out here. After all, I'd have been totally content to abandon the idea of capturing a good wildlife photo altogether.*

Keeping track of directions while following someone through the forest was like being a passenger in a car. If you weren't the one driving, you weren't as aware of which direction you were going or how you'd gotten somewhere after you'd arrived.

We wandered aimlessly in circles for over an hour. When we passed the same red-tailed hawks' nest for the third time, and the tree we'd attached the camera to twice, I said, "We are clearly going nowhere fast, and it's going to get dark soon. You need to call someone who can help us find our way out of here before it's too late and we have another encounter with wild animals that doesn't go as smoothly.

Many of them come out to feed at night, you know. So call someone already!"

"You're being overly dramatic, dear. And just whom do you expect me to call? Nine-one-one?"

"Well, yes. For starters, anyway. Surely there's a forest ranger in the area who knows these woods like the back of his hand. He'd surely come to our rescue before we can't see our hands in front of us."

Unfortunately, I was talking to a man who would rather face a firing squad than ask anyone for assistance. A man who felt perfectly at ease rescuing someone else, but uncomfortable asking anyone to help him. A fact I was reminded of once again when he said, "Let's give it another half-hour. I think I see a clearing off in the distance. Maybe we can get our bearings if we're out in the open."

I sighed heavily and trudged on.

After a few moments, Rip commented again. "It's probably a moot point anyway. I looked earlier and we weren't getting a signal. Didn't I warn you about signing up with the cheapest service provider? They're the cheapest for a reason, you know. The way we travel around the country now, we need the company that offers the best coverage."

My guilt about having ever judged my ability to outrun Rip, should we be chased by a savage animal, dissipated quickly. I was now seriously beginning to hope a bear would sneak up behind us and give me the opportunity to try my luck. With his recent hip-replacement, and ever-expanding belt-line, I felt I had a pretty fair advantage on him. With a bear behind me, my tired old legs would be pumping ninety to nothing by the time I got up to speed. Teed off, but not anxious to get into a heated argument that might draw predators to us, I simply said. "Like you said, at least you have your gun on you."

My comment made Rip instinctively reach for his holster and his binoculars case. He cursed loudly, and then said, "I've lost my field glasses somehow. They must have slipped out of the case."

I knew exactly where his binoculars were; still propped up against the lodge pole pine, next to the sycamore that had our game camera strapped to it. After using them to try and locate the source of the whistling sound, I'd forgotten to pick them up and return them to the leather case hanging from Rip's belt. But I wasn't willing to offer myself up for another round of finger-pointing. If he piled any more blame on me, I'd soon need a periscope to see the path ahead of me while we traipsed hopelessly through the woods. So, I simply replied, "Way to go, buster!"

Twenty minutes later we emerged from the woods into a small clearing approximately the size of six football fields. The ground was wet and spongy with only a few bushes and cattails scattered about. Glancing around, we spotted a man on top of a ledge who was scanning the area through a set of binoculars. He was our only salvation at this point, and as much as I hated to walk through the marshy field, I knew it was a necessity. Through ankle-high sludge, I headed in the man's direction.

"Hey!" Rip said. "You're going to ruin your shoes in that muck!"

Now I am not one to throw away hard-earned money, especially to replace a pair of shoes that still had several years' worth of use left in them. But at that moment in time, I would have sacrificed my entire wardrobe to get to someone who could help us out of our current situation as quickly as possible. I felt a sense of being stalked and didn't want to spend any more time in that daunting forest than I had to.

As far as I was concerned, that stupid critter cam that Cora had talked me into wasting twenty bucks on could stay latched to the sycamore tree forever and rot away right along with Rip's binoculars. I had no intention of ever entering that forest again, if we got out of it in one piece to begin with.

"You can stand there like a dummy with clean shoes if you want to, dear, but I'm going to see if that man can point us in the right direction. The sun will be setting in an hour or so and, if we're still among the living by then, we're apt to still be out here walking in circles, trying to find our way back to the campground."

Without waiting for a response, I trudged on, waving my arms back and forth to get the man's attention. I could see a dark green jeep just a few yards behind him and was afraid he'd hop in it and take off. I felt a little silly when he raised his binoculars and aimed them straight at me. I could only imagine how I looked stomping through the mud and muck, swinging my arms wildly, acting like a crazed lunatic in the middle of an emotional meltdown who was being pursued by Sasquatch.

I felt a great deal of weight fall off my shoulders when the man on the outcropping returned my wave and put his binoculars down against the side of his thigh. With hands on his hips, he studied us curiously as we drew nearer. Rip was right behind me, grumbling under his breath. "Would you please put your arms down, Rapella? You're embarrassing me."

"Fine." I agreed only because the ranger on the hill was clearly waiting for us. "Are those your binoculars in his hand?"

"No. Mine are smaller and a different brand. He probably carries his every day. That's a Bighorn National Forest uniform he's wearing, so I'm assuming he's a ranger."

"Oh, thank God! He'll undoubtedly be able to assist us then."

"Let me do the talking, okay?"

"Fine," I said again. I wanted to add, *But you better say what I want you to say or I'm butting into the conversation the second you pause to take a breath.*

"What brings you folks out here today?" The ranger asked in way of a greeting.

"My wife here, Rapella, is trying to get an animal photo with her game camera to enter into the wildlife photography contest. We came out to set it up in a different location than we've already tried because we haven't captured much yet."

"Well, good luck to you, folks. That's quite a prize they're offering, and this is a great location to capture a winning wildlife photo. This marshy valley is prime moose habitat. My name's Richard Myer, by the way, but everyone calls me Ranger Rick."

Rip shook the man's hand. "It's a pleasure to meet you, Ranger Rick. I'm Clyde Ripple, or Rip, and as I said, my wife's name is Rapella. What brings *you* out here today? Are you out looking for Bea Whetstone, the missing owner of the Rest 'n Peace RV Park?"

"No. My department hasn't been brought into the search yet, but I've heard we will be soon. It's a damn shame though, ain't it?" Ranger Rick turned to me and apologized for his language and I assured him I'd heard much worse.

"Yeah. It's certainly worrisome for her to go missing like that," Rip remarked. "So, what are you up to today, Ranger Rick, if not searching for Mrs. Whetstone?"

"Yesterday, a couple of my fellow rangers and I found a cow moose caught in a bear trap at the tree line over there, just at the edge of this valley." He pointed to the edge of the marsh on the south end. "Worse yet, she had twin calves with her."

"Oh, no! How sad," I said. "Was she still alive?"

"Alive, but weak and badly injured. We called out the vet and he sedated her with a tranquilizer dart and treated her wounds as best he could. Her lower leg was cut deeply by the teeth of the jaw-like leg trap, and we weren't sure she'd be able to stand under her own weight when she came to. We stayed and watched her from the top of this plateau and, although she was quite wobbly, she slowly made her way back into the woods, no doubt looking for her calves that had darted off when we first arrived. Hopefully she'll survive her injuries. Her weakened condition will make her vulnerable to predators."

"Oh, dear! I hope she found her babies and all three are all right." The thought of the mother moose dying, or being killed before she found her twin calves was heartbreaking, and I was nearly moved to tears. I'd already witnessed a cub being orphaned, and now hearing the ranger's story about the potentially orphaned moose calves was even more distressing.

I told the ranger about our close call with the bear family earlier in the day. "Rip's quick thinking probably prevented our encounter with them from having a much different ending."

"You did exactly what you should have done to deter the mother bear. Sure glad you had your wits about you, Rip," he said. "However, it'd probably be in your best interest to carry some kind of weapon with you when you're wandering about in the forest. You never know what you might encounter. A pack of wolves would not have retreated like those bears did. Wolves hunt in a pack and would have had you surrounded before you knew it."

"I do carry a handgun; my service weapon from my law enforcement days." Rip pulled his jacket back to reveal his holstered gun.

"You were in law enforcement?" Ranger Rick asked. He sounded impressed.

"Yep! For thirty-seven years in all. I was a sheriff in south Texas my last ten years," Rip said. "Happy to be retired now, however. So what do you think the cow's chances of recovery are?"

"I think she'll make it, but I came out here hoping to catch a glimpse of the threesome to assure myself we'd made the right call. If she hadn't had calves with her, we might have put her down so she wouldn't suffer. But without their mother, the calves wouldn't stand a chance in hell of making it." Ranger Rick apologized once again for his choice of words, before continuing. "They'd also become fodder for a bear, cougar, grey wolf, or possibly even a pack of wolves. It's the natural cycle of life though, even if it's hard to accept sometimes."

The very idea of wolves being in the area strengthened my resolve to sacrifice the game camera and stay as far away from the woods as I could for the remainder of our stay in the Rest 'n Peace campground. My voice was almost a whisper when I asked, "So there's wolves around here too?"

"Yes, we've seen a few wolves around here recently. Ever since the U.S. Forest Service reintroduced grey wolves into Yellowstone in the mid-nineties, they've thrived. Not only have they proliferated, but they've spread far beyond the national park's boundaries. In 2011, they opened up a season on them, but in 2014, a U.S. District Court ruling relisted them on the endangered species list in all of Wyoming, much to the dismay of local ranchers."

"Understandably, due to the risk they pose to their livestock," Rip said.

I was dismayed by the ruling myself, knowing we'd probably have to traipse through the woods once again to find our way home to the campground after I'd made sure we got explicit directions from the ranger. I have nothing against wolves, mind you, but I don't exactly want to be the guest of honor at one of their family get-togethers.

"Say, it's going to get dark soon. You two need a lift?" Ranger Rick inquired. I was so relieved at his offer I could have kissed him, even though he'd probably think twice before offering a ride to sketchy-looking strangers in the future.

My spirits were lifted instantly by the ranger's kindness. Then I nearly choked on my own saliva when my bull-headed husband replied to the man's offer. Too proud to admit he had no clue about the route back to the RV park, he said, "No, we're good. We were kind of looking forward to hiking back to the campground by ourselves."

"What?" I shouted, almost hysterical. If I'd had a shovel in my hand I might have utilized it on my husband's thick skull. Three or four times, in fact.

Rip looked at me, as if surprised by my exclamation, and then back to the ranger. "But you're probably right, Rick. Darkness is almost upon us and Rapella's already a little chilled because she didn't think to bring along a warm enough jacket. Sometimes my better half doesn't have the sense God gave a skydiver who'd actually pay someone to let him jump out of their perfectly good plane."

I'd been highly impressed with the forest ranger until he'd laughed at Rip's sarcastic remark. What I wouldn't have given for a shovel at that moment! I'd have laid both of them out with it. Then I'd climb into the ranger's jeep and drive myself back to the Chartreuse Caboose, leaving those two jokers on the peak of the outcropping to fend for themselves—after they gained consciousness, that is! *Who'd get the last laugh then?* I thought.

By sundown the area was crawling with detectives. Ranger Rick had just delivered us to the RV park. The first thing we saw was a large portion of the campground's guests who were milling around aimlessly and chattering amongst themselves with concerned expressions on their faces. After we thanked the ranger, he departed and we joined the throng of curious RVers. I was surprised the ranger didn't stick around long enough to find out what the commotion was all about.

I glanced over at a swarm of people surrounding a young man I felt sure was a reporter for the *Buffalo Bulletin*. He looked like a younger version of Clark Kent, excitedly interviewing bystanders and scribbling their responses on a well-worn pad of paper. It'd become apparent to all of us, including my skeptical husband, that something ominous must have happened to Bea Whetstone. It appeared likely to be a more puzzling situation than her having just retreated to her mother's house after an angry tiff with her husband.

As the former sheriff of a county a good deal larger than the one we were currently camping in, Rip felt compelled to engage in a discussion with a horde of policemen who'd gathered to discuss their plan of action. I followed him as he strolled over to speak to the group. In the mix were six male cops, a lady cop, and the female sheriff of Johnson County, Jaclyn Wright.

When Rip approached the circle of law enforcement officers, their discussion came to an abrupt halt. It was an awkward moment for my husband. After a few seconds of silence, he introduced himself as the former sheriff of a south Texas county and a career law enforcement officer. "I've had many years of experience and would be happy to lend a hand if you need assistance. My wife and I would be more than willing to participate in a search party, as well."

I felt sure they'd welcome him into their circle with open arms, and I'm certain Rip did, too. Instead, he was given a very cold reception. Sheriff Wright gave her fellow sheriff a disdainful look after giving him the once-over. It was as if she was sizing up her competition before stepping into the middle of a boxing ring. "Sir, this is a private discussion and we can handle the situation just fine without your assistance. You need to worry about the jaywalkers in your own little jurisdiction and let me and my officers deal with this missing person case without interference."

"Jaywalkers?" Rip was angry. I could tell just how pissed he was by the amount of spittle that sprayed out of his mouth as he continued. "Did you actually say jaywalkers? I don't know about you, but I never had time to worry about jaywalkers because I was too busy taking care of more serious offenses. I'm willing to bet Aransas County, Texas, has a much higher crime rate than Johnson County, Wyoming, where there are more antelope than people."

"I doubt that," Sheriff Wright replied. "We have our fair share of crime too, I promise you. Now go on your way, sir."

I never thought I'd see two sheriffs bragging about the crime rates in their counties. Although neither county was exactly a hot bed of murderers, robbers and rapists, it appeared as if they were trying to out-crime each other. Rip was practically snarling when he said, "I was in law enforcement for more years than you've been alive, Missy. I'm sure I have a lot more experience in crime-fighting and solving cases than you do."

Just then a burly Buffalo police officer, about six-and-a-half feet tall and three-hundred pounds, walked over to Rip. Looking down at my five foot, seven-inch husband, the goliath said, "You'd better listen to the lady and go on back to your camper. We're more than capable of taking care of this situation without your help."

I can't remember the last time I'd seen Rip so livid. As he walked away, I heard Bea's husband being questioned by a detective. Rip told me he was going back to the trailer. No one in the group of eight had even cast a glance my way, so I said, "You go ahead. I'll be there in a few minutes."

Rip walked away in a huff, still seething from the sheriff's discourteous remarks.

Out of pure curiosity, I inched my way closer to the group of law enforcement officers to listen to what was being said. Rip had handed me our cell phone before he left and I fiddled with it nonchalantly so it wouldn't appear as if I was eavesdropping, which, of course, I was.

I turned on the video function and began recording so I could play it back for Rip should anything interesting be discussed. I was filming the ground, but still picking up their voices.

If I could figure out how to do it, I wanted to delete the first part of the recording, when the sheriff said, "Who does that roly-poly twerp think he is? I don't need him or any other two-bit sheriff telling me how to do my job. Being female doesn't mean I'm incompetent or incapable of handling my position as well as any man."

The male detectives wisely remained silent, while the sole female cop nodded her head in agreement. Despite the disrespect she'd shown my husband, I had to agree with her last remark. In fact, I think we'd all be better off, happier and more at peace, if women ruled the world. I believed if every country was led by a woman, war would soon cease to exist. Women by nature don't feel the obligation to flex their muscles in front of other women, or in front of men, for that matter.

The sheriff then asked Boonie a question I couldn't make out. But I heard Boonie make a reply that jived with what Jan had told me in the laundry room earlier. "My wife had a habit of taking early morning walks in the woods. She said it not only kept her fit, but walking also helped reduce stress. You don't think an animal attacked her, do you?"

"We don't know anything about what happened to her yet, sir," a detective replied. "Does she normally carry any kind of weapon to fend off an aggressive bear, or perhaps a cougar?"

"Yes. She nearly always carried a gun for protection, but she could have been taken by surprise. For example, six or seven months ago, a cougar leapt from the lower limb of a tree, landing right in front of her as she was walking down a trail just beyond the tree line behind our house. The cougar got in one good swipe at Bea's left arm before she dropped him with one shot from her pearl-handled Colt revolver."

I found Boonie's past-tense responses, as in "my wife had" and "she always carried" a bit odd. It was if he'd had the same premonition I now had that Bea was no longer with us. I had a bad feeling in my gut that she'd be found, but not found alive.

Then an older detective asked the bewildered park owner, "Was that Colt revolver missing when you awakened this morning?"

"No, it's still on top of her chest of drawers, which is why I was immediately concerned for her well-being when I couldn't locate her in the campground. I made a couple of phone calls and she wasn't at her sister's house, or her mother's either. Still, I suppose it's possible that if she did go for a walk this morning, as she so often did, she might have just forgotten to take it with her." Boonie didn't sound convinced.

One of the detectives then asked Boonie if he knew if Bea had come to bed the night before, and he replied, "I can't say for sure. I'm a restless sleeper, so I couldn't tell whether her side of the bed had been disturbed by her sleeping there, or it was just my tossing and turning that had the bedclothes all tangled up. Last time I recall seeing her was when she left to go to the office to do her end-of-day paperwork last night. I hit the sack soon after she departed."

"You know, Mr. Whetstone, your wife may very well be out there in the woods, injured and in danger of further harm. Did you search the walking trail she usually follows in an effort to retrace her path after you noticed she was missing?" Sheriff Wright asked.

I'd wondered the same thing, and was as surprised as the sheriff when Boonie replied, "No. I guess it didn't occur to me. Maybe I should have thought of that."

"You think?" The sheriff asked in a sarcastic tone.

After they dismissed Boonie, the officers conversed among themselves. I had to concentrate to make out what they were saying. It was of their collective opinion the missing woman had most likely become the victim of a random animal encounter, rather than foul play. All the other avenues they'd gone down had resulted in a dead end. Even though her vehicle was still at the campground, it was possible someone may have picked her up there, so the detectives' search had begun with that thought in mind. But Bea wasn't at any of her friends or relatives homes and they all were now as worried as Boonie and the authorities about what might have happened to her.

The investigators discussed the fact that having left her gun behind, Bea would have had no way to protect herself from a surprise attack. And, after all, a close encounter had happened to the missing woman before. One detective said, "She was fortunate not to have been killed by the cougar her husband talked about leaping down practically on top of her a while back. You'd have thought she'd learned her lesson then, and never hiked in the forest alone again. Or, at least not without her gun."

My thoughts exactly! Still listening in, I could tell that should it turn out Bea hadn't been attacked by an animal, the police force had no clue as to where the missing woman could be. Had a predatory animal emerged from the woods and dragged her off into the forest? Had she instead been abducted by a predator of the human variety? Was she being held captive? Had she suffered an injury? Been raped, or worse, killed? At that point, there seemed to be more questions than answers.

When I returned to the trailer, Rip was preparing for bed in quiet contempt. I spooned some shredded tuna into Dolly's bowl, took a quick shower, and donned a cotton nightshirt. Rip was snoring raucously when I slipped under the covers on my side of the built-in queen bed. A niggling thought that the next few days could be quite a departure from our normally calm and comfortable routine was flitting through my mind just before I finally drifted off to sleep. I'm willing to bet I tossed and turned more that night than Boonie Whetstone habitually did.

CHAPTER 8

"Have you heard that the Crazy Woman Ranch, south of Buffalo, is up for sale?" Rip asked me as he turned a page in the *Buffalo Bulletin*. He'd purchased the newspaper from a rusty machine in front of the campground's office, which had been closed since Bea Whetstone's mysterious disappearance. Surprisingly, the puzzling situation regarding the missing campground owner had not been mentioned in the paper.

"I bet that'd cost a pretty penny," I replied absentmindedly. It was the automatic response of someone who was paying more attention to the grapefruit she was cutting in half to serve for breakfast than what her husband was saying. Shipped to the local grocery stores from California, grapefruit in Wyoming cost a pretty penny too. I wasn't going to waste one by bleeding all over it after slicing a finger.

"Yeah, almost nineteen million." As if he thought I was interested in the topic, he added, "But it *is* nearly fifty thousand acres of prime ranch land."

"That's nice. Would you like a packet of fake sugar on your grapefruit?"

"Yeah, that's fine. I—"

Rip ceased talking abruptly and pointed to the television screen where the Channel Thirteen news broadcast was announcing breaking news. Most often, their breaking news was something on the level of a mobile home on fire in a Casper trailer park due to the misuse of a twenty-year old space heater. But something in Rip's expression made me rush over to watch the broadcast.

"Missing Buffalo woman's body found ripped to shreds in the Bighorn National Forest!" The statement was plastered across the top of the screen as we watched the Johnson County Sheriff step up behind a podium to speak to the press and take questions. We listened in stunned silence as Sheriff Jaclyn Wright spoke in a serious and straightforward manner. We'd already seen how gruff she could be. We'd also heard she was tough as nails, and it was clear the scuttlebutt about her was accurate.

"The severely decomposed body was found by a participant in the search party late last evening. It appears as if local business owner, Beata Whetstone, suffered an ill-fated encounter with an animal, according to the county medical examiner. Considering the multiple slashing wounds on the body, it appears as if it was most likely a mountain lion that shredded her abdomen and legs with its claws. The body was discovered in dense foliage just south of the Rest 'n Peace RV Park. The campground, owned by the victim and her husband, is located just a quarter of a mile off Highway Sixteen." Sheriff Wright spoke in a highly professional and composed, but dispassionate, manner. She paused for a moment, as if to allow time for the paradoxical name of the victim's business to sink in with the crowd and television viewers. I know it sank in with me because I felt a chill run up my spine, down my spine, and then back up it again.

Rip and I shared a look that required no words. We listened intently as the sheriff continued. "We can't rule out foul play, however. Animals may have feasted on the body postmortem, after it had been dumped in the forest. It's unclear whether or not an autopsy will be able to determine the exact cause of death due to the condition of the body. But at this time, we are treating the death as an accidental animal attack."

Just like that, the Rest 'n Peace campground owner had gone from being referred to as Bea Whetstone, or "evil witch" in Jan's case, to simply being called "the body." I didn't think the female sheriff's description of Bea's body being "feasted on" was necessary, but with her matter-of-fact demeanor, it was not particularly shocking. An even colder chill raced up and down my spine at the thought of the fear and pain the poor woman must have endured prior to her passing. A bit nauseated by the news, I wasn't sure I wanted to hear any more of the details. But like a person unable to turn away from an impending train wreck, I remained glued to the TV screen.

"I've only got time for a couple of questions," the sheriff said to the group of twenty or more reporters in the crowd. The sheriff pointed to a rail-thin woman with hair the color of provolone cheese, and teeth, what few she had left, the color of coffee grounds. "You—over there."

"Did the animal or person kill her before or after the shredding took place?" The reporter asked as she tugged on her tank top to conceal the pink bra strap that had been peeking out behind it. The skinny gal had a distinct meth-head look about her, but it appeared she at least had a job, which could not be said for a large percentage of addicts.

"With possibly only two inquiries to the sheriff, that dumb bimbo asks a stupid question like that?" I asked.

"Definitely a true blonde." Rip smiled at me and quipped, "Honey, I'm sure glad you're a brunette bimbo instead of a blond one."

I returned his smile briefly, too unnerved by the news of Bea's death to laugh or make a smart retort in response. A seasoned lawman, Rip was more accustomed to coping with news of this nature. He ran his hand up my thigh to let me know he was only kidding me. It was an unnecessary gesture, for I'd never thought otherwise.

The sheriff responded to the reporter's ridiculous question with a question of her own. In an deliberately sarcastic tone, she asked, "What do you think?" She then pointed to an older man on the front row she was apparently acquainted with, and said, "Last question. Ted?"

"When will the autopsy report be available?" Ted asked.

"I can't answer that at this time." Apparently feeling as if the first question was ignorant, and her answer to the second one was not very informative, Sheriff Wright said, "I'll take one more. You—over there in the red jacket."

It became apparent the petite woman in the red jacket was not a member of the press when she asked with a trembling voice, "In the event it wasn't due to an accidental animal encounter, are there any suspects in Mrs. Whetstone's death? My husband and I own a campground in the same vicinity as Rest 'n Peace and I'm wondering if we should be concerned for our own well-being and, of course, that of our customers. Should we be taking extra precautions in case there's a serial killer on the loose?"

"The likelihood of a serial killer in our area is slim. At this stage in the investigation, we have no reason to believe a search for a suspect is necessary," Sheriff Wright responded. "But it wouldn't hurt to ask your customers to be alert at all times and call the sheriff's department if they see anything suspicious. It's always better to err on the side of caution. You should, however, inform your customers of the dangers of wandering outside the park's perimeter. There's also a possibility an aggressive animal could encroach on your property."

With that advice, the sheriff turned and stepped back from the podium. As she walked away, the buzz in the crowd was audible. It sounded like the hum of a high-voltage power line. It suddenly occurred to me that Rip and I were in the same boat as the nearby campground owner in the red jacket. However, due to our proximity to the scene of the woman's death, we were in even more potential danger. I asked Rip, "What if there truly *is* a killer on the loose? Shouldn't we be on the lookout for unusual activity, as well?"

"One should always be on the lookout for suspicious activity in this day and age. And the sheriff was right about erring on the side of caution. But I also agree with her that the chances of a serial killer being responsible for Bea's death are remote." Sensing I was anxious, Rip reached over and patted my leg. "Don't worry, sweetheart. I've had at least a small measure of experience in this kind of situation and I'll make sure nothing bad happens to us. Wyoming's an open-carry state, and also recognizes Texas concealed firearms permits. So there's no reason I can't routinely carry my Glock with me while we're searching for our stuff in the woods, or even while we're just hanging out here in the campground. Would that make you feel more comfortable?"

"The heck with the critter cam and your binoculars! What would make me comfortable is never getting within twenty feet of the park's perimeter again! I have no desire to experience the horror of what Bea might have endured. Promise?"

"Well, I don't know that—"

"Are you trying to make me more comfortable, or not?" I asked.

"Oh, all right. But I really did love that pair of binoc—"

"I'll order you a new pair exactly like the old ones!" I nearly shouted at Rip in my frustration. "I am not risking life and limb to recover a pair of binoculars that can easily be replaced."

"Okay, okay! Calm down, dear. I'll buy myself a new pair for an early birthday present. I've had my eye on a pair with night vision, anyway."

"Good try, Rip," I said after a long sigh. My relief was so palpable I felt compelled to tease my husband. "But July eighteenth is three months from now. You know as well as I do that by then we'll both have forgotten you've already purchased your birthday present."

We'd given up trying to pick out gifts for each other many years ago. Selecting our own presents insured we'd like what we got and prevented wasting money on something that'd do nothing more than collect dust.

Grinning like Lewis Carroll's infamous Cheshire Cat, Rip replied, "Forgetting about it was exactly what I was counting on."

I had to laugh at his response, despite the heightened state of my anxiety from having just learned about Bea Whetstone's death.

At least we have a good idea what happened to her now, I assured myself. But even as that thought crossed my mind, I had a hunch our involvement in her death had merely just begun.

CHAPTER 9

I bit my tongue when a knock on the door startled me. I'd
been dusting our 240 square feet trailer for an hour, a
few items two or three times. Even though I knew I
couldn't have scared up one dust mite if I tried, I was antsy
and felt the need to keep busy. It was obvious, even to Rip,
that I was more uptight and on edge than I'd let on when
he'd asked me how I was doing earlier while I was
finishing up our lunch dishes.

"Come in," Rip hollered, loud enough that the person
rapping on the door could hear. I was appalled to discover
he hadn't locked the door as I'd requested. I was even more
appalled that it would appear to our visitor that my husband
was too lazy to stand up and walk five feet to open the
door.

"Howdy folks!" Ranger Rick stepped inside and removed
his hat out of courtesy as he shook both of our hands. A
bulging Wal-Mart bag hung from his left hand. "I assume
you've heard the news about Mrs. Whetstone."

Rip assured him we had. He motioned to the ranger to
have a seat in the vacant recliner and asked him what was
on his mind that caused him to stop by.

"I just wanted to bring these to you." The ranger set the
bag down on a small stack of newspapers lying on the table

next to his chair. "I found your camera and binoculars as I was helping comb the woods for Bea's body yesterday evening. I put them in my Jeep for safe-keeping, afraid someone else would find them and you'd never get them back. A detective might have kept them as potential evidence, when I knew for a fact they'd played no part in her death."

I had to wonder how he could know without a doubt that the Ripples had not premeditated and executed a plan to knock off the campground owner. After all, she was a very disagreeable individual who might have rubbed a number of people the wrong way. She'd nearly made a habit of that with me.

I'm opposed to violence of any kind. However, Bea was so bad-tempered that I'd fancied stabbing her with a ball point pen myself one day in the park store, even though I'd never have actually done so. That particular morning I'd informed her that every time I'd put money in the vending machine next to the laundry room, I had received neither my soda nor my money back. She'd replied without batting an eye. "Then if I were you, I'd quit putting money in the vending machine."

Now wouldn't a rude response like that make you want to poke the woman in the eye with whatever sharp instrument was handy? It sure made me want to!

Rip and Rick had been discussing the best brand of binoculars, and before they got back to the subject of Bea's death, Rip said, "Thanks for returning our items, even though it effectively put a cork in my plan to buy myself a new set with infrared or thermal-imaging night-vision capabilities."

"Sorry 'bout that, bud," Rick said.

They both laughed before Rip continued. "Seriously, we appreciate your thoughtfulness very much, Rick. It was very kind of you to make the trip out here to return our stuff, as well as bring us home yesterday. I have to admit, in hindsight, I think it was probably a good thing we didn't attempt to get home before dark on our own."

No shit, Sherlock? I was dying to say. Left to find our own way home, we'd still be walking in circles in the forest, provided we hadn't already been reduced to big piles of bear poop.

"Have you heard anything new about her death, Rick?" Rip asked. "Why would they be collecting potential evidence if they were convinced she been killed in an animal encounter?"

"I didn't mean to imply they were actively searching for evidence of any kind. At the time, I had no idea what had happened to her. I really don't know any more than you do, I'm sure. After I discovered the body—"

Stunned, Rip and I interrupted him simultaneously. In unison, we asked, "*You* discovered her body?"

"Yeah. I just followed the smell. It's a hard thing to get out of your mind."

"I understand completely, son." Son, to Rip, was any man at least a year younger than his own age of sixty-eight.

With an expression I couldn't possibly describe to you with only the one million or so words I have at my disposal, Ranger Rick said, "It's the first time I've ever smelled a dead person, and—"

The visibly upset ranger stopped speaking, unable to finish. Rip gave the man a consoling smile and completed the sentence for him, "It's a smell you'll never forget. Been there, done that. I'm sorry you had to experience such a disturbing incident, Rick."

"I'm sorry, as well," I added. "If you don't mind me asking, after observing the condition of her remains, what do *you* think happened to Bea?"

Rip shot me a look that clearly was meant to admonish me for asking the already troubled ranger such an upsetting question. The look did not go unnoticed by the ranger, who caught Rip's eye and replied, "It's all right. I don't mind, Rip. It helps to talk about it. Anyway, I have no doubt at all she was killed by a bear. Possibly a cougar, but I'd place money on a bear. Around here, there are more black bears per square mile than cougars."

Rip and I merely nodded, not sure what to say. After an uncomfortable silence, I told him I found it ironic that she'd be killed by a bear, and related the story about the day she shot the mama bear who had stepped just inside the perimeter of the campground with her cub. Ranger Rick appeared genuinely angry at the idea she'd kill a sow who was visibly protecting her cub from harm as the two were backing away to retreat into the forest. He shook his head. "It takes someone with no conscience at all to do such an evil thing."

I wholeheartedly agreed. No matter how tempting it might be at times, I would never harm another creature, human or otherwise, unless I was in imminent danger of being harmed, or worse, and forced to protect myself. The mama bear had not been threatening anyone. She and her cub had accidentally happened upon the campground and had begun moving back into the forest as soon as she'd spotted humans, something she undoubtedly saw as a threat to her and her offspring.

The somber conversation shifted back to small talk as Rip and the ranger discussed their favorite types of firearms and exchanged stories about interesting situations their individual occupations had involved them in. I think Rip was deliberately trying to lighten the mood, because before Ranger Rick left, at Rip's subtle guidance, their discussion had deteriorated to the topic of how fun it'd be to pass gas in an elevator filled with nuns. I saw this as a sign they were quickly becoming not only acquaintances, but also friends. It doesn't take long to determine if two men were cut from the same cloth.

I listened to their banter as I occupied myself by scouring the sink for the fifth time and organizing the spices sprawled out in one of the kitchen cabinets. With limited space in the travel trailer, it helped to have contents of the cabinets in an orderly arrangement. More importantly, it took my mind off other, more unnerving, things.

* * *

Fifteen minutes after Ranger Rick departed, I was scrubbing the kitchen table with the abrasive side of a sponge. The fact that I was still restless was not lost on Rip. He said, "Honey, why don't we get out of the trailer for a while and find something to do before you scrub the veneer right off the table."

"Is it that apparent I'm on pins and needles?"

"Yes, it is, dear. By the sheen on the coffee table from numerous layers of furniture polish, and the overwhelming aroma of disinfectant spray throughout the trailer, it's clear you feel as if you're walking on eggshells. Let's do something to get your mind off of the horrid news about Bea."

"Got anything specific in mind?"

"Not really. You have any ideas?"

It had just occurred to me we might have acquired a zillion images on the game camera Rick had just returned to us. Maybe even a photo of whatever, or whoever, killed Bea. "Why don't we run into town for groceries and stop by Cora's on the way back? She can upload any photos we might have on our memory card. After all, it's been out in the forest for a while."

"Oh, that's right!" Rip exclaimed. "I forgot all about the camera. Great idea, honey. Put that blasted sponge down and let's go! I'm starting to feel guilty about lounging around watching this marathon of old John Wayne movies while you're working yourself to the bone. I don't want to feel obligated to straighten up all the junk in our storage compartments. The last time I did that I came across the leveling blocks I had accused you of throwing away."

"I *should* have pitched them, dear. I still can't understand why we have to haul those around when this trailer has built-in leveling jacks. We also lug around a tool box containing twenty-seven different screwdrivers, when any one of them could accomplish the same thing as the other twenty-six. That makes no sense to me whatsoever."

"And it never will. It's a man thing, you see. Besides, there are slot head screwdrivers, Phillips head, Torx, Hex sockets, Pozi Drive, Robertsons—"

"Okay, okay. I stand corrected."

"Besides, it's no different than us men not understanding why you ladies require twenty-seven different bottles of lotions and potions when any one of them can accomplish the exact same thing as the other twenty-six."

"*Touché*, my dear."

"Seven thousand, three hundred and six images?" I asked in astonishment. I was as giddy as a girl after her first kiss. I was so confident I'd have a slew of amazing wildlife photos to choose from, I was already considering what I'd do with the twenty-five thousand bucks I was hoping to win.

"Yep, that's what it says, Aunt Rappie. With over seven thousand images, there's bound to be some good ones," Cora said. Like us, she was anxious to see if we'd captured any good wildlife photographs. She pulled a transfer cord out of a kitchen drawer and plugged the memory card into it. "Might as well make yourselves comfortable. It might take a while for all of these photos to upload to your tablet."

We accepted Cora's offer of a cup of coffee and conversed with her as we waited. Willie was at baseball practice and was due to be picked up shortly. While Rip fiddled with her remote control, as men are wired to do whether it belongs to them or not, I related to her what we'd learned from Ranger Rick. After I finished my recital, I added, "Crazy, huh?"

"Yeah, but what's really crazy is that Bea Whetstone was the only sibling of Richard Myer's ex-wife. In other words, Bea was Rick's former sister-in-law. A friend of Bea's told me their mother, who has terminal esophageal cancer, is in her final days."

Rip's attention swerved away from the TV and back to Cora. "Are you for real?"

At the very same time, I asked, "Bea had a friend?"

"Yes, to both questions," Cora said. "Their mother was a pediatrician until her illness forced her to give up her practice five years ago. Up until then, she was the physician I always took Willie to."

"Does their mother have a substantial estate?" Rip asked.

"Hard to say, Uncle Clyde. She's been in an assisted-living facility for several years, and I'm sure that has sucked a lot of money out of her savings."

"No doubt," Rip said with a nod.

I was surprised to hear Cora knew both Ranger Rick and Bea Whetstone even though Buffalo is the kind of small town where everybody seemed to know each other. Not unlike our hometown of Rockport, Texas, where one couldn't even get fined for an overdue library book without everyone in town knowing about it before twenty-four hours had elapsed.

I listened as Cora went on to explain Richard Myer's relationship with the victim. "Rick never did cotton to Bea much. In fact, I'm not sure his loathing of her didn't have something to do with his divorce from her sister. But I heard a lady say at the hair salon that after the pair's divorce, Bea and Desireé had a falling out, as well. Something to do with their momma's will, they said. 'Course you can't believe everything you hear, particularly at a hair salon."

"Their momma's will? Sounds like there *was* a substantial amount of money involved if the woman's two daughters are squabbling about it. I can't believe Bea and Ranger Rick's ex are sisters." I was dumbfounded. Why hadn't Ranger Rick given us some indication of having known Bea Whetstone as anything other than just a local business owner?

Rip was puzzled too. When I broached the subject of the ranger not bringing up his relationship with Bea, Rip shrugged his shoulders, and in defense of his new friend, said, "Well, Rick probably has a very good reason to not want to advertise his former connection to the victim. He never actually said he *didn't* have some kind of tie to her and we never questioned him about it. However, it would explain why he was so emotional this morning. Like a person or not, the death of a former sister-in-law would have a disturbing affect on even the most cold-hearted among us. Then again, finding any dead body, whether you knew the victim personally, or not, would have a disturbing affect on just about anyone. Unless they were a sociopath, of course."

The photos had just finished uploading to our iPad when Cora apologized for having to leave to pick Willie up at the ball field. "You two are free to hang around. We'll be back in no more than fifteen minutes."

I was anxious to get home and review the photos, and I'm certain Rip was too. Besides, even though it was cool outside, I didn't want to leave the groceries in the back of the truck for much longer.

I thanked my niece for uploading the photos for us. Cora had offered to lend us a spare transfer cord, and I had quickly agreed to borrow it. I wasn't about to pay good money for one of our own when she was all too happy to let us take advantage of hers. I told her we hadn't intended to be underfoot all afternoon, and it was time to get home to stow the groceries away and take a roast out of our oven anyway.

"Okay. See you later. And hey, on second thought, why don't you just keep that spare transfer cord. I don't really need two of them, and I'm sure you'll need to have one in the future." Cora knew her aunt well enough to know it'd be difficult for me to hand over thirty bucks for a little four-inch cord, no matter how badly I needed one. If I did have to buy my own, the store clerk would have to wrench the cash out of my tightly clenched fist. Buying a thirty-dollar cord for a twenty-dollar camera didn't seem like a financially-justifiable expenditure to me.

"Thanks, sweetheart," I said. "That is so thoughtful of you. No wonder you're my favorite niece."

"We love and appreciate you more than you know," Rip added.

"Love you guys more, Uncle Clyde and Aunt Rappie. Stop by any time. And don't forget, Willie's team competes for the league championship this weekend."

"We wouldn't miss it," I assured her.

"We'll be there with balls on," Rip quipped, using a sport's reference.

"Speak for yourself," I said.

"Sorry. I meant bells." Rip cracked himself up with his play-on-words, and Cora and I both groaned at his cheesy quip.

We spent most of that evening scanning through photos. We hadn't come across anything of significance after reviewing the first five thousand. I thought if I saw one more photo of the same leaf in slightly different positions I'd scream. Finally, we saw a black blur on image number five thousand, two-hundred and four. When Rip skipped right by the image as if it amounted to nothing, like all the previous photos, I asked him to go back to it.

"What do you think that blurry black thing is?" I asked.

"I don't know. A bird flitting by, perhaps."

"I don't think so, unless it was flying about two feet off the ground. Let me see if I can enhance and sharpen the image like Cora showed us."

"Okay, go ahead. I need to take a break anyway. We are an hour overdue for our afternoon cocktails, and that's one appointment I hate to be tardy for. I'll prepare our drinks while you mess with the photo. Tequila sunrise as usual, my dear?"

"Yes, of course," I replied. Rip had asked me the exact same question every day since we'd first begun the daily ritual shortly after we'd retired. I'd never once requested a different drink, but someday I was going to ask for a Long Island Iced Tea just to see how he'd react. My guess is that, having no clue what goes in that cocktail, he'll respond, "Tequila Sunrise coming right up!"

Once I'd improved the clarity of the photo as best I could, I pulled a lighted magnifying glass out of one of my three junk drawers, which in a travel trailer doesn't leave much space for important items like silverware. Studying the image carefully, I finally felt certain I'd accurately distinguished what had caused the blur. I proudly announced, "It's a woman's fingernail with black polish on it."

"Okay, if you say so." Rip was clearly not convinced. "How can you determine the fingernail belongs to a woman?"

"What part of 'fingernail polish' didn't you understand?"

"The fingernail polish part. If you could see some of the young hooligans I've dealt with during my career, you'd know that fingernail polish is not just for women anymore. I can't count the guys I've seen with their nails polished. And black seems to be a popular color with males for some reason. Maybe they think it's less emasculating than pink or red. I think any color looks ridiculous on a guy. If they're worried that the color of the nail polish might make them appear less manly, they shouldn't wear any at all."

"I second the motion. But then, maybe that's just our age showing. When I was a teenager and asked my mother if I could get my ears pierced she said no, because she didn't want men to think I was easy."

"Even without pierced ears, I thought you were easy," Rip said, grinning sheepishly. "You proved it, too, when you let me get in your knickers on our third date."

I would have walloped Rip if his words weren't spot on. "Yes, that's true. But we wouldn't have Regina if I had played hard to get that night."

"Aha! So, you're admitting she's your fault, and not mine?" Rip teased, echoing the words we'd recently heard Willie use.

I did wallop him this time, and then added, "Besides, I find all that body piercing that's so prevalent amongst the younger generations today even more ludicrous than pierced ears. It doesn't look cool. It doesn't look attractive. To me, it just looks painful and ridiculous. But, again, I'm sure it's just my age talking."

"Darn it!" Rip spoke so emphatically I thought he was being serious, until he continued. "I was going to give you a gift certificate for a tongue piercing for our upcoming fiftieth anniversary."

"Oh, so very thoughtful of you, honey. But I think the Alaskan trip you've been planning is more than sufficient."

"Well, all right. If you're sure. Don't say I didn't offer it." Rip chuckled with amusement. "But back to the fingernail. It could belong to a woman *or* a man."

"Well, either way, do you think it's possible that it belongs to someone who might have killed Bea and dumped her body in the woods? Sheriff Wright did say that they couldn't rule out homicide due to the condition of her body after a number of days of being exposed to the elements, and the wildlife that might have happened upon it. Like Ranger Rick, they might have been drawn to the decomposing body by the smell."

"Naturally, the fingernail could be attached to the killer, but I think it's a long shot even if it does turn out to be a case of homicide. Practically nothing is out of the realm of possibility, though." Rip was right, of course, but I wasn't going to just accept that the fingernail had no correlation to Bea's death. I wrote down the image number on the back of a grocery receipt and began scanning the photos again.

Six photos later there was a very sharp image of the cuff of a blue shirt, most likely a man's, but, like the polished fingernail, we couldn't be positive. After all, it wasn't unusual for me to wear long-sleeved shirts myself. I was getting increasingly excited by our findings and Rip appeared intrigued, too.

We resumed reviewing the remaining images, hoping we had even better photographs of the finger and shirt and, more importantly, who they belonged to. I naturally assumed we'd captured evidence of two people in the woods for whatever reason, until Rip reminded me that both could belong to the same person. "Do you realize how probable it is that the motion-activated camera captured one of the members of the search party who were combing the woods for Bea's body? With its camouflaged casing, it could have blended in with the foliage so well no one but Ranger Rick even noticed it."

"Yeah, you're right. I hadn't thought of that," I replied. "But I'm glad the ranger didn't overlook the camera. It was nice to get it back, along with your binoculars, without even having to step foot inside the tree line."

"For that matter, it's even more likely the shirt cuff belonged to Rick, who would have triggered the motion sensor when he reached down to remove the camera from the tree."

I found Rip's reasoning to be sensible, but disheartening at the same time. I suppose the adrenalin rush of being intricately involved in the investigations of two former murder cases, and the satisfaction of being the person most responsible for solving them, had gotten into my blood. If you're still a spring chicken, you'll one day see how once a person becomes a senior citizen, it becomes more satisfying to be useful and beneficial to something or someone. There comes a time in one's life when the thought of having their legacy based on the delectable fruitcakes they pass out every holiday season just doesn't seem satisfying enough.

After we viewed the next one hundred photos, I gave Rip's reasoning a little more thought and realized his theory made no sense at all. If the ranger had picked up the camera and turned it off, there'd not be another fifteen hundred photos or so left on the memory card. And if Ranger Rick had left it on, as we had on our first attempt, the following images would have been similar to the ones we'd captured on our first attempt: photos of grass, legs and arms, tree trunks, animal scat, shoes, and so forth. Instead, the images following the fingernail and blue shirt photos were that of the flitting leaf each time its motion was detected by the motion sensor. Had Ranger Rick discovered the camera and binoculars but waited until later to go back and retrieve them?

After we'd scanned through another thousand images and had seen nothing but the same leaf moving about in the breeze, Rip suggested we call it a day. "It's apparent we're not going to find anything else worth viewing. Why don't I refill our drinks so we can sit out on the patio in our lawn chairs and enjoy the sunset?"

It sounded like an appealing idea, even if it could potentially put us in the crosshairs of a serial killer's rifle scope. I decided to roll the dice on that remote possibility because I wouldn't want to insinuate that I didn't trust Rip to shelter me from harm. I'd never want the man, whom I'd known by our third date would be the love of my life, to think I didn't have the utmost faith in him. And, most importantly, I was in desperate need of some alcohol to calm my nerves.

CHAPTER 10

"**D**o you think we should hand the memory card over to the police department?" I asked Rip during breakfast the following morning. "It might be of some benefit in a search for a perpetrator."

"No, I don't. For one thing, they aren't looking for a perpetrator. They've pretty much concluded Bea was attacked by a wild animal, and I have to agree they're probably correct. Secondly, they'd most likely laugh me out of the police station and tell me they didn't need any assistance from the former sheriff of Petticoat Junction."

"But, honey, they should respect the fact you've spent thirty-seven years in law enforcement, even if it wasn't in a big city like Dallas or Houston. You'd think they'd appreciate a fresh set of experienced eyes looking at the case."

"You'd think. But they made it excruciatingly clear they don't. And, besides, there's currently no investigation taking place other than waiting for the autopsy results to come back. Even then, according to this morning's paper, they don't expect to find much in the report that leads to a specific cause of death. They found hair in the body's wounds from a number of different species, including bear, cougar, and some opportunistic smaller scavengers. As

Sheriff Wright indicated, Bea's body was ripped to shreds and eaten by animals. Postmortem, of course."

"Thank God for small favors!" I exclaimed.

"As far as the authorities are concerned, it's an open and closed case of being in the wrong place at the wrong time, with Bea falling victim to an unexpected encounter with a bear or cougar. Granted, it was a horrific and tragic incident. But it looks as if that's all it was."

"Okay. But I'm just not one-hundred percent convinced she was killed by a four-legged animal. I think the case needs to be delved into deeper, with the idea it might not have been accidental after all."

Rip studied my face for a moment. "I don't like that glimmer in your eye, Rapella. Please don't tell me you're going to drag me into another murder case, investigating Bea's death on our own. I know how satisfying it was to you to have been primarily responsible for solving the mysteries behind both Trotter Hayes and Cooper Claypool's deaths. But both those cases involved people close to us. Seriously, Rapella, what do we personally have to gain by jumping headfirst into a case like this one? As far as I could tell, you didn't care for the woman to begin with."

"I don't know why I feel so compelled to dig further into this situation. It's not like I knew Bea very well, and what little I did know about her, I felt was abominable. Still, no one deserves to die like that. If by chance somebody was responsible for her death, I think they should be held accountable. Even a person as repulsive as Bea deserves justice if their life's been savagely taken from them. The victim's family deserves closure, as well."

"I spoke to Boonie this morning. I got the distinct impression he's already gotten all the closure he needs."

I grimaced at Rip's remark and felt a lone tear run down my cheek. I could never explain why I felt so disconcerted by the woman's untimely death. Perhaps it was the fact no one seemed overly upset about her demise that bothered me so much.

Rip sighed and covered my hands with his. He looked me straight in the eyes. "Honey, I don't disagree with you one bit. But that's why God created a little something called law enforcement. Why not just let the Buffalo Police Department handle it? I'm sure if they have any inkling a crime has been committed, they'll investigate it thoroughly. As much as I hate to admit it, I'm sure Jaclyn Wright is a competent sheriff."

"Oh, all right," I said. "I'm sure you're correct. Besides, we've got better things to do while we're here. For starters, we need to cheer Willie's ball team on to victory this weekend. They're ranked third in the tournament, Cora said, but we already know they can whoop Worland, and if the Buffalo boys are all in it to win it, I think they can kick butt and take names in the game against Gillette too."

Rip let out a sigh of relief. He was happy to see my mood brighten and for me to concentrate on something less distressing. "I hope so. I'm sure the championship means a lot to Willie. I know he's interested in a career in mechanical engineering, but I believe he has a good shot at going to college on a baseball scholarship."

"I agree. For his age, he's an incredibly talented ball player, both offensively and defensively. Willie's like a Hoover vacuum at third and can hit the leather off the ball, too. Who's to say he can't earn a degree in mechanical engineering while attending the university on a baseball scholarship?"

"That's true. I think I'll try to stress the benefits of doing both simultaneously the next time I have a discussion with Willie about his future."

After a few more minutes of chit-chat, I cleared the dishes off the table while Rip got dressed. As usual, he had consumed his grapefruit and orange juice that morning in nothing but a well-worn t-shirt and his Fruit of the Looms. I'd watched him painstakingly cut his grapefruit into perfect little wedges as if he were performing delicate brain surgery, and then slurp his juice like a hog at a water trough.

When finished, he stood up, scratched his behind, let out a juicy belch and walked back into the bedroom. *Yep*, I thought. *After fifty years together, the honeymoon is definitely over.*

I'd ignored the overflowing basket of dirty clothes until I couldn't get a single sock to balance on the top without toppling the pile. On Thursday morning, I decided I'd better not put it off any longer. Rip had driven into town to pick up some rubber gaskets at the hardware store to replace one in the kitchen faucet that had dried up and cracked. He planned to store the spare ones in his metal tool box for future leaks. I'd been complaining about the constant dripping for three weeks and gotten nowhere. So that morning I threatened to call a plumber, at seventy-five bucks per service call, to complete the simple task. My ruse worked.

When I first arrived at the laundry facility, all of the washers were already operating. I recognized the petite woman monopolizing the machines but it took a few moments of studying her to recall where I'd previously seen her. She was a wisp of a thing, probably no more than ninety pounds soaking wet. She had long wavy hair and had utilized a pale blue visor to keep the loose tendrils off her face. She wasn't what one would describe as pretty, but she had a cute tomboyish appearance. She wore a white sweatshirt with a Denali National Park emblem on the front, and there was a small stain on the brim of her visor. I finally realized she was the female half of the couple who had snatched the gun out of Bea's hands after we'd all observed the woman shoot and kill the mama bear.

It's not that I'm prone to gossiping, as I'm sure you've already figured out for yourself, but I thought engaging the woman in conversation might result in some interesting information. And as it turned out, it did exactly that!

The lady introduced herself as Barb Harris and, when asked, explained to me why she and her husband, John, were staying at the campground. "We're employed by an organization that deals with protecting animals of every variety from abuse and neglect."

"That must keep you two busy, considering the vast number of animal species."

"Yes, extremely busy. There are nearly nine million recognized species in the world, so we don't have a lot of time to let grass grow under our feet. We recently were involved in two projects: studying the decline of the Asian black bear, and how the diminishing habitat in South Africa has affected the baboon population, whose primary predators, unfortunately, are humans."

"What a fascinating vocation you two are involved in." I was sincere. It sounded like an incredibly interesting way to make a living.

"Yes. It's exciting to work toward the goal of preventing the extinction of any of the many, many species, from the black rhino down to the tiniest minnow. When our preservation efforts work, it's quite rewarding. For example, John and I were heavily involved in increasing the numbers of whooping cranes after their numbers dipped to a mere thirteen birds in 1941. They estimate there are now just over six hundred whoopers in existence, although about a quarter of those are being held in captivity."

"Really? That's awesome! My husband, Rip, and I know all about whooping cranes because our hometown is Rockport, Texas. As I'm sure you're aware, a large portion of the whooping crane population winters at the Aransas National Wildlife Refuge just north of Rockport."

"Oh, sure. We've been to the refuge on several occasions to study the whoopers' breeding and nesting habits, and monitor the number of surviving hatchlings. Our preservation efforts have helped increase their numbers, but not nearly enough to take them off the endangered species list."

"Well, we certainly appreciate your efforts. I think the entire Coastal Bend of south Texas is partial to the whooping cranes." I liked Barb Harris immediately and decided to bring up the topic of Bea's death. "Speaking of protecting animals, I was horrified by the way Bea executed that mama bear a while back. Now I'm even more horrified by what happened to the woman herself. Aren't you?"

"I suppose, but John and I are too busy to keep up with what's going on around here. I'm just glad to know she'll never get the opportunity to kill another animal." Barb's response seemed a bit callous to me, but I admired her dedication to the cause.

"I agree with that part, but my husband, a former sheriff, and I have been involved in similar cases in the past and are looking into this situation, too. There seems to be a piece of the pie that's missing, and we're hoping to find it."

"Good luck with that!" As Barb spoke she turned away as if she were dismissing me. She didn't appear to be interested enough in Bea's death to discuss the matter.

One of Barb's washing machines ground to a halt and she proceeded to toss the load into a dryer. I filled the now empty washer with my own basketful of laundry. Just to break the silence when we'd both returned to our cheap, flimsy chairs to wait, I said, "You sure had a lot of laundry to do today. I'm glad I only have the one load."

"We spend a lot of time outside and doing research in the forest. We tend to go through clean clothes like nobody's business. And I seldom have the time to get caught up on the laundry."

I watched her pull out a bottle of stain remover and use a good portion of its contents to spray some stains on the sleeves of a man's flannel shirt. After I'd placed her face, I'd been trying to figure out why her voice sounded somewhat familiar. Suddenly a remote possibility occurred to me. "Do you guys do any research in the vicinity of the forest beyond the south edge of this campground?"

"No. The area our research is involved with is on the western side of the Bighorn Mountains. Unfortunately, there's no RV park in the vicinity. But this campground's close enough to suit our needs. Why do you ask?"

"My husband and I were hiking through the forest and overheard a couple conversing. Your voice sounds quite familiar. I thought it might have been you and John." Actually, their voices were so faint I couldn't have recognized my own daughter's voice from that distance. As far as Barb knew, we'd heard the entire conversation clearly. So, I wanted to judge her reaction to my remark. However, her demeanor never wavered and was disappointedly indifferent.

"No. It couldn't have been us if it was within hiking distance of this campground. I sure hope you two carry some kind of protection when you're out hiking around here," Barb said, with a concerned expression. "As you witnessed the other day, there are dangerous animals in the area. You'd probably be better off not putting yourselves at risk by walking around in the forest."

"We're cautious, and my husband carries a gun for protection. And yet traipsing around in the forest still scares the bewillikers outta me."

"I was thinking of pepper spray, or a flare, for protection, rather than a gun. I'd hate to see any animal killed unnecessarily. And that goes for hikers, like you and your husband, as well."

"I truly appreciate your concern, Barb. We'll be careful, and we'd never harm an animal unless absolutely necessary. So, what are you and John researching here in Wyoming?"

"We're mostly obtaining data involving the ecosystem of mountainous terrain such as is found in the Bighorns. At the moment, we're trying to get a reasonably accurate idea of the average number of black bears per square mile in this area, and scout around for possible grizzly sightings."

My face no doubt paled to the color of the white plastic chair I was sitting on. "Grizzlies?"

"We're not apt to spot one, but it's always a possibility, as they are moving farther and farther east from Yellowstone in their search for new territory. In fact, there have been a few reported sightings in the Bighorn Basin.

But, in general, they haven't inhabited the Bighorn National Forest since the early twentieth century."

"Good to know," I replied with a shudder.

"Don't worry too much. We've yet to spot one, but it's an exciting prospect for people in our field of work."

"No doubt. So, dare I ask? Have you determined how many black bears there are per square mile in this area?"

Barb Harris was well versed on the subject, and I found the information she shared fascinating. "So far we haven't had much luck tracking any down, other than the one Bea executed for no reason whatsoever. I hate that the bear is dead, but she and her cub still count in our survey."

"My husband and I came face to face with a mother and three cubs out there," I pointed in the general direction. "My husband thinks there's a good chance one of the cubs, who's quite a bit smaller than the other two, might have been the slain bear's baby."

"Oh, good. That sounds promising. I agree with your husband. It wouldn't be unheard of for the sow to adopt the orphaned cub. We'll have to see if we can track those four down and tag them. Tagging them helps us keep track of the individual bears and is very beneficial in our research. The more we learn about them, the better we can protect them. Can you give me a little better idea on where you crossed paths with them?"

After I attempted to pinpoint the area where we met the bear family, which is not easy when you were totally lost yourself at the time, I said, "Although I loathe the idea of hunting animals, I've heard if not for hunters, many species would become over-populated to the point they'd all die of starvation or disease."

"There is some truth to that," Barb replied. "But a lot of hunters will kill anything that moves whose head would look good above their fireplace mantels. They often kill the large, healthy animals needed to keep the population strong. I feel we could control over-population more humanely by taking steps to reduce the animals' fertility."

"I wholeheartedly agree, Barb." Then, without giving it any thought, I blurted out, "Now I understand why you and your husband were so pissed off after the bear-shooting incident here in the park."

Barb's friendly expression turned to one of aggravation in a split second. Then she shot me a look that made my toes curl inside my sneakers. Suddenly I wished I hadn't made the remark. She was still boiling mad about the incident, I realized. Could she and her husband have been enraged enough to harm Bea for needlessly killing the mama bear? I was anxious to see what Rip thought about this possibility, even though I didn't feel it was very probable. My guess was the couple were against killing altogether.

Barb shook off her initial reaction of anger and simply shrugged in response to my comment. Without a word, she walked over to put more quarters in the three dryers. It seemed to me that the park owners had intentionally set the dryers on the lowest temperature possible to ensure it'd take several dollars' worth of quarters to dry each load. I kept threatening to string a clothesline from the back of the trailer to a nearby tree, but Rip didn't think either Boonie or the RVers in nearby sites would appreciate the view of his stained boxers and my stretched out, faded brassieres blowing in the breeze. He'd said, "This is a classy RV park, not an old run-down trailer court. Despite what some people might think, there is an immense difference between the two, you know."

When Barb Harris finished stuffing coins in the machines, she turned toward me and I glanced at her hands. Although trimmed barely above the tip of her fingers, her nails were well-manicured. They bore no sign of polish, but who's to say she hadn't recently trimmed her nails and removed black polish from them?

I probably should have left it at that, but I now had reservations about Barb and her husband, so I asked, "Didn't I see you in the nail salon on Main Street a while back?"

"I don't believe so," Barb answered. "Because I just had them cut down and the polish removed yesterday. My work makes it difficult to keep them clean and looking good."

"I understand completely." I was trying to come across as if I were only making small talk to be polite. I tried to sound curious, but not accusatory. "So, tell me, do you think an animal got Bea or that someone who didn't care for her took her out?"

While studying me carefully, Barb appeared to mull over her reply for several moments before speaking. Apparently she'd come to the conclusion I was just a nosy old broad with nothing better to do than sit in a laundry room and jabber about things that didn't concern me. Finally she said, "The news coverage indicated it was an animal. If the investigators are correct about that, she had it coming as far as I'm concerned. On the other hand, I wouldn't be surprised if one of her enemies killed her."

"She had enemies? As in more than one?"

"I've heard Bea Whetstone had many enemies, Ms. Ripple. She wasn't exactly at the top of my list of favorite people, either, but I'd never hurt anyone, or anything. However, a lady I met at my hairdresser's a while back named Jan might have wanted Bea dead badly enough to kill her."

"Jan?" I was taken aback by the familiar name. "You mean the fancy-dressing widowed lady with the long brunette hair? Nice, but a bit on the uppity side?"

"I didn't know she was widowed. I just assumed she was divorced. But yeah, that's probably the one you're referring to. Don't know her last name, but I heard she was having an affair with Boonie Whetstone. The gal who trimmed my hair thinks she's a gold-digger and looking for her next sugar daddy. Kerri said that if history repeats itself, Boonie will be history soon after Jan manages to drag him to the altar. Being that you're familiar with this lady, do you happen to know if that's true?"

"No, I don't have a clue. I only met her a couple of times, and I was under the impression she'd just arrived in

Wyoming for the very first time. But she sounds like a real piece of work if what your hairdresser told you is correct."

That didn't jive with what Jan had told me. But one would not expect a woman like her to tell someone she'd just met that she was on the hunt for a new man with deep pockets, and that the owner of the campground was her latest conquest. Intrigued by this information about the woman I'd conversed with the last time I'd done laundry, I asked, "Would this RV park produce enough income to make Boonie appealing to a conniving woman on the prowl for a well-to-do husband?"

"Probably. Take what you paid to stay here times the number of sites in this jam-packed campground and it amounts to pretty impressive revenue. Since they meter the electric on each of the monthly sites, and we all foot the bill for the power we use, there can't be a ton of overhead in this sort of business either. Not to mention, Boonie's pretty easy on the eyes."

When Barb was through speaking, she turned away and busied herself with hanging shirts and folding towels. I was practically foaming at the mouth in anticipation of more scandalous details to come, but my laundry room companion didn't seem inclined to want to discuss the sordid affair between Jan and Bea's husband any further.

Watching her, I was amazed by her efficiency at folding her clean laundry. All she had left was a heap of about a dozen washcloths. As she rapidly emptied the pile, I was mesmerized by her fastidiousness. Her growing stack of folded washcloths were in precise and color-coordinated order; three red, three green, three yellow, and so forth. Barb stopped twice during this procedure to adjust the stack and make sure each washcloth was in perfect alignment with those beneath it. Obsessive compulsive disorder, perhaps?

I continued to observe the meticulous animal activist. Her movements were in razor-sharp cadence; fold, fold, fold, stack, fold, fold, fold, stack. It was like watching a robot on speed, or a young army recruit fresh out of boot camp. She completed her task quickly and left with a simple, "See you later."

"Thanks for the warning," I jokingly replied as Barb Harris walked out the door.

As you can imagine, thoughts were whirring through my head as I finished up my laundry at my own pace and technique, which were not nearly as fast or neat as Barb's. Folding our own hand towels was less fold, fold, fold, stack, and more wad, wad, wad, stuff.

I was wondering why Jan had told me, when I'd first met her, that she'd just arrived at Rest 'n Peace RV Park the day prior to our meeting? She'd also indicated it was her first time in Wyoming. Was she hiding something other than her clandestine affair with the park owner?

Not telling a stranger in a laundry room about her covert intentions was to be expected, but being dishonest about her time spent in Wyoming didn't seem quite as logical to me. Rather than spouting outright lies, why didn't she just tell me nothing at all? We all know what happens when the web we're weaving gets too tangled. Sometimes it's the deceiver himself who gets caught up in his own labyrinth of lies. As Walter Scott said: "O, what a tangled web we weave when first we practice to deceive!" *Is it even remotely possible his quote could apply to Jan in the mystery behind Bea Whetstone's death?* I wondered.

As I continued to wait for my second load of laundry to finish drying, I ruminated over what Barb Harris had just shared with me. I had to wonder if the rumor was true. Could either Boonie or Jan, or perhaps the two together, have perpetrated a plan to eliminate the main obstacle keeping them from taking the next step in their relationship? Rip had been of the opinion Boonie wasn't acting like the grief-stricken widower one would expect him to be. Granted, every individual mourns in their own personal manner, but to appear as if he wasn't grieving in any manner whatsoever seemed odd to me.

Was Boonie aware of Jan's strategy, according to Barb's hairdresser, of landing men with money so she could seize a great deal of it later on when she ultimately dumped them? Should he be *made* aware of that rumor going around—in local hair salons, at least? Should Rip and I bring it to his attention somehow, just in case he was totally in the dark? Had Boonie accidently stepped into a trap, much as the cow moose with the twins had done? With this possibility in mind, I could hardly wait to get back to the trailer to share what I'd learned with Rip. A spooky squeaking sound behind the temporarily closed office as I exited the laundry room didn't make me want to linger any, either.

Rip was out and about when I returned to the trailer. I'd turned on the stereo system and was singing along, enthusiastically off-key, to *Uptown Funk*. Because it's nearly impossible not to, I was busting a move in beat with the Bruno Mars tune and hoping I didn't bust something else in the process—like a hip or an ankle. I stopped abruptly when it occurred to me that someone passing by might be watching me through our open window and call 9-1-1, concerned I might be experiencing a life-threatening seizure.

The RV sites were close enough together that the previous evening I had observed the woman in the motorhome next to us as she was preparing supper. Through her open window, I saw her accidentally drop a fried pork chop on her kitchen floor, pick it up and fan it like it was a Polaroid picture, flick a stubborn piece of debris off of it with her index finger, and then place it on the plate in front of her oblivious husband. I'm not passing judgment on my neighbor, mind you. Because, after all, who of us hasn't done that exact same thing a time or two ourselves?

On the contrary, I'm just giving you an example of the limited amount of privacy in the occasional camping facility, like the Rest 'n Peace RV Park, who stuffs too many units in too little space. In a few cases, particularly where the newer parks are concerned, it's a matter of pure greed, in my extremely biased opinion.

However, in many other cases, the lack of elbow room is the result of a campground that was built in 1962, when the typical RV consisted of a station wagon towing a primitive fifteen-foot travel trailer or a boxy pickup camper clamped to the bed of a Chevy C10. That same prehistoric campground is now doing its best to accommodate today's forty-five-foot motor-coaches with four slide-outs, more bells and whistles than Winnebago Industries could have ever imagined when the company was founded in 1958, and a tow vehicle, like a Jeep Wrangler, attached to its hitch. By the time all the motorized slide-outs are extended in some of these newer high-falutin' RV's, the owners are "camping" in more square footage than was in our first two homes combined.

I was daydreaming and placing a couple of folded dishtowels in a kitchen drawer when Rip walked in a couple of minutes later. If you can picture a mood that's a mixture—in equal parts—of anger, excitement, bewilderment, and determination, that combination exactly describes Rip's disposition as he explained the factors behind his mixed emotions to me. I'd been anxious to tell him about my interaction with Barb Harris but could tell whatever he had bottled up in him would boil over if not released soon.

"I went to the police station and asked the desk clerk if I could have a word with the sheriff about the death of the campground owner. To my surprise, Jaclyn Wright opened her office door and escorted me right inside."

"Oh, good. What made you decide to go to—"

"Because you asked me to. So, after I explained my career in law enforcement to her, I showed her the two questionable images we captured on the critter cam," Rip said. He was wound up tighter than an Egyptian mummy. I could have told him the sofa he was sitting on was on fire and he wouldn't have skipped a beat in reciting his story.

"What did she say about—"

"She barely gave them a glance, and then responded even

ruder and more arrogantly than I had anticipated. Believe it
or not, she replied, 'Really? Two undecipherable, blurry
images off a game camera is what brought you barging into
my office this morning, thinking you'd discovered some
earth-shattering clue that'd turn this tragic incident upside
down?' Can you believe that, Rapella?"

"No, she should have—"

"For starters, I didn't barge in. She invited me in."

"I know, sweetheart. Don't let it—"

"She told me if her competent detectives followed up on
every silly little tip that was brought to their attention,
they'd get nothing else done. I saw one of her 'competent'
detectives in the parking lot, picking his nose and sending a
text—to his under-aged girlfriend, no doubt. He couldn't
have been over twenty-one. If he wasn't still wet behind the
ears, he was at least damp."

"You were a young recruit at twenty—"

"Then Sheriff Wright told me Bea's death had been ruled
an accidental animal attack because they had no evidence
to suggest otherwise. She had the gall to say that my
assistance was not necessary or beneficial to the case, or to
the Buffalo Police Department in general."

"Calm down, dear," I said. "You need to—"

"She had the nerve to tell me I should go back to the
campground clubhouse and play bingo with the other old
fogeys."

"Take a deep breath, honey." I finally got a full sentence
in. I was afraid if he got any more riled up, his blood
pressure would shoot through the roof. "It sounds like she's
as strict and straightforward as everyone has said."

"Straightforward? Whose side are you on? Wasn't it you
who thought we should run those photos by the police
department?"

"Honey, I'm on your side, of course. I just meant she was
not an easy-going person to deal with, and you did the best
you could."

"Not easy-going? That's an understatement if I ever
heard one. I guess that's what I get for doing what you

requested," Rip said in obvious disgust.

"Hey, I—"

"To be an effective sheriff you need to be able to deal with the public and show people you appreciate their willingness to assist in cases like this. You don't just steamroll over their efforts to help and send them packing when they come in on their own accord with information that might aid in solving a pending case. That's precisely what she did to me today. By the way she acted, you'd think Sheriff Wright was the Captain of the New York City Police Department. "

"Heavens, no! That'd be Tom Selleck."

The look Rip shot me made it clear he didn't appreciate my reference to *Blue Bloods* even though it was his favorite prime-time TV show, which should come as no surprise to anyone. After a seething glare and ignoring my remark, which should also come as no surprise to anyone, he finished his comment.

"But actually, the high and mighty Jaclyn Wright is just the sheriff of a one-horse town half the size of Rockport."

"Actually, Buffalo seems to have horses all over the—"

"Please don't interrupt." Rip chided me as if he hadn't just interrupted me half a dozen times in a row. I'd known as soon as I'd opened my mouth that Rip was in no mood for levity and I should have kept my fly trap closed.

I was surprised Rip had made the trip to the police station, given the fact he wasn't nearly as quick as I to think there might be something ominous about the two photos. However, the promise of a lengthy foot rub from me could usually persuade Rip into doing anything short of bungee-jumping off the Bay Harbor Bridge in Corpus Christi, dressed only in a Speedo and pink flip-flops. The man loved to have his feet rubbed more than anything in the world besides me, his daughter, an aged bottle of Chivas Regal Scotch, and a good Cuban cigar—and not necessarily in that order.

Rip reached for the remote control, switched the channel to the news station, and then hit the mute button.

He turned back toward me and said, "Oh, I almost forgot. I heard something very interesting at the barber shop today."

I usually complained every time he paid to have his hair cut. With only a handful of hairs left, I felt like he was paying a dollar for each hair the barber snipped. Truth be told, I think Rip enjoyed going to the barber shop for the entertaining gossip that came free with every haircut. Today I didn't care if he'd paid fifty bucks for the haircut. I was too intrigued in the ever-increasing bizarreness behind Bea's death to bicker about something so insignificant. "What did you hear?"

"It has to do with that lady in the red coat at the televised press release."

"Wasn't she the lady who asked the sheriff what safety concerns she should have at the campground she and her husband owned?"

"Exactly. Their names are Leo and Charly Brown."

"Charlie Brown?"

"Charly's spelled C-H-A-R-L-Y, according to Elmer, the barber who trimmed my hair. Marrying a man named Leo Brown was just a comical coincidence. No pun intended. But, anyway, the Browns own a campground called the Sweet Sixteen RV Park."

"Sweet Sixteen is an unusual name."

"It makes sense in this case," Rip countered. "The campground's just over two miles west of Rest 'n Peace on Highway Sixteen, which is affectionately referred to as the Sweet Sixteen Highway."

I was confused as to why Rip thought this bit of news was so fascinating. I assumed he'd eventually explain so I continued to listen. He veered off into a lengthy explanation of all the well-known landmarks along the highway that ran from Devil's Tower in Eastern Wyoming to Yellowstone National Park on the western side of the state.

"There's the Ten Sleep Canyon, the Cloud Peak Skyway—"

"Excuse me, Rip. I need to get a meatloaf in the oven for supper. Can I expect you to get to the point sometime in the near future?"

"Oh, yeah. Sorry. Didn't mean to go off course like that," he said, an impish grin on his face. "So, anyway, it seems the Browns recently lost a civil law suit against the Whetstones. Because they're in close proximity to each other, they naturally compete for the same customers. Late last spring, the Browns dropped their overnight rates by twenty percent to encourage RVers to drive past the Whetstone's park to stay with them instead."

"That ploy would have worked with me."

"In return, the Whetstones began offering one free night with every three you paid for, which basically would amount to a twenty-five percent savings. Then when the Browns cut their monthly rate, the Whetstones cut theirs even more drastically."

"Gee, I wish we'd been here then!"

"It got to the point both parks were almost paying customers to stay at their facilities. Something had to give before they both went belly up."

"What happened next?" His story reminded me of a pricing war between two competing gas stations years ago in Rockport. Both stations ended up folding. Working out an equally fair solution together, they could have figured out a way that both stations could continue to flourish. It was a prime example of biting off your nose to spite your face.

"Finally, they came to the conclusion neither park could make it with the rock-bottom camping rates and both went back to their original rates. But the conflict didn't stop there. The Whetstones put in the large indoor swimming pool with slides and dual diving boards to attract families with children. People, including you, enjoy utilizing it for the exercise, too. Adding the pool appeared to work, as more and more customers chose Rest 'n Peace over the Sweet Sixteen park. So the Browns emptied their nest egg to add brand new machines in their laundry room, and a new clubhouse with an exercise room, bar area, pool tables, ping pong tables, and a variety of other activity options for RVers."

"How did the Whetstones counteract all the enhancements made at the Sweet Sixteen park?"

"They got down and dirty," Rip replied with an ornery smirk. "They put up that huge sign about a quarter mile before the entrance to Rest 'n Peace that reads, 'Don't miss your last opportunity for miles to stay in a fully-appointed RV park. REST 'N PEACE at the best campground in the Bighorn National Forest.'"

"And?" I had seen the sign and was on the edge of my seat, anxious to hear how the Whetstone's strategy had worked out. It was a clever idea, albeit a little too radical in my opinion.

"Their scheme was successful. There's no safe or easy place to turn a large recreational vehicle around for many miles. Like us, most RVers were hesitant to bypass what sounded like their last chance to find satisfactory accommodations without having to drive another hour or two. The Sweet Sixteen RV Park became a ghost town within days. The Browns claimed defamation and filed a lawsuit to have the sign removed. Although the judge found the sign objectionable and morally contemptible, there was no law preventing the Whetstones from displaying it."

"But the Whetstones' sign is based on a lie," I said, appalled at the court's decision. "Insinuating they're the only decent campground *for miles* is untrue."

"The term 'miles' is technically accurate whether you're referring to a thousand miles, or only two. There's two and one quarter miles between the two RV parks. So, by law, it's a factual statement."

"Wow," I said in astonishment. "Talk about a couple of sneaky snakes!"

"Yes, but it has to make you stop and think. Could the bitter dispute between the campground owners have escalated to the point of murder? I've heard of many motivations for murder that are a lot lamer than that over the years. Money makes for a powerful motive."

Rip was right. I knew how nasty Bea could be, and if the Browns were anywhere near her level of maliciousness, who knows what could have developed. As the smell of our supper baking filled our comfy little home, I told Rip what I'd learned in the laundry room.

With an oven mitt on each hand, I removed the pan from the oven. I almost dropped the steaming meatloaf on the floor after Rip's next remark. "Maybe doing a little snooping around isn't such a bad idea, Rapella. The list of people with motives to want Bea eliminated is growing longer all the time. Not to mention, I'd rather enjoy watching that mouthy, overbearing sheriff eat a little crow."

One should never underestimate the power of wanting retribution to avenge a wrong committed against them. In this case, all it took was the desire to serve up a heaping plateful of crow to sway Rip over to my way of thinking.

CHAPTER 11

The sound of heavy rain and small hail pelting the aluminum roof of our trailer woke me up early the next morning. I slipped on some jeans and a sweatshirt before going into the small bathroom to use the toilet, insert my dentures, and run a comb through my curly mop of salt and pepper hair. Rip was already watching CNN and drinking coffee in the living room when I ambled out to join him.

I picked up the coffee carafe to pour myself a cup just as there was a knock on the door. I opened it, and was surprised to see Ranger Rick had stopped by again. I asked him if he'd like to join us for a cup of coffee. After he accepted my offer, Rip held his now empty cup out and asked if I'd mind pouring him a refill while I was fixing a cup for the ranger.

"Good morning, Ranger." Rip greeted him in a jovially fashion. "What's up?"

"Not much. Just happened to be in the neighborhood. I saw your lights were on and thought I'd stop by."

I knew the two men had instantly clicked the day the ranger came by to return our binoculars and camera. I had grown fond of Rick, as well. Still, it seemed odd to me to have him drop by before seven in the morning for no reason whatsoever. Odder still was why the forest ranger would be in the neighborhood that early. He'd have to have been driving around in the RV park to notice our lights were on.

However, I was happy to see him. I thought it'd be an opportune time to question him about his relationship with his former sister-in-law. Having shown interest in looking into the woman's death, I thought Rip might bring up the subject, but was disappointed when their conversation drifted far away from that topic.

I wanted to seize the opportunity to learn anything we could pertaining to the case. Reluctant to jump right to the point, I adopted a playful bantering tone and asked, "Do you have a family, Rick? Any budding forest rangers, or rangettes?"

"Rangettes? I'm pretty sure the females in my department refer to themselves as rangers, just as their male counterparts do." That was the extent of Rick's response after chuckling at my remark. It seemed to me as if he was trying to avoid discussing his personal life. But then, I have a tendency to automatically suspect everyone of duplicity.

Rip, who's not usually so quick on the uptake, understood I was trying to segue into a conversation about his ex, so he added, "If you're anything like me, Rick, the last thing you'd want a son to do is follow in your footsteps. It'd scare me to death to have a child go into law enforcement these days. It's 'damned if you do and damned if you don't', it seems. When it comes to defending themselves, police officers' hands are almost tied now. They have to wait until after they've been shot dead before responding in kind. If a cop *is* forced to shoot a suspect who's threatening them, a large portion of the population wants them to serve more time than the thug they were trying to protect that very same population from. One time, when I was still a beat cop, I—"

Oh, boy, I thought. *I can see where this is going if I don't put the brakes on his anecdote right now.* I'd heard the long and winding story he was about to tell so many times I could have told it myself, verbatim. The tale usually preceded a dozen more accounts of incidents that had happened during his career in law enforcement. Rip might have been quick to pick up on my objective, but being easily distracted, he was even quicker to drop it like a red hot poker and focus on his own.

I knew it was only a matter of minutes before Rick looked at his watch, feigned alarm, and said, "Oh no! If I don't head out right this second, I'm going to be late to a very important appointment. I'll take a rain check, though, because I'd love to hear the rest of your story." Then he'd drive to a popular local cafe and relax over a second cup of coffee that he could have gotten free at our place, relieved at escaping our trailer before his eardrums turned to stone.

"Oh, yes!" I exclaimed. Both Rip and Rick's heads pivoted toward me in surprise. "Now I remember what I wanted to tell you the next time we saw you. I was at the beauty parlor yesterday—"

"Really?" Rick replied in bewilderment. I hadn't taken into consideration my hair looked like a nest of field mice had taken up residence in it. With nearly fifty years of practice at reading Rip's mind, I could read Ranger Rick's pretty well, too. He was thinking, *I don't know what you had to pay, lady, but you got royally screwed.*

"Of course, I haven't had time to comb it out this morning." I knew my face was flushing so I quickly continued. "But what I wanted to tell you was that I was chatting with another lady in the salon who appeared distraught. I asked her if she was all right and she told me her sister, Bea Whetstone, had recently suffered a gruesome death."

"What?" Rick looked as if I'd just informed him I'd seen his photo on a wanted poster in a Tijuana post office. "Did she give you her name?"

"No." I was surprised at his reaction to the story I'd concocted.

"Leggy redhead? 'Soiled Rotten' tattoo on the side of her neck?"

"Soiled rotten?" It sounded to me as if he'd misspoken. "I saw only the top of her tattoo because the cosmetologist had just put a towel around her neck. But don't you mean spoiled rather than soiled?"

"Unfortunately, no. You'd understand if you'd ever met her."

"She was a redhead, however," I said, fabricating to match the description he'd given of his ex.

"What else did the woman say?"

"Not much. But when I casually mentioned a new friend of ours, named Rick Myer, discovered Bea's body, she appeared as though she was quite familiar with you. Truth be told, she acted as if I'd slapped her when I told her it was you who discovered her sister's body." After my remark, I watched carefully for the ranger's reaction.

Rick smiled when I mentioned we considered him a friend now, because I thought he probably could use a friend to lean on. He'd given me the impression he was a very lonely man. But other than the smile, he showed little reaction to my provoking comment except for a barely discernable hint of contempt.

"Yeah, I guess you could say she's familiar with me since Desireé and I were married for ten years. She filed for divorce last August. She then immediately hooked up with a plumber in town. I'm certain she'd already been cheating on me with him for several months. The hardest part is missing our eight-year old daughter, Olivia. Dez makes me jump through hoops to spend any time at all with her. I see my son even less often. He's older though, and the result of a short relationship I had with a classmate during college."

Rick looked more hurt than angry. I felt sorry for the man. I couldn't imagine being separated from my own daughter, Regina, especially when she was still a young child in her formative years. And the very idea of being divorced from Rip made me sick to my stomach.

"I'm so sorry I mentioned it, Rick. I didn't know—"

"Don't worry about it. It's water under the bridge. Desireé owns a shop in town now and lives with her new boyfriend, Marco Paules. It's been hard for me, but Dez had no problem moving on."

"I'm so sorry." I apologized again, almost wishing I hadn't even brought the subject up. But that sudden tinge of regret didn't stop me from wanting to know more. "If you don't mind me asking, what kind of shop does she own?"

"It's that gaudy building with the brown trim about two blocks west of the Chamber of Commerce building on Main Street. You've surely seen it. It's been a bone of contention with a lot of residents since it opened. I had a lot of reservations about it myself."

"Are you talking about the building that's surrounded by the Ponderosa pines?" Even as I asked him, I was curious if Rick found the color of our travel trailer as gaudy as his ex-wife's shop. As I recalled, their color combinations were nearly identical. But, then, I realized her shop probably didn't have any painted sunflowers to class the place up like the Chartreuse Caboose had.

"Yes, that's it. It's appropriately called the Knotty Pine Playhouse." Rick sounded scornful, but I thought it was a cute name for a shop surrounded by pine trees that most likely sold toys and games for children in their daughter's age range. I wondered what kinds of items were sold there and why it'd be a bone of contention to residents, unless, like Rick, they thought the color of the building was atrocious. I decided I'd have to stop in sometime and look around. I needed to purchase a birthday gift to mail off to a ten-year-old nephew on the Ripple side of the family, and figured this might be the perfect place to pick something up.

I started to ask Rick more about Desireé's shop, when he suddenly glanced at his watch and said, "Oh, my! It's almost eight. I need to go right now. If I don't get to work on time, my boss will be on me like shit on a shingle. Oh, sorry, Rapella. Please pardon my language."

"Quit apologizing for your language, Ranger. A colorful choice of words has never bothered me one bit, and I enjoy a good old cliché as much as anyone."

"You can say that again!" Rip said, with a dramatic roll of his eyes.

"I enjoy a good old cliché—" Before I could jokingly finish repeating myself, the door was shutting behind Ranger Rick. He was, undoubtedly, breathing a deep sigh of relief at having escaped before being faced with even more uncomfortable questions he wasn't anxious to answer. I knew he was probably on his way to the cafe for that second cup of coffee I mentioned earlier.

"Sure seems like Rick left rather abruptly," Rip said.

"I thought so, too."

"Must have a tough boss. He never really mentioned why he stopped by to begin with. Reckon he wanted to ask me something? It was obvious he was uncomfortable talking about his ex, Destiny."

"Her name's Desireé."

"Whatever. I wish now you hadn't even brought the subject up. I don't want him to think we suspect him of anything. Especially now that we know why he didn't want to own up to knowing the victim. Having Destiny up and divorce him out of the blue like that was probably hard for Rick to accept."

I didn't correct him, but I made sure to let him know he'd said the woman's name wrong again. "Maybe he thinks Desireé was influenced to divorce him by another party, perhaps her sister, Bea."

"Really? You think Bea influenced his ex?" Rip asked sarcastically. "You don't think the plumber who was reaming out her pipes might have had something to do with Destiny's decision?"

"Well, yeah. There's that too. And once again, her name is Desireé."

Rip reached for the remote and turned up the volume to listen to the details of the latest mud-slinging episode involving a candidate in the upcoming presidential election. It was time for me to get breakfast prepared, knowing Rip would moan and groan about his cup of strawberry-flavored yogurt with granola sprinkled on it. His complaint would be in the nature of, "I'm a retired cop, not an anorexic sorority girl. I need more than a dollop of sour, bacteria-laden milk with a teaspoon of bird food on top of it to sustain me."

And my response would be, "Have I told you lately how incredible you're looking since you've lost ten pounds? Another fifteen or so and you'll look twenty years younger. Svelte enough to grace the cover of *GQ Magazine*, I'd bet."

He'd chew on my compliment for a few moments and then grudgingly begin to eat his breakfast. Where Rip is concerned, flattery will get you everywhere.

As soon as the breakfast dishes were washed and put away, I planned to head into town. I had no reason to doubt anything Rick had told us, and I really couldn't imagine him hurting a flea. But something seemed amiss to me, and I wanted to check out his ex-wife's shop and engage her in a conversation if given the opportunity.

In hindsight, I might have been better prepared for this visit had I known that the shop was called "Naughty Pine Playhouse" instead of "Knotty Pine Playhouse," which is what I'd assumed when Rick mentioned it. I was right in thinking the shop sold toys. Unfortunately, they weren't the sort of toys you'd buy your ten-year old nephew for his birthday.

CHAPTER 12

"Welcome to the playhouse," the sultry voice said as I entered the shop five minutes after its posted opening time. By the reddish-blond color of her hair and the absurd "Soiled Rotten" tattoo on her neck, I knew immediately it was the owner, Desireé. I was pleased I'd gotten lucky on my first attempt to locate her.

"Thank you," I said. I didn't want to get off on the wrong foot with Ranger Rick's ex-wife, but I felt obliged to offer advice so she wouldn't make the same sort of mistakes in the future. "I hate to bring it up, dear, but I noticed the sign on the front of your little shop and feel you might benefit from investing in a dictionary. Then you could double-check your spelling before you make important decisions, like naming your business or having a tattoo inked on your neck. And here's another piece of advice from someone with much more life experience and wisdom than you. I'm sure you think that tattoo is cute now, but you might not be as enamored with it when you're my age. For starters, with the wrinkles your neck will have acquired by then, your tattoo won't even be legible. Although, in your case that might be a good thing since 'spoiled' is misspelled. You'll be trying to cover your silly tattoo up with foundation or wearing turtlenecks year round, and regret your hasty decision from decades past. Mark my words, dear! You might want to keep that in mind the next time you're tempted to step inside a tattoo parlor. Turtlenecks can get mighty sticky and icky when it's ninety in the shade on the outside patio of the assisted living facility you'll likely be residing in."

Desireé flushed. "You may be right, ma'am. But enough about me. What are you in here looking for today?"

"A toy."

"Then you've most definitely come to the right place. Are you planning a partie à deux, or perhaps a ménage à trois?"

I was at a loss for words. I had no idea what language this woman was speaking or what she'd just said, and was afraid communicating with her might prove quite difficult. It could be extraordinarily challenging when it came to her helping me pick out a present for little Tommy.

I waited a few moments for her to translate what she'd just asked me. When she just silently stared at me, I asked, "You speaka da English?"

Desireé laughed, as if I'd been joking. "On the other hand, you may have flying solo in mind, in which case, we need to look around in an entirely different department."

Flying solo? What is this woman talking about? I asked myself. *Surely she doesn't own a flight school, too.*

"I have no desire to learn how to operate a plane, my dear. I'm only interested in finding a gift for my nephew."

"Sounds a little kinky, but I like it!" Desireé gave me a knowing wink. In return, I threw my hands up in the air. Literally.

"I think we have a failure to communicate, dear. My ten-year-old nephew, Tommy, has a birthday coming up, and I'd like to find an appropriate present for a boy of that age."

"Then I'm afraid you're in the wrong store, lady. The Naughty Pine offers erotica-type merchandise; from sex toys and pornographic literature, to barely-there lingerie. Sorry, but we don't offer a single item that'd be appropriate for a child."

I glanced around, taking in the merchandise on display in the Naughty Pine Playhouse. Some of its contents looked more like weapons than toys. My scanning stopped at a rack of men's magazines, including *Hustler* and *Penthouse*. Ernest Hemingway would have turned over in his grave if he'd heard this woman referring to that smut as literature. Mouth agape, I listened as Desireé continued. "Thank you for stopping by, however. Come back when you're in the market for a toy of your own."

I didn't even have a response for a remark like that, or for the knowing smile she'd flashed me. But I realized she was dismissing me before I'd had a chance to ask her one question about her ex-husband, Richard Myer. I wanted to find out if she, her ex, and her late sister had shared a tenuous relationship with one another. Had Bea encouraged her sister to leave Rick? And if so, why? Was Desireé determined to be the sole heir when her ailing mama died? Was the size of the treasure trove she was set to inherit worth killing her only sibling? I couldn't imagine any amount of money being worth killing for, but there were all kinds of money-mongers, misfits, and mental cases in the world who may feel differently. There are even those who would throw their own mama under a bus for a mere fistful of dollars; just enough for a snort or two of heroin, for instance.

I could only think of one option to keep her engaged in conversation. So, trying not to gag on my own words, I said, "Well, now that you mention it, there is something I've been meaning to purchase. I have all of the sex toys I need already, but I would like some new lingerie. Kind of want to spice up the old love life, you see."

Just having sex twice in the same month would be all it'd take to put our libidos in overdrive at this stage of our lives. Not having the get-up-and-go I once had, I needed to save what little energy I did have for tasks like mopping the kitchen floor and dusting off venetian blinds. But, for now, I needed to pretend I was interested in acquiring something more alluring than my high-waisted bloomers that I could practically tuck my boobs in to.

"I have the perfect teddy for you!" Desireé exclaimed in delight.

"Teddy? I thought you said you didn't carry any toys appropriate for children."

"Not a teddy bear, ma'am. A teddy is a one-piece type of sleepwear. Very sexy and a real turn-on for your man. Do you have any preferences on style or material? Lace? Satin? Silk? Or are you the S & M type that likes to kick it up a notch with leather lingerie?"

"Leather lingerie? I'm not one of the Hell's Angels, dear. And I'm not certain what S & M stands for, either. Is it 'sweaty' and 'manhandled' perhaps? I know I'd sweat like a cold-water tank in the summer if I wore leather to bed, especially if I were being manhandled by my husband at the same time. After about seventeen seconds of that kind of nonsense, there wouldn't be a dry thread left in one of those ludicrous leather 'teddies', as you like to call them. So, whatever S & M is, my dear, I'm guessing by the saucy way you asked me, it's a relatively safe bet I'm not that type."

"It stands for sadism and masochism, ma'am." I didn't appreciate the way the shop owner rolled her eyes and shook her head as she spoke, or the mocking tone in her voice.

"That's nice," I said. "Although it doesn't help me much. So let's just assume I'm not the S & M type. Just show me something appropriate for my age bracket. I have almost no experience at all with frilly, uncomfortable pajamas that I wouldn't be able to sleep in if I had to."

"Sleep?" The redhead asked in puzzlement. "Who said anything about sleeping in them?"

"Excuse me?" Now I was even more puzzled. But according to Desireé's description, a teddy, made out of something other than cowhide, sounded fairly tame to me. After all, my cotton night shirt with a sleeping Calico kitten appliquéd on the front was a one-piece style of nightwear.

"I have an idea you might like." She motioned for me to follow her to the far corner of the store. I seized the moment to make a casual comment that I hoped would lead into a more enlightening exchange. "Wasn't that just awful about that poor woman who got eaten by a bear, mountain lion, or something of that nature?"

Desireé stopped mid-step and turned to face me. "More awful than you think. For me, anyway. Bea was my sister. I can't get the image of her final moments out of my head. I've hardly slept a wink since I heard the news."

No surprise there, I thought, *especially if you've been wearing some of the leather sleepwear you're selling in this store*. The leather lingerie brought a whole new meaning to the phrase "back in the saddle again".

I studied the woman's expression and noticed she looked genuinely distraught. I felt I should offer my condolences. "Oh, my! I am so very sorry for your loss, dear. I hope she died doing what she loved. I don't mean to imply she loved trying to fend off a wild animal that was intent on devouring her, of course. I mean something she enjoyed doing, such as hiking through the forest, even though that pastime sounds absolutely dreadful to me, considering all the animals that are champing at the bit to wolf down an intruder. Oh, goodness, I certainly didn't mean to use 'wolf down' as a pun. I suppose 'gobble up' would be a better—"

I stopped abruptly when I saw the horrified look on Desireé's face. It was clear I wasn't doing a good job at consoling her with my babbling. Finally, I said what she'd no doubt heard a couple of dozen times already. "At least Bea's in a better place now."

Her soul is in a better place anyway, I thought. *The rest of Bea is probably distributed among various piles of bear and cougar poop, and possibly a little raccoon scat, as well. And that's because someone, perhaps even you, Desireé, left her dead body in the forest, at the mercy of the wildlife populating it.*

Desireé remained motionless. I wasn't going to learn anything from her if she didn't speak. So I decided to inquire about something a little more pleasant. I asked, "How is your mother doing, dear? I've heard she was a remarkably-skilled pediatrician in her day. Unfortunately, I've also heard she's not doing well at the moment."

With a hand over each ear, the redhead finally responded. "What? How do you know my mother? I'm sorry, ma'am, but I just can't stand to talk about my family anymore. Bea's death is still too fresh in my mind. That horrific tragedy and my mother's declining health are too painful for me to even think about. Let me show you the teddy so I can get my mind off my sister and my terminally ill mother."

Darn it! The window of opportunity to gain a little insight into the matter of Bea's death had slammed shut on my fingers before I could even squeeze my way through it. I'd made no headway whatsoever into the possibilities of sibling rivalry when it came to their dying mother's estate.

"Here you go! What do you think?" Desireé asked in a disheartened voice. She then flashed a seemingly forced smile as she proudly held up a lacy, see-through pink "onesie" that left absolutely nothing to the imagination. And when it comes to my nearly seven-decade-old body, you wouldn't want to even attempt to imagine me wearing it. As if the sex shop proprietor thought it'd seal the deal, she turned the teddy around so I could see the back of it, and added, "It's even got a thong. A little extra enticement for your man."

Without even looking into a mirror, I knew my expression was that of a woman who'd just been handed a twelve-foot python and told to drape the harmless reptile around her neck. "Enticement? The only thing that teddy's liable to entice my husband to do is go into cardiac arrest. Particularly if I came to bed wearing it."

"Oh, come on! You still have a killer bod! He'd rip this sexy teddy off you so fast it'd make your head spin. Try it on before you decide whether or not to buy it. It's on sale for eighty-nine dollars, today only."

"Eighty-nine dollars?" I was astounded at the price and didn't mind telling Desireé what I thought about it. "Why there ain't eighty-nine *cents* worth of material in that thing, even if they hadn't chopped most of the backside off. And, believe me, if I paid eighty-nine bucks for it, I'd be stashing that teddy in our safety deposit box at the bank where no one, including my husband, would be doing any ripping on it."

"What if I let you have it at my break-even price of sixty-five dollars?"

"Lady, I wouldn't give you a nickel for that thing."

"But, but, ma'am. It has a thong on—"

"Having that tiny strip of tickly lace creeping up my crack would have me battier than Carlsbad Caverns in about three seconds."

"You'd get used to it after a while."

"Not in this lifetime, I won't! Maybe I should look elsewhere. This is not exactly what I had in mind." Not even the lure of possibly finding out additional useful tidbits of information from Desireé could keep me in her store another minute. I wanted to get out of there before she asked me to try out some of her toys before deciding whether or not to buy any. The vast majority of them resembled something I wouldn't feel comfortable using or even mentioning in my story, and I assume you get the picture without me doing so. The remaining products available in the shop would absolutely scare the pants off me. And, just so you don't get the wrong idea, I meant that last comment figuratively.

"You know, there's a Wal-Mart about thirty-five miles away in Sheridan. You could get both a toy for your nephew and some flannel jammies for yourself," Desireé said in an effort to insult me.

"Now you're talking. And I wouldn't even have to rob the First Northern Bank to pay for them," I replied as I walked toward the front entrance. Desireé probably didn't hear my snide remark because her cell phone was ringing. As I opened the door to leave, her response to the caller stopped me in my tracks. She was clearly upset as she said, "You promised me you'd keep your end of the deal. We had an agreement, Ricky, and you'd better stick to it. After all, because of you I have a lot of debt to pay off. But even then, you have more on the line than I do, you know. Why don't you stop by the shop this afternoon so we can discuss the matter?"

Not only did I think the likelihood of the caller being Ranger Rick was good, the way Desireé pleaded with him not to break their agreement made my skin crawl.

I stepped back into the store and walked toward Desireé. She quickly whispered into the phone, and afterward, angrily jammed it down into her ample-sized brassiere. I winced in reaction to her forcefulness. Then, in a sickening sweet voice, she asked, "Did you change your mind about the teddy?"

"Do earthworms have elbows? Not hardly."

If not for it being totally intrusive, I'd have asked where she was on the day of Bea's death and if her whereabouts could be corroborated. While I was at it, I'd have also asked if killing Bea was a plan she and her ex cooked up together for a mutually beneficial reason. Like, for instance, her sister's half of their momma's estate.

I knew that was over-reaching, even for me. Instead I asked something less threatening. "No. Actually, I was wondering if you've spoken to law enforcement since your sister's death."

"No. Why would I have spoken with them?"

"I was just thinking that due to the close relationship you clearly had with your sister, you might be able to share something that helps them determine for certain if it was an animal that killed her or something else. You know, just in case it *wasn't* an animal attack. As I'm sure you've heard, they couldn't pin down the exact cause of her death because of the deplorable condition of her body. My husband was in law enforcement his entire career. To be perfectly honest with you, we are helping investigate Bea's death. So if you have something to share, and would feel more comfortable sharing it with me than a couple of intimidating interrogators, by all means, go ahead. I'm ready to listen."

I ceased talking when tears starting forming in Desireé's eyes. It was hard to judge whether her sorrow was sincere, or she was merely shedding crocodile tears to appear grief-stricken about her loss. Either way, I didn't have time to wait for her to compose herself, so I continued. "And if by off-chance she *was* murdered by someone, I know you'd want to see the perpetrator of such an atrocity captured and punished. Am I right?"

Desireé sniffed, wiped her eyes, blew her nose loudly, took in a long, deep breath, and then repeated the entire sequence twice before speaking again. I almost got the feeling she'd been using the time as a stall tactic to give her a few moments to compose her next remark, in the event I didn't tire of the whole process and go away. I was even more convinced this was the case when, following the third long sigh, she reached into the other side of her brassiere to extract lip gloss and ran it back and forth across her lips a half-dozen times, before checking her cell phone for any new messages. All the while hoping I'd give up and leave. I wondered if before the woman responded, she'd pull a cotton ball and bottle of make-up remover out of her bra to dab at the smeared mascara under her eyes.

To force a reply, I stared silently at her until she finally said, "Yes, of course I'd want the killer punished if Bea was murdered. She was the only sibling I have and we were very close. And, with my mother in grave condition now, I feel helpless and alone. I could sure use my sister's shoulder to lean on. But it doesn't sound as if the authorities believe murder was the cause of Bea's death, and for that I'm very thankful."

Desireé dug around—in her bra, of course—until she found a compact with a mirror to inspect her face for smeared makeup. I was beginning to think this gal must actually be flat-chested. Otherwise, I couldn't see how there'd be enough room in what appeared to be a 38D cup-sized brassiere to not only secure her breasts, but also to serve as her well-stocked toiletry bag. I've heard of "fanny" packs, but "booby" packs? Not so much!

After finally returning the compact to its former place, she spoke again. "As for speaking with the detectives, I answered their questions on the day she went missing and again after her body was discovered by that miserable son-of-a-buck I was married to. I have absolutely nothing more to relate to them that'd be of any benefit in putting the cause of Bea's death to rest. I think they've already determined it wasn't murder, anyway. Besides, like them, I too have no doubt it was an animal attack. I don't know how anyone could want to hurt Bea. She meant the world to me. Everybody, and I mean *everybody*, loved her."

Everybody loved her? Are we talking about the same Bea Whetstone? I wanted to ask. I'm sure somewhere in the sisterhood code of ethics there's a clause obligating Desireé to love Bea. But I certainly didn't love the woman and had even fancied killing her myself. Not seriously, of course. The point is, I had just recently met the gal. If I'd had the time to get to know Bea better, I've no doubt I'd have despised her even more intensely. I could also attest to the fact she wasn't high on several other people's lists either. Both Jan and Barb Harris had made no secret of the fact they had little use for Bea. And Desireé and I both knew her ex, "Ricky", wasn't a big fan of her sister.

I watched Desireé straighten up a pile of packages in her "toy" department, clearly an attempt to speed up my departure. Forget Tommy, I'm not sure *I'd* even know what to do with some of the toys sold there—nor would I want to know! I studied Desireé's nails as she restacked the doodads. They were the exact shade of purple as her blouse. And, as you know, there are about eighty different shades of purple to choose from. There was a nail salon two doors down from the Naughty Pine, but my guess was she polished her own nails on a daily basis, in order to match whatever outfit she was wearing at the time. She easily could have been wearing a black blouse on the day of Bea's death, which she might have complemented with matching nail polish.

Before I departed, I encouraged Desireé once again to think about contacting the police. As Bea's sister, I told her, she should feel duty-bound to give a statement in case the investigators found it useful in the case. She may know of some seemingly inconsequential detail she hadn't already shared with them that could prove to be a crucial clue to what exactly happened to Bea. Without waiting for a reply, I turned to walk back to the door. I could feel her eyes burning holes in the back of my shirt. For a second I even thought I smelled smoke. Before I could exit the building, Desireé was already talking on the phone again. As the door closed behind me, I heard part of her first remark. "Sorry, honey, I had some crazy, senile old woman in here asking me if—"

I considered myself neither senile nor old. I'll admit I was still on the fence about "crazy", but I resented being called insulting names by some red-headed bimbo whom I'd discovered was most definitely "soiled rotten." I'm not proud to tell you this, but I felt compelled to give her the finger through her shop's plate glass window. So I did! In fact, I wiggled all of the fingers on my left hand, giving her a whole flock of birdies. To my dismay, Desireé mistook my obscene gesture as an enthusiastic wave, and responded with a half-hearted one of her own.

After my uncomfortable experience with Desireé, I was anxious to get home and see what Rip thought about my conversation with her. I'd leave out the part about the teddy, complete with a thong, or I'd never hear the end of it. I suddenly had a strong desire to reach down into my jeans to insure my underwear wasn't all "tucked in," so to speak. Resisting the urge, I climbed into the cab of the truck and fired it up.

"I think I know Rick well enough by now to judge his character."

I'd just informed Rip I'd stopped by the shop to visit with the ranger's ex, and he was annoyed I had any doubt the man wasn't entirely above-board. He was also appalled that

I'd suggest Rick could, or would, ever hurt another human being. In an irritated tone, he said, "Don't you think that a man who'd demonstrate such genuine concern for a moose and her babies has to have been blessed with a pure heart and a deep desire to protect all living creatures? Good grief, Rapella. I sure hope you didn't give Destiny—"

"Desireé."

"—your name. I wouldn't want it to get back to Rick that you were snooping into his and his ex-wife's relationship."

"Was comparing the types of firearms you and the ranger both like all it took to convince you that you know what makes the man tick? Was sharing a laugh about passing gas in an elevator all that was necessary for you to conclude he's incapable of having another, darker side? Is a man's opinion of tighty-whities the new litmus test for determining his ability to kill? I have to say, dear, your quickness to absolve the ranger sounds a little hasty to me."

"Think what you will, Rapella. Richard Myer seems like a decent fellow to me, and I choose to take him at face value."

"I like Ranger Rick too, Rip, but it doesn't mean I'm going to judge him through rose-colored glasses. During your underwear debate, did Rick happen to mention he has arranged a pow-wow with his ex-wife? Apparently, they made a deal to keep something strictly between the two of them. Something sinister, I'd bet. And tonight he's going to her place to hash it out."

"Your over-active imagination is running away with your common sense, my dear. So the former spouses have some sort of agreement. What does that prove? They have a daughter in common, for goodness sake! Their meeting tonight could easily be to discuss a custody agreement. And both are probably close to his older son, as well. I'm sure their post-marriage relationship is based on a long list of compromises to make sure the decisions they make are what's best for their children. In my opinion, you should be looking into the conflict between the campground owners. The rift between them sounded serious and unrelenting.

Hard to say how far the Browns might have gone to retaliate after the justice system failed to protect them from unfair business practices being perpetrated against them by the owners of a competitive campground. Especially when the Browns' livelihood depends entirely on their ability to lure RVers into staying in their campground."

I nodded in agreement. Rip's assessment of Desireé and Ranger Rick's situation was reasonable. I've never been through a divorce, thank the Lord, and never plan to be. I could only imagine the degree of cooperation that must be worked out between divorced parents with regard to the well-being of their children. Granted, there were times during Regina's upbringing, I considered begging Rip to run away from home and take our rebellious daughter with him. But in the event of a divorce, I would have fought tooth and nail to retain custody, or at least joint custody, of the spoiled, noisy, messy, ungrateful and aggravating brat that I loved unconditionally.

I also had to agree with Rip about the feud between the RV park owners. It wouldn't hurt to look into the extent of the contention between the two parties, if I could think of a conceivable reason to arrange a meeting with Leo and Charly Brown.

I prepared tuna-salad sandwiches for lunch while I mused over possible ploys to get an audience with one or both of the Browns. Dolly, who'd been giving me the cold fur since she'd finished her breakfast, suddenly rushed into the kitchen and attached herself to my left leg like a large, furry growth. She knew from past experience she was about to be the recipient of the juice I'd drained from the tuna can. I glanced over at Rip, who was seated at the table, licking his lips and waiting impatiently for me to set his plate down in front of him. My gaze drifted back to Dolly, now licking her chops as well, while winding in and out of my legs. Clearly, she was impatient for me to set the bowl of juice down in front of her. Gee, I wonder from whom Dolly had picked up her exasperating habit?

CHAPTER 13

"**M**a'am, what would you say are the best-selling souvenirs here in your store?" I asked. "Preferably those that would appeal to children."

I picked up each item in turn, checked its price and quality before returning it to its designated spot on the shelf. I was the lone customer in the store at the time. The sales clerk sat at a desk behind the counter with her back to me as she added up receipts on an adding machine and notated the resulting figures in a ledger. She had her hair all tucked into a teal-colored ball cap, presumably to keep it up off her shoulders. It was warm in the store that morning as a fire crackled in the pot belly stove in the middle of the room.

"Sorry, I really don't know much about any of them. This is just my third day helping out in the store until permanent help can be found," the woman replied. I recognized the voice immediately and turned to walk toward the front counter as the lady continued to respond with her back to me. "Frankly, everything is so over-priced, I haven't sold much of anything. So far today, only a toothbrush and a four-pack of biodegradable toilet tissue have left the building: two items it'd be hard to put off buying until a later time."

"Jan?" I asked. "Is that you slaving over a hot ledger?"

"Oh, hello, Rapella!" Jan stood up and chuckled when she heard her name. "I didn't see you come in and was too wrapped up in what I was doing to recognize your voice. I'm trying to make heads or tails of the receipts piled up all over this desk. It's a rat's nest, let me tell you. How are you this morning?"

"Fine. And you? Other than being buried in paperwork, that is. I was surprised to hear your voice because I'd never have expected you to be working in here. But I have to say, it's nice to find someone with a much more cheerful disposition working in the store today." Before Bea's disappearance, I'd begun to dread having to come into the store for any reason whatsoever and had avoided it as much as possible.

"Thank you. However, I can't imagine too many folks with a less cheerful disposition than Bea Whetstone. Can you?" We exchanged smiles, but I instantly felt remorseful for disparaging a woman who'd just recently met with such a gruesome demise. No one deserved a fate like that. Not even the disagreeable woman who had co-owned the campground and spent much of her day running its store while ripping off and haranguing the customers.

Not meaning to use a play on words, I solemnly responded, "I really do hope Bea didn't suffer too much and I pray she now rests in peace."

"Me, too." Jan agreed, although the joyfulness in her voice said otherwise. "I'm only here for another forty-five minutes. Boonie asked if I'd fill in on occasion until he has hired someone to run the store on a regular schedule. A work camper in site B-2 comes in at eleven-thirty to work the remainder of the day."

"I see. How's Boonie doing? He must be devastated. I feel so badly for the poor guy."

"I do, too. He's lost without Bea. That's why I felt I should ask him if I could fill in here at the store while he deals with more pressing matters, such as the many responsibilities and obligations regarding her death."

"I thought you just said *he* asked *you* to help out?"

"Um, well, I, uh, I meant, what I meant was, I meant he asked me to run the office after I offered to help out in any way I could. Yes, that's what I meant to say. You know, well, um, you know, because, like you, I felt so sorry for him, being so lonely and depressed and all. And, of course, you know, that he's, well, um, he is so very, very upset about the loss of his wife, as you can imagine."

As Bea stumbled through her remarks, I crouched down, squatting on the floor, to sort through the souvenirs lined up on the bottom rack of a metal stand. In that position, I was hidden from Jan's view from behind the counter. I nearly toppled over when I heard the creaking of the back door as it swung open and Boonie's low-timbered voice say, "Hey, sweetie, you getting that mess all straightened out? I know I'm repeating myself, but you look incredibly sexy this morning. Your beautiful baby blues match your cap perfectly."

I froze, now too embarrassed to stand up and make my presence known. But I had the distinct feeling Jan had wordlessly alerted Boonie about me when he stopped speaking abruptly in the middle of his next sentence, "Maybe we can find something funner to do this—"

More fun, I wanted to say to correct him, and no doubt scare the dickens out of him in the process. But, because I might hear some more interesting exchanges between the two if he didn't know I was in the room, I remained silent.

Jan giggled nervously, and made light of his comments. "Oh, you big flirt. I'm happy you're at least trying to lighten your spirits by kidding with me like that. But you can't fool me. I know how devastated you are, and I just can't imagine how hard it is for you to go on without the love of your life."

You can't fool me, either, I thought. I wasn't sure if she was trying to convince me or Boonie about how distraught he really was. He'd certainly sounded jovial to me when he greeted the temporary help; a woman with whom he couldn't have been well acquainted if this was truly her first time in Wyoming. When my bent knees began to cramp, I stood up and faced the pair, trying not to appear as uncomfortable as I felt.

Boonie glanced over at me, and then replied to Jan's remarks. In a total about-face, his voice had morphed from one of good-humor to one of deep, but unnatural-sounding, despair. "Yes, it's been so difficult for me to go on without my one true love. The support I've received from so many people like you two lovely gals has helped a bit, but it certainly doesn't erase the pain of losing her."

I'm not sure what kind of support he'd received from Jan, but I knew I hadn't offered him support of any kind. In fact, we hadn't even spoken since news of his wife's disappearance first broke. And I wasn't buying his pathetic attempt to convince me of his devotion to Bea, or his grief at losing her. Both he and Jan appeared flushed and wore expressions of apprehension, undoubtedly worried I had figured out the truth about their relationship. I faked a look of compassion, and said, "My heart and prayers are with you, Mr. Whetstone. At least you have the comfort of knowing that Bea is in a better place now."

"Yes, that's true. Thank you." With his head hung low, Boonie took a brief sideways glance at Jan and walked out the back door.

Jan turned to me and asked, "Isn't that sad? The poor man's so broken-hearted. So, have you found what you're looking for today?"

"Not yet." Actually I'd found more than I was looking for. I'd found more evidence of a compelling motive for two suspects in Bea Whetstone's death. "I'd like to buy about a half-dozen or so souvenirs, preferably a variety of popular items. I have a couple I'm interested in. If you don't mind, I'll just set the ones I want to purchase here on the counter."

"Sure, no problem. Are they for your grandkids?"

"No. Actually, I'm going to use them as an excuse to chat with the owners of the Sweet Sixteen RV Park. I have a sneaking suspicion there's more to Bea's death than meets the eye. My husband, whose career was in law-enforcement, and I have had very good success in solving murder cases in the past. We thought we might look into Bea's bizarre death as well, because it appears to us to have too many untied loose ends. I guess now that we're retired, we just have too much time on our hands."

Jan looked baffled, but merely nodded. I don't know what had made me decide to open my big mouth about investigating Bea's death, but I hoped it wasn't a decision that would come back to bite me in the kiester as so many of my impulsive decisions had done in the past. I'd really just wanted to judge Jan's reaction to my statement, but as it turned out, she showed very little reaction at all. She just gazed at me with a blank expression before returning to her chair behind the desk that was covered with piles of receipts.

As I continued to appraise the souvenirs on display, I wondered if and why Jan had lied to me about this being her first visit to Wyoming the day I first met her in the laundry room. If she hadn't lied, could she realistically have established a seemingly romantic relationship with the new widower this quickly after Bea's death and Jan's own arrival in Buffalo? Had telling me it was her first time in the state been an attempt to distance herself from her soon-to-be victim so as not to give anyone a reason to suspect her of any involvement in Bea's death?

The awkward scene I'd just witnessed seemed to confirm Barb Harris's remark about an alleged affair between Jan and the victim's husband. I had no doubt at this juncture the rumor was true. Jan and Boonie had almost assuredly been carrying on an affair behind Bea's back. But had their relationship been a casual "no-strings attached" fling, or serious enough that one or both of them wanted Bea out of the picture? Enough so that perhaps they'd instigate a plan to do it themselves? We'd also have to bear in mind that anyone could have hired a hit man to take her out, in lieu of killing the woman on their own.

As these thoughts ran through my mind, I selected a canvas hiking-style back pack with "Bighorn National Forest" stitched across the flap, and three stuffed animals: big horn sheep, moose, and bison, each with a "Buffalo, Wyoming" patch on one side. The rest of my purchases consisted of a pack of three Wyoming-themed coloring books, a deck of playing cards with a photo on top depicting the Old Faithful geyser in Yellowstone, and a large snow globe that had shiny white speckles raining down on an elk standing in the middle of a meadow.

I wasn't happy about spending almost ninety bucks on useless souvenirs, but I needed them to carry out the scheme I'd concocted to get my foot inside the door at the rival RV park. Plus, if I wasn't allowed to return them, I figured I could always pass out the frivolous gifts to the members of my bunko club the next time we visited Rockport.

As Jan totaled up my purchases on the old-fashioned cash register, she casually asked, "So, you're doing a little investigating into Bea's death, huh?"

"Yep!"

"Were you involved in criminal investigation work before you retired, like your hubby?"

"No. But I think I'd have been very successful in that line of work instead of all the dead-end jobs I did hold," I replied truthfully. The list of jobs I'd been hired to do over the years was nearly as long as the list of side effects on nearly every available medication. I'm positive that if swallowing one's own tongue was truly possible without cutting it off first, it'd be listed as a potential side effect of every drug, too.

When Jan made no further comment, I paid for the souvenirs, wished her a nice day, and left.

I'd parked our truck right outside the store, having planned to head straight to the Browns' campground. But as soon as I stepped outside, I realized the Chevy's front tires had both been slashed. I was baffled as to who would do such a thing, and why. The campground was nearly full, but no one appeared to be stirring outside of their RV's, so the likelihood of a witness was slim.

I rushed right back inside the store to report the issue. Jan seemed as perplexed as I was. She called Boonie to inform him of the incident and he quickly returned to the store, indicating he hadn't seen anyone messing around the vehicle. But then, he'd been busy working on a weed eater that'd been refusing to start and hadn't been paying a lot of attention to anything else, he told us. Shaking his head in disgust, Boonie said, "Ornery damn kids!"

"Kids? What kids?" It was late April and school was still in session. I hadn't seen any children in the park in days who were old enough to wield a knife, and I couldn't quite picture the few toddlers I'd seen in the campground out slashing tires just to amuse themselves between diaper changes.

Boonie then asked if I'd like to file a police report, but I thought it best to let Rip make that decision. Jan lent me her cell phone to call my husband and I explained the problem to Rip. He cursed, as I'd expected, and told me Ranger Rick had stopped by to shoot the crap and was just leaving. He told me he'd have the ranger drop him off at our disabled vehicle on his way out.

Rip didn't end up filing a police report, after all. He knew from his law-enforcement experience it was just a formality and rarely resulted in the apprehension of the responsible party. He agreed with Boonie that it was probably the work of rowdy teenagers. I wasn't so certain.

I was surprised Boonie was anxious to be of help, offering to call AAA for us. I got the impression that for some reason he felt somewhat responsible: because the crime occurred in his campground, he was concerned about protecting the reputation of his business, or he'd had a hand in the tire-slashing episode himself or knew who did. And I suppose I should add, he could have just offered to help because he was a kind, stand-up sort of guy. Whichever was the case, his assistance was appreciated. Rip always carried a spare tire for both the truck and the trailer, but had never felt the need to haul around two spares for either one.

Boonie took one of the park's golf carts to a nearby maintenance shed and brought back a heavy-duty floor jack. Rather than waiting for the auto service to do it, he and Rip removed the ruined tires and waited for a representative of the auto club to arrive with two new replacements. My plans for the afternoon thwarted, I carried my bag of souvenirs back to the trailer and put some potatoes on the stove to boil. I decided I might as well make use of the time and prepare a bowl of German potato salad to go along with a couple of grilled fish filets for supper.

Then I filled a quart-sized canning jar with equal parts of orange juice and tequila, and topped it off with a dash of grenadine syrup. It was quite a bit stronger than I usually mixed it. Nonetheless, it went down smoothly and I looked forward to an equally strong refill after Rip returned with the truck and was more than ready for his afternoon highball.

The next morning I was up and around early, eager to put my plan into action. Now I'll bet you thought my plan was to go to the Sweet Sixteen RV Park pretending to be a souvenir salesman in hopes of getting to meet with one of the owners, didn't you? And, truthfully, I *had* considered that option. But knowing my luck, they'd have wanted to place an order for fifty of each item, and I'd find myself in a real fix when I had no forms to fill out or any way to fill the order even if I'd had the forms.

As it turned out, I did find myself in a fix, but it had little to do with the souvenirs I'd purchased.

CHAPTER 14

I walked into the Sweet Sixteen's campground store twenty seconds after the "open" light was illuminated. I'd arrived a half hour too early and had to wait impatiently in the truck until the store opened at nine. Much like the store at Rest 'n Peace, it had separate shelves for the different types of products available—for example: toiletries, RV supplies, snack items, and souvenirs.

"Good morning, ma'am," I was greeted by a young wisp of a girl, no older than twenty in my estimation, wearing a name badge telling everyone her name was Gretchen. Despite her age, she was polite, friendly, and professional. After a few minutes of small-talk about the unseasonably warm weather that day, I got down to the business at hand.

"I'm searching for a specific item this morning, Gretchen. Let me look around for a bit and see if you carry it here."

"If you tell me what the item is, I may be able to save you the trouble."

"Thanks, but I might find something else I'm interested in too. You probably know how it is. Like me, you might be one of those shop 'til you drop kind of gals." We exchanged smiles, and she told me to let her know if I needed any help. In reality, I hated to shop. I was too financially conservative—okay, cheap—to buy anything we didn't absolutely need. And buying necessities was as dull as watching two slugs race down a sidewalk. I was one of the few women who could walk into a store with a list of five things to buy, and walk back out with less than seventy-eight items, distributed among fifteen plastic shopping bags.

I was mentally marking off the souvenirs I'd bought the day before in my head and was down to one final chance at finding what I needed. After I'd completed a second and third search and failed to locate a stuffed buffalo with the "Buffalo" patch affixed to its side, I had to refrain from clapping in delight.

"Darn it!" I said loud enough for Gretchen to hear.

"Couldn't find what you were looking for?" She asked.

"No. But I have a notion I might be able to order what I need from one of the souvenir vendors you guys use. Is the person in charge of stocking the store available by any chance?"

"That'd be the owner, Charly. I'm not positive, but I think she's collecting quarters from the pay phone."

"Pay phone? They actually still have pay phones in Wyoming? Wow, Gretchen! You Wyoming folks need to see what's going on in the rest of the world. Pay phones have disappeared like dinosaurs during the Ice Age."

The young lady laughed and assured me that, like the rest of the world, nearly every person over four in Wyoming had a cell phone. Give or take a couple of years, she'd said the same thing, almost word for word, that Jan had said to me in the laundry room. Gretchen went on to say, "Speaking of dinosaurs, there are still a lot of elderly folks, like in their sixties or so, who couldn't figure out how to make a call on an iPhone if their lives depended on it. A few are still reliant on public phones, which is why the Browns still offer one. Let me call Charly on the radio."

Yes, please do, young lady, I thought, *before I feel compelled to clock you with my handbag*. Considering her cheeky comment, I had to wonder if Gretchen saw a prehistoric mammal when she looked at me. I considered myself a young sixty-eight. I could not only make phone calls, I could actually take a photo with our iPhone. As a matter of fact, on occasion I could even locate where the photo went after I took it if given enough time to push all the buttons or, of course, ask a four-year-old for assistance.

Gretchen picked up a two-way radio and paged Charly, who assured the clerk she'd be over momentarily. Rip and I had worked as work campers on numerous occasions during our nearly seven years of living a nomadic life on wheels. We'd put in quite a few hours of work here and there in various campgrounds in lieu of paying rent. In some cases, we were paid a little cash, as well. As you know, if there's a little extra cash involved, I'm all over it!

From my experience, I knew the vast majority of campgrounds normally employed only a handful of people, and it was usually the responsibility of the owner to deal with the vendors. I had taken this into consideration when devising my scheme.

I introduced myself to Charly Brown when she entered the store. I recognized her immediately from the news release on television. Charly, who looked to be in her mid-fifties, was nearly a foot shorter than me, standing at about four-foot nine, and she probably weighed no more than ninety pounds after polishing off an entire Thanksgiving feast. I actually did feel a bit dinosaurish as I towered over the petite lady. I reminded myself to be careful I didn't wipe out any of the store's display racks with an inadvertent swish of my tail.

Despite her diminutive size, I could tell she was an enterprising ball of fire. I had gone out to the truck and retrieved the stuffed buffalo I'd purchased the previous day while I waited for Charly to arrive. I was relieved there was at least one item I'd purchased that was not duplicated in her souvenir selection.

I showed her the toy and explained I wanted to purchase another twelve of them so I could give one to each of my thirteen grandkids. Actually, my only two grandkids, Dusty and Tiffany, were well beyond the stuffed animal stage, but Charly had no way of knowing that. Thirteen had always been my lucky number, even though I couldn't really recall it ever bringing me good luck. On the other hand, I couldn't remember it bringing me any bad luck either. For the record, I'd soon discover the number thirteen wouldn't turn out to be overly auspicious for me on that particular day.

"I might be able to help you out, then," she said. "In fact, I have a number of similar stuffed animals. We're out of buffalo, but there's several other stuffed animals: moose, cougar, elk, big horn sheep, and several more. That way the kids wouldn't all have identical toys, which might prevent a lot of squabbling amongst them."

"Hmm, yeah. You obviously don't know my grandkids," I said. *Thank God! Or you'd wonder why two people in their twenties would squabble over stuffed animals.*

"Trust me, ma'am, I understand. My young grandchildren fight over everything, including which one of them is my favorite. I always tell them that none of them are. I say that my favorite grandchild is a well-behaved, well-mannered boy who never, ever, sasses his grandmother. Of course they just laugh, knowing they're my only three grandkids."

I chuckled at her humorous story, and then said, "I did see the other stuffed animals while I was looking around. But, unfortunately, they just won't work."

"Why not?"

Why not, you ask? Good question, Charly, I thought. *Could you give me a few seconds to concoct a reasonable, rational reason that you might readily believe?* Finally, speaking matter-of-factly with a disappointed tinge to my voice, I replied, "You see, our last name is Bison, and—"

"Bison? Seriously? What an unusual name," Charly replied. She appeared hesitant, as if waiting for me to tell her I was only joking and explain the real reason I couldn't possibly give a stuffed elk to one of my grandkids. So much for a reasonable, rational reason she'd readily believe. However, it was the best I could come up with under pressure. And at the moment, it was the only story I had at my disposal, so I was obligated to stick to it.

"Yes, isn't it bizarre? Rapella Ann Bison's my full name. My husband's Native American, you see. Bison wouldn't have been my first choice for a surname, of course, but you can't pick who you fall in love with, can you? I guess you learned that first hand, Charly, when you married a man with the last name of Brown." That last remark was probably uncalled for, but it drove home my point.

"So, you see, there's a specific reason why I want all thirteen toys to match. Several weeks ago, when we still had a camper on the bed of our truck, we stayed at the Rest 'n Peace campground down the road. According to the billboard just before the park's entrance gate, we thought it was the last campground we were likely to find for another hundred miles or so."

"Yes, I know," Charly said. "That billboard still chaps my hide."

"And with good reason," I agreed. "So, anyway, I bought this stuffed buffalo there and once I knew we were planning to come back here for a family reunion, I decided I wanted to get one for each of my thirteen grandchildren who all share the same last name of Bison. I had all boys, you see."

"You were so lucky to have only sons. We only have two daughters. Girls are so dramatic. So did you all pick this town for your family reunion because of its name?"

"Excuse me?"

"You know, because bison is another term for buffalo, which is the name of our town."

It took me a second to make the connection. "Oh, yes. Exactly! Seemed appropriate, as you astutely picked up on. We're staying in a motel this time, by the way, or we'd be staying here. So, as I was saying, before coming to your campground, I stopped at Rest 'n Peace, and the lady in the store told me they don't carry this item any longer. Oh, and I have to tell you, I was shocked to hear her say the owner, that Bea lady we'd met when we stayed there in March, was found dead not long ago. The gal working the counter—I think she told me her name was Jan—said initially the authorities had concluded Bea had been attacked and killed by a wild animal. Is that true?"

"Yes, sadly it is. Isn't that just awful? Wait, a minute. What did this lady mean by 'initially'?"

"Well, Jan told me she'd just heard that some new clue had surfaced indicating Bea's death might have been caused by a human perpetrator instead of a wild animal. According to her, the homicide detectives involved in the case are getting ready to begin an all-out search for potential suspects. In fact, Jan thought they may already have a likely perpetrator in their sights."

Charly's expression never changed, I noticed. Not even the hint of a flinch. "It wouldn't surprise me one iota if someone killed her. Beata Whetstone was a vicious and vindictive person. Hateful broad, to be perfectly honest. I don't know how much interaction you had with her when you stayed there, but—"

"Enough to know she wasn't the friendliest person in the world," I cut in. "Trust me, I couldn't agree with you more. And, besides that, her stuffed animals like this one were four dollars higher. But then, I felt like I got gouged every single time I had to buy something in their store."

"No surprise there. Did the lady named Jan who waited on you today happen to tell you her full name?"

"No. Jan's all I know. Why do you ask?"

"I was just curious if it was Janelle Tyson-Simms, who also goes by the nickname, Jan."

I had assumed Jan was short for either Janice or Janet, but it made sense to be a nickname for Janelle, as well. I asked Charly, "Tall, uppity brunette who just lost her husband?"

"That's the one! Although 'lost' is a rather odd way to say 'divorced', don't you think? And then she took him to the cleaners, I might add." Charly didn't appear any fonder of Jan than she was of Bea.

"She told me she was a widow." I was confused as to why nothing about Janelle, or Jan for short, seemed to be adding up to match the gal I'd spoken to on several occasions. "Are you saying Jan's husband, Mr. Simms, is alive and well?"

"Paul lives in one of the fanciest homes in Buffalo. As far as I know he's doing well. The mix-up was probably just a misunderstanding on your part. As we get older, it's harder to remember everything correctly. Jan's first two husbands did die, and both of their deaths involved mysterious circumstances. But she divorced Paul Simms, who owns a number of hotels in Wyoming, after just two years of marriage. She received a huge settlement and now gets a hefty alimony check every month."

I might seem like a prehistoric mammal to people in Gretchen's age range, and apparently Charly's, as well, but I was certain I didn't misunderstand Jan explicitly telling me she was a widow. I asked Charly, "Were all three of Janelle's husbands local dudes?"

"Yes. She was a year behind me in high school. Her first marriage occurred three months after she graduated."

"So much for this being her first time in Wyoming."

"What?" Charly was obviously confused by my remark, but I didn't care to go into that aspect of it. My time talking to this friendly lady was limited, after all.

"Never mind. Am I correct to assume all three of her husbands were well-to-do?"

"Very. Husband number one was the CEO of an investment firm. He accidently fell off a cliff during a trip they took to the Grand Tetons to celebrate their seventh anniversary. There was no way to prove otherwise, so his death was never subjected to an intensive investigation."

"Hmmm. That's an interesting way to scratch a seven-year itch. What happened to husband number two? Accidently fall chest first onto a sharp icicle?"

Charly laughed. "Something like that, only more grotesque! He accidently fell into a vat of boiling oil in a potato chip manufacturing plant he owned. Not surprisingly, Janelle had stopped by the plant to speak to him that day and was the only witness to the tragic mishap."

"Her late husbands seemed to have had the same bad habit of losing their balance. I'm surprised Paul Simms didn't fall off the balcony of one of his hotels' penthouse suites. Accidentally, of course. Even if the couple's divorce was not his decision, Paul Simms was fortunate to get out of the marriage before he became the victim of a tragic accident."

"My sentiments exactly!" Charly agreed. "So, come with me. Let's see if I can help you out."

"Thanks! I really appreciate it!" I hadn't gotten as much insight from the kind lady as I was hoping to get, but I'd gotten enough to propel Janelle Tyson-Simms higher up on my suspect list.

If I'd been on top of my game that morning, I would have claimed a sudden migraine and promised to return the following day. And, of course, broken that vow before I found myself in a fix, as I so often do. So instead of leaving while the leaving was good, I followed Charly to her office as if she were the Pied Piper of Hamelin.

The dark-haired woman waved me back to a small enclosed office in the corner of the store which was currently void of customers. Charly was bubbly and very personal, truly a ray of sunshine compared to Bea. As I took a seat next to the desk, I felt a twinge of guilt that I was playing her like a five-string banjo at a hillbilly hoedown.

After taking a reservation over the phone, Charly said, "I think I might be able to figure out which vendor I got these from. If so, I could order a dozen of them for you at my cost, which is about half the retail cost. And, of course, I'll just have you pay the wholesale price. And, better yet, they are cheaper by the dozen."

I had no intention of ordering anything, but I gave her an appreciative smile. She couldn't have been more friendly, generous, or accommodating. I felt sure no one this kind could savagely slash anyone to shreds, even if she was a fierce rival with a competitive nature. However, I had to remind myself I couldn't judge a campground owner by her demeanor any more than I could judge a cozy mystery book by its cover.

Letting her search for the item would give me a little time to question her and feel her out on her opponent's death, even though it turned out I'd have been better off to have left well enough alone. While she dragged out a number of catalogs, I asked, "You seem to have known Mrs. Whetstone well. As a fellow RV park owner, that's totally expected. So, just between the two of us, who do you think might have done the dirty deed if it turns out she really was killed by someone?"

"I couldn't even begin to guess," she replied. "If it does turn out to be a case of murder, I'd imagine there will be a long list of candidates who might have been vying for the opportunity. Neither my husband, Leo, nor I would ever carve somebody up with a knife like that, even though we have had unpleasant dealings with her in the past. We tried to get that sign you mentioned taken down. We were forced to take the Whetstones to court, but we lost the case. As you probably noticed, it's still there, and we're not but a couple of miles farther down the road."

"Yes, I did see that. In fact, I wouldn't have known about this campground if the lady working in the store this morning hadn't told me about you and advised me to check here for the stuffed bison."

"Well, bless Janelle for small favors then. If Bea were still alive, she'd have never uttered a word about us, I guarantee you. Her business acumen was shrewd, I'll admit, but it was also cut-throat, and she didn't care whose throat she had to cut to get a leg up."

Her comments were intriguing, but hardly informative or unanticipated. So, I dug a little deeper. Which basically means I lied even more outlandishly. Even as I spoke I knew my tone sounded more accusatory than conversational. "It seems you already know about the new twist in the case. They've determined Bea was killed with a knife even though the majority of the slashes covering her body were the result of marauding animals post-mortem. What do you know about that development in the case?"

The appraising gaze from Charly was hard to decipher. I couldn't tell if it was an expression meaning, "how much does this old buttinsky know?", "is this old lady wired and working undercover for the police?", or "why in the hell am I going out of my way to help this nosy old busybody?" I was waiting for her to throw the catalogs back into her desk drawer, point me to the exit, and caution me not to let the door hit me in the hind end on my way out.

I was completely taken off guard when, instead of being angry, Charly laughed. "Who are you? Nancy Drew? Like everyone else in town, I heard the sheriff say that Bea's body had sustained slashing wounds, most likely by an animal. If it was a human perpetrator who ripped her to shreds, I'd hazard to guess he or she didn't do it with a gun."

"Good point!" I relented.

"The sheriff hosted a televised press release that Leo and I attended. I even asked the sheriff if we should be taking extra precautions for the safety of our customers. We'd yet to hear any recent news about the possibility of human involvement, though. Trust me, Leo and I had nothing to do with her death, if that's what you're insinuating."

Charly laughed again, but it wasn't in an "ain't I funny?" way. It seemed more like a "you ain't got nothing on me, lady" sort of way.

Following Charly's cue, I chuckled and said, "You got me, Charly! As a young reader, I always dreamed of being a detective when I grew up. And, yes, Nancy Drew truly was my idol. Pardon me if I sounded like I suspected you of murder and mayhem. Nothing could be further from the truth."

Nothing could be more spot on, I said under my breath. "But after speaking with you, I'm more convinced there's something more devious behind Mrs. Whetstone's death.

Technically, everyone she knew is a potential suspect. As they say, you're guilty until proven innocent."

"I'm pretty sure no one says it that way, particularly the United States justice system." Charly appeared weary of me all of a sudden and I couldn't imagine why.

Deciding I'd better veer away from the subject of Bea's death, I said, "So, enough about Bea Whetstone. Let's see if we can locate the buffalo toy in one of your catalogs."

I was praying she wouldn't be able to find the toy. Unfortunately, God clearly was once again busy performing more important miracles at the time. Obviously he'd not checked out the price of the toys I was about to get hung with or he'd have been as aghast as I was and most likely have done something to intervene. After scanning a couple of catalogs, Charly turned a couple pages in the third one, and exclaimed, "Bingo! Here it is!" She then spun in her chair to face a computer monitor on her desk, and furiously typed in a web address. Pointing to an image on the screen of the exact same stuffed animal I held in my left hand, she said, "Fifteen bucks apiece. A dollar cheaper per toy if purchasing ten or more at one time. Cool, huh?"

"Very. But I don't think it's going to pan out, after all. I need them in a couple of days to pass out at the reunion, and I sincerely doubt they'll arrive that quickly." I thought I would chatter a short while, thank her for her efforts, and bid her *adieu*. In line with that idea, I said, "I'm looking forward to seeing everyone. I rarely get to see all thirteen grandchildren at one time. Giving them each a stuffed animal at the Bison family reunion was just a passing fancy. No big deal, really. Well, I best be going so my husband doesn't worry about—"

"Done!" Charly exclaimed excitedly as she forcefully tapped the left side of her mouse, clicking the cursor on the "submit order" tab.

"What?" I had just stood up and headed toward the office door. At her exclamation, my head whipped around to face her, like an owl who'd just heard a mouse squeak behind him.

"I ordered them for you!" She said this in the same self-satisfied tone she'd have chanted, "Hip, hip, hooray, I saved the day!"

"What? You did what?" I was alarmed. I'd never actually meant to order any of the dorky-looking critters, especially one hundred and sixty-eight clams worth. In fact, I'd planned to return the one in my hand if I could get the Rest 'n Peace park store to take it back, along with the rest of the silly crap I'd purchased there. Assuming all the Wyoming RV parks ordered their souvenirs from the same vendors, I'd bought a variety of items in hopes of showing up at the Sweet Sixteen campground store with at least one their store didn't also carry. I'd pulled it off, too. But, actually ordering a dozen of them was never part of the plan.

"I ordered them! Twelve of them at only fourteen bucks apiece, and free shipping because the order is over one hundred and fifty dollars. Isn't that awesome?"

"But, but, but didn't you hear me say I needed them—"

"No worries, Mrs. Bison," Charly assured me. "As a loyal customer of the Out West Supply Company, I get overnight shipping at no additional cost. Which means—in this case—you benefit, too. You can pick them up here anytime after ten tomorrow morning, and have them in plenty of time to take to the reunion."

"You don't say."

Charly beamed, proud to have been able to help take care of my dilemma for me. "Now every Bison grandchild will have a bison of their own."

"Swell," I replied, forcing an expression of gratitude, wondering if it was too late to cancel the order. I couldn't think of any logical way to tell her I'd changed my mind, post-order. "Thank you. I'll see you tomorrow around noon, or shortly thereafter."

I could be sly, cunning, even downright deceptive. But I wasn't the type to stick Charly Brown with another dozen stuffed animals she wasn't apt to sell in the next decade or two. I'd bite the bullet and pick the stupid things up the following afternoon and pretend to be happy to have them.

Then, because we couldn't spare the space in our trailer to haul them around for years on end, I'd pass them out like Halloween candy to any of the toddlers I saw "toddling" around the campground. I'd start with the young girl I'd nearly made swallow her binky when I screamed that one day I thought I was about to come face to face with a cougar after leaving the laundry room.

I walked out of Charly's office, mentally kicking myself for not having anticipated such an outcome. I needed to bone up on my scheming skills.

My jaw dropped when I looked up to see that both tires on the driver's side of our Chevy truck were flat. Again! The vandal, or vandals, had shown mercy on me, though. They hadn't slashed them this time. Only the air had been let out.

I turned to head back into the store, when a handsome, dark-haired man, walked by and stated the obvious. "Looks like you got a couple of flats there, ma'am. Sorry about that! I'd like to wring them mischief-making punks' necks!"

I'd seen a photo on Charly's desk and recognized the man as her husband, Leo. I was surprised to hear him make the same inference Boonie had. What kids did both men suspect of these tire-assaulting pranks? Was there a gang of hoodlums on the loose who were sneaking into one campground after another and flattening random people's tires? It didn't seem feasible to me. In fact, it seemed deliberate, as a way to warn me or impede my progress in my investigation venture.

I borrowed Leo's cell phone to send a "yelling" text to my husband. AT SWEET 16. TWO FLAT TIRES AGAIN. JUST NEED AIR. Leo had offered to air them up himself and, in retrospect, I should have accepted the offer. But I told him my husband always carried cans of Fix-a-Flat and would take care of the flats himself. I wanted Rip to see them with his own eyes. Maybe then he'd agree with me that our tires were being flattened intentionally.

It was evident to me someone was sending us a message.

I had an idea why we were being victimized, but needed to find out for certain and figure out who was behind it. Most probably, whoever assaulted my tires was the same individual who assaulted, and killed, Bea Whetstone.

Just as Charly exited the store and joined her husband and me in the parking lot, Rip and Boonie pulled into the campground in a four-wheel drive Dodge Ram with a "Rest 'n Peace" logo on both of the truck's doors. I swallowed hard. It hadn't occurred to me until that moment that I'd taken our only vehicle, with the cans of Fix-a-Flat under the rear seat, and Rip would have had to hitch a ride with someone to come to my aid.

Boonie jumped out of the driver's seat. He and Leo exchanged hard glares, as if the two adversaries were involved in a bar fight and trying to intimidate each other before the brawling began. After a few tense seconds, Boonie turned his attention to me. "Sorry this happened to you again, Mrs. Ripple! Ornery no-account kids! But don't fret; me and your husband will take care of it and have you back on the road in no time."

I swallowed hard a second time when I recalled I'd told Charly Brown that my last name was Bison and my husband was Native American. I don't think she saw a man with Indian heritage when a short, chubby, ghostly-white guy with a bald head, whom Boonie had just referred to as my husband, stepped out of the truck.

"What the—" I heard Charly utter. The fierce look she gave me said it all as it sank in that I'd fed her a load of crap. Without even a "howdy-do" to either man, Charly turned and strode angrily back toward the campground store. I watched as Leo followed her without making further eye contact or exchanging one word with Rip or Boonie, his rival campground owner.

I felt bad, because I had sincerely liked Charly and would have chosen her as a friend over Bea any day of the week. Just before she reached the front door of the shop, I shouted out to her, "Sorry, Charly. Probably best if you cancel that order right away!"

CHAPTER 15

"Those no good sons-a-bit—"

"Now, now, dear." I reached over to pat Rip's thigh in a calming manner. He was careening around a curve on the edge of a steep cliff as we made our way back to the Rest 'n Peace campground, on a set of brand new tires that were filled to the gills with Fix-a-Flat. Boonie had bidden us farewell shortly after helping Rip air up the tires in the Sweet Sixteen parking lot. In parting he'd said, "Can't stand to be on enemy soil any longer than necessary."

No longer convinced a gang of juvenile delinquents were responsible for our two pairs of flats in one morning, Rip was livid. "I'm beginning to think whoever's behind Bea's death is on to the fact we're sticking our noses into the investigation, and they're trying to put a stop to our meddling."

I was delighted. Even though I was a world-class meddler, I would have preferred he refer to our investigating as probing rather than meddling. Still, I was pleased that Rip had come over to my way of thinking and hopped aboard my "let's put 'em away" train. Or, so I'd thought. I excitedly exclaimed, "All the more reason to step it up a notch!"

"All the more reason to remove our noses from where they don't belong," Rip countered. And just as quickly as he'd hopped aboard my train, he'd bailed off. "We can't afford to put new tires on this truck every day. And I don't know about you, but I have no desire to stir up a hornet's nest. We know for a fact this particular hornet would not hesitate to sting anything or anyone that gets in its path."

"But don't you think this is a sign that Bea was killed by someone, like the same 'someone' who's trying to derail us?"

"Not necessarily. Even though that was my first inclination too, we mustn't jump to conclusions over what could easily have just been a coincidence."

"We also mustn't ignore the fact it could just as easily *not* have been a coincidence," I said in rebuttal.

"I suppose. However, I still think it'd be in our best interests to take a step back and let the homicide detectives handle it. If any evidence is discovered that points to foul play, they'll have to re-evaluate their 'animal encounter gone bad' deduction."

So, here was my dilemma. I couldn't disagree with Rip's reasoning, or balk at his decision to take a step back and let the Buffalo Police Department handle the case. Rip was a smart man and, as a career law-enforcer, he made sound decisions, not rash ones like those I had a tendency to make on occasion. He'd been my protector and the love of my life since we were both eighteen. He would never put me in harm's way, or allow me to place myself in a dangerous situation, even when I was dying to do so.

All of this raced through my mind as I sat silently in the passenger seat, looking straight down from my window at the sheer wall of a rock cliff just a few feet to my right. I held my breath as Rip sped around curves like he was Mario Andretti. I was holding on to the door handle with a death grip. If the need arose, I was prepared to fling the door open and then jump, drop, and roll; a sequence of moves I'd learned many moons ago in a self-defense class for women. I'd still end up dying, most likely, but at least I'd look better doing it.

Even though my mind told me to listen to Rip and follow his advice, I couldn't quite wrap my head around the homicide department's conclusion that Bea was the victim of an animal attack.

For one thing, there appeared to me to be scads of people anxious to see the last of the highly intolerable Bea Whetstone. It was practically one of those situations where decent, law-abiding folks felt compelled to line up and take a number to see who got first crack at the detestable woman.

And what could be a more workable plan than to slice and dice her in a private location, then dump her in the woods behind her campground and make it appear as if a cougar or bear had ripped her to shreds? With no one to witness the murder, the perpetrator could've high-tailed it out of the forest, knowing the smell of fresh blood would draw predators from far and wide to attend the picnic, with Bea as the main entrée.

Even though I was not a big fan of the victim, I wouldn't want a terrible fate like that to befall anyone—even her. I still find it abhorrent that someone could steal another human's life and get away with it scot free. Free to go on with their own life, until old age or until some meddler who was approaching old age—like me—caught up with them.

So there lay the dilemma I found myself in. It was the age-old question people often ask themselves: do I follow my head, or my heart? Unfortunately, in my case anyway, the heart won every time.

CHAPTER 16

It was about four o'clock and we'd just returned from watching Willie's ball game. That afternoon, Willie's team beat the Worland Warriors ten to three in round one of the championship tournament. Despite the team's victory, Willie was upset with himself for fumbling a grounder, allowing the base runner on third to score, striking out twice, and hitting into a double play. Rip reinforced the importance of good sportsmanship to his nephew when the four of us stopped at the ice cream shop for cones following the game.

"It's teamwork, Willie. There's no 'I' in 'team'. I've seen you pick up the slack when one of your teammates was in a hitting slump. Today it was Jason, who was errorless at shortstop and hit two homeruns, who carried the load and led your team to victory. You need to shake it off and come back ready to pound it out of the park in your game on Sunday. Your team won, for goodness sakes! Celebrate and be content with the victory."

Willie nodded. He'd always looked up to his Uncle Rip and had taken his advice to heart on many occasions. I knew this time would be no exception and was anxious to see how he bounced back in the next round of the tournament.

While the fellows conversed about the game, Cora and I chatted about what to get Tommy for his tenth birthday. While Cora was listing suggestions, I studied her fingernails. They were long, perfectly manicured, and had pale, almost skin-toned, pink polish. When she noticed my fascination with them, she said, "I just got them done this morning. I always get this color because it nearly matches my cuticles, and that makes it less obvious when I'm overdue for another manicure."

"It's a very nice color, dear," I said. "Much better than the woman I saw in the post office the other day who had her nails all painted black. Can you imagine that? Black fingernails? I was afraid she was going to cast a spell on me, so I skedaddled back to the truck after I'd picked up our bundle of mail. We use a mail service in Livingston, Texas, that was designed with RVers in mind. They forward our mail to us wherever we are."

"That's awesome. Do they—?"

"So, anyway," I interrupted. I'd strayed far afield from the topic I'd worked so hard to segue into. Rip and I were keeping the full scope of our investigative involvement in Bea's death under the rug as much as possible, so as not to cause our worry-wart niece unnecessary concern. "How about those black fingernails? Ever seen the like?"

"Not often, but once in a while. I've run into this one gal a couple of times at the salon in the past few months who got a manicure and pedicure with a black gel polish the last time I saw her there."

"Really? Was she a tall, slim brunette?"

"I don't really know. Both times I saw her she was sitting at a station while a manicurist worked on her nails, so I couldn't judge her height. I couldn't see her hair color, either, because she wears a scarf wrapped around her head. But I did hear her say she worked nearby, which made it convenient to get her nails polished or her hair cut at the salon next door on her lunch break."

"Hmm, that's interesting. I find black fingernails a little ghoulish, don't you?" I asked Cora.

"Maybe a little, but it *is* the twenty-first century, Aunt Rappie."

I seethed internally every time someone reminded me what century it was. It was as if they were inferring I was old and out of date, lingering behind the bulk of the general public and permanently stuck somewhere back in the 1960s. It made me feel like a can of creamed corn that had been on a grocery store shelf so long, it was covered in a thick layer of dust and you couldn't see that it was eighteen years past its expiration date. In my defense, I said, "Yes, Cora, you're right. I reckon I need to stay more current with today's unbelievable, unexplainable, and unattractive trends and fashions. I do try though, dear."

"You do great," Cora said, patting the top of my wrinkled and liver-spotted hand. She must have sensed she'd offended me. "I think you've stayed very much in touch with the younger generations."

Once again we'd gotten off-track from the topic of fingernails, and I didn't have the time or patience to wait while Cora climbed her way out of the hole she'd dug for herself. In a conversational tone, I asked, "So tell me, Cora. Do you know anything else about this gal who likes to wear black fingernail polish?"

"No, but I remember hearing the girl doing her nails call her Babs a couple of times."

Babs, like in Barbara Streisand? I wondered. *Barbara like in Barb? Barb like in angry animal activist?*

I needed to find a reason to get closer to Barb Harris, and possibly her husband, John, as well. Perhaps she, or both of them, were taking their responsibilities of protecting the well-being of local wildlife too much too heart. So much, in fact, that they'd kill a two-legged creature to protect those of the four-legged variety.

CHAPTER 17

With one hand on my pepper spray holster, I scurried up to the office and found a young gal I'd seen a time or two around the campground. She was busy taking what sounded like a complicated reservation. I listened to her end of the conversation after she gestured to me she'd be with me as soon as she'd completed the call.

"So, you're saying there are twenty-two Airstreams in the group?" The gal asked the caller.

"*****************"

"I see. There'll be seven who want full hook-ups, twelve want electricity only, and three will be dry-camping. But you'd all like to be together in the park in side-by-side sites. Is that correct?"

"*****************"

"I'm sorry. I'm pretty sure the owner won't let me put the twelve who only need electricity, or the three who prefer to dry-camp, in the full hook-up area."

"*****************"

"No, I understand. The problem is that it would render fifteen full hook-up sites unavailable for folks coming in who *do* need all of the amenities we offer. In essence, we'd only be getting significantly reduced rates on those sites for five days, and turning away customers who'd have paid full price for them. I'm almost certain the owner won't go for that."

"*************"

"Really? You're the wagon master of this caravan and Bea gave you a free site the last time your group stayed here? I'm sorry to say, following a tragic accident, Bea is no longer with us, and I don't have the authority to approve free sites."

"*************"

"Sorry. Can't do that either." Her frustrated response was accompanied by a roll of her eyes.

"*************"

"All right. The number for Sweet Sixteen is 307-555-1022. I truly believe everyone would be happier if you stayed there instead." Clearly annoyed, the young gal pointed toward herself and nodded as she verbalized her last remark. It was a scornful barb, cleverly disguised by her polite tone of voice. I wanted to give her a high five for the way she'd handled the exasperating caller.

She placed the phone down in its cradle a tad more aggressively than necessary and shook her head in bewilderment. "Some people!"

"Yeah, I know. Don't you just hate cheap-ass folks like that?" I (the pot) said referring to the caller (a.k.a. the kettle.) As if I wouldn't have tried to weasel a free site out of her myself, I continued, "Always wanting something for nothing."

"I know that's right! I've worked in a number of other campground offices as a work camper but I just recently signed on at this one. I don't want to be fired for offering customers free sites on my first day."

"I can't blame you, dear." We then exchanged some small talk and introduced ourselves. Her name was Cheri Beets, and she and her husband were spending the entire summer and fall in Buffalo. Her husband, Don, had taken a temporary welding job on a nearby pipeline project. When there was a pause in our chit-chat, I asked, "Do you happen to know what site John and Barb Harris are in?"

With no questions asked, Cheri scanned a schematic of the campground on a large dry-erase board behind her desk where they kept track of what sites were filled, and by whom. She erased several names and replaced each with a new name. "Needs a little updating. I'm not used to their system yet, and I'm getting behind. There's a lot more to running an RV park office than you'd imagine."

"I'll bet! Glad it's you and not me." I'd experienced working in campground offices and their stores as a work camper on numerous occasions, too, but I didn't want to waste time going into that.

"Looks like the Harrises are in C-23. That's one of the long, 50-amp service sites on the north side," she said. As she spoke, she pointed toward the northwest corner of the campground.

"Thank you, dear. I won't keep you. Looks like you're busy, and I didn't mean to interrupt your train of thought."

"No problem. Assisting customers is what Mr. Whetstone's paying me to do." She flashed a toothy smile, which I returned with one of my own. The only difference was Cheri's involved real teeth and mine didn't, which reminded me I needed to let my dentures soak for an hour when I returned to the trailer.

Rap, rap, rap. I banged on the door of the Jayco Fifth Wheel that belonged to Barb and John Harris. Before returning to the trailer to soak my choppers, I wanted to speak to at least one of them, which is why I was standing at their door, knocking. I waited nearly a minute but no one responded. I tried again, in case they were napping. But this time, in lieu of tapping, I hammered on the door loudly enough to wake the dead. *Bam, bam, bam.*

After a few seconds, I heard something heavy and metallic scrap across the floor, the rustling of paper, a couple of cabinets closing, and some other unrecognizable activities going on inside. I'd have thought they were rearranging the furniture if it wasn't pretty much all affixed in place. If it weren't affixed, your RV would rearrange its own furniture every time you drove it from one place to another.

When my knocking still remained unanswered, I wondered if I was being deliberately ignored. It was clear someone was home, unless they had a pet large enough to move heavy objects. Our cat was probably large enough, but she wouldn't expend any energy unless there was a yummy treat in her future to reward her for her efforts.

You know I'm not one to give up easily. So, this time I beat on the door like I was trying to kill a rabid Tyrannosaurus Rex with my bare hands. While I waited for another minute or so, I tried to think of a way to launch into a conversation with the couple in the event they ever finished whatever they were doing and answered the door. Finally, the door, which was in dire need of some WD-40, creaked open and Barb greeted me. "Hello again. Sorry for the wait."

My response was probably not the best approach at breaking the ice, but it *was* effective. I jokingly said, "I was beginning to think you two were trying to hide a body and clean up the crime scene before you responded."

The expression on Barb's face that followed my remark was priceless. For a second, I thought she was going to slam the door in my face. Out of instinct, I quickly yanked my hand off the jamb to keep my fingers from being squashed. Barb's silent stare made me uncomfortable. I swallowed hard and said, "Only joshing you, of course."

"What do you want?" Her voice was neither friendly nor amused at my lame attempt at levity. By this time, John was standing next to her, wearing an identical scowl to the one his wife now wore.

Unable to come up with anything better, I pulled one of Rip's socks out of my back pocket and held it up. I'd shoved it in there earlier while I was searching the trailer for its match. "Umm, well, I just, um, I just wanted to see if this sock belonged to you, Mr. Harris. I found it between two washing machines in the laundry room and thought I remembered Barb folding socks just like it when we were both doing laundry at the same time. I'm sure you know how dryers have a bad habit of eating socks. Looks like this time it just—"

"Not mine," John said. He dismissed me without any sign of gratitude for my efforts to return the sock to its rightful owner, which in this case was actually my husband. I thought it was rather boorish of the inhospitable couple.

Before I could utter another word, the door slammed closed. I was fortunate I'd removed my hand from the jamb or I'd now have four fingers that looked like they'd been run through a meat grinder.

If you're hearing a strange noise right now, dear reader, it's the sound of the Harrises being ratcheted up another notch on my suspect list. I was convinced something was rotten in Denmark, at least as far as those two cagey characters were concerned, and I hoped to find out what was causing the stench.

"It's happened again!" Rip said as I walked through the Chartreuse Caboose's door.

"Oh, my God! Who was it this time?"

"Huh?"

"Was it someone we knew? Someone associated with the campground?"

"What are you talking about?" Rip asked, confused by my queries.

"What are *you* talking about? I thought you meant another body was found in the forest."

"No, nothing like that. Rick Myer called and told me another animal was found snared by a bear trap not far from where Bea's body was found. This time it was a raccoon that had already died from its injuries. It's apparent someone is trying to illegally trap bears."

"That's awful! Raccoons are so adorable," I exclaimed.

"Except for the rabid ones, as this one tested positive for. Its death turned out to be a blessing in disguise, but it certainly wasn't what the trapper had in mind."

"Who would do such a thing?" I asked. I was saddened by the news, even though it was better for all concerned, even the animal itself, that the coon was dead.

"Money truly is the root of all evil," Rip simply stated in response.

I was furious at the thought of someone killing animals for financial gain. "Cruelty to animals should be a crime punishable by death. A slow, painful, and agonizing death, at that. Maybe they should have their fingernails ripped off and their eyes gouged out, and of course, acid poured in—"

"Good grief, dear! Should I be sleeping with one eye open? You're beginning to sound more brutal than the bear trappers." Rip had a feigned look of horror on his face.

"Yeah, I suppose you're right. I guess a firing squad would be sufficient, without the torturing and all. So, does the Forest Service have any clues as to who's behind the poaching?"

"Unfortunately, not yet, but Rick was able to follow a path of weeds and foliage tromped down by the poachers for a fair distance."

"And how does that help in tracking down the trappers?" I was also curious how one makes money off a dead bear, but got distracted by Rip's next response and forgot to pose the question.

"It won't necessarily help track them down, but they might find incriminating evidence if and when they are apprehended. The interesting thing is the well-worn path was leading back toward this campground. But, he lost the trail when he came to a thick patch of sage brush. Rick's stopping by later to ask a favor of us. He had to get to a meeting this morning and couldn't talk long on the phone."

"That sounds intriguing. What do you reckon he's going to ask us to do?"

"I have no idea, honey. But I'm intrigued by his remark as much as you are."

"I sure hope we can help them find out who's behind the poaching." I was astonished at how upset I was. I'm not sure what this says about my character, but I was more in hopes of the poachers being punished than I was of the person behind Bea's death being held accountable. If indeed there was one, of course. "I can't wait to see what favor Rick has in mind."

Rip appeared interested, but not as excited as I was by the idea of the two of us being involved in the hunt. I didn't mention my interaction with Barb and John Harris. I'd learned nothing of any value or interest, and there was no sense getting Rip riled up by my aggressive and reckless behavior. Or at least, that's what he'd have called it. Personally, I considered it to be fearless fortitude on my part. But that's just my opinion of my actions, which on most occasions was the polar opposite of my husband's.

Rip left an hour later to go to the ball park to watch Willie's team practice for the upcoming championship game. With Willie's father, Dirk Beaufont, away on a job in Texas for several months, Rip enjoyed serving as a surrogate male influence in the boy's life. He did his best to instill integrity and good values in his nephew, and showed a genuine interest in all of Willie's activities, from restoring an old Buick in the Beaufonts' garage to volunteering at the local food shelter for the underprivileged. In fact, Rip restocked shelves right beside Willie every Thursday morning.

At the end of their shift, they routinely rewarded themselves with chocolate shakes at the ice cream shop before Rip dropped Willie off at his house. Despite the fact I was trying to help Rip shed some extra baggage, I knew he'd never forfeit this weekly treat. It was "a tradition", he'd probably say should I ever chastise him for cheating on his diet.

With Rip at the ball park, I decided to use my free time beneficially. My intent was to see if Janelle Tyson-Simms was in the office or laundry room that morning. As I walked past the Harris's Fifth Wheel, I noticed the accordion blind over their living room window was about three inches shy of being pulled down completely. Their truck was gone, so I decided to take the opportunity to stand on the picnic table beside their rig and peer through the opening. Naturally, I'd never do something this flagrant unless there was something as crucial as solving a murder mystery hanging in the balance.

Looking through the void beneath their living room blind, I saw two large cardboard boxes on the kitchen table and a small Styrofoam cooler on an end table. Affixed on the side of the cooler was some kind of sticker. A national park decal, perhaps? Even if I weren't overdue for a new eyeglass prescription, the lettering would not have been clear enough for me to decipher.

Rip had taken our cell phone so I rushed back to our trailer and grabbed my iPad before returning to the Harris's Fifth Wheel. Cora had shown me how to utilize the tablet as a camera and I'd already known how to use my fingers to manipulate and enlarge a photo. I figured that maybe if I snapped a photo or two, I might be able to enlarge the sticker on the cooler and make out what was written on it. If nothing else, Cora had that app she'd used to enhance the images of the fingernail with black polish.

Note to self, I thought. *Have Cora install that app on our iPad for future use.*

Back at the Harris's site, I stepped back up on the picnic table bench to look through the window opening. Just as I raised the iPad and snapped a photo, a sudden presence on the screen startled me. I fell off the bench, clutching the iPad to my chest to protect it. Cuts and bruises would heal, but the expensive tablet would be forever rendered useless and a brand new one was not in this month's budget.

Second note to self. Try to remember this old body doesn't bounce back the way it used to decades ago. Accidental falls is not one of the leading causes of death for senior citizens without good reason.

I was no Olga Korbut, even in my younger days, so I didn't exactly nail the landing when my body crashed down on the hard concrete. My right wrist had taken the full impact of the fall as I'd instinctually tried to brace my fall with my dominant hand while I held tight to the iPad with the other. The sudden impact also knocked the breath out of me and jarred my dentures loose. I bit my lower lip a split second before my upper plate was ejected, landing in the middle of a fire pit beside the picnic table. It took me a few seconds to recover my senses. I then reached over into the fire pit to retrieve my dentures and put them back in my mouth, something I'd have been wise to put off until the clinging fire pit debris had been rinsed off.

As I cocked my left arm to judge the severity of the nasty scrape on my elbow, the door opened and Barb gazed down at me. I was lying half-under the picnic table on their concrete patio, spitting out ashy saliva and trying to staunch the blood running down my arm. With venom in her voice, she asked, "What in the bloody hell are you doing?"

I opened my mouth to reply, but nothing came out except blood and black, gritty spittle. I couldn't think of one feasible excuse she'd accept. I was usually better prepared than this. Under normal circumstances, I had the ability to come up with some reasonably believable B.S. at the drop of a hat. But this situation was not normal, so I did the only thing I could think of. I stood up, dusted off my jeans with my hands, including the right one, which was now throbbing and beginning to swell, spit out a mouthful of bloody grime, wished the bewildered woman a good afternoon, and limped away without one word of explanation for my actions.

"What the —?" I heard Barb drop an F-bomb as I hobbled away.

Back at the trailer, after disinfecting and bandaging my elbow, I cleaned my dentures. I dropped them in a glass with several antibacterial, effervescent tablets that I usually rationed as if I were lost at sea and they were my few remaining morsels of food. I realize the tablets are only a nominal expense, but I feel they're an unnecessary one when tap water and baking soda usually does the trick.

While my stained and gritty teeth soaked, I reviewed the photo I'd snapped just as I'd lost my balance. From what I could tell, a whitish smear was the right corner of the two cardboard boxes atop a brown sheet that was draped over something like a table. The small Styrofoam cooler on the end table that'd hold seven or eight cans of beer, at best, was cockeyed and blurry in the photo. The label on it that was still impossible to make out, but it resembled Chinese lettering to me. No surprise there, as nearly everything Americans purchase these days was made in China. It made sense the couple would carry a small cooler of cold drinks with them if they planned to spend an entire day in the forest, completing their research work involving the bear population in the area.

Crapola! It'd been all for naught. My disappointment was palpable. I wouldn't have minded the ill-fated outcome of my failed attempt at snooping if I'd at least captured something worthwhile on the single photo I'd managed to obtain. Instead, all I'd ended up with was a sore body, nasty dentures, and a great deal of embarrassment.

I ruminated as I sat at the kitchen table, soaking my right hand in a tub of water and Epson salt, while my teeth soaked in a glass next to me.

Final note to self. Give your impulsive decisions a little more thought next time. Just because their vehicle was missing didn't mean one of them wasn't still in the RV. Our vehicle is gone, isn't it? And I'm still here, ain't I? I must need my head examined. Not only was it a stupid idea, but now I'll have to avoid running into Barb and John Harris completely. Not an easy task in a private, secluded campground where, like Rip and I, RVers wandered around at all hours of the day and night. I'd also have to explain my current condition to my husband when he returned home, which wasn't apt to be a barrel of fun. Rip's right! Sometimes I am my own worst enemy.

CHAPTER 18

When Rip returned from Willie's baseball practice, I noticed he had incriminating chocolate stains on his chest. I often wondered why more and more food ended up on the front of his shirts the older he got. Had the target—in this case, his mouth—gotten smaller and harder to hit? Surely not. And you'd think with all the practice he'd had shoveling food in his mouth over the years, his aim would be dead-on by now.

"What in the world happened to you?" He shook his head as he gave me the once over. "Are you in pain, sweetheart? Do you need me to take you to the ER?"

"No, I'll be fine," I replied. Without going into a lot of detail, I said, "I was out and about on the campground property earlier and for some unexplainable reason, right out of the blue, I lost my balance and took a tumble. Not paying attention, I guess."

I didn't mention to Rip that it wasn't explainable because I couldn't quite put what happened into words, but rather *unexplained*, because I had no desire to put it into words. Despite the fuzzy line between truth and deception, he was satisfied with my account of the mishap, and I was relieved I hadn't had to tell him a bald-faced lie.

To divert the conversation away from my injuries, I asked Rip how Willie's baseball practice went. "Do you think they stand a chance at winning the championship game?"

"Yes, of course," he replied. "But they stand just as good of a chance at losing it. It depends on which team shows up for the game. Today the boys seemed more interested in discussing the upcoming high school prom and who they might ask to be their dates to the dance. Willie is the youngest kid on the team, only a freshman, and the only player seemingly devoted to improving their skills at practice today."

"You, of all people, can't blame the boys for being distracted by their potential prom dates. If you remember right, the first time you asked me out was to accompany you to the prom our junior year. And look at us now! Still joined at the hip over fifty years later."

"Yes, I guess you're right. And to think everyone said it'd never last! I guess we showed them, didn't we?"

Rip's expression was one of smugness and triumph, until I jokingly replied, "Don't declare victory quite yet, dear. We're still on the right side of the grass, and no one but God knows what tomorrow will bring."

After a less than fulfilling bowl of oyster stew, sans the high-carbohydrate mini crackers, Rip shared some information he'd garnered at the local greasy spoon that morning. On occasion, he liked to banter with the local men at a small diner where a brood of them congregated at the crack of dawn every morning to discuss the news of the day. I refer to the group as a "brood" because, no matter how Rip describes the gathering, we all know it's nothing but a gossip session among grown men. Not one of whom would ever admit to behaving precisely like a group of chattering women—described by them as "old hens"—exchanging rumors, speculations, and hearsay.

Now that's a prime example of a hanging rack full of pots calling an entire stovetop full of kettles "black", wouldn't you say? I know I certainly would.

"So what earth-shattering revelation did you fellows discuss today?" I asked.

"You'd have been hanging on every word of our conversation, Rapella."

"Really? Go on!" My interest was instantly piqued.

"You remember Fred from the hardware store?" Without waiting for my reply, he continued. "Well, he was speaking to Elmer the other day, who'd had a discussion with Gordon about something Gordon had heard from Ned."

It sounded to me like the brood's grapevine was operating on all cylinders. I asked, "So from whom had Ned heard the news?"

"No one at the table seemed to know."

"Aha! So there's the weak link in the gossip chain."

Rip stared at me in disgust for a few seconds before exclaiming, "How many times do I have to tell you we do not engage in gos—"

"Very well," I interjected. I was anxious to hear the details and didn't want him to veer off on a tangent. "Go on with your story."

"All right. Ned heard that the medical examiner who performed the autopsy on Bea Whetstone had made a notation in the report that Bea had a broken wrist and a crushed ankle bone. Along with several other non-extenuating injuries, he believes they were inflicted prior to her death and the subsequent damage inflicted by animals."

"So has it actually been declared a homicide now? Have they arrested, or at least interrogated, any suspects yet?"

"No one seemed to know that either."

"I hate to say this, dear, but your boys club's gossiping technique needs a little work."

Ranger Rick stopped by about an hour later. He was clearly dead set on tracking down the party responsible for the illegal poaching He'd asked us if we'd do him a favor, to which I'd exclaimed, "You bet!" and Rip simultaneously replied, "Depends on the favor."

As I've mentioned on several occasions, Rip was much more cautious than I was. Perhaps a lifetime of protecting law-abiding citizens from those among us who don't feel an obligation to obey the laws of the land had made Rip think twice before agreeing to become involved in certain situations. Being intimately involved in numerous crime scenes that could turn a person's heart inside out, and at times their stomach as well, had also played a part in molding Rip into the man he was today.

In the same vein, perhaps it was a lifetime of not really giving a rat's behind what hazards and pitfalls might lie ahead that had helped make me the self-sufficient, courageous, and persevering individual I am today. As I'm sure you could guess, Rip had phrased my personality differently. He'd described me as an impulsive and reckless, act-first-think-later, wild-hair-up-the butt, devil-may-care sort of character who didn't have the sense God gave a dandelion, if I remember right. And due to the fact I'd brooded over his depiction of me for days, I'm fairly certain I've remembered it precisely.

Ranger Rick asked if we'd follow him to a site near the swampy valley, where both illegal bear traps had been discovered. He'd wanted us to set our game camera up at such an angle we might capture a photo of the trapper, or trappers, as the case might be. "I want to catch this bastard, and will stop at nothing to do it. Oh, sorry, ma'am, please excuse my lang—"

"Please, Rick. Quit apologizing for being honest and saying what you're thinking," I cut in. "If I wasn't such a lady, I'd say I'd like to catch that mother—"

"Shush!" Rip had placed his hand over my mouth before I could continue. "I think the ranger gets the idea."

Rick smiled and said he and a few fellow rangers were scouring the area on an every-day basis now, searching for illegal traps before they were triggered by an unsuspecting animal. He hoped the motion-sensing camera would detect movement as the perpetrators wandered into its field of vision. "If we could somehow catch an image of the trap in the possession of its owners, we'd have compelling evidence of guilt. Capturing photos of the trap actually being set up by the guilty party would be rock-solid proof of culpability."

As the three of us discussed the scheme, the two men quaffed down several beers each and I nursed a key lime margarita I'd found hiding in the far back corner of the refrigerator. Since tequila was my poison of choice and it was too early for our customary afternoon highball, I'd decided not to check the expiration date on the bottle for fear it'd take some of my enjoyment out of downing it.

I unconsciously played a word search game on the iPad while directing my attention to the discussion taking place between the two men. Rip related the news (a.k.a. scuttlebutt) he'd heard in the cafe that morning via the old crows' rumor mill. The ranger admitted he'd heard something of the same nature at the barber shop the previous afternoon, except that the pre-death injuries had been a dislocated kneecap and a couple of fractured ribs. The Buffalo barber shop, as you've probably figured out by now, is one of the major lifelines of that aforementioned grapevine. I wasn't convinced either one of the stories had an iota of truth to them, but paid attention just in case.

"Have you heard if they've put together a task force to investigate the possibility of her death being a homicide rather than a lethal animal attack?" Rip inquired.

"No. But my friend, Kelly Rohr, heard that Paul Pardee told Winston Aldrich he'd been told by an acquaintance of his that Sheriff Wright, the Simon Legree of Johnson County, had refused to accept the findings as evidence of foul play. She'd stated that Bea's death had undergone sufficient examination and the ruling of accidental death would stand with no further funds being 'wasted frivolously' on the cut and dried case."

Rip shook his head in disbelief. "Even with my limited personal experience with her, I've seen she can be a real battleaxe. I also found her to be a bit lackadaisical. You can learn a lot from tips received from the public. On occasion, they can even help solve complicated cases. She seems unwilling to take the time or make the effort to pursue any of the incoming tips, even ones with overwhelming merit. I took her two photos captured by our game camera after we set the camera out the day—"

Rip stopped mid-sentence, as if something important had just occurred to him. I could almost visualize the glow of a light bulb turning on over his head.

"What?" I asked.

It was clear the ranger was mystified by Rip's abrupt halt, as well. He asked, "What is it, Rip?"

"Something just occurred to me. Rapella, think back to the day when we discovered the images on the memory card."

"We've made so many attempts to capture a good wildlife photo, I can only vaguely recall that day. Why?"

"It's the timing," he responded, as if that told me all I needed to know to put two and two together.

"What timing? I don't know what you're talking about."

Ranger Rick sat silently, watching the exchange between Rip and me as if we were engaged in a tennis match.

"We set the camera out the day we first met Rick on the other side of the marshy valley. Remember? We spoke with him about Bea's disappearance that afternoon, although we didn't know at the time what had happened to her."

"Yes, I do recall that now. And?" I was thinking back to that first conversation with the ranger.

"If we spoke to him directly after we sat up the camera that day, it was after Bea had gone missing. Remember, we asked Rick if his department was involved in the search? So, after the camera was activated that day, it remained on until Rick found it during the search party sweep of the surrounding forest."

"Okay. So?" I was having difficulty following his line of thought.

"So the images of the black fingernail and blue shirt cuff weren't captured until after the fact. I'm sure whatever happened to Bea took place the night before she was discovered missing by her husband. We set the camera out the next day, and it wasn't until after her disappearance those two images were captured."

"Yeah, I guess you're right. So the images most likely had nothing to do with her death. The fingernail and cuff belonged to hikers, out on a trek through the forest, no doubt. Gee, Rip, aren't you kind of glad now that the battleaxe didn't pursue your tip? That might have been a little embarrassing for a career law enforcer once the timing error had been realized."

My teasing was not well-received by the former sheriff, as you can imagine. It was a little uncalled for on my part since, like Rip, the timing error had flown over my head like a Phantom jet, too. Feeling contrite, I added, "Just kidding, honey. Kudos to you for figuring that out, because I never would have thought of it."

I ignored the look he gave me. It wasn't one of gratitude for my pitiful attempt at praise. As I've said before, I've had a vast amount of experience in analyzing his expressions and reading his mind, and to be frank, you don't want to know what I'm certain was going through his mind at that moment.

While the two men each opened up another beer, I went back to my memories of the day we met the ranger. I remembered Rick saying how sad the situation with the missing woman was and that it was a "damn shame", almost as if he'd already known she was dead and wasn't just at a friend's house, or possibly even ticked off at her husband and holed up at the Comfort Inn. Bea could have done just that without informing Boonie in an effort to get retribution for whatever grievance she'd had with him. I'd spent several nights at my parents' house in the early years of our marriage. After Rip had apologized for being wrong about whatever issue we'd argued about, I'd returned home. Funny how, now that I had reflected back on those incidents, I realized it had been Rip who'd been wrong every stinking time. *He's lucky I've put up with him all these years*, I thought.

If I've completely confused you with my irrelevant blathering, the point I'm trying to make is that my own thoughts that day had naturally leaned toward a situation like that rather than immediately assuming Bea Whetstone had suffered a devastating injury, or worse, been killed. But Ranger Rick had immediately assumed the worst, which, as it turned out, was the correct assumption. I'd have to bring this up with Rip after the ranger left, even though I knew my skepticism would be met with angry denial.

Was Ranger Rick more intimately involved in this case than we'd realized? Had he been the individual responsible for discovering his former sister-in-law's body based on the fact he knew exactly where he'd left it? After all, he might have felt that if it were he who found the woman's body, it might throw suspicion away from him instead of the other way around. A reverse-psychology type of scheme. On the day in question, Rick never mentioned having any knowledge of, or relationship with, the missing woman. He gave no clue of Bea being his ex-wife's sister, and someone he felt might be responsible for his divorce. *Why had he not mentioned knowing Bea?* I wondered. I listened more intently now to the two men's exchange.

Rick leaned forward in the recliner as he launched into a rather lengthy commentary. "Although I agree with you that it's lazy police work, I don't doubt the ruling is correct. I'm convinced it was nothing more than Bea being in the wrong place at the wrong time. You told me about the bear she shot that stepped inside the perimeter of the campground a few weeks ago. That's proof enough that it's not unheard of for them to encroach on the park's property. If not a bear encounter while she was on her customary morning hike, it could have taken place the evening before. When Bea left the office late that evening, I'm guessing alone and unarmed, she could have been taken by surprise by a marauding bear. Possibly a bear on the hunt for a meal, because it's likely it would have been heading to the campground dumpster to pillage for food. The large trash container has a locking lid, of course, but the bears don't know that. Their sense of smell is so acute, they can smell food in a dumpster from miles away. It wouldn't take much of a blow by a hungry or startled bear to fracture someone's ankle or wrist before it dragged them into the forest to feed on."

The very idea of Bea experiencing something so horrific made my stomach roil and I hope telling you about it doesn't have the same effect on you. I don't want to upset you, but you need to hear exactly what happened to Bea Whetstone to understand and appreciate what Rip and I went through to seek justice for her.

"Hmm," Rip said after careful deliberation. His face had a slight greenish tinge to it, as if the ranger's words had made him queasy. "You make a valid point, son, but I'm not so certain there isn't more than meets the eye in this particular case. I've witnessed a lot of mind-boggling things during the thirty-seven years I served as a law enforcement officer. Enough to know that truth really is stranger than fiction more often than you'd think."

Apparently, Ranger Rick had tired of the topic because his next words, as he popped the top on his fourth bottle of pale ale, were, "Did you know you can use beer to loosen rusty bolts?"

"No," Rip replied. He was so easily distracted, I often wondered if he might have a touch of attention deficit disorder. This was just another one of his frequent "squirrel!" moments. "But that does make sense. I've heard that beer's basically a diuretic, so it's also beneficial for helping someone pass a kidney stone."

"Yeah." The ranger laughed. "A twelve pack of brew would definitely help dull the pain of passing it, too."

The men's discussion went downhill from that point. I eventually tuned them out and concentrated on composing an email to our daughter. Regina had a tendency to worry when she didn't hear from us every few days. She was akin to a mother hen with three-day-old chicks who didn't have enough sense to not walk straight up to a salivating fox and chirp a warm greeting.

By the time Rip and Rick had wrapped up their conversation, they'd polished off enough beer they both could have passed a baby porcupine without feeling a thing. In fact, I was concerned about the ranger driving home in his tipsy condition. I offered him the couch for the evening, but he assured me he'd make it home without incident. Despite their slurring speech, I could decipher their plans to meet here at our trailer the following morning at the crack of dawn, about the time of day when I usually got my best sleep. But I had a feeling I wouldn't be getting much sleep that night anyway because, although I was looking forward to our next adventure, I was apprehensive about the outcome.

At least I'd be able to focus on something else for a while besides my aching body and who might have broken Bea's bones before leaving her body to the forest-dwellers. My restlessness was due to having too many thoughts running amok in my head, and nothing I did seemed to quiet them.

Meanwhile, as I tossed and turned for hours that night, Rip lay beside me, snoring so loudly I swear I saw all 205 pounds of him levitate off the bed at least twice.

CHAPTER 19

The throbbing in my wrist had subsided somewhat during the night. I was up, dressed, showered, and sipping on my third cup of coffee by four in the morning. I have to admit I was a little irked that Rip could still be in such a deep slumber, despite the four or five times I'd inadvertently slammed one of the cabinet doors in the kitchen.

Sleep is totally over-rated, after all. Particularly when you have bigger fish to fry, like we did! We were angling to reel in a doozy of a catch, namely a heartless, bear-poaching shark. I could hardly wait to get the show on the road.

It was unseasonably cool that morning, and I was wishing I'd worn a sweatshirt under my jacket for extra warmth. I had my arms folded across my chest as I followed Ranger Rick and Rip down a well-worn path in the forest. The ranger must have heard my teeth chatter. He came to a stop and turned to me. "Are you cold, Rapella?"

"A bit."

"I guess Rip was right when he said you didn't have the sense God gave a skydiver when it came to wearing appropriate clothing on a chilly day." After he and Rip shared a chuckle at my expense, he continued. "I remember him saying that because I actually *have* paid a friend of mine one hundred bucks to let me jump out of his perfectly good plane."

I didn't appreciate the laughter the two men erupted into again, but I was grateful when, like a well-prepared Eagle Scout, Ranger Rick pulled a folded poncho out of the canvas hiking pack he had strapped to his back. He told me it would help insulate me to the point I'd feel sufficiently warmer, and he was correct. I also accepted a bottle of water from his back pack, as did Rip. But I should have given drinking another twelve ounces of fluid a second thought. I'd indulged in four cups of coffee earlier that morning, and my bladder was already becoming uncomfortably full.

After zigzagging through the trees and foliage for another twenty minutes, I felt like a water balloon that could burst at any moment. "Can we stop for a minute or two? Just long enough for me to make a nature call. It would be very much appreciated."

"Of course," Rick said. "I can't think of a better place to make a nature call than right here. If you continue on about thirty feet and veer off to the right I think you'll find a decent spot to, um, well, a decent spot for you to, um—"

"Pee?" I asked. The tougher-than-nails ranger's face flushed as he nodded and turned away. I thought his bashfulness was adorable.

I found the spot he'd indicated, and as he'd said, it was a decent spot to relieve my bladder. Except for two things, I should add. One, there was a pile of bear scat about three yards to my left. It had dried up to a certain extent, but still had a pungent odor that made the hairs in my nostrils recoil. And, two, where there's bear poop, there's been a bear. I knew the animal that left that huge calling card might frequent the area. And, for all I knew, it might have had its eyes on me even as I crouched down beside a tree with Kleenex in hand. The very thought terrified me. I've never been inflicted with a shy bladder before, but that morning it refused to relinquish a single drop. The harder I strained, the more stubborn my urethral sphincter became.

"You okay over there?" I heard Rip shout.

"Yes, I'm fine. I'll just be a minute." I thought about asking him to come accompany me. He had a gun to protect us. I had an antiquated metal finger nail file. But just then my bladder relaxed and I was able to relieve myself.

I rejoined the men and we continued along the path. On several occasions two paths crossed, but the ranger appeared to know exactly where he was going and which path to follow. If not for that observation, I'd be tossing out a Skittle or two every three or four yards to mark our trail. I'd stuck two boxes of them in the over-sized fanny pack I'd chosen to carry that day. If not used for marking our trail, it'd make a good pick-me-up snack later on in the day.

My suede leather bag carried all the essentials that made up my survival kit: lip gloss, Kleenex, several different-sized bandages, Neosporin, a lifeguard-type whistle, the two boxes of candy and the finger nail file to potentially use for protection. Even though I was realistic enough to know I couldn't fend off a charging gerbil with the file, much less a full grown bear, it gave me a little comfort knowing it was available in a crisis. The crisis, in this case, being a torn nail that would bug the crap out of me until it'd been smoothed out. There was also a stick of gum that'd been in the bag so long it was as stiff as a metal rasp. I'd been meaning to pitch it, but never remembered when I was near a trash receptacle. And I loathed litterers.

I also had my pepper-spray can nestled into the leather holster Rip had fashioned for me. Even though I'd been warned the deterrent might do nothing more than provoke the animal I used it on, it really did give me peace of mind. It also gave me comfort to know that once I'd ticked the animal off with the pepper spray, its deadly attack would be quick and thorough. There'd likely be no drawn-out agony before my demise. It wasn't a great plan, but it was the only one I had.

We finally reached the boggy swamp we'd crossed the day we'd lost our way in the forest. Ranger Rick picked out the location he thought would give us our best chance at capturing a photo of the perpetrator. Rip attached the game camera to the trunk of a lodge pole pine that was predominantly camouflaged by various-colored foliage. If I hadn't known it was there, I'd probably have overlooked the critter cam myself.

Rip activated the camera's motion-sensing capabilities and we reversed our direction to follow the ranger back to the campground. The trek back was enjoyable and without incident. We did observe a northern spotted owl fly across the path ahead of us.

"That was a rare sight to see," Rick said. "Owls rarely come out during the daylight hours, and the influx of barred owls has caused a sharp decline in the number of these spotted owls in the northwestern forest regions."

"The two owl species don't co-exist in harmony?" I asked.

"Pardon my language, Rapella, but the barred owl is one badass bird. It's much bigger and meaner than the spotted owl, and has driven the smaller birds off their own turf."

Having Rick, a trained biologist, as our guide was a treat. He was very knowledgeable about the flora and fauna in the region. When a couple of yellow-bellied marmots, sniffing around a mossy log from a toppled sycamore tree, became aware of our presence, one of them stood up on his back legs and emitted a shrill, high-pitched sound. I remembered that exact same sound scaring the heck out of me on one of our trips to reset the game camera.

Both the marmots then scampered into a nearby burrow partially concealed by a cluster of shrubby plants that Rick referred to as a hybrid species called Bonneville sagebrush. "He was warning his clan about trespassers in their territory. That's why we often refer to marmots as 'whistle pigs'."

"You are fascinating to listen to, Rick. You'd make an excellent nature guide, for adults and kids alike." I was sincere in my praise. The experienced ranger was passionate about his job, the wildlife, and the environment, and it showed in the way he explained the variety of wildlife and plant life we encountered.

"Thank you, ma'am," he replied. "I actually do volunteer. I take elementary school classes on field trips and teach them about the importance of protecting our environment and all of the different species indigenous to the area. I find it rewarding and hope the experience has a lasting effect on them."

"How could it not?" I asked. "It's so captivating. My guess is that you'll be responsible for some of them growing up to be forest rangers like you. By the way, there is a couple in our park named Harris, whose mission is to protect all the endangered species on the globe. Have you ever had any interaction with them?"

"Of course! Barb and John are incredible. A few years ago I worked with them on a project involving the decline of those northern spotted owls I told you about. They've also assisted me a couple of times with the summer camp program I'm involved with. We take the kids hiking and point out different plants and animals and, naturally, answer all of their questions. Except for one question a kid asked, that is."

"What question was that?" Rip inquired.

"One day we came across a mother fox, with three kits who were playing on a log. After watching the kits scurrying all over the place, wrestling and having fun for a few minutes, a young boy about seven asked me where the mother fox got her babies."

"Oh, goodness!" I exclaimed with an amused grin. "What did you tell him?"

"I asked him if he'd heard of the phrase 'sly as a fox'. Then I told him the phrase referred to the fact that foxes are so sneaky and devious that people could never figure out where a female fox, called a vixen, got her kits from. With a poker face, the teacher who accompanied the class nodded and said, 'That's what I've always heard too.'"

We enjoyed his story, along with a number of other ones he related to us during our trek in the woods that morning. Even though I couldn't remove him from my suspect list quite yet, I found it difficult to imagine that this kind man would harm even the tiniest living creature, much less his ex-wife's sister. I marveled at the way he'd deliberately walked around a fire ant crossing the path ahead of us. I'd have intentionally squashed its brains out with the heel of one of my hiking boots had I been in the lead. Afterward, I was kind of glad I hadn't been leading the way. The ranger might not have appreciated my inclination to brutally execute every bug or spider I came across.

John and Barb were practically saints, I realized, and I felt guilty for having ever added the ranger to my suspect list, too. But even if I could remove Rick from the list, could I remove Desireé, his ex, as well? I wasn't so certain. I couldn't get past the conversation I'd overheard—or at least Desireé's side of it—when she reminded "Ricky" he had as much at stake as she did regarding an agreement they'd made. I couldn't comprehend why Desireé would want to involve her ex-husband in a plot to kill her sister, but as Rip had pointed out to Rick, truth can often be stranger than fiction.

It was conceivable that the debt I'd heard Desireé mention on the phone call was hanging like an ominous cloud over her head, and her being the sole heir of their mother's estate was too tempting to resist. Maybe she used the fact there was no love lost between her ex and her sister to coerce Rick into eliminating Bea for jealousy, money, or whatever else. Could she have offered him a portion of her inheritance to lure him into killing Bea, or at least participating in the plot with her? I just couldn't see the kind, gentle ranger accepting an offer like that—for any amount of money.

I was leaning more toward Desireé being behind her sister's death alone. It appeared to me she was extremely self-absorbed and in dire need of some cash. But was she desperate enough to bump off her sister so she'd be the sole heir of their dying mother's estate? Maybe. After all, the greedy woman was asking eighty-nine dollars for a quarter's worth of lace at her scandalous sex shop. If that doesn't say money-hungry, what does?

I still wanted to get to the bottom of this conundrum. *Maybe,* I told myself, *I want a sex toy more than I'd first thought.* I'd have a little spare time before Willie's ballgame and decided it wouldn't hurt to go give Desiree's shop another look—even though the very idea of inquiring about one of her sleazy toys made me want to slash my wrists with a switchblade. It might be less agonizing than the humiliation I was apt to experience at the Naughty Pine Playhouse that afternoon.

"You again?" Was the greeting I received from Desireé when I entered her shop two hours later.

"Um, yes. Nice to see you too!"

"Still don't have anything appropriate for your ten-year-old nephew."

"No, of course not," I said. "Actually I'm here looking for a little something for myself."

"Oh?" Her tentative tone was accompanied by a raised eyebrow that had a pierced earring shoved through the middle of it. It looked painful to me, and comical as well. On the bright side, it was a perfect match to the one protruding from her right nostril. A nose ring would drive me nuttier than a bag of trail mix within an hour. Again, that's probably just my age talking. But, still, it made me wonder how she and Rick had ever peacefully cohabitated. They gave the impression of having been from two different planets. Personally, I thought Rick was fortunate to be rid of her.

"Yes, maybe you can just show me a few of the more popular toys. Preferably the ones you mentioned that had something to do with airplanes." I turned away from her as I spoke, although I thought any toy that had to do with planes couldn't be too repulsive. Just asking about sex toys embarrassed the crap out of me, and I didn't want her to see my crimson face, or that I was gagging on my own words.

"Airplanes?" She asked, clearly confused.

"You know, the 'flying solo' toys."

"Aha!" She exclaimed, with a seductive wink that made me want to upchuck the ham salad sandwich I'd eaten for lunch. "I know exactly what you want!"

I followed Desireé across the store. Not wanting to waste an opportunity, I asked, "Have you heard about any new developments in your sister's homicide case?"

"No. I hadn't even heard it was now considered a homicide case. Last I knew it was ruled an accidental death in connection with an animal attack. What have you heard?" She had stopped and turned to face me, obviously shaken by my statement.

"I heard the medical examiner uncovered something in the autopsy that pointed toward Bea's death being declared an intentional murder. Something to do with injuries she sustained before her death."

"Wow! When I spoke to her the day before her disappearance, she told me she'd bumped her head on a kitchen cabinet in the cabin. But I hadn't heard about any other injuries she'd sustained."

"I think they were implying the perpetrator was responsible for more serious injuries right before he, or *she*, killed Bea." I hate to admit it, but I felt compelled to return the facial gesture she had just bestowed on me. So when I drew out the word "she" as if it were fourteen syllables long, I added a knowing wink.

She gasped in horror. Then she closed her eyes tightly, like she was attempting to shut out the image she was visualizing. Her reaction was intense. She lifted a trembling hand and placed it over her mouth as her complexion paled. She was genuinely taken aback by my comment. But why? Did she know more about Bea's death than she was letting on? Was she deeply involved, but thought she had successfully flown under the radar? Or was she truly shocked by my announcement out of concern for her late sister? After she composed herself, she whispered, "Who do they think killed her?"

Although it was a total falsehood, I replied, "I heard someone say the detectives were looking at the whereabouts and potential motives of her closest relatives and friends. I'm surprised they haven't questioned you already."

Desireé was motionless, as if she'd accidentally stepped in front of an elephant being shot at with a tranquilizer dart. After several anxious moments, her stunned expression morphed, ever so slowly, into one of distrust. Her distraught demeanor quickly vanished like a mirage in the Mohave Desert. "How do you know they *haven't* already questioned me?"

"It was just an assumption."

"Well, you assumed wrong. They did contact me. Yesterday, in fact. But I had nothing useful to share with them, like I told you before. I hadn't seen my sister in over a week when she disappeared. It's true I had spoken to Bea over the phone the previous day, but she said nothing that might indicate she was afraid someone was out to get her. I'd have contacted the police myself if she had."

"What kind of relationship did your ex have with the victim?" I asked. Her response was completely unexpected, but I tried not to appear astonished. If the detectives had questioned her the previous day, I had to wonder if they had indeed discovered something that made them suspect Bea's death might have been something other than first thought. Maybe they had changed their conclusion about the accidental animal attack being her COD.

"You know Rick?" Desireé asked, appearing more stunned by that question than she did my statement about the detectives questioning Bea's family and friends.

"We've met."

"Have you spoken with him recently? Did he say anything about Bea's death?"

"Yes, I have spoken with him, and although he informed me and my husband it'd been him who discovered her body, he said nothing else of any consequence. Didn't seem to care much for your sister though."

"*Rick* found her body? He never mentioned that to me. But I haven't spoken to him in a couple of weeks, or more."

Liar, liar, lingerie on fire! I wanted to chant. "He didn't mention it to my husband and me either. At first, anyway. I think it's hard for him to talk about. Either that or he was involved in some way in your sister's death."

My comments seemed to make Desireé want to open up about her ex-husband. She said, "There was quite a rift between the two of them. Still, I know he'd never have hurt her in any way, even though he mistakenly believed she was behind our divorce. He thought she encouraged me, and eventually persuaded me, to leave him. She did think Rick wasn't the right man for me, which was probably obvious to everyone, but it was ultimately my decision to file for divorce."

"Did having your pipes reamed out by—"

"What?" Desireé's eyes bugged out and her mouth dropped open so wide I could see her tonsils quivering.

"Never mind, dear. Go on with your story."

"Uh, okay. So, anyway. After Rick told me that—"

Desireé's phone rang, silencing her mid-sentence. I wanted to know what Rick had told her, but she chose to take the call instead, which turned out to be the ranger himself. I eavesdropped as she responded to the caller. I was not surprised to hear it was Rick Myer calling again. She was nearly whispering as she spoke into the phone, but I could still make out her words. "Of course, I will, Ricky. Just do what I asked you to do, or I won't uphold my end of the deal, either."

She listened for a few moments, and then responded, "I realize that, but that excuse is not going to fly with me. Stop by later on. Okay? Olivia's spending the night with a classmate."

"Ricky" must have agreed to stop by her house, because Desireé went on to tell him she'd get home about six and then the two of them could go to the Bozeman Trail Steakhouse. They'd discuss the matter over supper. She'd make reservations for two at six-thirty, she informed him.

As I'd been concentrating on Desireé's side of the conversation, I'd been mindlessly picking up various packages off a shelf, trying to not look as if I was hanging on to her every word like a floating life ring. After Desireé stuffed her phone back in her brassiere, she said, "Are you interested in one of those? Good for you for being so remarkably indulgent at your age."

I looked down and almost dropped the package on the floor. I'm sure my mouth was gaping open even wider than hers had just been as I locked eyes with the soiled-rotten lady. As a refined and dignified woman of sixty-eight years, I found the "toy" to be quite offensive. Not to be too graphic about something I'd rather not mention to you in the first place, I'll just say the contraption looked as if it could have been hacked off that aforementioned elephant.

I stood motionless, and Desireé could clearly tell I had been rendered speechless. After studying my reaction for a few seconds, Desireé asked, "You just reacted like that package seared your hand. Did you really come in my shop to buy a toy, or was it just an excuse to question me about my sister's death?"

"Heaven's n-n-no! I ca-ca-came in to b-b-b-b-buy this th-th-th-thing!" I held up the package with two fingers as if trying to limit my exposure to any cooties it might be coated with. Feeling a gazillion miles out of my comfort zone, I stuttered my way through my response. "How mm-mu-much is this 'thing'?"

"It's forty-nine, ninety-five. Today only."

"Fifty bucks?" My stuttering came to a screeching halt and for a second I was afraid I might prove to the medical field a person actually could swallow their own tongue. There was no way I was paying that much for something I'd have to toss into the nearest dumpster after I exited the store. I certainly couldn't show up at home with it. Rip would take one look at my purchase and have to be resuscitated. It'd be a 9-1-1 call waiting to happen.

"No, not fifty dollars. It's forty-nine, ninety-five," Desireé corrected me, as if there was a hill of beans worth of difference between the two. Five cents wouldn't buy you a gumball these days. Even as cheap as I am, I have to think twice before bending over to pick a nickel up off the sidewalk. And, yes, I always opt to do so.

"That's fifty bucks anyway you look at it, dear. I'll have to give this a little more thought before I decide if I want to splurge on something this expensive."

"I guarantee it'll be the best forty-nine ninety-five you'll ever spend."

No, it'll be the best fifty bucks I ever saved, I thought. But I somehow managed to take a deep breath, and say, "You're probably right. I'll give it serious consideration and then most likely stop back in to purchase it."

I'd come back and purchase it right after I climbed Mount Everest, zip-lined across the Royal Gorge in Colorado, and hand-fed Killdeer eggs to a badger. Afterward, I would jump out of her ex-husband's friend's perfectly good plane.

It'd been a mortifying experience, but I had learned something at least. I learned I'd be having supper at the Bozeman Trail Steakhouse. With any luck at all, we'd be seated within eavesdropping range of the divorced couple. And if so, we might be able to find out more about the agreement Desireé had made with her ex-husband, the seemingly wholesome forest ranger. The pair might be surprised to see us, but it's not that unusual to run into people you know in a town the size of Buffalo.

After I backed the truck out of my parking spot, I drove to the restaurant on East Hart Street to make reservations for six-forty-five. I'd taken liver out of the freezer to fix with onions that evening, but I felt relatively certain Rip wouldn't balk at having to take a break from his diet to devour a mouth-watering T-bone at the steakhouse. In fact, I'd have bet a bundle on that one!

CHAPTER 20

As expected, Rip jumped all over my idea to go to the steakhouse for supper. His words exactly were, "Hell yes, I'd like to have a juicy steak for dinner! That gross-looking slab of yuck that's been thawing on the counter all day has done nothing to stimulate my appetite. Quite the opposite. As a matter of fact, I was planning to fake a bellyache at suppertime, and then get up after you'd fallen sleep tonight to sneak a couple of bologna sandwiches."

I'm pretty sure Rip was kidding, but don't you go thinking that the idea hadn't crossed his mind a time or two. As a matter of fact, I was so convinced, I said, "I think you've already snarfed down a couple of sandwiches while I was out."

"My lips are sealed," he returned with a smirk.

"Uh-huh. Your lips are not only sealed, you scoundrel, they also tasted like mustard when you kissed me a couple of minutes ago."

When the waitress met us at the door of the steakhouse, she asked if we'd prefer a booth or a table. I quickly scanned the restaurant and saw Desireé sitting across from a dark-haired man at a booth by the kitchen. I was sure her dining companion was the ranger, even though I could only

see the back of his head. There was a vacant booth next to
theirs that would have Rick's back to us. It was ideal for
eavesdropping on their conversation. I requested that
particular booth even though Rip always preferred a table.

"Why a booth?" He asked. "And especially one in such a
high-traffic area?"

"I know it's right next to the kitchen, but it's also close to
the restrooms. I'm a little concerned about the rumbling in
the pit of my stomach, dear, and would feel more
comfortable having the bathroom nearby in case of an
emergency."

He looked at me queerly. I hadn't mentioned an issue
with my stomach earlier so I figured he had doubts racing
through his mind. But after an impassive "whatever", he
took my elbow and led me to the chosen table.

As we approached, Desireé looked up and caught my
eye. Without smiling she nodded. I adopted a "so surprised
to see you here" expression and nodded back. Having never
met Rick's ex-wife, Rip was oblivious to the exchange. I
was surprised to see the stunning woman dressed in a
conservative outfit: blue jeans and a light blue high-necked
sweater, complemented by her severely toned-down eye
makeup. It was if she thought it necessary to dress up like a
call girl when working at her X-rated shop, and a sensible
human being elsewhere. She was actually a beautiful lady
with just a hint of eye shadow and the absurd tattoo on her
neck concealed. She'd even excluded the facial piercings
that evening. Maybe Rick was opposed to the "tramp" look
and she hadn't want to squabble over her appearance that
evening when they had more important issues to discuss.

Once seated, I leaned across the table and whispered, "I
believe that's Ranger Rick and his ex-wife, Desireé, behind
us."

"Aha! I knew something was amiss!" Rip replied. "I
should have known you didn't choose this booth because of
an upset stomach. Destiny is very pretty, isn't she?"

I didn't bother to correct him on Desireé's name. As long
as Rip's known my brother, Seward, he's referred to him as

Steward. He couldn't seem to let go of the "t" that had no place in Seward's given name. I finally gave up correcting him when I realized it was a losing battle. Fortunately, my brother never seemed to care one way or the other.

"Yes, she is," I replied to Rip's remark about Desireé's attractiveness. "At least when she doesn't go out of her way to look like a prostitute."

"Huh? What's a hostile toot?" Rip looked puzzled. He had a hard time hearing me under the best of circumstances, much less when I was whispering in a crowded restaurant.

"A 'hostile toot' would be what you told Rick you'd like to do in an elevator full of nuns. However, what I actually said was 'prostitute'."

He still looked confused, but let it drop, and said, "I suppose I better get up and greet Rick."

"No, don't do that. Rick doesn't know we're here and will be careful what he says if he finds out we're behind him. I was curious what their tête-à-tête was all about and hoped maybe we could overhear—"

"Eavesdrop."

"Okay, eavesdrop, on their conversation. They've made some kind of mutual agreement about something important. That much I know for certain."

"Rick would never—"

"I know how you feel, dear. And I don't disagree. I'd just like to eliminate Rick from our suspect list once and for all."

"We have a suspect list? I didn't even realize we had suspects."

"Of course we do. The way I see it we have several of them. Boonie, for one. As you once told me, the spouse is almost always considered a suspect when someone is murdered."

"That's true. But I can't imagine why Boonie would want to kill his wife. He needed her help to run the campground efficiently. And if he was already seeing that woman you told me about, Janet Talley-Sands—"

"Oh, good grief, Rip. It's Janelle Tyson-Simms."

"Well, whatever her name is, my point is if he was already having his cake and eating it too, what would be the point of knocking off his business partner?" As Rip spoke I put my finger to my lips to remind him to keep his voice down. He spoke quieter as he continued. "Plus, to me, he doesn't seem the type to do such an unspeakable thing."

"Do I seem that type to you, dear? I love you more than you'll ever know, and our marriage has been fifty years of pure bliss, as far as I'm concerned. But that doesn't mean I haven't wanted to kill you a time or two along the way."

"Seriously?" With mouth wide open, Rip looked as if I'd poked him in the eye with my salad fork. "There were times you wanted me dead?"

"Well, not permanently. Only for a few hours, perhaps. Just until I'd had enough time to get over whatever had made me want to kill you in the first place."

"Good to know. I am definitely keeping one eye open while I sleep from now on."

"You know I'm only joshing you. Still, I thought coming here for dinner was too good an opportunity to pass up. There's no telling what we might learn."

"I understand. I don't necessarily agree with your methods, but I do understand why you're anxious to prove to yourself that the ranger wasn't involved. I, too, thought it odd he didn't mention his relationship to the victim the day we first met. Still, I can't imagine a fine man like Rick—"

"Me neither, Rip. I am fond of him, too." I interrupted him because he was speaking too loudly again, a tendency not uncommon for someone with a hearing impairment.

I'd been speaking softly so the man we were discussing, who wasn't two feet behind me, couldn't hear me over the clatter of dishes and several simultaneous conversations going on around us. I knew Rip was having extreme difficulty in understanding me. Unfortunately, hearing one word I said throughout our entire evening meal had not been enough incentive for him to wear his hearing aids to the restaurant. I could tell he was reading my lips more than anything. Rip confirmed that suspicion with our next exchange.

"I don't seriously think Rick was involved in Bea's death," I said. "But, as Lexie Starr once told me, one should leave no stone unturned when on the hunt for a perpetrator."

"Why would I want a purple tater? I don't see anything like that on the menu, and wouldn't want one even if I did."

I practically hissed when I responded, enunciating each syllable as if his understanding of my words was of critical importance. "I didn't ask you if you wanted a pur-ple ta-ter, Rip. I said 'on the hunt for a perp-e-trator'."

"Oh."

"Wear your hearing aids next time, for goodness sakes! Now hush up so we can hear any conversation between Desireé and Rick, or Ricky, as she calls him."

"I can barely make out what you're saying, Rapella. How am I supposed to hear anything those two are discussing?"

"You don't have to hear them. You just need to be quiet so I can. Look through the menu and decide what you want to order."

The couple behind me appeared to be focused on eating their meals and I hadn't heard any conversation between them by the time the waitress returned to take our order. I chose the grilled salmon and house salad and Rip decided on a large porterhouse with steak fries, followed by apple pie á la mode for dessert. He'd instructed the waitress to "Hold the salad and green beans, but pile on the vanilla ice cream."

It was so fulfilling to hear how seriously he was taking the diet I had him on. I really wasn't restricting his carbohydrates, saturated fat, and grams of sugar to be mean. His doctor had warned him he was a dead man walking if he didn't lose weight and eat healthier. I just wanted him to stick around a while. It was tougher than I'd imagined to save a guy who wouldn't help save himself. Rip seemed perfectly content with the notion he'd likely die with a smile on his face and vanilla ice cream dripping down the front of his shirt.

I leaned as far back in my chair as possible after the waitress shuffled off with our order. I could just make out Desireé's raspy voice. She said, "You promised me you'd enroll in that final class to earn your doctorate, Ricky. And, in return, I said I'd continue to support you in the interim. I'm giving you one week to comply. If you haven't enrolled by then, I'm pulling the plug on your monthly allowance. Like Bea suspected after you dropped out of college with one class to go, I'm beginning to think your plan all along was to be a career student. I can't afford to carry you forever, you know. Not to mention, I still have a large portion of your huge student loan to pay off."

"Yeah, I know. Sorry about that, Mom."

"The least you could do is try to become independent of me, Ricky. And your father, I should add. I know he's been forking it over to sustain you too. It's time to get your degree and an engineering job. No more screwing around. You understand?"

When Ricky didn't respond, Desireé asked him again. "I said, do you understand me, Ricky?"

"All right, all right, Mom." I heard a voice respond. The voice was similar to the ranger's but about an octave higher. "I'll sign up tomorrow, even though I think it was none of that woman's business how I live my life. By the way, how's your mother doing? Have they called in hospice yet? Put her on a morphine drip or anything?"

"Oh, my!" I said under my breath as I leaned forward toward Rip.

"What's up?" He asked.

"I had it all wrong. Ricky is not Ranger Rick, after all. I'd assumed it was a term of endearment Desireé used for her ex-husband, in the same way I heard Rick refer to her as Dez a couple of times. But in actuality, Ricky is a nickname for Richard Myer, Junior, the son the ranger mentioned to us when he dropped by that one day. I remember he said his eight-year-old daughter was named Olivia, but never told us his son's name."

"Oh, yes. Now that you mention it, I do remember. Although I thought he said his daughter's name was Olive."

"I'm sure you did. And, actually, that's closer than you usually get."

With his selective hearing electively turned off, Rip ignored my comment, and said, "And I also recall him saying his son was the result of a short-lived fling in college."

"I remember that too. I have to admit, it is very nice of Desireé to help her step-son out the way she appears to be doing, even after her marriage with his father went kaput. Sounds like she took on a huge debt to put him through college. But rather than finish the doctorate program he was nearly through with, he decided to just bum around and let both his step-mom and father support him."

"It's nice that she cares for Rick's son as if she was his own biological mother. But I can see why she's fed up with him at this point. He had better comply with Destiny's wishes, or he might be learning a lesson the hard way," Rip whispered. I had officially given up trying to teach him Desireé's name and just nodded in response.

A few minutes later our waitress sat our plates down in front of us. Rip tore into his steak like a starving wolverine while I picked at my salmon, reflecting on what we'd just learned. I felt relatively safe now about scratching both Rick and Desireé off my list of potential suspects.

While I was propped against the back of the padded bench, in quiet contemplation, Rip devoured his apple pie and the huge mound of ice cream balanced tentatively on top of it. The sound of Desireé's voice saying the name "Janelle" brought me instantly out of my reverie. We'd just seen that very woman less than a half-hour earlier, carrying a basket of clothes to the park's laundry room as we were driving toward the campground's exit gate. Atop the pile was a shirt that resembled the one Boonie had been wearing the last time I saw him. For a widowed lady traveling alone, Jan sure seemed to have a lot of dirty laundry. And by "dirty laundry" I mean in the literal clothes-washing way, and possibly in a rhetorical way, as well.

I leaned back and concentrated on Desireé's words to her former step-son to see if I could pick up what she was saying about Janelle. *There couldn't be too many women with that uncommon name in Buffalo*, I thought.

"Did I tell you I ran into Janelle at her weekly hair appointment last Wednesday? I just needed a quick trim, but arrived ten minutes early for my appointment. I chatted with Jan while she was letting the highlight solution permeate."

"That's nice." Ricky's tone made it apparent he couldn't have cared less. But his next remark made me plug up my left ear with my index finger to more easily isolate his and Desireé's voices, and block out as much of the droning of surrounding patrons' conversations as possible. In a blasé manner, he said, "I assume she's still running around with Boonie Whetstone, particularly now that Aunt Bea's gone."

"I told you that was just hearsay, son," I heard Desireé reply. "There's no actual proof the two were having an affair behind Bea's back. I can't believe Boonie cheated on her, or you'd think she'd have had some idea of his infidelity. After all, they ran their campground together for many years, and that's practically a 24/7 responsibility. And if Bea had any suspicion of Boonie having an affair behind her back, she'd have told me about it, I'm certain."

"Maybe Aunt Bea had no clue about it, or maybe she knew about the affair and didn't care. You know how much they'd seemed to have grown apart. Well, no offense, but I know I'd have cheated on that intolerable bitch if I were Uncle Boonie. With just about any woman that caught my eye, in fact." Ricky clearly despised his Aunt Bea.

"Watch your mouth, boy, or you've seen your last dime from me. That's my sister you're talking about. Besides, you shouldn't speak ill of the dead, Richard! You're beginning to sound like your father."

I barely heard the young man's grumbled response, but it sounded like a remorseful apology. He surely didn't want Desireé cutting off his funds, particularly with her mother on her death bed. I'd noticed that when he asked about Desireé's mother, it hadn't sounded if he was upset about her impending death. Quite the opposite, in fact. I wondered if he had some reason to believe he'd benefit financially from his step-grandmother's death. To me, he'd sounded impatient for her to kick the bucket. His conversation with Desireé ceased when their waitress brought their check and they stood up to leave.

The decision to have supper at the popular steakhouse had been an advantageous one. I was mentally patting myself on the back for my cleverness. So imagine my mortification when Desireé stopped next to our booth as she prepared to depart. I watched all of the color drain out of my husband's face after she said, "I'm holding that (blankety-blank-blank) you wanted for you, so stop by whenever you're ready to pick it up."

Rather than tell you the exact words Desireé used, I'll just leave her very graphic remark to your imagination. But I *will* tell you I'd never been more embarrassed in my entire life than I was at that moment. Not only did Rip nearly choke on the long swallow of beer he'd just taken, Desireé's remark was a shocking jolt to all of the diners within earshot, as well. For the next ten seconds, every eyeball in the joint was fixed on me. It was so deathly quiet in the room you could have heard a fly doing the breast stroke in someone's chicken noodle soup.

CHAPTER 21

On the drive back to the campground, after Rip's blood pressure had come back down to near normal, I explained the ill-mannered remark Desireé had made as she and her stepson were leaving. I didn't want him to think I'd turned into a past-her-prime, wanna-be porn star right before his eyes. He got a good chuckle out of my story, knowing how humiliated I'd been following Desireé's parting jab. She was on to me, Rip pointed out. "And she clearly didn't appreciate your fanatical tactics. Foolish, too, I might add."

"Well, my approach was a bit brash, but it served its purpose." I felt compelled to defend my actions for, if nothing else, I was putting my heart and soul into it. Rip was acting willy-nilly, just showing an intermittent interest in the case when it suited him. I needed him to be as adamant about getting to the bottom of Bea's death as I was or our time and effort would likely all be for naught.

"Okay, I can almost see your point about Desireé. But, tell me, sweetheart, what purpose did intruding on the Harris's privacy serve?" Rip had finally gotten Rick's ex-wife's name right, but as much as I wanted to change the subject, this was not the proper time to commend him for it. Besides, I had the feeling I wouldn't be able to segue my way out of this conversation no matter how hard I tried. Considering the circumstances, Rip wasn't apt to be as easily distracted as he usually was.

"Oh, um, so I guess you heard about that, did you?" I looked down at my feet as I spoke. "That one didn't quite work out the way I planned."

"So I assumed. Have any of your shenanigans, while investigating murder cases at least, ever panned out the way you intended them to?"

"Yes, they have!" I could only come up with a pitiful three-word retort, so I said all three as emphatically as I could. "How did you find out about the Harris fiasco?"

"I was in the office buying a canister of butane for the grill this afternoon while you were sorting through (blankety-blank-blanks) at the Naughty Pine Playhouse," Rip said, teasing me unmercifully and using the same obscene words the sex shop owner had used earlier. I could tell my face was beet-red. It felt like you could have fried an egg on it. Rip studied me for a moment and said, "I'm just kidding you, sweetheart. So, anyway, while I was in the office, that gal with the laundry, Jane—"

"It's Jan. Janelle Tyson-Simms, to be exact. Even her name has a snooty ring to it, doesn't it?"

"Jane, Jan, Janelle, whatever. The point is, I thought you told me she was only a temporary replacement for Bea, and Boonie had hired a full-time office clerk."

"I did. That's what Jan told me, and I met the new girl, a work camper named Cheri Beets, a day or two later. Maybe it didn't work out. As big a flirt as Boonie seems to be with pretty young ladies, she probably felt uncomfortable around him."

"Very possible," Rip concurred. "Boonie was hanging all over Jane today, and she didn't appear to be very thrilled about it either."

I was astounded that Rip couldn't remember Janelle's nickname for more than the nine seconds that had elapsed since I'd corrected him. I was also surprised by his observation. I asked, "Why would that be? She's been having an ongoing affair with him, even before his wife's death, and I think their clandestine relationship might have played a part in Bea's death. Maybe Jan was disgusted that Boonie was being so transparent about his attraction to her when she thought he should be behaving more discreet about it, particularly when his wife's untimely death was still fresh in everyone's mind."

"Possible, but not probable. Now let me get to back to how I found out my wife was a Peeping Tom."

"I am not a Peeping Tom!" I spoke very defensively for someone who had got caught red-handedly peering into another camper's window. I knew Rip was once again being intentionally cynical, mocking my actions, and I didn't appreciate it one bit.

"Oh, I'm sorry, dear. Would you prefer being classified as a voyeur instead?"

"Knock it off, buster!"

"Okay, okay." Rip chuckled. "I'll cut you some slack. So, anyway, a man was in the shop complaining that some woman with wavy salt and pepper hair, who was probably in her late fifties, was standing on their picnic table bench and looking through their blinds into their RV while his wife was home alone, packaging up gift bags to send overseas to a few of the American veterans stationed on foreign soil."

"He said late fifties? Really?" I asked, flattered to be mistaken for a woman a decade younger. "Okay, so they send packages to vets. Very admirable. And?"

"And what?" Rip asked. "Mr. Harris's description of the meddlesome culprit was all I needed to hear to figure out who he was referring to. After the man left, Jan told me John Harris, and his wife, Barb, are heavily involved in researching wildlife statistics in order to help prevent the extinction of different species."

"Yeah, I know. It's a noble undertaking, I admit. And kudos on getting Jan's name right."

"You're avoiding the issue, Rapella."

"Okay, okay. I'll admit prying into their business turned out to be totally uninformative and extremely painful."

"My point, exactly! Which reminds me, John also asked Jan about the closest shipping store. He said he needed to know where he could ship gift boxes off to veterans stationed around the globe. It appears he and Barb put together collections of toiletries, phone cards, snacks, and other essentials for the vets as a way of showing their appreciation to the men and women who put their lives on the line every day to protect our freedom here at home. They're the kind of philanthropic people the world needs more of."

"Yeah, I agree." I realized Rip was right and I now felt confident in removing them from my suspect list, too. It felt good to be eliminating suspects one by one. Eventually, with any luck at all, I'd have only one suspect left: the killer.

Barb and John's humanitarian efforts explained the boxes I'd seen on their table. I felt a little silly about having them on my list in the first place, as well as embarrassed by my impulsive decision to peer into their window. But, in line with the slogan, 'no pain, no gain', if you don't risk a few thorn pricks, you can't gather beautiful rose blossoms. I just hoped I'd find the guilty rose before I needed a blood transfusion from all the pricks I was accumulating.

Even with Ranger Rick, Desireé, and the Harrises crossed off, I still had a number of people left I'd been unable to justifiably clear. I was determined not to quit trying to cross off suspects until that lone suspect remained. There were Janelle and Boonie, along with the owners of the competing campground, Leo and Charly Brown. To my mind, there was at least one other suspect we might be overlooking, who had sufficient motive to kill Bea Whetstone. I just couldn't quite put my finger on who it was.

The Browns seemed like nice people, incapable of murder, but how many times do we hear people on television saying they would never have believed their next-door neighbor was capable of dismembering a slew of sorority sisters and storing their body parts in a chest freezer in their basement? And yet that sweetheart of a neighbor next door was ultimately convicted of doing that very thing to a dozen or more victims. See my point? Even the vilest among us may be skilled at putting on a front, convincing acquaintances that they're a kind, friendly, stand-up kind of individual. In fact, those are exactly the kinds of people one should be most distrustful of in some instances. But don't misunderstand me. I don't believe you should automatically be wary of the little old lady next door just because she bakes you a plateful of snickerdoodles while you're recovering from your appendectomy. Although, given the opportunity, it wouldn't hurt to check out the contents of her chest freezer.

I really wanted another chance to speak with the Browns, but wasn't sure how I could arrange it after the last fiasco. In my gut, I really didn't think the couple were guilty of anything, other than retaliating with tricks of their own when the Whetstones tried to steal all their customers.

However, if I made another trip to their campground, I'd half expect to be forcefully removed from their property. On the other hand, maybe they'd be somewhat relenting if I made the effort to say I was sorry about the incident. I did owe them an apology, after all.

But first I wanted to speak with Janelle Tyson-Simms again and planned to head straight to the office after I'd had my quota of two cups of coffee the following morning.

"Where's Jan this morning?" I asked Cheri Beets, who was standing behind the cash register, counting the money in the till and notating the totals on a yellow post-it note. "When you weren't here yesterday, I thought maybe you'd decided this job wasn't for you."

"Oh, it's all right. Owner's a little too touchy-feely for my taste, but other than that it's not so bad. Yesterday, he asked another person to fill in for me so I could go have my vision checked and order a new pair of glasses."

"That'll cost you! What I had to pay for my last pair would have made a nice down payment on a new car." While I was nonchalantly making small talk, I was exaggerating, as I am wont to do, but not by much. "Well, I won't bother you any longer."

"You're no bother," she replied. Cheri was a sweet and polite young lady, and much easier to deal with than Beata Whetstone, or even Janelle Tyson-Simms. "If you were needing to talk to Jan, she told me yesterday she had a hair appointment today."

Her comment triggered a memory of a question Desireé had asked Ricky at supper the previous evening. "Did I tell you I ran into Janelle at her weekly hair appointment last Wednesday?" I recalled her asking her step-son. Today was Wednesday.

"Thank you, Cheri. Do you happen to know what salon she uses? I need to get something done with this mess and am not familiar with the hair salons in town." I ran my hand across the top of my unruly mop of hair as I spoke.

"I use Donna Duca at the Hair Affair Salon on Klondike Drive," the affable young lady said. "She's great! You should go to her salon."

"No, offense, dear, but I'd prefer to go to the same salon Jan uses." Even as I was speaking, I knew there was no way Cheri could help but be offended by my remark. I might as well have just said, "Your hairstyle is absolutely atrocious and I'd rather go to someone who has at least some clue about styling hair properly."

"Oh," Cheri said. As I'd feared, she had taken my comment personally. And who wouldn't have? I felt bad because she was such a friendly gal. Cheri was jovial and polite, yet helpful and professional. She was the ideal individual for dealing with the public.

"I should clarify my response," I said contritely. I certainly didn't want to insult her and leave a sour taste in this sweet lady's mouth. "Your hair is gorgeous! Mine could never look that nice no matter who took a crack at it.

Thing is, if I go to the salon she uses, I'll be able to talk to her while we're both being worked on."

"Oh, of course. I understand completely." The crestfallen expression disappeared from Cheri's face and one of gratitude replaced it. She glanced up at a large clock on the wall. "I'm almost positive Jan said her ten o'clock appointment was at the Snip Joint on Main Street, right next to the nail salon. If you leave within ten minutes, you'd both get there about the same time."

"Oh, good idea. Thanks, Cheri. You are a real sweetie."

Rip reluctantly approved of my idea to "accidentally" run in to Jan at the hair salon. He pleaded with me to use diplomacy when conversing with her, and under no circumstances, accuse her outright of murdering her boyfriend's wife. Sometimes my husband shows very little faith in my ability to use tact and decorum when the situation calls for it. Not wanting to give him the time or a reason to change his mind, I didn't remind Rip that I could tip-toe around a dicey subject as delicately as anyone.

But I did have to ask, "So, John Harris really thought I was in my fifties, huh?"

"Late fifties," Rip replied dryly.

"Even so, that's ten years younger than my real age. Very flattering, don't you think?"

"I guess. But, then, I've never thought you looked anywhere near your age, darling. I've always suspected you'd discovered the fountain of youth and never thought to share it with me."

"You look much younger than sixty-eight too, honey." I gave Rip a longer than usual kiss before I left. His compliments had me smiling all the way to the salon. I was anxious to return home with a new hairstyle that made me look even younger.

I didn't have much time to spare if I wanted to get there at the same time as Jan. I slipped out of my faded Dallas Cowboys t-shirt and put on a tangerine-colored blouse. I gave my dentures a quick once-over with my toothbrush.

Lastly, I studied my current hairdo. I could think of no conceivable way a stylist could make it look worse, so decided to make a last-minute choice of styles once I got there. Because, after all, what could possibly go wrong with this strategy?

A lot, as it turned out.

I couldn't make a last-minute appointment, naturally, so was relieved to see a "walk-ins welcome" banner stretched across the green awning over the entrance. I greeted the perfectly proportioned black woman at the reception desk just inside the front door. I told her I'd like to get a more fashionable hairdo. I admired her long, dark brown dreadlocks, and commented on how beautiful her hair was. I wished I had enough hair to pull off such a youthful style, but doubted Rip would be overly enthused if his bride of fifty years came home from the hair salon with dreadlocks. She thanked me for the compliment. I smiled, and then said, "I'd opt for your figure too, if I could have my druthers."

"Druthers?" She asked, with a confused look on her face. "What's that?"

"Never mind. Not important," I replied with a smile. I wasn't sure I could come up with a definition of the word. At least not at a moment's notice. But, as someone who habitually used clichés, I wondered when "if I had my druthers" had become an archaic idiom of the past.

I scanned the customers at the individual stations and discovered I'd beaten Jan to the salon. As I walked over and sat in a chair in the waiting area. I told the receptionist, "I'm going to wait until my friend arrives if that's all right with you."

"Of course. What's her name? I can check to make sure we have her on today's schedule."

I hadn't really wanted to let on I knew Jan and infer we had planned to meet here at ten, but I didn't have a choice at this point. "Her name's Jan."

"Jan? We actually have two people named Jan on the schedule for ten. Jan Dorsey hasn't arrived, but Janelle Tyson-Simms, who occasionally goes by Jan, is having her hair done by Kerri this morning."

"Yes, that's the one. We've been friends for so long that I always call her Jan. I'll just wait for her to arrive. Her appointment's at ten, right?"

"Um, yes. So, ma'am, exactly how long have you been friends with Janelle?"

"It seems like forever. Why?"

"She's already here, sitting in that second chair over there." The receptionist pointed toward a willowy brunette who was chatting with her hair stylist. "I'm surprised you didn't recognize her."

Uh-oh. I actually *didn't* recognize her. Apparently, just as I'd confused Ricky for Richard Myer Senior, I had apparently mixed up Jan Dorsey with this Janelle Tyson-Simms. I'd experienced my second mistaken identity in as many days. Janelle did resemble the Jan I knew from the campground, except for the squarer face and dark-rimmed eyeglasses. "That's Janelle Tyson-Simms?" I asked, just in case there was some kind of misunderstanding on the receptionist's part. But there was no mix-up on her part, I realized, after she nodded.

"That's definitely Janelle. She's been patronizing this salon for years." She gave me a sympathetic smile, probably assuming I was in the latter stages of Alzheimer's. I was beginning to wonder about that possibility, myself.

"My goodness! You're absolutely right! That is Jan!" I exclaimed after removing my glasses as if they were hindering my vision. "I really do need to get my peepers checked. My eyesight has deteriorated so much in the last year, I can barely distinguish between a field mouse and a hippopotamus."

The befuddled lady stared at me for a few seconds. "You really do need glasses if you can't tell the difference between a mouse and a hippo, given one is like a zillion times larger than the other."

I merely chuckled, not sure how to respond to her inarguable statement. Then I pointed to the vacant styling station next to the one Janelle was seated at. "I would like that gal next to Jan to do my hair, if possible."

"Sure. If that's who you want." She sounded uncertain, but not nearly as uncertain as I felt. "Her next client doesn't come in until eleven."

As I walked toward the empty chair, I studied the gal I'd chosen to do my hair. I considered saying I didn't have time for a new hairstyle after all, and then bolting from the small building like there was a wrecking ball about to crash through the window. Even though my impulse to flee was intense, I managed to resist the urge. I sat down facing the mirror with a sense of dread.

My hair stylist had light blue hair with vivid orange tips. The hair on the right side of her head was about the length of the bristles on your toothbrush. The hair on the other side, however, was more like the bristles on your straw broom. It was hard to judge the left side's length, though, because it was secured on top with some kind of stretchy-scrunchy band. The best visual I can offer is to picture a grown-up Pebbles Flintstone after a run-in with a couple of open cans of paint. To top it off, everything that could possibly be pierced was pierced. There was enough metal bisecting her body to build a Mini Cooper convertible—the tiny, original model, of course.

And her outfit was nearly indescribable. A combination of stripper, color-blindness, and flea market enthusiast is the best I can do. With a skirt that short, if she were to drop her brush, she'd just have to dig in her drawer for another one. No way she could bend over without flashing everyone in the room and taking the risk that one of her breasts might pop out of her way too tight, and way too plunging, tank top.

She introduced herself after I had done the same. Her name was impossible to pronounce, and I'd forgotten it before she'd even draped a cape around me. She ran her fingers through my hair and asked what kind of style I wanted. I hadn't given it much thought, so I looked across the room and saw an older woman who had hair about the color and length as mine. The cosmetologist was rolling her hair and chatting with her. I assessed the woman in the chair for a few seconds. She passed my inspection, appearing relaxed and, more importantly, sane, so I pointed at her. "I'd like what she's having done."

"If you say so," my stylist, who I'll simply refer to as Freak, remarked. "Let's go wash your hair and get started then."

Walking to the sink basin, I passed Jan Dorsey, a.k.a. Laundry Room Jan, who had just arrived for her ten o'clock appointment. She sounded very chipper as she greeted me. "Hey, Rapella! Long time, no see!"

I smiled and nodded, realizing I'd totally misjudged her. She was not the Jan rumored to be having an affair with Boonie Whetstone, after all. Just a friendly lady who happened to share a nickname with the woman who *was* seeing Boonie on the sly. Most likely, Jan truly was a widow visiting Buffalo, Wyoming, for the very first time.

Freak washed my hair and I believe in giving credit where credit is due. Her scalp massage was calming, and I'd have been content to have her continue kneading my hair for another hour or two. But soon we were back at her station and she removed a tray of tiny curlers from a cabinet below the mirror. While she gathered all the other necessary items, I scanned the four small framed photos propped up against the back of her counter. I assumed the four individuals in the photos, three girls and a boy, were her children; a fact Freak later confirmed.

All four children, aged from about seven to fourteen in my estimation, looked perfectly normal. They had typical hairstyles and outfits for children their ages. I wondered if they were ever embarrassed by their mother's out-there appearance. I could see them asking her to drop them off three blocks from their school every morning. I know I would have if she were my mother.

I struggled to come up with a way to chat with Janelle Tyson-Simms, who I now knew to be the gold-digger whose first two wealthy husbands had met with ghastly ends. Then, I had a clever idea. Most people love to be praised, especially about their appearance, so I turned to her. "Excuse me, ma'am, but I have to say you have the loveliest hair I've ever seen."

"Thank you so much," she replied with a broad smile. Her voice was much different from Laundry Room Jan's. Deep and sultry, it had a southern drawl to it. My guess was she was one of the Naughty Pine Playhouse's most loyal customers. Janelle studied me briefly before replying."You have, um, well, you, um—"

"Yes?"

"You, um, have hair too." She stumbled through her response. Although she apparently had no problem being deceitful when it came to men, she clearly found it impossible to lie about my hair by returning the compliment.

"Thank you for noticing I have hair," I said, as if I weren't already aware of that fact. "You sure do look familiar."

"I do?"

"Yes, I'm trying to think of where I've seen you before." I tapped a finger on my chin and pretended to be in deep thought for a few seconds. "I've got it! You remind me of a lady I saw cuddling with the guy who owns the RV Park my husband and I are staying at. Your boyfriend, I assume, is quite handsome. Don't you think?"

As her stylist turned toward me in astonishment, Janelle gulped, not sure what to say. "Hmm, I'm sure you must be confusing me with someone else. I really don't know who owns the Rest 'n Peace campground."

"I didn't say which RV park we were staying in, but you're absolutely correct about the name of it." I could think of a number of other campgrounds in and around Buffalo. Her mentioning the one Boonie owns was all the verification I needed to know the rumors about their illicit affair were true. So I plunged in. "You've surely heard about the missing woman whose body was discovered in the forest a couple of days later. As I'm sure you already realize, the park owner I'm referring to was the victim's husband."

Kerri, Janelle's stylist, made her client turn her head so that she was looking straight at the mirror, and Janelle seemed more than happy to comply. I'm certain Kerri did so to try and prevent an ensuing catfight in the middle of the hair salon, but I found it easier to fib to someone when you aren't looking them directly in the eyes, anyway.

When Janelle, with her back to me now, remained silent, I asked, "You were aware of that, weren't you?"

As if she were composing her response, and then re-evaluating it, she eventually replied, "I do kind of recall hearing about her death. What a horrible thing to happen."

What a horrible thing to do, I wanted to reply. Charly Brown said she and Janelle were only a year apart, and both had attended Buffalo High School. Was it instinct that made Janelle mention the Rest 'n Peace RV Park rather than her schoolmate's Sweet Sixteen RV Park, or the popular Deer Park Campground? Why had she automatically assumed I wasn't referring to the owner of the Buffalo KOA or the Indian Campground, two other highly-regarded RV Parks in town? It could be coincidental, but I didn't think so.

And in a town the size of Buffalo, with no more than five-thousand residents if you counted a few of them twice, incidents like that didn't occur often. In a huge city like New York, news of a missing person found dead in the woods would be forgotten as old news by the next day. But it'd be "water cooler" conversation in Buffalo for weeks, if not in all of Johnson County. Given the demographics of the town, it seemed too big a deal for someone who'd been a local citizen for many years, possibly forever, to make a remark like, "I do kind of recall hearing about her death."

So, I plunged deeper. "I heard they've determined the woman's death wasn't the result of an animal encounter after all."

Janelle's head turned toward me so fast she was fortunate Kerri didn't snip her left ear off with the sharp scissors. She was intense when she asked, "What do you mean?"

"Just that. Someone killed her. Before my husband retired, he was the sheriff of Aransas County, in south Texas. He has an 'in' with the local detectives, you see." Rip had no such thing and it was a state of affairs that irked him so much he was seeing red and berating Sheriff Jaclyn Wright every chance he got. But Janelle was in the dark about that situation and I wanted her to think we were privy to all the juicy details about an intense investigation going on within the local police department.

Janelle gulped once again, quite audibly this time. "Do they have any suspects?"

"I dunno. But the detectives told my husband they were looking into a tip they got over the hotline. It has something to do with some local woman who was having an affair with the victim's husband. In fact, she's the woman I mistook you for. It's not clear to us whether they believe it's the husband or his mistress, or both, they're zeroing in on."

Janelle's eyes were as big as half-dollars. She seemed unable to speak. So I added, "As far as I'm concerned, if that skanky whore had anything to do with the woman's death, she should get the needle. Don't you agree?"

I don't particularly like the "W" word, and had probably only said it out loud once or twice in my entire life. I've said the word to myself, in reference to some shady lady, or another, more times that you can count. But that's beside the point. In this instance, I wanted to get under Janelle's skin, and my plan seemed to work. She obviously didn't like being referred to as a skanky whore—but then, who would?

"Just because Boonie and this woman were involved with each other doesn't mean she was a 'skanky whore,' as you put it. Maybe Bea didn't fulfill Boonie's needs. Perhaps they'd grown apart and were living separate lives. They could have even had an open marriage, where each of

them was free to see other people. You don't know what
went on behind the Whetstone's door."

"No, I don't. But you sure seem to! Especially for
someone who professed to not know who owned the Rest
'n Peace Park just a few moments ago. Yet you just
mentioned both of the park owners' names." I had
intentionally not said their names and my intuition had paid
off. "The tipster told the dispatcher the mistress in question
was a tall, slim, brunette woman named Janelle. Does that
name ring a bell with you?"

Janelle glared at me for a few seconds before ripping the
plastic cape off and throwing two twenties on the stylist's
station. "I'm done here. I'll see you next week, Kerri."

"If you say so, Jan," Kerri replied. The stylist stepped
back, stunned by her client's reaction to the exchange she'd
just overheard. Me, not so much. But I was a little surprised
she'd walk out with only half of her long hair trimmed. The
mane hanging down her back was lopsided, one side three
inches longer than the other. But then, I suppose Boonie
could easily even the sides out with a pair of office scissors
the next time she saw him. I had a feeling that would be
very soon. In fact, I'd have guessed she was heading
straight to the Rest 'n Peace RV Park to tell him what some
interfering old lady in the hair salon had just told her.

Kerri's eyes followed Janelle out the front door, as did
mine. Then she and I locked eyes. I just shrugged and
looked away. I'd have left then had my hair not been
wrapped around numerous curlers. I will concede it was
time I tried something different with my hair, and Rip was
pleased earlier to hear me say I was planning to get a new
style. I didn't, however, appreciate his quip. "A *new* one? I
didn't know you *had* a style to begin with."

Freak led me over to a waiting area with a stack of
magazines on the table next to it. "I'll be back in about
fifteen minutes to rinse your hair and apply stabilizer."

"All right." I sat down and watched as Kerri swept up
Janelle's hair from the floor. Barb Harris had indicated that
Kerri thought Janelle was a con artist and only interested in

hooking up with Boonie for monetary gain. I went over my conversation with Janelle in my head. Even though I knew it might turn out that neither Boonie nor Janelle had any part in Bea's death, I still felt no remorse about the way I'd spoken to the woman. Taking up with another woman's husband was a low-down thing to do. I thought she had a dressing-down coming, no matter if she were guilty of murder or not. And I'd bet you, my dear reader, feel the same way.

Twenty minutes later, I was back at Freak's station. With my back to the mirror, she used the clippers, the hair dryer, a curling iron, a fistful of gel, and a couple of different kinds of spray. Still musing about my conversation with Janelle Tyson-Simms, I sucked on a peppermint candy I'd dug out of my purse, and paid little attention to what she was doing. In retrospect, I should have taken heed to the expression on Jan Dorsey's face earlier when she'd glanced over at my hair as Freak was laboring over it. The look on Jan's face had been one of shock, as if she'd just witnessed a loved one's hand reach out from under their own tombstone to pick a dandelion.

Looking pleased with her work, Freak finally whipped my chair around so I could admire my new hair style in the mirror. Suddenly I understood the reason behind Jan's incredulous expression. I was so stunned by my appearance, I inhaled the peppermint and it got wedged in my throat. For a few seconds I was afraid I'd need someone to administer the Heimlich maneuver to dislodge it. I hacked several times and at last the candy broke free. The peppermint disc shot out of my mouth, ricocheted off the mirror, and began rolling across the floor behind me. As I turned instinctively to follow its path, the sticky disc began gathering loose strands of clipped hair as it slid across the linoleum to the far side of the salon. For the second time in as many days, ever eyeball in the room was fixed on me.

I looked back at the mirror, hoping my hair didn't look as outrageous as my first glance had indicated. No such luck. Like Freak's, the hair on the right side of my head was cut short. Not as short as hers, but definitely shorter than the opposite side. She'd given me an extremely tight perm on that side. The loops were so tiny and taut, I was certain the right side of my head would adhere to the hook side of a Velcro strip. On the permed side, she'd left about two inches of the hair closest to my face much longer. Running the length of that longer hair were fluorescent purple streaks.

I glanced over at the woman whose hair style I'd asked Freak to duplicate. She had a tight perm, but none of the other, crazier features I'd been treated to. I pointed at the older woman, looked up at Freak, and muttered, "But—"

My hair stylist smiled, patted my shoulder. "No worries. I'm only charging you for the perm. The other special touches I'm throwing in for free. I know how elderly ladies tend to like the color purple, so I knew you'd appreciate that extra flair. And I was correct in thinking this new style would make you appear much younger."

"But, but, but, I wanted to look like I was in my fifties, not sixteen! Because, after all, I'm pretty sure the remainder of my body would have let the cat out of the bag, anyway. I look absolutely preposterous!"

"Awesome! I knew you'd love it!" I'm not sure what Freak thought the word preposterous meant, but she was obviously as daft as she appeared.

"Uh-huh. I wish I could tell you how much." I knew if I *did* tell her what I thought, I'd probably be driven away from the salon in a paddy wagon. I wanted to laugh, sob, throw up, and slap the self-satisfied smile off Freak's face all at the same time. I would have thrown a hissy fit and demanded to have something done about my hair if not for the fact I knew it was probably beyond repair and my own stupid fault to begin with. If I'd made myself clear and paid more attention to what Freak was doing, I wouldn't look like a freak now, too. Getting arrested for a public disturbance would only delay my investigation into Bea's death, and too much time had passed already. Not to mention, having to bail me out of jail had a tendency to turn Rip into a cranky sourpuss.

I was so shocked and dismayed by my appearance, I could barely catch my breath. I might prefer a little color and "flair" on the outside facade of the Chartreuse Caboose, but I had absolutely no desire for "hair flair". My knees were shaking as I stood up from the chair, but I felt an overwhelming sense of relief when Freak warned me, "Don't wash your hair for two or three days or it will not only loosen your perm, it will wash out the color, as well."

I paid the sixty-dollar tab, which I felt was seventy dollars too much, left the Snip Joint Salon, and sprinted to the truck. If I hadn't wanted to be seen by as few people as possible, I'd probably have stuck around a few extra minutes; just long enough to caution them about the repercussions of overcharging their clients. They surely wouldn't want patrons to refer to the salon as the "Gyp" instead of "Snip" Joint behind their backs. It wouldn't be very conducive for positive word-of-mouth advertising.

I drove twenty miles over the speed limit on my way back to the campground so I could wash my hair as soon as possible—a dozen times if need be. I prayed I could wash some of the perm and *all* of the purple dye out.

We'd been planning to attend Willie's two o'clock ball game that afternoon. If I couldn't come up with a feasible reason to stay home, other than being humiliated by my atrocious hairstyle, I'd have to try on all of my various hats to see which one covered up my hair the best. I knew Rip would be adamant about me attending the championship baseball game because it meant so much to our nephew.

As I walked through the trailer door, I braced myself for Rip's reaction. I stepped inside and faced my husband stoically, as if daring him to make a smart remark about my hair. As expected, he rose to the occasion and laughed heartily. "Well, you most definitely have a new style now, my dear!"

CHAPTER 22

I'd managed to return my hair to its normal color, and the curls had loosened up somewhat, but there was no growing back the hair on the right side anytime soon. As I've said so many times before, only our Lord could perform miracles, and once again I had a sneaking suspicion this prayer would go unanswered, as had many of mine in the past. No doubt God had some drowning kid to save, or some nursing home fire to rain out, and didn't have time to waste on a foolish woman old enough to know better.

It dawned on me the only option I had now was to have the side Freak had left long cut short to match the other side. I'd never worn my hair that short in my entire life and was a bit apprehensive about how I'd look. It's not like I could change my mind once it was chopped off.

Cora stopped by shortly after I'd dried my hair, and eventually got to the point she could control her laughter long enough to speak. "I cut Willie's hair all the time to save money, Aunt Rappie. I can trim yours up on the left side good enough to get you by until you have time to visit the salon again."

"That would be wonderful, honey. But I guarantee you, I won't be returning to *that* salon ever again. In fact, if it looks passable enough when you're done, I might not need to go back to any salon." Like Cora said, if I could get by I'd rather save the money. She was definitely a chip off my old block. Besides, I'd already wasted sixty bucks on my hair that day.

Cora did a bang-up job trimming my hair and making me look reasonably normal again. In fact, both Rip and Cora thought a short cut was an attractive style on me, and their praise sounded genuine. When I took a look at myself in the mirror, I had to agree. I thought I might just keep it short from then on. It would definitely be much easier to care for.

Shortly afterward, Cora left and said she'd see us in a few hours at the ball field. I felt confident enough now to accompany Rip and Cora to Willie's game. But first, I wanted to place a call to the Browns. I wouldn't feel right until I issued an apology to both of them. However, I'd totally understand if they were unwilling to accept it. Although I can barely remember what we had for breakfast that morning, I recalled the number Cheri Beets had given to the wagon master of the Airstream caravan over the phone the day I'd walked into the office as she was taking a reservation. I think I subconsciously knew I might need to call it in the future. I picked up the iPhone and dialed 307-555-1022.

Charly Brown answered after the first ring, no doubt assuming someone was calling to make a reservation. "Sweet Sixteen, may I help you?"

"This is Rapella, the gal who you were kind enough to order the stuffed buffalos for."

"Oh, it's you. What do you want now?" Charly's voice was icy and impatient. But then, I hadn't expected to receive a warm greeting from a woman I'd deceived so blatantly.

"I want to apologize, and offer to pay for the stuffed buffalo toys if you were unable to cancel the order. I wasn't comfortable telling you we were staying at your competitor's campground, particularly after you told me how badly they'd treated you."

"That wouldn't have bothered me," she replied in a wee bit friendlier tone. "Despite the Whetstones' business practices, we stay plenty busy. Besides, we were just as guilty as they are, you know. We were pulling some uncalled for stunts against them, as well. I'm just thankful I eventually offered Bea an olive branch and she and I had made amends before her unexpected death, or I'd have lived with the guilt forever. Truth be told, we are both better off if the two parks work together. That way I have a place to send folks who are needing a site when all ours are already full, and vice versa."

That didn't sound to me like someone anxious to eliminate her rival business owner. We hadn't heard the two couples had patched things up prior to Bea's unexpected demise, and neither Boonie nor Leo had appeared as if they'd reached a truce the day our tires were flattened twice. Apparently there'd been a breakdown in the barbershop grapevine that had not been brought to Rip's attention.

"But you told me the highway sign still chapped your hide," I said.

Charly laughed. "It does, but since it hasn't stopped us from filling up every night in the last few months, I decided to just let it be. If our business starts slacking off again though, I'm going to approach Boonie about it. Like I said, Bea and I made amends, but that doesn't mean I cared for her much. She was a mean-spirited woman even before the war that erupted between our two campgrounds. And atonement didn't change her personality at all. Boonie, on his own, is tolerable. Not sure what he saw in her to begin with, truthfully. The ill-will between Boonie and Leo has lingered, but they seem content to just act as if the other one doesn't exist. If that works for them, I'm fine with it."

Charly's comments confirmed that my observation about the two men was spot on. There'd been a definite chill between them the day Boonie drove Rip to Leo's campground. But I had a feeling I'd been too hasty in suspecting the Browns. After all, I'd felt an instant kinship with Charly the moment we met. She was kind, friendly, and accommodating; all the things her rival hadn't been.

"I understand completely, Charly," I said, grateful she hadn't slammed the phone down in my ear, as I might have done if our roles were reversed. Even though I wanted to make amends, I didn't want to tell her my visit to her store had been a ploy to try and determine if she, and/or Leo, were guilty of murder. "That's exactly why I placed this call. I felt bad about what happened and wouldn't rest easy until I'd apologized. Please let me compensate you for placing an order of stuffed animals that I don't need after all. As it turned out, the family reunion was canceled when my cousin Benjamin became gravely ill."

"Oh, my. I'm so sorry. Is there anything I can do?" Charly sounded genuine, and I had no reason to doubt her sincerity. I only wish I could be as forgiving as she was after someone had given me a bad shake the way I had her.

"No, but I appreciate the offer. He's on the road to recovery now. So, figure out how much I owe you and I'll drop off a check."

"Oh, heavens no! I was able to cancel the order with no problem. I do a lot of business with that company and they wouldn't want to lose me as a customer, I assure you."

"I'm sure you're right. You and your husband are such nice folks. My husband and I will definitely stay at your campground the next time we're in the area visiting my niece." I was sincere about staying at the Sweet Sixteen RV Park the next time we visited the Beaufont family. It was a pretty, well-appointed park, and more importantly, it had a fence surrounding the perimeter to keep the bears, cougars, and other dangerous critters at bay. "Once again, I am so very sorry, Charly. I wish you and Leo only the best."

"Thank you. I wish you and your husband the same. And, your cousin too, of course."

"Who?" I asked, confused by her remark.

"Your cousin, Benjamin. The one who's so sick."

"Oh, yes, of course! Benjamin. My sick cousin." I hoped I didn't sound as much like a dingbat to her as I sounded to myself. It was mind-boggling to me how I could remember the Brown's phone number days later, and forget what I'd just said moments earlier. Once again, the prospect of progressive memory impairment left me shaken.

"Sorry about the flat tires you experienced in our parking lot, too. It's happened several more times since your encounter with those young hoodlums. Leo just set up a new security camera and is waiting with bated breath for the culprits to strike again so he can identify them and nail the ornery jerks. He's trying to entice them by leaving his truck parked out front, directly across from the camera. Is your husband as conniving as mine, Ms. Bison?" I joined Charly in laughter at Leo's scheme to catch the tire-assaulters.

"You can call me Rapella, dear," I said when our laughter ended. I'd forgotten she still thought my surname was Bison. If we did stay at the Brown's campground during our next visit to Buffalo, I'd have to remember to register us for a site as Rip and Rapella Bison. I'm sure Rip would be thrilled about being called Mr. Bison by the Browns for the duration of our stay.

Charly's remark about the flat tires convinced me that having the air let out of them really was just a prank carried out by a group of young punks with nothing better to do. I wasn't as certain the same young pranksters were responsible for the slashed-tires incident at the Rest 'n Peace park, however.

"By the way," Charly said. "Have you had any luck determining who might have killed Bea?"

"No, not yet. But we're getting close."

"Hmm. Good to hear. Well, I best get back to work now. Thanks for calling, Rapella."

One second after I ended the call with Charly Brown, the cell phone rang in my hand. I instantly recognized Ranger Rick's deep voice. "Were you anticipating my call? There was barely a full ring before you answered."

"Yes. Did I forget to tell you that I'm physic? I've been talking to dead people like some of those scam artists on TV."

"Ha! That must be interesting. So, have you spoken with Bea recently?" He laughed at his own light-hearted question.

"Yes. Just this morning, as a matter of fact. She told me to get off my can and see that whoever killed her is punished accordingly." Even though it didn't feel right to joke about someone's death, it helped calm my nerves, and I imagined it did the same for Rick. We'd all been on edge since he'd discovered his former sister-in-law's body.

"Gee, did she mention me by chance?" Rick asked. "I was never her favorite person, you know. Bea's probably still congratulating herself in heaven for managing to break up my marriage. And by the way, I still think her death was due to an animal encounter. I've seen or heard nothing to convince me otherwise."

Rick had good-naturedly chuckled about my claiming to have spoken to Bea's spirit, but I could see through his levity. He was still hurt by Desireé's rejection. "Actually, although I'm positive Bea encouraged my wife to divorce me, I'm sure everyone could see our break-up was inevitable. We'd been growing more distant from each other for several years, so Bea probably did us both a favor. And I do appreciate that Desireé has remained close to my son, Ricky. His biological mother was killed in a car wreck when he was only three, and I took full custody of him afterward. But it was Desireé who became a bigger factor in his life than I was. Ricky could barely stand to look at his step-aunt, Bea, though. Bea would say things to my ex like, 'How long are you going to let that loafer walk all over you? Ain't it about time you shoved that deadbeat out of the nest?'"

"Wow! Bea called your son, who's also *her* step-nephew, a loafer and a deadbeat?"

"Those were some of the nicest things she called him. She also referred to him as a leach, a bum, a mooch, a lazy slackass, and worse."

"Worse than a lazy slackass?" I asked. "Can it even get worse than that?"

"Much worse. Her total disregard for Ricky kind of drove a wedge between the two sisters, after awhile. Desireé has always been very fond of Ricky. She practically raised him by herself because I was traveling all over the country for the U.S. National Forest Service. Being home with my family so seldom was a real bone of contention between us. It was only a few years ago I began my current job, which doesn't require any traveling."

"You'd think after you landed a job that allowed you to spend more time with your family, your bond would grow stronger," I said.

"Yeah, you'd think that, wouldn't you? Instead, once we were able to spend more time together, she realized she really didn't like having me around all that much. Truth is, I think it made us both realize just how far apart we'd drifted. I found myself wishing I was anywhere but home. It certainly wasn't a marriage made in heaven. We've stayed on good terms for the sake of the children, especially our eight-year-old, and actually get along better now than when we were married."

"Sounds more like a *divorce* made in heaven to me." Then jokingly I said, "But enough about you. What was the reason behind your call?"

"You are a hoot, Rapella. I pray someday I'll find the right one for me and have as strong of a union as you and Rip have." The longing in Rick's voice was undeniable.

"You will, Rick. Have faith in the Lord and it will happen one day."

"Thanks, Rapella. I have been praying for that very thing, and I hope you're right. But the reason I called was to see if you two were available to check the camera for any beneficial photos. Purely by accident, we found and confiscated another trap this morning. It was raining steadily and the trap was camouflaged so well we didn't even see it until a fellow ranger stepped right into the middle of it. Had it not already been triggered, and the jaws released, he'd have been badly injured. So, in other words, time is of the essence."

"Oh, my goodness! I'm so glad your fellow ranger wasn't hurt. And also that you guys found it before another animal was maimed or killed."

"I'm afraid we were too late for that," Rick said, before continuing in a rueful tone. "There was a lot of blood on and around the trap, I'm afraid. We don't know for sure if it was a bear or not, but that's why it was already disarmed when Roger stepped into it. We know an animal suffered a lot due to that damned trap. But at least it was able to free itself somehow."

"Oh, no! You are absolutely right, Rick. Time really is of the essence. We need to capture the responsible party before another animal is victimized. Rip walked up to the office to pay lot rent for two more weeks. He should be back any time. Come on over and we'll be ready to head out when you get here."

"That's terrific! I'm on the way!"

Rip walked in the door just as I ended the call. I told him the ranger was coming over, and rehashed my conversation with the man. Then Rip told me he'd chatted with Boonie for a few minutes. The campground owner had just gotten off the phone when Rip arrived. Boonie was clearly stressed out by whatever discussion had transpired during the call. When Rip noticed Boonie's tenseness, he inquired about his state of mind and asked if there was anything we could do for him.

"No, but I surely do appreciate the offer. I'm getting by, but it hasn't been easy. I've been carrying around a lot of guilt," Boonie said. He then asked Rip if he could tell him something in confidence, to which Rip naturally agreed. Rip has always been the kind of guy people opened up to, especially when something heavy was resting on their shoulders.

To Rip's surprise, Boonie confessed to him about his affair with Janelle Tyson-Simms. He explained that he and Bea had drifted apart to the point they couldn't exchange a kind word with each other. Working side-by-side for many years had taken a toll on their relationship. While Bea was alive, he'd had no qualms about cheating on her, but overpowering guilt was eating him up now that she was gone. He'd said to Rip, "I've tried to break it off with Janelle, but she's persistently calling and ragging me. Says I owe it to her to put a ring on her finger, which was not an option that was ever on the table. She shows up here at the campground nearly every day now and argues with me in front of my customers. Yesterday she came storming in my house, screaming that some crazy woman at the hair salon told her the detectives think that she, I, or both of us, intentionally killed my wife, which couldn't be further from the truth."

"I can definitely see why you're upset, buddy," Rip had said when he was finally able to get a word in edgewise. But his window to speak had closed quickly as Boonie began to speak again.

"Now I'm scared to death I'm going to be hung for a murder I didn't commit. Janelle's a bit flighty, but I seriously don't think she'd do something that heinous, either."

"I'd hope not. Running around with someone else's spouse is heinous enough," Rip had replied. According to Rip, Boonie had hung his head in shame for a few moments before responding.

"I know you were in law enforcement your entire career, Rip. Do you have any advice on what I should do?"

Rip had convinced Boonie there was no truth at all to what the crazy woman had said to Janelle. Naturally, he didn't tell the tormented man the crazy woman was his wife of fifty years. About Janelle's persistence, Rip suggested a restraining order, but warned it was only as good as the paper it was written on. It was often like trying to plug a leaking dam with a wine cork, he'd told Boonie. Rip also advised him not to take Janelle's calls and have his small staff tell her he's away from the campground when she shows up uninvited. Eventually, she'd probably tire of the process and leave him alone. Finally, he'd truthfully told the distraught man, "Unfortunately, it's a situation you've brought upon yourself. Once you've made your own bed, it often becomes difficult to lie in, and on occasion, even more difficult to get out of."

I felt sorry for Boonie even though I was disgusted by his self-professed infidelity. It was one of those unique situations where you'd like to sympathize with someone while simultaneously christening their noggin with a champagne bottle.

"Oh, and by the way, Boonie told me it didn't make it any easier that Bea disappeared on her birthday."

"Oh, my! That's so sad. I do recall her telling me her birthday was in April, hence the big honking diamond in a bracelet her grandmother gave her that she told me she always wore for luck." The irony of my last remark to Rip made me wonder if she'd forgotten to put her lucky bracelet on the day of her disappearance.

Before we knew it, Rick had arrived. The three of us began our hike to the site where we'd set up our game camera. The rain had subsided, but a heavy mist still permeated the air. The ground was saturated enough to be a nuisance. First, the soles of my hiking boots got caked with mud, and then the wet leaves adhered to the muck. As my boots got heavier and heavier, each step became more taxing than the last.

All the animals in the forest must have taken refuge from the rain or at least hunkered down to lessen its effect on them. We saw no signs of life, not even a bird. The silence was deafening, almost eerie. Rick suggested we stop and take a breather at the same location we'd taken a break the day before. He recommended I make a nature call, if necessary. I didn't feel as though I needed to go, but knowing I wouldn't get another chance any time soon, I took his advice. I walked down the path and crouched next to the tree at the exact same spot I'd used previously. I knew this to be true because beside the tree lay the wad of biodegradable tissue I'd used the previous day, and the nearby pile of bear poop was even more pungent.

With my back against the tree, I glanced over at the bear scat, which almost looked, and smelled, like a fresh new deposit because of the rain and lingering moisture in the air. Then I noticed something protruding from the dung pile. After I completed my business, which didn't amount to much, I walked toward the scat to get a closer look.

When I recognized the object I was flabbergasted. I'd have peed my pants had I not just emptied my bladder. Protruding from the top of the pile of bear dung was the gold bracelet Bea had been wearing the first time I met her. The very piece of jewelry we'd just been discussing before Rick arrived less than an hour earlier. Leaving the bracelet undisturbed, I yanked up my breeches and sprinted back to get the men.

Scrutinizing the scene, Rick and Rip were unsure how to proceed. Rip feared if he placed a call to the police department or county sheriff, he'd once again be told to go to the campground's clubhouse and play bingo with some other old fogeys. So he recommended that Rick call and notify the lead detective of our findings.

Rick appeared hesitant to call the authorities. "I guess this is proof she was at least partially eaten by a bear. Huh?"

"I guess," Rip replied mechanically, his thoughts obviously elsewhere.

"Her bracelet must have passed through the bear's digestive system, and been deposited in that scat," Rick continued. "This makes me even more convinced it was an accidental bear attack, not the work of a killer."

"Not necessarily, Rick," Rip said, suddenly realizing what Rick was assuming. "Whether she'd initially been killed by a bear or a human, if a scavenging bear gnawed on her body, the bracelet would have ultimately ended up in the same place."

"Oh, yeah. I guess you're right." Rick seemed disappointed by Rip's reasoning.

The thing I couldn't understand was that I was 99.9 percent sure the bracelet had not been there the previous day. Granted, my vision wasn't flawless. But I couldn't have missed the bracelet from no more than ten feet away. I'd stared at the pile of bear poop the entire time I was relieving myself as if afraid it'd come to life and attack me. Not to mention, the clouds hadn't set in until earlier that morning. The sun was bright yesterday and would have been glinting off the gold, as well as the solitaire diamond between the smaller emeralds. The diamond that represented Bea's April birthstone was large and clear, a real sparkler.

The diamond! Where is the diamond? I wondered. The emeralds were intact, I noted, but the diamond was gone. Could the diamond have been dislodged from its setting during the initial attack, or inside the bear's colon where it might have ended up in a different pile of scat? It didn't seem likely to me.

I pointed out the missing gem to the men. The way the bracelet was stuck in the scat, it was difficult to tell the impressive diamond that had originally been mounted between the two smaller gems was no longer there. I'd been so amazed by its size and clarity that I remembered the solitaire vividly.

Rip looked at the bracelet closer without touching it. "It looks to me as if the diamond was pried out of its setting with a pocket knife or some other small tool. My guess is, if Bea was killed by a human, that person is in possession of the diamond. The way you described it, Rapella, it's a valuable gem. For that matter, it's not beyond the realm of possibility that the diamond's value was what had prompted someone to kill Bea. There's a good chance, if my theory is correct, it's already been hocked. When the detectives arrive, we'll bring it to their attention. They can check with all the nearby pawn shops. If they find the diamond, the individual who brought it in was most likely captured on the store's security video. An employee at the shop might have even known or recognized the person. At the very least, a diamond of that magnitude would be remarkable enough in a small town like Buffalo that whichever pawn shop clerk made the deal on it should be able to describe the customer hocking it to a sketch artist."

Rick studied Rip's face for a few seconds. "So you think she was actually murdered?"

"Well, I certainly think it's possible, buddy. Do you know anyone who despised her enough to actually murder her, or needed money badly enough to kill her for the diamond?"

"I know a number of people who didn't care for her, including me, Rip. But any of them hating her enough to take her life? I don't think so. As far as someone needing money badly enough to kill her, I'm not quite as certain." After he finished speaking, Rick became quiet and pensive. He appeared to be musing over the fact that even the seasoned lawman was not convinced his former sister-in-law's death was due to an animal encounter gone bad. Really, really bad. Either that, or the ranger was deliberating about whether or not to tell us about someone he knew who might be desperate enough for money to kill for it. I decided not to press him on the matter. Not yet, anyway.

Knowing it'd take a while for the investigators to arrive on the scene, we decided to go remove the memory card from the game camera, upload any images it captured on the iPad I'd brought with me, and ensure the camera was ready to operate again. There turned out to be only twelve images on the memory card, and none of them were of any substance.

Afterward, we tromped through the marshy field and waited for the investigators to arrive on the same outcropping where we'd first seen the ranger. It was the most logical place to meet. From there, Rick could lead the officers to the pile of bear scat so they could process the scene.

Rick encouraged us to wait on the other side of the mucky valley so we wouldn't ruin our footwear, but I think we both felt more comfortable in the company of the experienced ranger, even though only one of us would admit it. Rip is what you'd call a man's man. A testosterone-driven man like him doesn't ever own up to fear. Instead they lie through their teeth to preserve their manhood, just as Rip did then.

"I'd like to tag along," Rip said. "I really need the exercise, and you don't get a physique like mine without working at it. On the other hand, I don't feel comfortable leaving Rapella here alone."

I saw through that story like I'd been peering into space through the Hubble telescope. Being responsible for my husband's "man card" being revoked seemed kind of heartless to me, though, so I said, "Actually, I need the exercise, too. I'm getting out of shape by not walking as much as I used to. Let's all go."

After the detectives arrived and were led to the scene, one of them barked out orders to a younger cop. "Get the photos taken, then bag up some bear crap, Bill."

Rip leaned over toward the fellow named Bill, and grinned. "Welcome to the police force, son. You must be the rookie in the group."

"Gee, was it that obvious? I can hardly wait until I have enough seniority to order some new recruit to 'bag up some bear crap'." Everyone laughed except Bill, who donned latex gloves and tried not to gag as he reached deep into the soggy pile to withdraw a healthy sample for the crime lab.

I told nobody about being certain the bracelet wasn't sticking out of the nearly dried up excrement the previous day. For one thing, I was trying to chew on the significance of that matter myself. And for another, it's hard for a woman to retain any dignity whatsoever when she has to announce to a group of men that she's pretty sure the bracelet wasn't present in the bear poop when she took a leak in the same spot the day before.

I did discuss it with Rip in the truck while driving to the ball field. He said he thought we should keep it under our hats for the time being. What he really thought, I'd bet, was, "Rapella's bat-crap crazy! Of course the bracelet was there yesterday. It's her over-active imagination at work again. How in the world could a bracelet end up in bear scat by itself?"

It was that last question I visualized him thinking that bothered me. It *couldn't* end up there by itself. Someone had to place the bracelet in the scat pile in the interim between our two visits to the site. But why? And, more importantly, who? I knew I wasn't bat-crap crazy, but convincing anyone else of that was not going to be easy.

CHAPTER 23

We missed the first three innings of Willie's game due to the time it took for the detectives to arrive and process the scene. When we arrived, the Buffalo boys were behind with one run to Gillette's two. The opposing team outscored them through the next five innings and at the top of the ninth, it was eight to four in favor of Gillette.

The lead-off batter managed to place a base hit over the third baseman's head for a single, and the next batter laid down the perfect bunt to move him to second base and outrun the throw to first. With runners on first and second, the enthusiasm in the bleachers grew intense. The clean-up batter, a solidly-built boy named Chad, struck out on three straight pitches to the dismay of the crowd, and the following batter was hit by a pitch, loading the bases.

Now the Buffalo crowd was buzzing with anticipation. Their cheering turned to silence when Willie's best friend, Anthony, was called out on a pop-up to the pitcher. As one, every fan on both sides held their breaths. Cora was as still as a pillar of salt, more nervous than her son, whose turn it was to bat.

"You can do it, Willie!" Rip hollered. Willie looked over to the three of us and flashed a confident smile.

Willie swung and missed two straight-down-the-pike pitches. He then took three straight balls just outside the strike zone and fended off a third strike with a foul ball into the crowd. Facing a full count, Willie stepped away from the plate. He took a couple of practice swings and waited for his nerves to calm down before facing the Gillette pitcher again.

As if in slow motion, the pitcher wound up for the pitch, released it, and with all the onlookers standing on their feet cheering, Willie swung with all the power he could muster. Making solid contact with the bat, the ball sailed over the center fielder's head, cleared the fence by twenty feet, and rolled out of sight.

With his fist pumping, Willie cleared the bases behind the other three base runners. It was a game-changing grand slam. He'd put his team in contention for the win by tying the score. Gillette had the last at-bat, leaving the Buffalo boys three outs away from extra innings and a good chance of becoming the league champions. "After all," Rip said optimistically, "they'll have momentum on their side going into extra innings."

Unfortunately, the lead-off batter for the Gillette team hit the first pitch for a line drive, clearing the left-field fence by mere inches for a walk-off home run, and leading his team to a nine to eight victory over Buffalo, as well as the conference championship.

Following the game, Willie's face was long and his head hung low. He fought off the urge to cry, not wanting to look like a baby in front of his teammates, two of whom were already sobbing. He blamed himself for hitting into a double play in the third inning. Rip spoke to his great-nephew man to man, reminding him it was just a game and telling him the Buffalo boys should be proud of how well they'd played all season just to earn the right to play in the championship game.

"Your grand slam was the most exciting play in the game. Maybe even in the entire tournament," Rip said. "In my day, it was every boy's dream to step up to the plate in the ninth inning with two out and a full count. And then, under intense pressure, to knock the ball out of the park for a grand slam. With the entire Buffalo crowd on their feet and screaming, you did exactly that, son. No one can ever take that moment, or that feeling of accomplishment, away from you."

"Yeah, I guess you're right. That really was a once-in-a-lifetime kind of moment, wasn't it?" Willie's grin stretched from one ear to the other, his spirits instantly lifted by his uncle's words.

"I seriously doubt it was a once-in-a-lifetime moment for you, son. To be honest, Willie, I believe it was just one of many moments like that in your ball-playing future. Now let's go celebrate that grand slam at the ice cream shop. I want to see if we can all finish a cone before that baseball you pounded comes to a rest just this side of the Montana border. Because it was still picking up steam when it flew over the parking lot, heading north toward downtown at an amazing clip."

Willie laughed, punched my husband in the shoulder. "You're nuts, Uncle Rip!"

At the ice cream shop, we all chatted while Rip, Cora and I enjoyed our single-dip cones. Willie, a growing boy who, like a hummingbird, could eat twice his weight in food daily and not pack a spare ounce on his slim frame, was snarfing down a triple-decker. He was trying not to miss out on a single drop of it, but it appeared to be a losing effort. The bottom dip was melting faster than he could consume the top two.

Every time Willie accompanied his mother to our place, I tried to empty the entire contents of the fridge into him, hoping to put a little more meat on his bones. That, too, appeared to be a losing effort. When Willie asked if he could order a cheeseburger after he finished his cone, Rip just shrugged. "Go for it, kid! That ball you clobbered has probably just sailed past Sheridan, so we still have lots of time to get out of here before it comes to a stop."

Willie knew his uncle was being facetious, but he welcomed the praise all the same. After Willie polished off his cheeseburger, we lingered at the shop discussing the topic of the bear poachers the forest service was trying to nab. Willie, who was always conjuring up a scheme of some kind, came up with a very intriguing idea. I couldn't wait to call Ranger Rick and summon him back to our trailer. But first we had to stop by the Beaufonts' home to borrow the bear rug that lay in front of the fireplace hearth in Dirk's "man cave" downstairs.

I was excited about putting Willie's suggestion into place. It was at that moment something occurred to me. My great-nephew would make a good detective when he grew up, if his dream to become a renowned classic car restorer or a professional ball player didn't work out.

Rick found Willie's idea more promising than anything else we could come up with. He told us he'd pick us up in a half-hour, and together we'd ride back to the spot where we'd met up with the detectives earlier in the day. From the vantage point atop the outcropping, we could better put Willie's inspiration into action.

Rick arrived in twenty minutes and we headed toward our desired location. After we stopped and exited the vehicle, Rick and Rip removed the confiscated bear trap from a trailer being towed behind the Jeep. It was coated with dried blood. Rick explained it was from the unidentified snared animal he'd told us about earlier. It had escaped the trap, but not before losing a great deal of blood. Together, the two men lugged the fifty pound trap back to the spot where Rick had discovered and confiscated it earlier that morning. I trailed behind them with Dirk's bear rug, which wasn't all that lightweight either.

It was easy to find the trap's previous location, as the blood was still on the ground. By the amount of blood lost, I couldn't imagine any creature surviving the incident. Certainly nothing small, like a raccoon or marmot, could spill that much blood and live to tell about it—tell other coons or marmots about their near-death experience with the trap, that is.

The rain had stopped a couple of hours before Willie's ball game and the field had been dried out so the championship game could commence. But the valley, already marshy, was difficult to traverse after being saturated with moisture. Rick agreed with Willie that the odds of the poachers trudging through the forest into the even sloppier valley that day were slim. Chances were, they'd opt to wait until the following morning to check the trap, giving the ground a little extra time to dry out. The fact there were no existing footprints in the muck when we arrived seemed to confirm the notion.

As Willie had suggested, we placed the trap in its former location, but didn't arm it so as to be sure no other animal could be injured in its powerful steel jaws. The steel trap was designed to trap a poacher now, rather than a bear. Not literally, of course.

Rick gathered up some brush and piled it next to the trap before placing the rug over it. The brush gave the rug "body" so it looked like a complete bear, not just a pelt. He arranged the pelt to look as if a bear had been immobilized by the trap. Then, when the trapper approached what he thought was a real bear, the camera's sensor would be triggered and snap photos of the guilty party. Or, at least, that was the plan we'd set into motion.

Before we left, I picked up a sycamore leaf that had been kept dry by a layer of brush the rangers had moved aside earlier that morning. I folded the leaf and placed it in my back pocket. We lumbered through the sludge to retrieve the critter cam from where we'd set it up earlier, then relocated it to a tree about twenty-five feet from the disarmed trap. Rip camouflaged it with sagebrush before activating it.

Now all we had to do was sit back and wait for our prey to walk into our trap. And, lo and behold, the next morning, as Willie had predicted, they did just that!

CHAPTER 24

Once again we accompanied Rick out into the forest. It was early afternoon the following day, and we had hopes the poachers had checked their trap, or traps, earlier in the day. I knew I was risking the poacher discovering my camera and removing it, and effectively eliminating any evidence of their wrongdoing that might have been captured in photos. But it had been well hidden from view, and I truly didn't give a hoot if my camera was stolen. I'd have paid five times that much for an incriminating image of the guilty party.

As we followed the path, which by then we knew by heart, I asked Rick what a person had to gain by poaching bears. He explained that it was strictly for monetary gain.

"Seriously?" I asked. "How much dough could someone get from a single bear? Surely the pelt, or even the meat, doesn't bring in enough money to make it worth the effort."

"The poacher, or poachers, probably deal in black market trading of viscera, or internal organs, along with selling the pelt and meat."

"I don't understand, Rick. I can see why the pelt and meat might bring in a little money. But who'd want to buy a bear's kidneys or liver?" I asked. "Can they somehow be utilized in human organ transplants?"

"No. That's not the reason behind the demand. It's not a bear's kidneys or liver the buyers are interested in. They might get a thousand or two off the pelt and meat, but they can earn a greater amount from harvesting their gallbladders. Three or four thousand bucks per gallbladder, in fact. Have you heard about the medicinal benefits derived from rhinoceros horns?"

"Sure. It's horrific, and it's resulted in near distinction of the animal," I replied. "But I've heard it's questionable whether or not the substance found in the rhino horns has any actual medicinal benefit."

"You're exactly right. But as long as people hold the belief that it does have medicinal value, the animals will continue to be slaughtered for their horns. The bear population has a similar issue to contend with. The bile from a bear's gallbladder contains high concentrates of urosdeoxycholic acid, which is thought to be effective in treating gallstones, cirrhosis and other diseases. It's also believed to help prevent colon cancer by inhibiting the growth of tumors. Its healing power has created a great demand for the substance in Asia, where it's still legal in some areas to farm bears for the bile from their gallbladders. It's a cruel, torturous process for the animal that conservationists are trying to put an end to. However, due to supply and demand, it sells for a substantial amount in countries that have made the entire industry illegal, such as Vietnam."

As we huddled together so we could all view the images simultaneously, I thought about what Rick had said. The idea of torturing an animal for financial gain made me want to catch these poachers even more fervently, and maybe poke their eyes out with a bear claw, as well.

As we scanned through the handful of images, the men became more and more discouraged with each photo they scrutinized. It'd become apparent the poachers had realized our "bait" was a rug, rather than a fully functioning bear, just as they had entered the camera's field of vision. Once they'd figured out it was a ruse, they hastily departed without approaching the trap.

"Most likely, they thought the authorities had eyes on them even as they retreated," Rick pointed out. "Anticipating an ambush, they'd probably never even considered searching for something like a camera."

One photo showed the rim of a light blue ball cap, which narrowed our field of suspects down to about a zillion and nine individuals. The next photo was of a denim-covered leg with a hard-to-distinguish white object apparently dangling from the subject's hand. None of the other six or seven images captured anything of consequence. After the images had been uploaded to the tablet I'd brought along, Rip absentmindedly put the memory card back into the camera as we all were studying the images, hoping to find more damning evidence.

"Well, that was a foiled effort," Rip finally said. "And now that they're on to us, they'll probably leave the area and move on to another place to resume their poaching efforts. We may have blown our only chance to catch them."

"Gosh damn it!" Rick exclaimed, for once not taking the time to apologize for his foul language. "I agree, Rip. They've probably already hightailed it out of town. I don't think there's anything we can do now to stop them."

"Not so fast, boys. I think there might be a way to stop them," I said.

I was hoping my suspicions could be verified. There was one question that had been bothering me. Why would Bea go for her habitual hike that fateful morning without her gun for protection? Wouldn't that be the last thing she'd forget after a close brush with death during her previous cougar encounter?

"Just for kicks, let's fan out and scour the area within about a fifteen-foot diameter of the trap before we leave," I said.

"Why?" Both men spoke in unison, with identical puzzled expressions.

"Just humor me and do it. I'll explain later."

Both men appeared hesitant about my request, but

scoured the area as I'd suggested. After ten minutes or so, Rip found a gun buried in the mud about twelve feet from the trap. He was clearly puzzled as he asked, "Whose gun do you think this is?"

"That gun belongs to our victim, and convinces me that the bear poacher is the same individual who's responsible for Bea's death. Now we can get the heck out of this quagmire and go request an audience with Sheriff Wright."

"Huh?" Rip asked. "What are you talking about? For starters, I don't want to speak to that battleaxe again unless I can put that gun in the poacher's—and/or killer's—hands without a shadow of a doubt about who it belongs to."

"I think we can!" Trying not to sound too smug and full of myself, I explained my hypothesis and the reasons behind it. They both agreed my deduction was most likely correct. So the three of us returned to the Jeep and headed straight for the Buffalo Police Station.

CHAPTER 25

In our excitement to take our theory to the police station, we collected Dirk's bear rug, but forgot to pick up my game camera. I was relieved when Rick told us he planned to return for the trap the following day, anyway. "I'll drop your camera off tomorrow on my way back to the office."

When we arrived at the police station, we were directed to Sheriff Wright's office. Buffalo is the county seat of Johnson County, and her office was in the same building on Fort Street as the town's police department.

After we arrived at the police station, we were seated in Sheriff Wright's office. She didn't appear particularly delighted to see us. I thanked her for letting us have a word with her, and said, "Your poachers are named John and Barb Harris, who use the guise of being animal activists to explain their actual objective of trapping bears to exploit. I will show you the proof in a minute. I also believe these same two individuals are responsible for killing Bea Whetstone, and I'll show you how I reached that conclusion, as well."

I felt as if I was giving a power-point demonstration to a class of criminal law students. It was an empowering sensation. Trying not to appear overly emphatic, I continued with my explanation. "The first time I laid eyes on the couple, they were forcefully snatching a gun out of Bea's hands. She'd just killed a mama bear who had wandered into the campground with her cub. Killing that bear was completely unnecessary, I might add. Everyone's impression, including mine, was that the Harrises were upset at the idea she'd hurt a defenseless animal who was protecting her young from harm. However, I now believe they were upset that Bea brought down a bear they'd been tracking themselves and were eager to capture for their own personal gain. I have no doubt that, given the opportunity, they'd have also killed the cub."

Sheriff Wright nodded, noted something on a pad of paper in front of her, and said, "Go on."

I pulled a gallon-sized Ziploc bag out of my large satchel. Inside was the gun Rip had found in the mud near the trap. "This is the gun Bea used to kill the mama bear that morning. According to Boonie, she usually took a pearl-handled Colt revolver with her on her morning hikes. And, also according to Boonie, that pearl-handled handgun was still on her chest of drawers the morning following her disappearance. However, the fact this gun with the gold-plated barrel was the weapon she'd killed the mama bear with proves she occasionally used this gun as well. I had a hunch Bea took this gun with her the morning she disappeared, and that's what prompted me to ask the guys to search the boggy area around the bloody trap this afternoon."

"Are you one-hundred percent positive that's the same gun she killed the bear with?" Sheriff Wright asked.

"I could never be one-hundred percent certain of anything. But I'd be willing to bet my life on it. I distinctly remember the gun she used that day. The Colt revolver had a silver handle with a gold-plated barrel instead of a pearl handle. Exactly like this gun. The sun was glinting off the barrel, which is why I looked it over so carefully. I'd never seen a gun with a gold barrel like this one before." As I spoke, I handed the bagged gun to the sheriff, who appraised it intently.

"Interesting," the sheriff said. She then turned the bagged gun over to study the other side. I waited until she was done to continue.

"The second time I crossed paths with Barb Harris was in the laundry room at the campground owned by Bea and Boonie Whetstone. She was there when I arrived with my laundry. I remember she was wearing a light blue visor that day." I brought up one of the images and sat the iPad down in front of the sheriff before continuing. I briefly explained the ploy we'd used to bring out the poachers. "I noticed this image we captured today matches Barb's visor perfectly. Just like in this photo, the visor she wore that day in the laundry room had a stained area that looks like a print from a muddy, or even bloody, finger as she was adjusting the visor on her head. See?" I pointed to the image of the visor's bill on the iPad's screen.

"Are you absolutely certain you saw this exact stain on Harris's visor that day?" Sheriff Wright appeared hopeful, but skeptical at the same time.

"Like I said before, I can't be absolutely certain about anything. But I remember being surprised that a woman who had exhibited fastidious OCD-like mannerisms, as Barb did that day in the laundry room, would not be compelled to remove this stain on her visor by any means necessary, or wear another visor in its place. Particularly after she used nearly half a bottle of stain remover on the sleeves of one of John's shirts. Now that I think about it, the stains on his shirt were probably made by Bea's blood, and the same could well hold true for the small blood-drop sized stain on Barb's visor."

When she made no reply, I continued. "I believe now that my husband and I also crossed paths with the pair in the forest one day while we were trying to set up a game camera. I'm convinced now that they were scoping out a location to place one of their traps. We didn't see them, but heard a few words they'd spoken from a short distance away. The male voice, John Harris's I'm sure, very clearly said, 'I don't like the location. Too close to the campground'."

"How can you be certain it was Mr. Harris's voice?" The sheriff was obviously intent on disproving my theory, but I realized she couldn't arrest the pair without solid proof of culpability.

"One day I stopped by their RV to see if I could question them about any involvement they might have had in Bea's death, and—"

"You did what?" Jaclyn Wright appeared aghast, and Rip looked at me like I'd just dropped my drawers and mooned the sheriff.

I ignored both of their reactions and forged ahead with my explanation. "And when John spoke that day, I recognized his voice but couldn't recall where I'd heard it before. It came to me this afternoon as we were viewing the images my game camera captured."

"That's intriguing," the sheriff said with a nod. "But I need more evidence."

Ignoring her cynicism, I kept talking as if she'd never spoken. "That morning in the woods, I also heard what sounded like the word 'jaw' as in the clamping part of the trapping apparatus, and an even harder to decipher word that sounded like 'tap'. I now believe the word she'd said was 'trap'. You see, it was a woman's voice we heard then, and high-pitched like Barb's. The only word I understood explicitly was 'valley', as in where they seemed to prefer to place their traps." I paused to let the significance of the overheard words sink in.

"Is that it?" Sheriff Wright asked, clearly unconvinced.

"Of course not," I replied. I'm sure I sounded irritated with the sheriff, because I was and couldn't disguise my annoyance. "In the laundry room, she and I discussed her employment as an animal activist working to prevent the extinction of various species. She was very knowledgeable about various species of wildlife and the efforts to protect them, as was evidenced by her comments on whooping cranes, which winter near our hometown in south Texas. One location she and John had recently been to, she told me, was Asia. She said their mission there was to study the decline in the black bear population in the region, which I now believe was due to the demand for bear bile."

"Bear bile?" Sheriff Wright looked perplexed. Because I couldn't remember the exact details, I had Rick explain the powerful healing qualities of the substance before I picked up where I'd left off.

"My guess is their income from working on behalf of wildlife everywhere, paled when compared to what they could make by trapping and selling the bears' gallbladders to the black market for the production of pharmaceutical products. I truly believe they were passionate about their work until greed reared its ugly head. I imagine they'd become frustrated too. It probably seemed to them as if they were whacking moles in their efforts to prevent others from killing bears only for their gallbladders. And that's when I think they decided to cross over to the dark side and become predators of the animal instead of their protectors. After all, from the experience they'd had tracking bears for their research, they surely felt confident they'd be able to locate many bears and obtain a lot of the valuable substance."

"That makes sense. But it's still not enough evidence to arrest them on poaching charges, much less murder."

"Cool your jets, sister. I'm not finished yet."

The sheriff looked as if I'd slapped her. I knew she considered throwing us all out of her office, but her curiosity and desire to get to the bottom of both issues took precedent. "All right, Mrs. Ripple. But get to the point before my patience wears out."

"Okay, okay," I said. I picked the iPad from her desk, brought up another image, and laid it back down in the same place. Rick had already explained the connection between bear bile and the black marketing of the substance in Asia. So, to connect the dots, I now gave a vague explanation of how I'd captured a photo of the inside of the couple's Fifth Wheel trailer. I didn't want to recite unnecessary details and give Rip's heart a jolt it might not survive.

Then I leaned over the desk to enlarge the image on the screen with my fingers. "This small white cooler seen here in this image was inside the couple's trailer. At first I assumed it was used to carry water or other beverages as they completed their studies in the forest. But, as I close in on it, you can clearly see the label, which has Chinese characters on it. Naturally, with so many of the products we purchase in the United States having been manufactured in China, I hadn't initially considered this unusual. Ranger Rick is now convinced the cooler was intended to be used as a container in which to ship the frozen gallbladders overseas to an Asian dealer. Rip was present in the campground's office when John Harris asked where a shipping facility could be found, supposedly to ship care packages to veterans stationed overseas."

"I see," the sheriff said.

"Now I will show you a photo captured this morning in the field. Here you see the bear rug we arranged on the trap that we used to bait the poachers. Over in the corner of the picture is the leg of a person dressed in blue jeans, who was carrying a container that matches the one I photographed in their trailer. As I close in on the container, you can see it's a small cooler with the identical Chinese marking. Unfortunately, that's as far as they got before realizing the bear was a prop, placed on their trap to trick them. They turned and fled at that point, so we weren't able to get any more incriminating photos."

"I'm listening," the sheriff said with a little more enthusiasm. "Now you have my attention. This is powerful evidence that the Harris couple is behind the poaching, but what makes you think they had anything to do with Bea Whetstone's death? I can't seem to connect the dots."

"Then let me connect them for you," I replied smugly. "We heard the medical examiner determined that Bea's wrist and ankle had been injured prior to her death. Is that correct?"

"Yes. But what does that have to do with anything?" Sheriff Wright asked.

"Rick was telling us about he and some fellow rangers discovering this trap earlier this morning. He said it was so well-concealed that one of the rangers stepped into it, which could have caused great harm to the ranger's foot and ankle if not for the fact it'd already been tripped by an animal that had been snared and ultimately managed to escape the trap's powerful jaws. I now believe that the creature who was inadvertently snared was none other than Bea Whetstone."

"Seriously?" The sheriff's dubious response made it obvious she was not going to be easy to convince the poaching couple were the killers of not only bears, but a human being. But I wasn't finished with my theory yet.

"Yes. Seriously. When you and the investigating team came to the campground the day following Bea's disappearance, I overheard Boonie say that Bea always wore rubber boots when she hiked so she could meander about in the marshy valley. I actually have a video of that discussion on my phone if you'd like to review it."

At this point, the sheriff didn't even look surprised I had taped their conversation. She shook her head, and said, "I remember that remark. But could you send that video to this phone number?"

After she scribbled the number on a post-it note and handed it to me, Rick spoke up to say, "I was the one who discovered Bea's body during a search, and can verify she had boots on that day. But they were no match for the strength of the trapping apparatus."

"Hmm." The sheriff was leaning forward in her seat now, just as anxious to hear the rest of my story as I was to tell it.

"This made me wonder if perhaps, while out on her daily morning hike through the forest, Bea accidentally stepped into the trap, triggering it and causing the sharp, jagged jaws to clamp down on her ankle. Despite the rubber boots, those powerful jaws could easily have caused the damage to her ankle that the medical examiner determined had occurred prior to her death. While I was snapping the photo I showed you of the Styrofoam cooler inside the trailer, I took a tumble and sprained my right wrist when I tried to break my fall. That could explain Bea's wrist injury. It was also her right hand, and I don't know that Bea was right-handed, but due to the fact only four percent of people are left-handed, I'd say the odds are very good."

I looked up as the sheriff wrote something on her notepad. She caught my eye, nodded and smiled. It was the first genuine smile I'd seen on her typically stoic face. "Yes, I'm one of those oddball lefties."

I was hoping the sheriff was far enough away she didn't hear what I heard Rip mumble under his breath, which was, "You got the oddball part right!"

Just in case she did have acute hearing, I quickly continued. "Unfortunately, because I was so shocked by the shooting, I really can't recall which hand she held her gun in when she killed the mama bear."

"Not important. Go on." The sheriff appeared to be putty in my hand now.

"So, anyway, if John and Barb found the woman snared in the trap, they had two options to choose from. One, they could free her from the trap and seek medical attention for her wounds. Or two, they could kill her, drag her body to another location in the woods, and hope no one ever put two and two together. As I did," I couldn't resist adding. "A large man like John Harris would have no trouble snapping her neck with one quick twist."

"There was no evidence of a broken neck during the autopsy," Sheriff Wright said. There was a definite hint of disappointment in her tone.

"Okay, but I'm sure there are other ways the pair could have killed Bea. So, as I was saying, the couple had two options. Option one, freeing her, would be paramount to turning themselves into the authorities. They'd have been arrested and ordered to stand trial in front of a jury of their peers, as you in the justice system like to say. And the pair had to realize they'd almost certainly face severe punishment. Rick said they'd get serious prison time and their lives would be adversely affected forever."

"The ranger's correct," the sheriff agreed. "Their atrocious actions were deplorable. And I'll recommend that the judge throw the book at them."

"Absolutely!" I exclaimed in response. "So, given the consequences of option one, my guess is they chose the other option and killed her. Then they dragged Bea's body to where Rick discovered it, leaving her remains to the carnivorous predators to devour."

"That's all well and good, but it's only a supposition. We have no way to prove that theory." Sheriff Wright appeared anxious to find a way to tie the cases together.

"I think there is," I told her. "No doubt you've seen the bracelet we discovered in a pile of bear scat this morning. I guarantee you that bracelet did not travel through the digestion system of the animal who left the dung pile. I took a nature call in the identical spot, not ten feet from that very pile of scat yesterday and then again this morning. At some point between those two occasions, that bracelet, which Boonie can confirm belonged to his wife, was intentionally placed in the scat. Bea had informed me earlier that her grandmother had given it to her to wear as a talisman. Granny promised her it would bring her good luck, Bea said."

"Granny lied," Rip muttered.

"And the missing diamond?" Not surprisingly, the sheriff ignored her fellow sheriff's sarcasm.

"This part is only speculation, but we believe that because of its value, the impressive gem was pried out of the bracelet before it was used in hopes of distracting the detectives when they discovered it sticking out of the scat. I'm sure the Harrises thought the investigators would assume the mauling by the bear had dislodged the gem, or the acid in the animal's digestive tract had eaten away at the mount just enough to loosen it. You might want to have someone in your department check with any local pawn shops for the missing diamond."

"I definitely will." Sheriff Wright scribbled furiously on her notepad. "But I don't see any reasoning behind placing the bracelet in the scat."

"Not only would this action serve to potentially throw the authorities off-track, it'd also probably give John and Barb long enough to pack up and move on. I'm sure they already thought the authorities were closing in on them. You see, I kind of told Barb the detectives had determined it was definitely a homicide, and also that Rip and I were involved in an investigation of our own."

"You were involved in what?" The sheriff stood up and pointed to Rip. "I specifically told you to stay out of it. You may have been the sheriff in some Podunk county in Texas that—"

"That what?" Rip broke in. He was standing up now, pointing at the sheriff as he yelled at her. "That had a population three times that of Johnson County, Wyoming?"

I waved my hands before an all-out confrontation erupted between the two sheriffs. "Let's keep to the subject. Please hear me out, Sheriff Wright. And Rip, please calm down and have a seat."

"Oh, all right. Finish your story and make it quick," Sheriff Wright said as Rip reluctantly sat back down. Wisps of steam seemed to be escaping the sheriff's ears and floating around her face, distorting the scowl on her face. Of course, that might have just been my imagination because of my fervent desire to convince the sheriff of John and Barb's guilt. The sheriff tapped the tip of her pen on her desk several times before speaking again. "I still don't see how you think you can positively tie the bracelet in the bear poop incident to the Harris couple."

Bracelet in the bear poop? I thought. *There could be a country song in there somewhere just waiting to be written.* I waited for the sheriff to settle back down and then continued with my theory.

"The bracelet was removed from the dung by a rookie detective wearing latex gloves and then placed in a plastic bag to keep from destroying any trace evidence. If I'm correct, and I believe I am, the last person to touch that bracelet was either John or Barb Harris. The bracelet has an unusually wide band that consists predominantly of smooth gold. If a fingerprint matching one or both of the Harrises can be taken off the bracelet, I think you'd have enough evidence to arrest the pair. Don't you?"

"Perhaps. Is there anything else?"

"Yes. I'm sure Boonie can confirm this revolver with a gold-plated barrel belonged to his wife. I had Rick and Rip search for a weapon in the trap's vicinity because I couldn't imagine Bea not having some form of protection with her after her close encounter with a cougar. I now wonder if that close call might have prompted her lack of hesitancy when she killed that bear in the campground. I know after Rip and I came face to face with a mama bear and three cubs, I was much jumpier on subsequent treks through the forest."

"And who wouldn't be?" The sheriff said in agreement. "Please continue."

"When Bea stepped into the trap, she most likely flung this gun out of her hand so she could use her dominate hand to brace her fall. Since the gun was buried in the muck in that marshy valley, and neither the Harrises nor the rangers knew to look for one, it was still lying where it'd landed when it flew out of Bea's hand. I have a hunch only the victim's fingerprints will be found on the gun."

"Hmm," the sheriff muttered as if in deep thought.

"One last thing," I said, reaching into my pocket for the sycamore leaf I'd placed in there earlier. "When the rangers discovered the trap this morning, it was covered in blood. They naturally assumed it was from the animal, or animals, the poachers had previously snared. I think if you have the blood tested on this leaf that I found right next to the trap, you'll find out it belonged to Bea Whetstone."

The sheriff thought for a moment. Then, without replying, she made a call to request the bagged bracelet be brought to her from the evidence locker. She then pressed a button on her intercom. "Millie, send someone from the crime lab to my office with a fingerprint dusting kit."

A timid voice could be heard over the speaker. The woman started to say something like, "I'll take care of it after I finish handling some other pressing matters." But Millie got cut off by the brash sheriff, who practically growled into the microphone, "I want it yesterday!"

"Yes, ma'am. I'll get right on it!"

"I'm almost certain I can pull a decent enough print off this bracelet to run it through IAFIS," the crime lab technician said about twenty-five minutes later. Having been married to a career law enforcement officer, I knew he was referring to the largest criminal fingerprint database in the world.

"What if they've never been arrested before and aren't in the system?" I asked. I didn't want a technical detail like that to throw a monkey wrench in my theory.

The sheriff replied to my inquiry while looking straight into my eyes. "Don't worry, we'll handle it. We'll obtain the couple's fingerprints one way or the other. We've known it was a homicide all along, but have been keeping the details of the case under wraps. We wanted to prevent the media from insinuating a serial killer might be on the loose and terrifying everyone in the county when there was nothing to suggest that was the case. We also thought if we put it out there that we were convinced the woman's death was due to an animal attack, the real perpetrator wouldn't feel as pressured to immediately cover their tracks."

I heard Rip whisper to Rick behind me, "What'd she just say about a purple tater?"

I shushed my husband, and directed my attention back to the sheriff, as she continued. "We were hoping some clue would pop up that'd lead us to the killer, or in this case, killers."

Rip couldn't resist needling the sheriff. " Is that why you blew off my suggestion to study a couple of images we captured earlier on the motion-sensing camera?"

"Sorry about that." The sheriff looked directly at Rip and had the decency to look ashamed. Judging by Rip's smug expression, it was obvious her apology was a tad bit of redemption for him.

"Were you looking at John and Barb Harris as potential suspects?" Rip asked.

"No." Sheriff Wright appeared uneasy. It was clear that admitting to failure was not an easy pill for her to swallow. "To be honest, we were looking at the husband and trying to build a case around him. Unsuccessfully, I might add. Our attention then shifted to a local lady who was believed to be involved with the husband prior to his wife's murder."

"Janelle Tyson-Simms?" I asked.

"You knew about her, as well?" The sheriff appeared bewildered.

"Of course!"

"Hmm. All right. I guess I shouldn't be surprised to hear that. So, anyway, to this point John and Barb Harris have been flying under our radar."

"Really? They've been on our suspect list for quite a while, but—"

"Your suspect list?" The sheriff was clearly aghast by my statement. "Don't take this wrong, Mrs. Ripple. I do appreciate your efforts and the time and thought you two put into this murder case. But I'm not particularly happy that you and your husband took it upon yourselves to dabble in an official investigation without my approval. Interference by the public can often be more of a hindrance than a help. This time may turn out to be an exception to that rule. Still, don't make a habit of it. In my county, anyway."

Her praise had a double-edged sword effect. Her words of appreciation pleased me no end, while making Rip want to tear her a new one. The word "dabble" had clearly put a big, fat burr under his saddle.

The sheriff, oblivious to the daggers being cast her way from Rip's eyes, continued, "I'm sending the leaf to the crime lab for testing, as well as the bracelet. I'm also sending a couple of squad cars to the RV park to question the Harris couple. We'll fingerprint them and try to verify any alibis they might provide. My guess is that if they are guilty of one or both crimes, they've flown the coop already. I sincerely hope your theory is correct, Mrs. Ripple, and I am fairly confident now that it is. You've been able to provide a lot of incriminating evidence. And I must say, I'd really like to put this case to bed."

Jaclyn Wright sighed. The fact we'd been more successful in our investigation than her entire team of "competent" detectives had in theirs seemed to take the wind out of the sheriff's sails. But I was thrilled beyond words at her remarks. I could already visualize myself carving another notch in my imaginary belt. I was proving to be quite adept at solving cases, if I must say so myself.

I'd missed my calling, I thought. I briefly wondered if my age was too advanced to hire myself out as a private detective. Better yet, a traveling gumshoe who was paid to stay in local RV parks while serving as a private eye on individual homicide cases. That'd be a more satisfying way to earn a little cash, or free rent, than selling toilet chemical and water regulators to other RVers.

After a couple more minutes of discussion, Sheriff Wright recommended we head back to Rest 'n Peace RV Park. I think she was about to say we should go to the campground's clubhouse and play bingo with some other old fogeys while her men handled the situation from here on out. However, after a quick glance at Rip, she'd thought better of it.

Instead, she said, "Thank you. I believe we can handle it from here without your assistance. But we do appreciate your help in this challenging case. If it turns out the way I suspect it will, I'll be recommending you both for a special commendations plaque from the department. And, Ranger Rick, your part in this case is appreciated as well. I'll put a bug in your supervisor's ear that your efforts are worthy of a raise or an advancement."

Rip began to say something, but I elbowed him in the ribs before he could turn down her offer. As far as I was concerned, the plaque was well deserved. We had put ourselves in danger more than once, even looking a mama bear with cubs in the eye on one occasion.

I knew that every time Rip looked at the plaque, he'd be visualizing the iron-fisted sheriff, or battleaxe, as he preferred to call her, eating a plate of perfectly seasoned crow. Regardless of his negative opinion of Sheriff Wright, I think he was placated by her next words. "Hope I didn't offend you."

That apology, as lame as it sounded, would have to do, for there were no more conciliatory remarks forthcoming. I told Rip she'd meant the comment as a plea for forgiveness, and added, "I know how much you hate to be criticized by a woman."

He gave me a pointed look. "No, big Rip! I'm used to it."

Rip chuckled at his own tongue-in-cheek humor even though I was certain the sheriff's jabs were still burning a hole in his stomach like an ulcer that wouldn't heal. But I knew the man who'd been shackled to me for the last half-century well enough to know he appreciated the sheriff's pitiful act of contrition.

"Ready to head home to the Chartreuse Caboose, my dear?" Rip asked. "I'm proud of you, you know. Figuring out the connection between the two crimes is another feather in your cap."

"And yours, too," I added.

"It was you who put the pieces together, not me. Another job well done!"

Rip whistled *Girl on Fire*, the popular Alicia Keys song, as we strolled out of the police station, hand-in-hand. I was amazed he'd even heard the song, much less was familiar with its melody. Even after fifty years together, I still learn something new about my man every day.

CHAPTER 26

When three squad cars rolled into the campground a few minutes later, they met Barb and John Harris in their truck with their fifth wheel hooked to the hitch, exiting the park through the campground's gate.

We'd returned to the park prior to the detectives' arrival and noticed the Harris's site was vacant. At the time, we didn't realize they'd pulled their rig around to the park's dump station to empty their holding tanks and fill up their fresh water tank before heading out. They were planning to do some dry camping in a remote part of the mountainous range for two or three days until they were confident the coast was clear and they could proceed to their next scheduled hunting grounds.

You'd never have known their site had been occupied except for a small white cooler they'd left on the picnic table. I imagine they'd overlooked it in their haste to get the heck out of Dodge as quickly as possible. The cooler had both Chinese and English characters written on it. After a line of intricate designs that seemed as if they'd take a day and a half to pen, it read, "Pork Cutlets. Beware of hazardous dry ice."

Pork cutlets, my behind! Horrifically harvested organs, it should have read. I was relieved to see the cooler was an exact match to the one in both of the photos my camera had captured. And also that the cooler was empty, an indication that no bear had suffered or died to fill it. The corroboration of my surmised theory was duly noted by the sheriff, who pulled up in her own Johnson County Sheriff's SUV a few minutes after the detectives.

While we'd been awaiting the police force's arrival, I also noticed John and Barb had forgotten to remove their brass water regulator from the spigot. If the detectives didn't bag it as some kind of evidence, I planned to snag it the following morning, knowing it was only a matter of time before Rip left the used over-priced regulator I'd purchased from Bea behind in a campground somewhere.

A couple of minutes later, we noticed the commotion at the gate and walked over to see what was going on. The sheriff was reciting Miranda rights as two detectives placed Barb and John in handcuffs. Afterward, the two were helped into the back of a squad car to be driven to the sheriff's office for interrogation. Then they'd be booked into to the Johnson County Detention Center at the same location on Fort Street.

Early the next morning, we were summoned to report to the sheriff's office at our earliest convenience. I was ready to go in twenty seconds. Rip, on the other hand, was hem-hawing around. He took his own sweet time to shave whiskers that hadn't even grown out yet, cut his grapefruit into precise little wedges, drink two more cups of coffee than he usually drank, and read through the paper. When he began scanning through the society pages, it became apparent to me he was deliberately making the sheriff wait. I knew he was trying to make the point he was not at her beck and call and would arrive in her office when he so chose. It was a deep-rooted, mulish trait of his, and I'd had enough of it.

"Come on, Rip! I know what you're doing, and you're just making a horse's behind out of yourself. I'm anxious to hear what Sheriff Wright has to say, and I'm tired of waiting on you. If you really need to know who married who in Buffalo last week, the paper will still be here when we get back."

It was an hour later when we walked into the police station. It had taken Rip a good ten minutes to decide whether to wear his blue shirt or his gray shirt. Finally, I picked up the gray shirt and hurled it at him. "Put the blasted thing on before I leave without you!"

Sheriff Wright ushered us into her office, but not before turning the table on Rip's ploy to make her wait on him. I almost applauded when she said, "If it took me that long to get ready to leave the house, I'd never get anything done. But then, you probably didn't have nearly as much to do when you were a sheriff and could stroll in to work any old time you felt like it."

The expression on Rip's face after her cutting remark was priceless. The sheriff asked us to make ourselves comfortable and then told us she wanted to let us know John and Barb Harris had been charged with manslaughter in the murder of Beata Whetstone, along with numerous poaching violations. "After a couple of hours of interrogation, the couple finally admitted their guilt after all the evidence was laid out in front of them. We questioned them in separate rooms—"

"Duh," Rip cut in. I elbowed him in the ribs before he could say anything else. I didn't want to be booted out of her office before we'd heard all the details of the couple's arrest.

"Hush, Rip! Please go on, Sheriff Wright," I said, encouraging her to continue.

She glared at Rip momentarily, and then turned her attention to me. "As you correctly surmised, the pair had gone out to check their three remaining traps, upset about the loss of several others that the forest service had confiscated. When they approached the one in the valley, they found Bea snared in the trap, already deceased. The steel jaws had severed two of the three arteries that pass through the ankle; the peroneal and posterior tibia arteries. According to the medical examiner, she most likely bled to death quickly, and didn't suffer for very long."

I let out a relieved sigh. "Thank God. That's good to hear. I couldn't imagine the pain and suffering the poor woman endured."

"It wasn't painless, but it could have been much worse, Doc Stevens told me. And, yes, he said the broken wrist was no doubt caused by her trying to brace her fall. Also, the crime lab determined the print they'd been able to obtain off Bea's bracelet matched that of John Harris, and a large knife discovered in a tool storage bin in the rear of their truck tested positive for bear blood. The blood belonged to the mama bear Bea shot in the campground, a bear the couple had been tracking. It was John's truck the bear's carcass was loaded into that day. He'd volunteered to dispose of it properly after he and Barb had conducted some tests on it that were pertinent to their current research project. Naturally, they harvested its gallbladder. They also skinned and butchered it, and then left its remains in a ditch alongside a seldom-used road in mountainous terrain. After John Harris confessed, he described the location where the carcass had been dumped and I sent the new recruit, Bill Holsaffer, out to retrieve it."

That poor rookie can't catch a break, I thought with a snicker. I listened carefully to the sheriff's description of events after the couple had been driven away in handcuffs. I'll never forget the evil look Barb gave me out the back window as the squad car had passed by. It was clear she'd been told who had turned her into the authorities. I had smiled back and given her a thumbs-up gesture. It was my sign to her that I was happy she and her equally despicable husband had been apprehended.

As it turned out, the deceitful couple had never spent a dime sending gift packages to soldiers, either. As I'd suspected, that falsehood had served only to obtain the address of a nearby shipping facility and, conceivably, account for the boxes I'd seen inside their trailer. They also had no way of knowing how detailed, or clear, the photo I'd snapped that day had turned out.

As I'd suspected, what they'd learned during their research project in Asia had prompted them to begin poaching the animals they used to fight to protect. They were in cahoots with a dealer in Taiwan, where the practice of bear farming, trading, importing, exporting, or even possessing animal parts and derivatives had been banned. The ban did not eliminate the cruel activity, but it did drive up the price a seller could get for the illegal substance. And this reality had not gone unnoticed by John and Barb Harris. Money truly is the root of all evil, isn't it?

Cora called earlier that morning to tell me she'd seen the lady referred to as Babs in the salon again the previous afternoon. She was getting her nails painted pink this time. Cora spoke to her and learned she had recently moved to Buffalo and her name was Barbara Steinback, or Babs, to her family and friends. Barb Harris, on the other hand, had removed the black polish and trimmed her own nails after Bea's death because of the dried blood underneath them that was hard to get to so it could be eliminated.

As all of my suspicions were verified one by one, I could feel my chest swelling with pride. I was thrilled to know the Harrises would both be taking up residence at the Wyoming State Penitentiary in Rawlins for many years to come.

We also found out that after Bea killed the mama bear who had wandered into the campground, the animal activists, turned poachers, had not had any success in tracking down, or trapping, another bear. I was relieved to hear that, other than the mama bear Bea shot, they'd come up empty-handed. Despite the scare the sow bear and three cubs had given us that one day on the trail, I was happy they'd all been spared from the Harris's numerous traps.

I was also right on target about Barb's thought process on the bracelet. She'd hoped to throw the detectives off with the placement of the bracelet, but couldn't pass up seizing the large solitaire, which was found by the detectives in the bathroom soap dish in the Harris's trailer. Shoving a valuable diamond into a pile of bear poop must have seemed sacrilegious to the misguided woman, yet she thought keeping the costly gem in a soap dish just inches from an unforgiving drain pipe made sense. Really? I wouldn't even consider setting a pair of five-dollar studs on our bathroom sink. Five bucks is five bucks, after all.

Barb confessed she'd been planning to have a necklace designed using the diamond from Bea's bracelet. I couldn't understand how anyone but a sociopath could wear something around her neck that she'd attained by killing a fellow human being, even if the woman's death was unintentional. It was as if she'd wanted to keep it as a souvenir of the ghastly incident. *This particular gemstone could literally be classified as a "blood" diamond,* I thought.

Everything was falling into place to form an insurmountable case against the Harrises. I could finally relax, knowing the ordeal was behind us. At the time, I'd thought I'd never have to walk into the dangerous forest again. But you can't expect me to be right about everything, can you?

So far, in our personal involvement with murder cases, we were batting three for three. I knew Willie would be thrilled with a batting average like ours. And so was I!

EPILOGUE

R anger Rick stopped by one morning the following week. We'd been preparing to pack up and move on. He told us when he'd gone into the Rest 'n Peace campground store to speak with Boonie, he'd met a beautiful widowed woman working the counter named Jan Dorsey, or Laundry Room Jan, so as not to confuse you. They'd chatted for a while, and Jan had accepted his offer to take her out for supper the following night so they could get to know each other a little better.

"She's been having a tough time going on with her life since her husband passed a few months ago. To keep her mind off her loneliness and sorrow, she'd agreed to help out in the store and office, as well as take care of Boonie's laundry in exchange for a free RV site. It's been working out well for both of them, she said. She also told me she'd gotten used to Boonie's flirtatiousness and finally figured out he was basically harmless."

"Jan seems like a nice lady, Rick," I said. I was sincere and felt bad for having ever doubted her word, and now understood why I'd seen one of Boonie's shirts in her laundry basket one day. I'd wondered how she could accumulate so much laundry for a single woman. And if I'd looked closer that day, I'd probably have realized the entire basket was filled with his dirty clothes, not hers. "I'll pray it works out for both of you, Rick."

"Thanks. I will too."

I was happy to see Ranger Rick with a new gleam in his eye. I truly hoped he could find true love, if not with Jan Dorsey, then with some other woman worthy of a good man's devotion. "Have you heard how Desireé's mother is doing?"

"Yeah. I talked to Desireé this morning, in fact. She called to tell me her mom had passed late last night. She said she was going to split Bea's half of the estate between Bea's two daughters, both in their twenties and living on the east coast. I've met them both and they're good kids, both well-deserving of their mother's share of their grandmother's estate. Desireé told me she knew that's what her sister would have wanted, and I agree."

"That's very thoughtful of your ex." I'd judged the woman too harshly, I realized. It'd been hard for me to look past what Desireé did for a living to see the goodness in her heart. It appeared as if I had yet another apology to make before we left town.

"Yeah, she's a good person," Rick replied. "She took on a lot of debt on behalf of my son. I'm mailing out a check tomorrow to cover most of it, even though it was her idea to finance him for so long."

"That's because you're such a good person yourself." I'd judged Rick unfairly at times, too, in my desire to find out the truth behind his former sister-in-law's death. I vowed that in the future I'd try to keep that bad habit of mine in check. And, as the law proclaims, I'll bear in mind that everyone is innocent until proven guilty.

"Thanks, Rapella." Rick smiled, knowing I was sincere. "The reason I dropped by was that I just remembered this morning I'd forgotten about your game camera. Sheriff Wright had Bill Holsaffer go out to retrieve that trap we used as a prop to trick the Harrises. It was the last one, thank God. Because of that, my intentions of retrieving your camera slipped my mind. If you'd like me to go get it for you today, I'd be happy to."

I was about to jump all over the ranger's thoughtful offer, until my foolish husband said, "Thanks, Rick, but we'll go retrieve it. It'll give us an opportunity for one last trek through the forest before we have to pull out in a few days. For old time's sake, you know."

Where was a shovel when you needed one?

Our hike through the woods the following morning was not only uneventful, it was actually quite enjoyable. The birds were singing, the sun was shining, and my body had quit aching. We collected the camera and made it back to the Chartreuse Caboose in time for lunch. Rip could not have been less thrilled when I set a bowl of split-pea soup in front of him. Yet, just that morning he'd been bragging about another five-pound weight loss. It seemed that trying to keep the bull-headed fool alive was turning out to be a thankless job. But, still, it was worth all the toil and trouble because I loved that stubborn ass more than life itself.

When Rip went outside to put the critter cam in an under-carriage storage compartment, he realized he'd somehow activated the motion-sensing device when he'd inserted the memory card back into its slot the day we 'trapped' the Harrises. He'd been too busy concentrating on scanning the few images we'd uploaded on the iPad to realize what he was unconsciously doing with the game camera. The camera now indicated there were sixteen new images on the card.

It was a lazy afternoon and all my chores were done, so I decided to upload the new images, just out of curiosity.

I nearly fell off the kitchen chair when I discovered a sharp, clear image of a cow moose grazing in the background, while in the foreground, two calves were checking out the camera, partially visible through the sagebrush we'd concealed it with. The fifteen remaining photos were also of the same moose family, but not nearly as sharp and vivid.

"Rip! You're not going to believe this! I have good news and even better news."

"So, tell me already!" Rip said impatiently.

"The good news is that we captured what could be a twenty-five thousand dollar photo!"

"Congratulations, honey. That's fantastic news! So what news could be even better than that?"

"The mama moose made it! There's still a visible wound on her leg, but otherwise she appears perfectly healthy. And guess what? She and her twins are together again!"

We marveled at the photo and couldn't wait to show it to Cora and Willie, so we drove to their house to share it with them. That once-in-a-lifetime photo would end up taking third place in the wildlife photography contest Cora had entered me in. Personally, I thought it was the best of the entire lot of entries, but I certainly didn't stick my nose up at the five-thousand dollar prize! I offered to return Cora's thirty-dollar entry fee along with an additional two hundred dollars. She refused the offer, saying, "No way, José. That was an Easter present, Aunt Rappie."

So instead, I ordered a gift basket full of candles, scented skin lotions, two bottles of Chardonnay, and a box of fresh chocolate-covered strawberries to be delivered to her home the following day. In the card accompanying the basket of goodies, I told her I thought they might come in handy with Dirk, who she hadn't seen in three months, returning from his stint in Texas the following day. And, if that collection of items wasn't enough to turn her man on, I knew where she could pick up a lace teddy, complete with a thong, for a mere eighty-nine dollars.

Rip and I decided to give Willie five-hundred dollars to put in his savings account. He'd be getting his driver's license in less than six months and could use it as part of his down payment on a used car. It was a well-earned reward for his ingenious idea to catch the poachers.

Cora told us she would not allow Willie to accept the money, but we convinced her we couldn't have done it without him, and she finally relented.

"I don't call him Slick Willie for no reason, you know!" Rip had countered with a chuckle.

Afterward, because Rip will use any excuse he can come up with to appease his sweet tooth, he suggested the four of us celebrate my third place finish by making a visit to the ice cream shop. And, I have to admit, it tasted pretty good to me too!

When we stopped by the office on our way back to the Chartreuse Caboose to see how Boonie was getting along, he appeared to be coping as best he could. Knowing the couple responsible for his wife's death were behind bars gave him a sense of closure, he told us. He was also happy to report the police had apprehended three seventeen-year-old boys after they'd been caught on camera letting the air out of all four tires on Leo Brown's truck. Discovering that the trio had skipped school on the exact days the numerous flat tire episodes were reported to the police helped tie the boys to the other tire-flattening incidents, as well. But they swore they never permanently ruined any tires by slashing them.

Boonie felt sure it had been either John or Barb Harris who'd slashed the tires of our truck the day I'd parked it in front of the campground office, and we agreed. John had most likely used the same blood-stained knife he'd used to clean the bear Bea shot in the campground, we decided. And after all, I had just made it clear to Barb that Rip and I were on the hunt for Bea's killer.

Boonie told Rip that Janelle Tyson-Simms had left the area and was now running around with a real-estate tycoon in Billings, Montana. At least this poor sucker was not married as her last boyfriend had been, according to Boonie. He was visibly relieved to have her out of his life, and we felt confident he'd be able to eventually come to grips with his loss and move forward.

Rip and I had enjoyed our stay in Buffalo and the time spent with Cora and Willie, but I was itching to start our next adventure. We'd be heading to Seattle soon. From there we would embark on a cruise up the Inside Passage to Alaska. May eighteenth would mark our fiftieth year of marriage, a partnership that was even stronger today than it was the day we exchanged vows. Through good times and bad, through sickness and in health, and despite a few nasty, name-calling incidents—the kind nearly every couple has on occasion—we'd stayed by each other's side and had no intention of ever living any other way.

To celebrate such a milestone, a rare accomplishment in this day and age, Rip had decided to go all out, with the help of the remainder of my prize money. There'd be no enduring a long trip up the often challenging Alaskan Highway. Instead, we'd drive to Seattle and park the Chartreuse Caboose in a campground. Then we'd board a cruise ship in the harbor there and sail to Alaska. We'd be wallowing in the lap of luxury, having booked a penthouse suite, where the cruise line representative assured us we'd be treated like visiting royalty.

I had a sneaking suspicion that having a personal porter to provide us with room service at any hour of the day, the all-you-can eat buffet on the Promenade deck, the midnight chocolate buffet on the third night at sea, and the round-the-clock access to food at various locations around the ship, might have been major factors in my husband's decision. No doubt we'd both be starting a new diet when we returned from our celebratory cruise. Also, no doubt, Dolly will be taking applications for new servants when she discovers the highly recommended cat-boarding facility we leave her at while we're gone doesn't feed her as if she were a Shetland pony instead of a housecat.

I was looking forward to the Alaskan voyage, and even though being personally involved in several murder cases had been rewarding in some ways, I prayed that kind of excitement was behind us for good.

So why did I have this feeling in my gut that, as per usual, it'd be a good long while before my prayer was considered, much less answered? I suspected I'd be waiting in line until after every human being on earth had enough food to eat and safe water to drink and every inhabitant of this rock we all share learned to live in peace and harmony.

And you know what? I was okay with that.

Turn the page for an
excerpt from

RIP YOUR
HEART OUT

A Ripple Effect Cozy Mystery
Book Four

Jeanne Glidewell

The view from White Pass Summit was breathtaking; a panorama of mountains, waterfalls, glaciers, gorges, tunnels and trestles. At the summit, nearly three thousand feet higher in elevation than the Skagway Harbor where our cruise ship was moored, we could see the headwaters of the Yukon River. My husband, Clyde "Rip" Ripple, and I were celebrating our fiftieth wedding anniversary in Skagway, Alaska, aboard the White Pass and Yukon Route Railway.

Skagway was one of five Alaskan ports we planned to visit on our seven-day cruise of Alaska's Inside Passage. The previous day, we'd gone whale watching in Juneau and traveled to the Mendenhall Glacier. With the digital camera we'd purchased as an early anniversary present to each other, we'd taken incredible humpback and orca photos. We'd also photographed dozens of bald eagles soaring above us or perched on tree branches ashore, a sleeping grizzly bear sprawled out on a fallen tree trunk along the shore of Auke Bay, and several sea lions snoozing on the base of a buoy.

The day before that we'd toured the town of Ketchikan on foot. We visited the Beaver Clan House, the Libby Salmon Cannery, the traditional totem poles of Saxman Village, and, of course, Dolly's House. Dolly's House was formerly a brothel but is now a museum, on Creek Street, which was the red light district of Ketchikan in the early 1900s. We have a chubby grey and white tabby named

Dolly, who was gracious enough to let us reside in her domain as long as we tended to her every need. With that premise in mind, I'd wanted a photo of Rip and me standing in front of the Dolly's House sign to use on our Christmas cards. I'd asked Rip, "Do you think 'her majesty' will realize the house was not named after her, but rather a long ago brothel owner named Dolly Arthur?"

"Probably not, Rapella," Rip had replied sarcastically. "After all, she *is* just a cat, you know. She only cares about two things; her next meal and a comfy place to nap."

"Are you describing Dolly or yourself?" I asked playfully. "I realize Dolly's just a cat. But the Dolly House *was* a 'house of ill repute'. And where do you think the term 'cat house' came from?"

Rip smiled at my bantering, but the smile didn't quite ring true. It seemed forced to me. It was as if he was trying to convince me he was enjoying the excursion as much as I was. But I knew better. My sixty-eight-year-old husband, and the love of my life, could not easily fool someone who'd been by his side for over half a decade. I was convinced Rip was not feeling up to snuff, and I decided to test the theory.

"Let's go out on that open-air area behind this passenger car so I can get a better photo of Dead Horse Gulch." The rear "porch" had a metal railing with spindles enclosing it, and I could run from side to side as we passed by different landmarks without the risk of making an early, unplanned departure from the train.

"You go ahead," Rip said. "I'm perfectly content to stay here for now."

"Do you feel all right, honey?"

"Of course. Just a little tired. We've been on the go so much that I'm kind of enjoying being off my feet for a spell. Besides, I'm conserving my energy to do some serious grazing at the midnight chocolate buffet this evening," Rip said with an ornery grin.

"There's nothing like a self-induced belly ache to finish off our anniversary celebration, is there?"

"Nope! My goal is to not stop eating milk chocolate until one bite *before* I've reached belly-aching status." Despite the twelve pounds he'd lost, while I'd gained three, on our self-imposed low-carb diet the last six weeks, Rip still suffered from "Dunlap Disease". As I'm sure you know, that's when your belly has done lapped over your belt. He patted his paunch and smiled. "You know I can't maintain this sexy spare tire without working at it."

I knew he was trying to alleviate my anxiety with his attempt at levity, but it was doing nothing to calm my concerns. Before I missed the opportunity for a magnificent photo, I patted his shoulder, and said, "You rest. I'll be back in a couple of minutes."

"Don't hurry on my account," I heard him say as I hustled down the aisle toward the door leading to the outside viewing area.

After the three-hour excursion along the narrow gauge railroad route, once used by the Klondike Gold Rush prospectors for transportation to the gold fields in Dawson City, we were going to do a little gold panning and enjoy a salmon bake in the Liarsville Trail Camp before returning to the cruise ship. If not for the fact we were on a shore excursion with twenty other passengers from our ship, I'd have opted to take Rip straight back to our cabin. He had appeared pale and lethargic all day, and I was hoping he'd get a chance to nap before our celebratory supper in one of the ship's specialty restaurants that evening.

After Rip had retired from a lifelong career in law enforcement, we'd sold our home and bought a thirty-foot travel trailer we affectionately call the "chartreuse caboose". Now we traveled around the country in our home on wheels as full-time RVers. The previous week we drove from Buffalo, Wyoming, to Seattle, Washington, where we'd signed up for a site in an RV Park near the Cascades Mountain Range. From our site we could see the tip of Mt. Rainier in the distance. We planned to park there for a couple of months so we could tour the area after we'd returned from the Alaskan cruise.

On our way to the Port of Seattle, where we'd boarded the cruise ship earlier that week, we'd dropped Dolly off at a pet-boarding facility that had great online reviews. I had tried to convince our eight-year old housecat she'd have a wonderful time there while we were on our trip, but I'm pretty sure I saw her raise her furry little paw to flip us off as we handed her carrying cage over to the nice lady at the desk. Pets have a way of capturing your heart in a way only they know how to do, and Dolly was no exception. Both Rip's and my eyes had gotten misty as we drove away from the Paw Spa Ranch and Resort.

It had been a hectic week for us, and it wasn't just Rip who was feeling the effect of a much busier schedule than usual. While he napped on our cabin's king-sized bed, I planned to sit out on our balcony and relax with a cup of hot tea from the single-cup hot beverage dispenser in our over-sized cabin, while reading the last few chapters of an Alice Duncan cozy mystery I was deeply immersed in. I might even place a call to our personal porter and request a refill of our complimentary fruit basket. Just because I could!

I could get used to all the pampering and individual service that came with booking a suite on a cruise ship. I'd already developed a sense of superiority in just four days aboard the floating resort, and wasn't sure how well I'd be able to adapt at being a mere "commoner" when the cruise was over.

Who, I wondered, *is going to place my linen napkin on my lap for me before every meal? Who's going to deliver an apple fritter when I have a hankering for a pastry? Who's going to attend to my every want or whim? And most importantly, who's going to make sure I have a chocolate mint on my pillow every night and a white cotton elephant or monkey crafted from one bath towel and two washcloths, at the foot of my bed?*

We had decided to splurge on a penthouse suite to properly celebrate our golden wedding anniversary. As promised, we'd been treated like visiting royalty from the moment we stepped on board the recently renovated ship. Upon arrival, we'd been quickly whisked away to a private waiting room, complete with scrumptious snacks and beverages, where we could relax, munch on refreshments, and mingle with other "suite" passengers while the porters transferred our luggage to our suite.

I'd noticed that with each day since we boarded the ship, Rip had seemed less energetic, less interested in the beautiful and fascinating sights we were visiting. However, I figured the following day would be a restful one for both of us. We'd be cruising Glacier Bay all day, enjoying the stunning scenery; bone-chilling clear water, glaciers, floating icebergs, breaching whales, and snow-capped mountains. What once was a single glacier of solid ice in the early eighteenth century has now retreated sixty-five miles to the head of the bay at Tarr Inlet and left behind sixteen much smaller tidewater glaciers. I was anxious to see what I considered to be convincing confirmation of the devastating effect of global warming.

As we boarded the bus that would transport us to the Liarsville Trail Camp, I prayed Rip would be back to his normal, lively self by the time we sat down for our anniversary supper at the popular onboard steakhouse. He'd warned me in advance when he said, "I'm planning to completely devour one of their thirty-two ounce porterhouses—or die trying."

Had I known at that time how ironic and prophetic his declaration would turn out to be, I'd have felt as if my heart was being ripped out of my chest. So, in retrospect, I'm glad I was unaware of the trials and tribulations that were about to befall us. Sometimes ignorance truly is bliss!

RIP YOUR HEART OUT

available in print and ebook

THE RIPPLE EFFECT COZY MYSTERIES

A Rip Roaring Good Time
Rip Tide
Ripped to Shreds
Rip Your Heart Out

Also by Jeanne Glidewell

The Lexie Star Mystery Series

Leave No Stone Unturned
Extinguished Guest
Haunted
With This Ring
Just Ducky
Cozy Camping
The Spirit of the Season (A Novella)

Jeanne Glidewell, lives with her husband, Bob, and chubby cat, Dolly, in Bonner Springs, Kansas. They spend every winter in their Rockport, Texas, waterfront condo to have fun with their Texas friends and wade-fish the bays off the Gulf Coast.

Besides writing and fishing, Jeanne enjoys wildlife photography and traveling. This year Jeanne and Bob traveled to Cozumel, Mexico, for a fun-filled week with friends, Dave and Cindy Colmer, and South America to visit Machu Picchu in Peru and Iguazu Falls in both Brazil and Argentina. They also spent a week in Homer, Alaska, celebrating their thirty-second anniversary in August. In January, they'll be traveling to Australia and New Zealand with Jeanne's best friend since seventh grade, Sheila Davis, and her husband, Randy.

Jeanne and Bob owned and operated a large RV park in Cheyenne, Wyoming, for twelve years. It was that enjoyable period in her life that inspired her to write a mystery series involving a full-time RVing couple—The Ripple Effect series.

As a 2006 pancreas and kidney transplant recipient, Jeanne now volunteers as a mentor for the Gift of Life of KC program, helping future transplant recipients prepare mentally and emotionally for their upcoming transplants. Please consider the possibility of giving the gift of life by opting to be an organ donor.

Jeanne is the author of a romance/suspense novel, Soul Survivor, six novels and one novella in her NY Times best-selling Lexie Starr cozy mystery series, and three novels in her new Ripple Effect cozy mystery series. She is currently writing book four in the Ripple Effect series, titled Rip Your Heart Out, and hopes to have it released in late summer of 2017.

Jeanne loves hearing from readers. Contact her at: JeanneGlidewell@epublishingworks.com